Carole was in the hall. Moving toward the stairway. Maybe it was all a dream, after all. And tomorrow they'd wake up, the sun shining, and it would be Sunday and she'd fix a big breakfast—

"Carole." Rolfe's voice stopped her. It sounded low and miserable, in pain. When she turned to look at him, he came toward her from the door.

And then he was holding her, at last, against his chest, at last.

Into her ear, a whisper: "Carole, I feel so awful seeing you like this. So . . . helpless. I'm sorry. I don't want to make anything worse—"

"Kiss me," she said. "Don't you want to kiss me, Rolfe?"

He kissed her then. On the lips.

But it was not Rolfe's kiss.

It was not their kiss.

And all of a sudden a wild grief went through her. She knew that her whole life had changed, was changing, and nothing would ever, could ever, be the same again. . . .

ACT of RAGE

JOSEPH HAYES

ST. MARTIN'S PAPERBACKS

ACT OF RAGE

Cover illustration by Jaime DeJesus.

Library of Congress Catalog Card Number: 89-34433

ISBN: 0-312-92341-4

Printed in the United States of America

St. Martin's Press hardcover edition published 1989
St. Martin's Paperbacks edition/September 1991

10 9 8 7 6 5 4 3 2 1

For Marrijane, who has again
made me believe in miracles

And to my three sisters: Benita, Margaret,
and Elizabeth

PART 1

LATER, UNDER POLICE INTERROGATION, when she had to try to recall in detail what had occurred during the morning and afternoon, the events leading up to the attack, Carole would not be able to get them into focus. Or to recall their exact sequence—

Because they were all so ordinary, so trivial really. It had been a Saturday much like any other. Well, she didn't prepare a dinner party every weekend, true. Informal, a small group, close friends only—the kind of party she really enjoyed. Herself and Rolfe, and two singles, both divorced, and two couples, one married, one living together.

After lunch, Rolfe had driven into Sudbury, the closest town of any size, eleven miles south, to the small electronics plant where he had worked for six years—the reason they had moved to Connecticut, the year after they were married in New York and the year before Sandy had been born. It was a habit Rolfe had fallen into in recent months and he had left cheerfully enough, even though it was a weekend. It didn't seem fair, though—to be under the gun, under such pressure, at thirty-five. Damn it, it *wasn't* fair! *The conglomerates are gobbling up the small fish,* he'd said a month or so ago, *and you'll see, us wizard executives, we'll be the first to get the axe.* When he'd kissed her goodbye this morning, standing tall and sandy-haired and loose-jointed alongside her chair, he'd said, *I'll be back in plenty of time to take care of the bar before anyone gets here at six.*

During the afternoon Carole had set the table and prepared the dinner herself. Which was her choice and which Rolfe never quite understood or approved now that they could afford help. The truth was that, having spent a childhood surrounded by servants, she didn't like anyone in her kitchen when she worked. And that included, when he offered, Aloysius Leo Cassady, weekend houseguest and borderline alcoholic, but oddly lovable and really loved by all their friends. His almost courtly charm, especially when tight, made everyone forget his off-center, downright homely, gnarled and slightly wizened face—and the cigarette eternally dangling between his half-amused, half-mocking lips. Rolfe's closest friend since high school days in Madison, Wisconsin, Cass had become a part of the family. On weekends when he didn't drive up the seventy miles from New York, Sandy would ask *Why, why, why* with a five-year-old's maddening insistence from Friday noon to Monday morning.

In the mid-afternoon Cass had disappeared for a while to the combined bathhouse and guest cottage on the pond —to write or to try to write or to sleep off the gin he'd been sipping like water since breakfast—but Sandy had routed him out in her own rambunctious manner and had tried to convince him to take her for a canoe ride on the pond. But instead they had gone for a walk in the woods. *Castles to lay siege to,* Cass had said. *Evil monsters to be slain in their lairs!*

From the kitchen window, Carole, her own shoulder-length black hair glistening with sweat and damp alongside her delicate face, had seen them strolling, hand in hand, over the rolling lawn behind the big old Victorian house. The sight touched her oddly. Divorced, no children, Cass would have made a delightful father. Author of a single passionate and angry novel when he'd returned from Nam, he'd become temporarily famous, a celebrity for a time, then nothing. Whenever Rolfe inquired, *You working?,* the answer was invariably the same: *Always, man, always working.* Which, sadly, was probably the sad, bitter truth.

Allison had appeared, punctual and cheerful and pleasantly officious as ever, to take Sandy to her house, where they were sharing a sitter for the evening. But this had sent Sandy skittering to the kitchen to protest and to turn on the charm. *Do I have to go? I love parties and I promise not to say one word. Please!* But Allison in her quick no-nonsense way had charged in and picked up the wriggling little body, held it head-first for Carole's kiss and had then thrown it over her wide competent shoulder and hauled Sandy off to her battered station wagon, where, Carole knew, Allison's Mike and Audrey would already be arguing about what they were going to do all evening. Allison Bonner, approaching forty, still looked and acted seventeen and, after two divorces, supported two children on her own by managing the office of a construction company. Where, she'd admitted once: *You can't win. If you roll over and play dead, the assholes think they've won, and if you give it back to them in kind, they get the idea you'll spread your legs.*

Once everything was more or less under control—beds made, wine chilling, litter removed in all areas, ashtrays glittering empty—Carole was about to relax when she discovered, with dismay, that someone had eaten the apples! Cass and Sandy probably. There were only three left. She'd warned them not to eat the walnuts or the French bread or the Camembert, but had she—

How the *hell* could she serve the new dessert she'd planned—baked golden apples stuffed with nuts and fresh pineapple chunks spiced with chutney? Eight people, three apples! Damn. But luck was with her. She still had time to dash over to the orchards in Bethel, and getting out of the house on this glorious Indian summer day was a terrific idea anyway! While she was out she could also pick up more anchovies and scallions for the Caesar salad—and at least two more quarts of gin, considering what Cass had done to the fifth she'd left on the bar in the den last night. Poor dear Cass—if only there was something she, or anyone, could do.

Should she change first? No. If she ran out of time, she could get by in the denim wraparound skirt she was wearing and maybe change out of the old plaid madras shirt she'd copped from Rolfe's closet, no second shower, but what the hell—

So, in the powder room downstairs she took a swipe or two at her hair with a brush and went outside and climbed into the new white Volvo wagon that she loved. Crossing the long narrow steel bridge over Lake Lillinonah—where the Housatonic River had been dammed up to form a narrow lake—she was wondering if she would be able to find some bittersweet on her way back, perhaps at the Woodall Orchards stand. Bittersweet would look fantastic in the centerpiece!

Excited now, driving uphill between bluffs of stone, she flipped on the radio and hit pay dirt at once: Chuck Berry's guitar. Then, exhilarated, she reached the top of Obtuse Hill and was sailing downhill, toward Sheffield Center, more often referred to as The Village, surprised that the light was fading so fast. After the bitter cold of late autumn, Indian summer was always unexpected, always exciting, but the sun still went down according to the October, not the summer, clock. The woods were no longer ablaze with color—muted, already darkening—and before she reached the foot of the hill, she could see the cluster of slanted rooftops, the spire of the Congregational church, and in the distance the soft roll of the Berkshire foothills in the fading display of their fall glory. Her heart lifting, she put her foot on the brake and slowed to savor the moment. A thin, purplish haze was moving mistily over the scene. Until she had met Rolfe and they had moved here, she had never had a sense of place. There was a Spanish word for it, but she couldn't remember it—having to do with a person's feeling not only "at home" but deeper, not attached-to but *one-with* a place. Growing up in the city, she'd never known it. Does anyone really *love* a New York apartment, even one as luxurious as her parents' Fifth Avenue penthouse?

After leaving the Village Store, with the small white clapboard police station alongside, she continued onto the highway. At Ye Olde Colonial Spirit Shoppe she always found herself tempted to ask for the best witch's brew in the house, vintage 1692. But she settled for the gin and a bottle of Courvoisier, feeling reckless and extravagant and foolishly elated and expectant.

A few minutes later, at the roadside stand on a narrow country road, she bought two jugs of chilled cider, one for tonight and one for Sandy tomorrow, and a small basket of Golden Delicious apples and, best of all, an armload of bittersweet, which took the last of her cash and to hell with it.

It was on the way home, on a different road, a shortcut that did not go through The Village, that she spotted the sumac. She slowed. Only a few scrubby plants along the pavement, but she could see others deeper in the woods, their elongated pods like clusters of berries red among the trunks of the trees. On impulse she stopped the wagon on the shoulder, making sure all wheels were off the blacktop. She leaped out, wishing she had brought a knife, and broke off a few stalks from the roadside shrugs, tossed her lovely swag through the open tailgate window, glanced at her watch, almost too dark to see the dial clearly—5:23—then decided she had the time, no cars passing, so she climbed over the low fieldstone wall and plunged excitedly into the woods.

Under the trees it was almost, but not quite, dark. She began to break off the brittle branches, the cracking sound loud in her ears. Some she had to fight as if they were live enemies, pulling and yanking, herself amused, and at herself.

Her arms were full when she turned to go in the direction of the road. Then, instead of seeing the white wagon beyond the tree trunks, she found herself facing a solid wall. It was all she could see. And then she recognized it—the Indian blanket Sandy used as a lap robe in the car.

It was moving. It was moving toward her.

She uttered a sound, dropped the sumac, heard footsteps crackling on the brittle leaves, out of sight, behind the blanket—was someone playing a trick?

She crouched, at first, still stunned at the unlikely, incredible development, and then she twisted around and started to run deeper into the woods.

But she had not taken more than three or four steps when, trying to cry out, she felt the blanket come down over her head.

Then she was struggling for breath, trying to scream, finally screaming, but only a muffled sound, she was smothering, she couldn't breathe, she was falling, she'd been pushed, she was falling and something around her neck, around the blanket, was tightening, choking her—

Was she awake or still dreaming? That's what it had been, a dream, a nightmare, and she was waking now and in a few minutes, when she was fully awake—

She was breathing again, too. She'd thought she'd never be able to breathe again. With the blanket over her head, while she was struggling frantically to loosen the leather strap that held it around her neck, choking her—there had been that moment after he'd gone, just an instant, when she had wished she would die before she got the strap off, the blanket off, if she didn't try, if she just stopped trying to breathe—

She was sick now.

The pain in her breast, her left breast, was excruciating. Unbearable.

She found herself sitting in a chair. A big soft leather chair. She was sitting there and yet she seemed detached from herself at the same time. As if she were watching, observing—

She was in a room she'd never seen. A handsome room, high beams, wooden walls, gray and weathered and rough. How had she come here? Or was this another hallucination? Like the one earlier, when she had come out of the woods, when she'd fallen, again, too weak to stand then, discovering the strange shapes and shadows around her, grotesque monsters, human size, some larger than human, terrifying, still and unreal, and she'd known she was hallucinating but it did no good to know because all she could do was go on screaming—

The room was a *good* dream. It was filled with soft golden light. Paintings on the walls. She could see colors but even the walls seemed far away. And the pain in her left breast, the one his hand had clutched harder and harder, until she stopped screaming, until she *couldn't* scream, twisting harder until her thrashing body stopped struggling, *that* pain had receded. But only slightly. That other pain, the less cruel but more shameful and terrible pain, was still down below, where the wetness was. She didn't want to think of that. She couldn't—

A shadow moved in the room and she flinched, and then her flesh was shuddering again and she was drawing back from the face, a man's face. Yes, him, she'd seen him before, but where, when? The small rust-red beard, the calm gray eyes frowning under shaggy red brows. He'd been the one who had picked her up after that terrifying time on the ground with the monstrous shapes on all sides—

"Try to drink this." A deep voice, a quiet voice, but annoyed, irritable. "Slowly, very slowly." Was that an accent? British?

She took the glass, a brandy snifter, and lifted it to her lips, her hand quivering, but the sharp-sweet bouquet made her gag. She felt his eyes on her. Who was he? Where was she? She ventured a single slow sip, then felt the hot shock in her raw throat, then scalding down to her stomach. For a second she was certain that she was going to retch.

Again. Now, for the first time, she remembered vomiting in the woods, in the dark, after she had the blanket off, and after she'd found her loafers by running her hands over the leaves, crawling on all fours. While she was pulling on the shoes, she had gone faint all over, gagging, coughing and rolling over, her body beyond control, disgorging everything inside, heaving till only a slimy sour liquid came, bitter and disgusting. Afterward when nothing more would come, her mind and body still felt the grinding need. Standing up then, she had seen the wavering yellow light through the trees, in the distance—

"May I ask you something?" Was that her voice? "Where . . . where am I?"

"You're in my house. Well, it was a barn once. My name's Clive. Duncan Clive. Those were my scoolptures that alarmed you so in the garden. They seem to frighten people in the galleries, too." His tone was more pleasant now, but distantly polite and self-mocking. "Anything else, Mrs. Jensen?"

"Yes." The blade turned over in her throat again. "How do you know my name?"

"Ye told me yourself."

She couldn't remember. She couldn't remember. . . . Now wasn't that strange? Weird? Eerie . . .

The voice came closer now. A face floated in the mist above her. "Shock plays tricks with the mind, Mrs. Jensen. Now, perhaps now ye'll allow me to summon the authorities."

"The authorities?"

"Ye shouted at me when I suggested it before." It was not an accusation, only a gentle reminder. Did he know that she couldn't remember, that it was blank space in her mind? "It's your decision, of course."

"I don't know." She was shaking her head from side to side. "I don't know. Rolfe will know." She took a long swallow of brandy, tried to stand up, and failed. "I'd like to go home, please."

"The police might prefer to talk to you here, closer to the site where—"

"Where I was raped?" Her voice was sharp, almost angry, hard. And she was standing, after all, her legs weak, her knees sore. "Why don't you say it?"

His face looked troubled then. "Ye're in a state of shock, m'dear, and from the way things appear ye're also in need of medical—"

"What did you say?"

"I said ye likely need medical attention."

"No, before that. What did you call me?"

"Call you?"

"My dear!" she shouted. "That's what he . . . that's what he—"

She looked around, frantically, in panic. For a weapon, a door, escape . . .

When she moved, he reached to take her arm. She saw thick red hair on the back of his hand.

"Don't touch me!" she shrieked, pulling away violently.

Then she bolted to the door, the closest door, she was tugging at it, it wouldn't open. She whirled around, and discovered him standing across the room staring at her, bushy brows drawn together, tweed jacket, black turtleneck sweater—

She was trying to remember. What had the man been wearing? She hadn't actually seen him. Did he roll his *r*'s? Did he have an accent?

"Mrs. Jensen," she heard Duncan Clive say, "if I said 'my dear,' it was only my feeble attempt to be reassuring."

The voice, that other voice, harsh and angry, echoed in her mind: *My dear, my sweet, my darling, my dear sweet girl*—an endearment with each terrible, painful, brutal thrust.

"Mrs. Jensen," Duncan Clive was saying, "I tried to ring your husband several times. The line was engaged. If ye'll allow me, I'll drive ye home, although I must say I still think . . ."

She was slumped against the door, certain she was about to slip to the floor. If he *was* the man, if it had been him inside her, driving, pumping, hurting—

As if reading her mind, he spoke in a whisper now: "Mrs. Jensen, please listen. I'm not the kind of man who goes about raping women."

"How do you know I was raped?" It was a whisper. She had him now. He *knew.* "How?"

"Ye just told me yourself," he said. "Not three minutes ago."

Oh God, it was too much, too much. She was too weak, too spent, to struggle.

"If ye'll step away from the door, I'll open it." She slid her body along the wall. Watched as he opened the door, and turned to her—such baffled miserable eyes now. "Ready?"

"Do you know the way?" Was that her voice?

"You told me that, too."

"I'm sorry." It was all she could say.

"Stop being sorry," he said. "Ye've done nothing. It's been done *to* you. Ye'd do well to bear that in mind, lass."

She felt her head nodding. "I'm sorry."

She went outside. When she reached the car, a tan station wagon that looked like a Jeep, he stepped back carefully after opening the door. "If ye'd feel more secure in the rear seat?"

She managed to shake her head and, slithering past him, she climbed into the front seat.

Would it always be like this now? Would she never be able to trust *anyone* again? Ever? Would she never be able to allow anyone, any male, to touch her?

What about Rolfe?

When, after an eternity of silence, her mind blank, the

car turned off the paved road into the familiar gravel driveway, she saw the lights and remembered the day she and Rolfe had installed the floodlights in the forks of the trees. And then she saw the cars parked in the circular area around the ancient oak tree. And remembered the dinner party. Tonight? Was this Saturday? What time was it?

As the car rolled to a careful slow stop, Duncan Clive asked, "Shall I come in?" His voice was reluctant. "Apparently ye have guests—"

Before she could summon the strength to answer, the front door opened and she saw Rolfe running, tall and slim, across the wide veranda and down the steps of the big old Victorian house and across the lawn toward the car.

Now . . . now everything would be all right. Now Rolfe would take care of her.

When he opened her door, she almost fell into his arms —no flinching, no hesitation, thank God, oh thank God! He held her, whispering into her ear, "God, we thought all sorts of things. You're alive! Where have you been, *where?"* Then, over her shoulder, in a different tone, to Duncan Clive: "Who are you?"

Breaking free, Carole said, "He helped me," and then she was running toward the house, surprised her legs were holding her up. Sandy! She'd forgotten Sandy!

Opening the front door, she was conscious that Rolfe was not following. In the wide center hall she stopped, staring through the broad arch into the living room on her left. They were all there, silent and waiting, her friends, bewilderment, anxiety, questions on every face. And love—

"Where's Sandy?" she heard herself ask, in a hoarse rasping voice, the blade scraping her raw throat.

At once Allison stood up from the sofa, rushing toward her, tall and wide-shouldered and wearing a red pantsuit, her long face filled with reassurance. "You know where Sandy is. She and Mike and Audrey are tormenting a sitter at my house. What's the matter with your voice?" Then she stopped, "Hey, look at you! Oh Jesus, what can I do, what?"

Carole shook her head, glancing around the big living room. Jerald and Karen, Esther and David, and in the corner, hunched over a glass, Cass, his small, knobby-gnarled face very still, very pale, his slate-blue eyes glittering with gin and concern.

Esther, who was sitting on the floor at David's feet, got up and came toward her, big brass earrings dangling, her short thickening body wrapped in a colorful peasant skirt, green headband holding her wild dark hair. "I'll put the steaks on whenever you tell me," she said, brown eyes sober and alert with questions. "Not what you planned, but you're the gourmet chef. God, girl, all we've done is drink and make guesses and drink and make phone calls. In a few words now, please. And pronto. What happened?"

Carole suddenly felt trapped. She opened her mouth but no words came. The room began to blur. An abrupt panic filled her. And her legs threatened to go. "I have to take a bath," she heard herself say, the words sounding idiotic, the impulse too powerful to deny, so she took a few steps to the broad stairway, fleeing, escaping, she had to be alone, she—

"I don't advise that," a voice behind her said. She turned. Jerald Dixon had come into the hall. Not so tall as Rolfe, nor so slim—a bulky linebacker's body going soft—Jerald was wearing his usual blazer and a white polo shirt. "Free *legal* advice," he said in his cool, almost teasing voice. His knowing pale blue eyes moved up and down her body, once. "Don't take a bath, Carole, unless you've already decided not to call in the police."

"Police?" The word came from the living room, out of view now—not a man's. Karen's then? Jerald's wife. "Jerry, why don't you bug off, darling?" Karen appeared between Allison and Esther—the blond beauty, quietly glacial, always exquisitely elegant, wearing a summer frock that, as usual, traced every slender line of her body, one tan shoulder bare. "I think we should all go home. How about that?"

But her husband ignored her, a faint smile flickering along his slightly bulbous lips. "Of course it's up to you, Carole. But if you are going to report it, the police will need all the evidence they can get."

"Evidence?" Esther cried. "Evidence of what?"

Carole was poised on the step, every pore longing for the gush of clean spring water from the shower. She felt filthy, she had never felt this dirty—her whole being, body and mind, and soul. And she had again become aware of a low, fierce anger deep inside. At everything. Everyone! She was tempted to run up the stairs, to hell with them, all of them, and to hell with the pain in her breast and in her groin. Rolfe, where are you? What are you doing out there? Why aren't you in here with me?"

But before she could decide, Cass emerged from the living room. "Leave her alone," he said. He came toward her. "Carole . . ."

Without thought or volition, she drew away from his extended hand. And stared. Cass stopped dead, frowning, and took the cigarette from between his lips.

"I rest my case," Jerald said and strolled into the den across from the living room. "How about a drink, Carole?"

"I don't believe it," Allison said in a whisper.

The front door opened then and Rolfe came into the hall. His slim, handsome face looked stricken. In the paleness, his freckles stood out. His sky-blue eyes held a stunned baffled fury. He looked at her. Was he asking? She nodded. He shook his head, then slammed his fist into his palm, and after the sharp explosion she heard Duncan Clive's Jeep-wagon going down the circular driveway. "I still goddamn don't believe it," Rolfe said.

But he didn't come to her. He didn't move.

Jerald returned, drink in hand. And Karen said, between thin lips: "If you say I-told-you-so, Jerry, I'm going to take my car and go home alone."

"Not me," Jerald said. *"The rest is silence."*

"Goddamn it," Cass said, under his breath. "Goddamn it to hell."

Rolfe moved then. At first she thought he was coming to her, at last, but he crossed in long strides to the telephone on the hall table next to the stairway. He was lifting it when Jerald followed, fast, and placed a hand on his shoulder. "Let's think it all over," Jerald said. "Let's be reasonable and consider all the possibilities."

Cass's voice, low and sharp, snapped: "I've got a better idea. Let's all take a *vote*—while Carole stands here and falls apart."

Rolfe turned, lifting his eyes to meet hers again. She was tempted to run to him. But didn't.

Jerald stepped to the stairs. "It's you I'm thinking about, Carole, what you'll be letting yourself in for if Rolfe dials the police." He turned to the others. "If you want to talk it over like reasonable adults, I'll be in here with David." Heavy shoulders hunched, he strolled into the living room.

"Carole, you must be starved," Esther said, taking a step or two toward her. "You don't want steak—what about some soup?"

Carole shook her head. The idea of food was nauseating. "Just . . . maybe a brandy. Please, I've had one and it did seem to help."

Rolfe, still holding the phone, replaced it with a clatter. "Your friend Mister Clive didn't mention a brandy. Although—" and he moved to face her "—although he seemed to have all the other *intimate* details." And when she didn't answer, couldn't: "Are you that sure *he* wasn't the one? It happened on his property. He admits that."

Carole was tempted again to twist away and run up the stairs. She still couldn't speak but now she didn't want to. The hall was silent. The whole house. And then she felt herself moving off again, not in body, in that same double vision she'd experienced before—detached, observing from a distance. *Shock plays tricks with the mind*—who had said that? She felt their eyes on her.

The anger was in her blood now. All through her.

She stepped down and crossed the hall diagonally, between them. As if from a distance, she saw Karen and Esther stepping back to let her pass.

In the spacious Victorian living room, David Slade, wearing a madras sportcoat of many colors, still sat alone on the window seat framed in the dark bay windows. She was conscious of Jerald seated on one of the sofas, but she ignored him. David's moonlike face—bushy black curly hair above and a shaggy black beard below—lifted to look at her. His dark eyes held a brooding, troubled intensity.

"Hi," he said.

"Hi, David."

It had always been very easy to be fond of David. He was a softly heavyset man, not tall and oddly gentle, and as devoted to Esther as any man could be, married or not. He took the pipe from between his teeth and an almost shy grin twisted the beard before he spoke. "I heard. L-L-Listen, Carole, do what your gut tells you. I know a scientist isn't supposed to believe that, but . . . I kinda t-t-trust your instincts, pal."

Carole turned away and sank into a deep chair. The wetness between her legs was no longer there. Or the pain —except in her breast, and in her knees when she bent them. "Is that your vote, David?" Her throat still hurt, but her voice sounded oddly brittle, oddly bitter, and hollow.

"Whatever will p-p-put it behind you faster," David said. "Why don't you go upstairs and sack out and d-d-decide tomorrow?"

"Do you imagine I could sleep, David?" Did anyone imagine she could ever sleep again?

He shrugged his huge, soft shoulders. "Rolfe's just excited," he said. "He's always been a l-l-little jealous. It's gotta be tough on him, too, y'know. And we're all a little bombed by now. Just cool it, pal."

The others were drifting in. She had no idea what time it was. Karen, making sure she didn't sit next to Jerald, was leaning against the frame of the opening into the hall, nibbling at a stalk of celery and washing it down with whisky. Rolfe came in, picked up a small stool, placed it alongside Carole's chair and curled his long body to squat down on it. He reached for her left hand on the armrest and covered it with his. The heat in his palm made her realize that her whole body was chilled.

Cass appeared, offered her a glass of brandy, which she accepted with her right hand while she watched him; avoiding her eyes, he retreated to a far corner by the fireplace to perch on the cobbler's bench. "Hear ye, hear ye, the Court will please come to order," he intoned, picking up a half-filled glass of gin from the floor. "I'll bet you were the captain of the debate team, Jerry,"

"Screw you," Jerald said, politely but fondly.

Cass lifted his glass in a mocking toast to Jerald, and took a long swig.

Suddenly, and very strangely, it was as if her world had returned to normal. She was still off there somewhere observing, but she was also here, with her dearest friends, all of whom she loved, all of whom loved her, and for the first time she began to feel, but very faintly now, that pleasant glow that always came when they were together. But even that did not touch the pervasive anger that seemed to be taking over.

"Where are Esther and Allison?" Jerald asked.

"They've decided to get on with the steaks," Karen said. "Rolfe, did I hear you say Duncan Clive? He's a very well-known sculptor, y'know. Scottish, I think. And talk about weird art—"

"For God's sake," Jerald said, uncrossing and recrossing his legs.

"If anyone's interested," David said from the window-seat, "I'll be glad to play h-h-host at the Sheffield Inn. Leave Carole and Rolfe here alone so they can—"

Jerald interrupted: "What I think you should know, Carole, Rolfe, is that most rapes in fact do go unreported. Four out of five, I think. And with good reason."

"Here we go," Karen moaned and took a long swallow.

"Why don't you go mix the salad?" Jerald asked. And then added, "Put a lot of garlic in it, *darling.*"

"Why don't you go out to the pond and fuck a duck or goose a goose or something?"

Jerald reached into his blazer pocket and brought out his gold-rimmed glasses. "The next thing I think you both should know is that rape is a crime of aggression, rage—not really a sex crime at all."

Then Carole did speak, in a sweet voice, astonishing herself: "Tell me about it, Jerry." But she was beginning to tremble again, deep inside. "Then why didn't he use his fists? Or a gun? Or a club?" Was she actually saying this? "If it's not a sex crime, why did he use his goddamn pecker?"

"Because," Karen said, "because all men think they're superior to the female. Just because they have one."

"Oh Christ," Jerald groaned. "Let's leave poor Sigmund out of this. I'm sorry I mentioned it."

"No female's ever safe, anywhere, anytime," Karen said firmly. "And every woman knows it from the day she starts to menstruate."

"I just thought," Jerald said, turning to Carole, "that it might help you reach a decision if you could put what's happened into some kind of perspective."

"Are you advising me, since *you* think it's not really a sex crime, to forget it? Eat dinner maybe, or play Trivial Pursuit? Maybe you could tell us more about your goddess, Ayn Rand, and the sanctity of greed. Or you and Rolfe could compare your stock market scores for the week."

Jerald held up a fleshy palm: "Hey, slow down. All I

want is for all of us to examine the facts, all of them." He stood up and looked down on her. "Now—tell us what really happened."

Carole considered, while she observed herself considering. Then she heard her voice. It was very composed. "On the way home from shopping I went into the woods to pick some sumac. Some sonofabitch threw a blanket over my head and nearly choked me to death while he raped me."

Jerald nodded, adjusting his glasses on his thick nose, and began to pace up and down, slowly. "Wasn't there sumac along the side of the road?"

Startled now, feeling the current of anger quivering inside, Carole heard Rolfe ask, "What the hell difference does that make? What the fuck is this?"

"They'll ask more than this, the cops, the prosecuting attorneys, and if they ever catch the bastard, his defense lawyer will too. Much more, and much rougher. That's what I want you both to understand." Jerald whirled suddenly and fixed his eyes on Carole. "Maybe you went into the woods to meet someone."

Rolfe and Cass both stood up at the same time. My two protectors, Carole thought, the anger swelling into rage. "You know better than that, Jerry," she said, between her teeth.

"I'm not me. I'm only the devil's advocate. I'm a stranger who doesn't know you the way we do. Look, let's say they do catch the bastard—can you identify him?"

"I told you I never saw him. I just *told* you! He put a belt around the blanket and—" She broke off. "Where's the blanket? That was Sandy's lap robe, where—"

The sense of distance and detachment was gone. Her mind was clear. She was fully alive again. And furious.

"Then you can't ID the perpetrator," Jerald said, in triumph. He stepped closer, as Cass left the room. "Listen to me, Carole. You, too, Rolfe." Rolfe sat down on the stool again. "Those questions, those implications, innuendos, they're nothing to what you're in for, *nothing.* Carole, could you identify his voice? Did he speak at all?"

"He spoke," she said, trying to recall—a whisper, just a whisper in her ear, not a voice. She took hold of Rolfe's hand, palm to palm, clutched it. "Sweet nothings. Darling-dear-honey-sweet." She was trying to force her mind to remember. Then she took her hand from Rolfe's. He, the stranger, he was inside her, thrust after thrust, growling through the blanket—what exactly *did* he say? Remembering, she said, "He also called me every rotten name in the book. Slut. Bitch. Whore. Hooker. Tramp. What's the biblical word? I forget. He sounded as if he hated me."

"Carole," Jerald said, softly, "this isn't even a sample of what they'll put you through. They'll demand specific crude explicit details—penetration, orgasm. Why do you think I didn't want you to take a bath?"

From where she stood Karen spoke one word, a warning: "Jer-ald."

He swung about to face her. "Goddamn it, to get to trial the police'll have to have something besides Carole's word. And *if* it gets to trial, the defense'll try to get into her whole goddamn sex life. And if the Court refuses to allow it, the bastard's attorney will make it seem she has plenty to hide. Which could be worse."

"Every man knows his own profession," Cass said from the hall, where he now stood with fresh glass in hand.

"Up yours," Jerald snarled.

The phone in the hall rang. "I'll get it," Cass said, and disappeared. "Nobody's home, right?"

Jerald was speaking directly to Rolfe now: "Look at her. She's already a basket case; they'll tear her apart. I damn well wouldn't put Karen through it."

Karen was staring at her husband, speaking in her cool mocking voice: "Darling, you just don't read the romance novels. All really torrid passion begins with a healthy rape. But thanks anyway, Jerry." She lifted her empty glass and winked at him.

Jerald shook his head again, adjusted his glasses with his thumb, and turned to Carole. "And don't forget—you'll have to prove you fought. Resisted with everything you had. Do you have bruises on your body, skin under your fingernails?"

Carole's mind resisted. She was not going to sit here and tell them about her breast. Which was still throbbing with pain. Damned if she would. "I have bruises" was all she said.

Esther and Allison, bearing trays, appeared in the hall and stopped to listen. Cass came into the room and stood in front of her.

"Your car's gone, Carole," he said. "That was the Scotsman on the phone. He looked when he returned home. Whoever raped you must have stolen it."

A silence.

Carole felt Rolfe's eyes on her as Cass moved away. "I don't know what to say," Rolfe said. "Personally I'd like to cut his balls off. But . . . Jerry's probably right. We'd better skip it, Carole."

Allison came into the room and set her tray down on the cocktail table. Her light brown hair was damp and askew and her long narrow face was beaded with sweat. "Is it really your decision to make, Rolfe?" She tilted her head and waited.

The rage in Carole, instead of abating, had mixed with the brandy and that metallic taste of poison that had been in her mouth and throat ever since she had vomited in the woods. Now it had become cold fury.

Again, all eyes were on her.

From the direction of the pond she heard the pleasant familiar sound of frogs croaking.

The smell of charred steak filled the room.

"Well, Carole?" Rolfe asked, placing his arm around her back. "Allison's right, darling. I'll go along with whatever *you* say."

Esther came into the room with another tray and Allison said, "Why the bloody hell do men always think they have the right to make these decisions?" Suddenly furious, facing Rolfe, eyes hostile, she cried, "*You* weren't the one who was raped!"

"You didn't hear what Jerry's been saying," Rolfe said, his voice baffled and filled with indecision again. His arm went around her: "I'm thinking of Carole."

Esther had placed her tray on the cobbler's bench and moved to where David sat in the bay window. "I never told you, Davey, but I was raped once. When I was eleven years old." She spoke very quietly, very casually. "My parents refused to report it because they knew the boy's family. That's why I left home when I was sixteen. You've often wondered why I don't like to see them any more than we can help it, haven't you? Well, I never forgave them, that's why."

"Jesus," Carole heard David whisper. She saw him reach for Esther's waist and draw her down onto the window seat.

"If he stole the car, too," Carole heard herself say, in a low, controlled tone, "they might be able to catch him then, mightn't they?"

"It's possible," Jerald conceded. "It'd give the police something to go on, anyway. But police don't always solve crimes, you know."

Carole said, "True . . . But if I don't go through with what . . . all that you said . . . then he'll never be punished, will he?"

"Oh hell no," Allison said. "He'll be free to go on looking for other pretty young women who imagine it's safe to act naturally in this man's world." She grunted a bitter laugh. "He'll even use your car to do it. Because you also know, don't you, you can't report the theft of the wagon without reporting the rape. Right, Jerry?"

Jerald, eyes on Carole, nodded.

Carole looked around the room, from face to face. Every one, with the exception of Allison and the possible exception of Cass, seemed to say, *To hell with it, let's eat.* Eat, drink and be merry—and live with it unresolved, never ended, *unpunished* the rest of her life. As Esther had done. She felt Rolfe's arm tighten around her. Urging her, in spite of his words, almost begging her to agree with his *We'd better skip it, Carole.*

She felt something give way inside. Then it exploded. A volcano erupting, spewing fire and black, shining, molten lava.

"The goddamn bastard's not going to get away with it!" she heard herself bawling. Was that her voice? Was that her standing up, shrugging off Rolfe's arm? "What makes him think he can do this to me and walk away?" She was quivering all over again, with a stillness at the core. "He can't, he can't, I won't let him!" Was she shrieking? "That slime, that cruel sadistic sonofabitch, he has to be *punished!*" The pain in her breast was back, as if his hard, brutal hand were again trying to silence her, while inside her his huge penis thrust and tore and pumped. "If he's not punished for this, there's no justice, no meaning, *nothing!* I'll never sleep again, I'll never be *able* to sleep. I'll never be able to tell Sandy what's right, what's wrong. I'll never *believe.* I'll never be able to make love again, I'll never believe in anything, I'll die inside!" She stopped to take a deep, shuddering breath, her throat on fire again, hearing her voice reverberating in a wild, murderous, animal-like howl through the house. When she spoke again, her tone was low and harsh: "If the police can't punish him, I'll do it myself. If they can't kill him, I'll do it myself, not you, Rolfe, me, *I'll* do it! I'll *kill* him!"

A long moment passed.

After the echo of her voice died in the other rooms, the huge house seemed suddenly very quiet.

Outside, a catbird called, high and faint, like a kitten at the door.

Rolfe placed his arm around her again, very gentle, but very tight. "Does anyone know whether nine-one-one is connected to the Sheffield Police or the State Police Barracks?"

"Sheffield," Jerald said. "I think you're making a b-i-i-g mistake, friend."

"Thanks, Jerry, but Carole has decided." Then he kissed her on the forehead, released her and went into the hall, his long steps determined.

Carole, exhausted now, suddenly numb again, sank down into the chair. "I'd like to talk to Sandy before we go . . . wherever we have to go."

"I'll keep her overnight," Allison said. "She doesn't need to know."

"I'll tell her myself," Carole said. "When I think it's the right time." Had she ever been so tired? "I just want to hear her voice now."

She closed her eyes and put her head back on the chair. If only she could sleep. She could hear Rolfe's voice, low and competent in the hall. She couldn't make out the words. It didn't matter.

Henry Lindheim—Chief of Police, Town of Sheffield, Connecticut—was a man who had been haunted for twenty of his sixty-three years. His affliction was the most terrible of any—memory. After his wife Luisa's death eighteen years ago—of grief, no matter what the doctors said—he had even gone to her pastor, as he had refused to do two years before when their daughter Teresa had been killed. *The will of God,* the good, kind little Father Esposito had assured him. *We must accept.* But Henry Lindheim, without ever saying it to the priest, of course, had decided that if all he had witnessed as a member of the police force of the City of New York—if all that violence and pain and unspeakable terror day after day reflected the will of God, then it was impossible, regardless of his own need, to believe in the goodness of that God. So Henry had resorted to other ways to deaden the memory, to detach himself. But the booze had become addictive, only intensifying his sense of loneliness and loss. The booze had also led to his early retirement, although not officially, of course. Burnout, the police psychologist had termed it, protecting Henry's pension.

After retirement, with a wrenching of will that would have made Luisa proud, he had stopped drinking, cold turkey. Possibly because by then he did not have to deal daily with the chaos over which a few men had the impossible responsibility to impose order, to contain the uncontainable mayhem.

But idleness had soon become a horror of a different sort. So he had applied for police-enforcement jobs in various towns in Jersey and Connecticut and Long Island. (He had to be within driving distance of Woodlawn Cemetery in New York, in order to visit the two graves at least once a month.) Now for seven years, he had been living a spartan life in a three-room flat, bare and simple, necessities only, over the Village Store in the small town of Sheffield, Connecticut. Like an exile, or refugee, in an alien land.

When the call had come in on the private line from the four-room, two-cell police station next door, he had been watching an old black-and-white Bogart movie on TV, sipping the first of the two ales he allowed himself each evening. And when Worley Walker, the officer on duty tonight, had reported, Henry had asked the usual questions. Worley had done the proper thing: he had instructed the victim's husband to take his wife to the emergency room of the Sudbury Hospital. Then Henry gave his orders: to inform the State Police Barracks in Ridgewood, dispatch one of the Sheffield officers on duty in a cruiser to cordon off the scene, then notify the hospital. "Tell them I'm on my way and ask 'em," Henry added, climbing into a cardigan instead of his uniform tunic, "ask 'em to try to get Dr. Herbert Stoddard to the emergency room. Ask him to come as a personal favor to me."

Sexual battery on a female. Henry was still trying to absorb the shock. He put on his uniform cap and went down to his black Ford squad car parked between the two buildings. In his seven years here, he had never had to deal with this particular crime. Not up here, not in this quiet beautiful rustic place. In Sudbury—well, that was something else. A much larger, and industrial, town, Sudbury was becoming rougher and more and more like a city every day.

By the time he reached the hospital, a four-story tan-brick building situated atop a knoll in a neighborhood of modest old New England homes, he had himself in hand. Until he saw the cemetery, shadowy in the dark, on a sloping hillside across the street from the lighted hospital.

Luisa and Teresa—he always returned from those silent melancholy pilgrimages to Woodlawn lonelier than ever.

He drew his mind back to the here and now as he parked. At least the victim, Mrs. Carole Jensen, had survived.

Henry Lindheim had no slightest human compassion, no regard or shade of sympathy, for any man who had the capacity, for any reason, to inflict that ultimate violation on any female human being. He had only a deep, quiet, stolid loathing and contempt.

In the emergency room, which was remarkably not busy for a Saturday night, he introduced himself at the curved counter and inquired whether Mrs. Jensen or Dr. Stoddard had arrived. The young nurse with frizzy blond hair said, "Dr. Stoddard's scrubbing, but Mrs. Jensen hasn't arrived yet. You want some coffee?"

Henry glanced at his watch. 8:42. Too early for the blood and weeping and agony around here. All of which he'd just as soon not witness. "No, thank you, nurse," he said, turning to go find Herb Stoddard, when headlights swept the wide glass entrance doors and a car appeared under the portico. Some kind of foreign car, metallic blue, Peugeot, Saab, Audi, one of those. So he waited.

If Mrs. Carole Jensen was the young woman he thought she was, she lived in a big white Victorian house on Harrow Road: wide porches in front and along both sides, bay windows on the first floor and dormers above. Homelike place, except for that square tower centered on the front facade. He'd often admired it, passing by.

The outside doors slid silently apart and a young woman appeared. Yep, she was the one Henry thought she was. Small, with delicate bones, a girl really, but her body had the soft curves of a woman. Black hair, somewhat disheveled, blue denim skirt and a man's plaid shirt hanging loose. On her oval-shaped face, which was either slightly tanned or had a natural tawny color, was an expression of dread and determination, though she also seemed poised to turn and run, as she glanced around. Like a young deer—alert, frightened. But then he caught a glint of anger in her almond-shaped brown eyes—defiance.

Henry stepped toward her and removed his cap and introduced himself. She only nodded, as if perhaps she had recognized him anyway. The word *violated* returned to his mind, and a tightening in his gut followed. "Dr. Stoddard's here," he said. "Try to just relax, Mrs. Jensen." Her brown eyes, liquid and stunned, questioned him. That skin, those eyes, that softness of face—she had a lush sensual beauty. And this fact, for no logical reason, stirred his anger further.

"My husband's parking the car." Her tone was flat. Without inflection. The voice of a child waiting to be told what to do.

"After you see the doctor," Henry said, "I'd like to ask you a few questions." Like to ask? He hated the necessity, dreaded the moment. "May I see your fingernails, please?"

She extended both hands. "I tried," she said, a defensive note in her otherwise softly melodious voice, "but I couldn't scratch him."

Henry leaned down and took her hands in his, studied them. No help showing. As she dropped her hands, her husband appeared behind her, stepped to her and placed his arm around her waist. A tall, slim man—not so tall as

Henry, who stood six foot five, but tall by any other standard. Narrow, handsome face, sandy hair, blue eyes, sharp and indignant, which remained fixed on Henry.

"Nurse," Henry called to the counter area—but then he saw another nurse approaching. Older, matronly, gray-haired. He felt a satisfying jolt of relief.

"My name's Erna," the older nurse said. "Mrs. Jensen? We're going to Room Three, honey."

"While your wife's in there, Mr. Jensen," Henry said, "I'd like to get a few details from you. If you don't mind, sir."

For a moment Henry was afraid the husband was going to object. Instead, though, he leaned down slightly to kiss his wife on the forehead. Meekly then, she turned to accompany the matronly nurse.

The young nurse behind the counter came through the swinging gate. "Chief Lindheim, if I could have Mr. Jensen's medical insurance card, I could get started. Pretty soon this'll be a zoo around here."

Mr. Jensen complied, then accompanied Henry into the little office Henry had used once before in an investigation of a DWI-vehicular manslaughter that had occurred in Sheffield. Henry sat on the swivel chair behind the metal desk, which was bare except for the telephone, and Jensen lowered himself into the only other chair.

Henry began by saying, "It's rough, Mr. Jensen, this whole thing. On everybody." He didn't tell him how well he knew. He didn't mention sitting across another desk, twenty years ago, not behind the desk but in Jensen's chair then, and not in a hospital but in a morgue.

"What do you want from me?" Jensen asked, his eyes revealing that his mind was elsewhere. "All I can tell you is what she told me."

"Fair enough," Henry said, feeling the tension in the tiny room. "Hearsay evidence is welcome here. This isn't a courtroom, sir."

But a suspicion had slithered into Henry's mind: "You

don't have any reason to doubt what she told you, do you?"

"Listen, Chief," the husband said, "listen: I know you got your duty and I know you're from New York and I've already been warned that the police might doubt Carole's story." He leaned forward, hands on his knees, his sky-blue eyes challenging. "But if you start trying to put the blame on my wife—well, I don't know whether I'm dumb enough to risk a punch, but don't push me."

"Mr. Jensen," Henry said then, beginning for the first time to like this fellow, "everything I might have to ask you is just to help your wife. Ain't that what you want, too?"

Henry heard the *ain't* and warned himself that he was getting excited. He waited.

"Right, Chief," Jensen sat back in his chair and crossed his long, lean legs. "Shoot."

But, as always, before he could begin, there was the time-consuming routine—the detailed filling out of forms. Then, with the formalities more or less out of the way, Henry sat back and, hoping to relax Rolfe Jensen, said: "Now I'd like to hear what you saw and heard from, say, five o'clock on. Just as you recall it, and excuse me if I interrupt now and then—"

It turned out to be, for the most part, a dead-end interrogation, but at least he learned exactly where the crime had occurred, confirmed the approximate time (between five and six-thirty), the circumstances surrounding the attack but not the details—except that the victim had not seen her assailant, a fact that invariably removed at least ninety percent of the possibility for arrest and reduced the likelihood of conviction to practically nil. He learned that one hell of a lot of time had been wasted while the Jensens had discussed with their friends whether to report the crime at all—which he somewhat understood, but he also knew that the time lapse between the commission and the reporting of a crime invariably worked mightily in favor of the perpetrator.

"Could I have the names and addresses of your male friends who were in the house when your wife came home? Addresses and phone numbers if you can recall them."

Rolfe Jensen was frowning, his blondish brows low over his blue eyes. "What the hell did they witness that I didn't?"

Henry was preparing to write again, in his own notebook this time. "You mentioned an attorney who advised your wife not to file that complaint—"

When the list was complete—only three names, really—he laid down his ballpoint pen and sat back again, wishing he had a cigar, and said: "Let's go back to the alleged theft of the car. Has *that* been reported?" When Jensen shook his head no: "I'll need the details. Description, registration, et cetera."

"She left her purse on the seat. Whoever has the wagon has the purse." And then he added: "Bastard took everything."

Henry picked up the phone and dialed 9. "Color and make and year?" He dialed the State Police Barracks in Ridgewood. "Registered in whose name?"

"Hers," Rolfe Jensen said. "White Volvo wagon, this year's model." He grunted a mirthless laugh. "Birthday present."

"We'll get the rest of the details from Motor Vehicles."

When he'd given the information, making sure to add suspicion of sexual battery to the auto theft data in the bulletin, he sat back and said, "Chances of spotting the vehicle this many hours after the theft're damn slim. But a white Volvo wagon—not too many of those on the roads." No reason to tell the husband now that, even if the wagon was located and the car thief arrested, they'd need more than that to tie him to the assault. "Where is the blanket or lap robe you mentioned—any idea?"

"No idea. Have you searched the woods where it happened?"

"It's being done. They haven't had enough time for me to have the report yet. Mr. Jensen, we're both on the same side. Don't fight me."

"Then why don't you ask about this guy Duncan Clive? He owns the property, he was there when she ran to his house, but that doesn't mean he wasn't out there in the woods earlier."

"His name's on my list."

"What list?"

"The one in my head," Henry said gently.

But Henry understood: a man whose wife has been raped has to feel a certain natural jealousy along with the rage and hate for whoever did it. On the other hand, no reason to discount his suspicion altogether, either.

"I'm afraid," Henry said, "that I have to ask you a personal question now, sir." He hated the necessity, but something, possibly the husband's attitude, had brought the idea into focus.

"Like what?"

"Were you and your wife getting along?"

Jensen stood up. "Hey now, back off. We get along just fine."

"Good. But all couples quarrel. Have you had any serious rows lately?"

"The answer is no and you can go to hell."

Spousal rape, Henry knew, was not nearly so uncommon as people think. And often the wife was afraid to talk about it. He'd known cases where, out of fear or loyalty, she'd blamed some stranger. "Were you at home around five?"

For a long moment Jensen didn't answer, his eyes clouded with fury. Then he said, "I was at Dyer Electronics here in town and I didn't get home till just before six, when the guests were arriving. I sometimes have to work on Saturdays. You know something? I'm not going to take any more of this. If you think I'd do that to Carole because I was pissed off or something . . . whatever you think, screw you."

So Henry, knowing he was also excited now, stood up, too, and said: "Until we can arrest or until the perpetrator confesses, it's my job to treat every male with motive and opportunity as a suspect. But if I were in your shoes, I'd feel just the way you feel now. And the chances are ten-to-one it was some stranger. So why don't you go out to the desk and take care of the paperwork and I'll have a few words with your wife."

Jensen changed. A plea came into his tone, his narrow face twisted. "Do you have to put her through that now, tonight?"

"I'll be as quick as possible." He heard his tone: it was gentle again, even a touch of regret in it. "Things she might remember tonight that she might forget tomorrow. Way it happens, kid."

Rolfe Jensen was glaring again. "You think I'm crazy? You think I'd have brought her here if I'd *raped* her?" Then he turned and left the office without another word.

Henry went out and along the corridor. The door of Room 3 was open, so he went into the small doctor's lavatory in the emergency room area, where he found Herb Stoddard scrubbing his hands with a brush. Seeing Henry in the mirror, the tall, stoop-shouldered doctor, roughly Henry's age, scowled. "Did I ever tell you? Gracie and I go dancing at the Lake Club on Saturday nights, damn you."

"The victim's under thirty and I just figured it'd be less of an ordeal, considering the circumstances, if some old sainted grandfather type like you examined her. What's the word?"

"Did you have any doubt she'd been sexually molested, Henry?"

"None. But I like evidence. Forcible penetration?"

"Definitely. Semen samples taken. But all that'll give you is the attacker's blood type. She'll deliver her shoes and shirt and skirt to you, unlaundered, tomorrow morning." He began to dry his hands on a towel. "The healing in the vagina is going to take time, but the most severe physical injury is to the left breast."

"Breast?" A picture flashed in Henry's mind of a photograph presented in evidence once: a woman's breast that had been chewed by human teeth almost past recognition. When it had been introduced in the courtroom, a woman juror had fainted. He felt anger shoot through him, all through him. "What did he do to her breast?"

"Henry, when you question her, go very easy on this, will you?" The doctor was removing the green surgical gown. "He used one hand to stop her yelling, struggling. Sadistic scum put so much pressure on the left breast that it's already discolored and swollen and will get worse. I think I'll bring in a specialist. But on Monday, when she's less traumatized."

"You washed that area, I suppose."

"It needed attention. Why?"

"Why? Because I blew it, that's why! No one mentioned a breast injury and I didn't ask. There had to be prints on the flesh."

The doctor was tying a black bow tie at his throat now. "I'm not in forensic medicine, you know. I cleaned and dressed the wounds, took vaginal smears, repaired the lacerations, douched with surgical scrub lotions. Very painful. Very. Did the best I could, Henry."

"I'm not blaming you, I'm blaming myself, goddamn it."

"Well, don't, but that child does worry me. She's too damn quiet. Dangerously composed. She had to be in terrific pain, but she's not even crying." For the first time emotion colored the doctor's tone. "Henry, I'm too old for a case like this and I've got a daughter and two granddaughters. Get somebody else next time."

A thought occurred to Henry then. Would photographs of a bruised breast convince a jury, the males on a jury, that she had resisted? Without proof of resistance, absolutely no consent whatever, a defense attorney could—

"I know what you're thinking." Herb pulled on the coat of his crumpled gray seersucker suit. "If I testify, the Court'll know she put up a fight. And, there are other injuries—"

"Such as?"

"She fell down over and over, running in the dark afterward. Her knees are a mess. Now, I'm going to the Club, have one more dance with Gracie, a double bourbon, and then go home."

As the doctor was about to go into the corridor, Henry said, "Isn't there something else we're forgetting?"

"What? Possible pregnancy? Well, she says she's on the pill, but I instructed her to be aware of her next period and to take it up with her own physician. So stop fretting, Henry."

"What about VD?"

"Also too early. There are just some possibilities that a woman unfortunate enough to be raped by a stranger has to face and sweat out. If you want my opinion, the mental torture comes later and it's even worse than the physical. It's not the strong who get through something like this without grievous suffering, it's the insensitive. Now, may I go, teacher?"

"What about AIDS?"

Dr. Stoddard, in the door, groaned. "God, you think of everything, don't you? Well, so do I. I've drawn blood. It'll be tested for the AIDS virus antibody. And I'll order a T-cell profile and get it to the lab. It'll take five to ten days to come back, but even that won't be conclusive. The incubation period's five to seven weeks. But she and I *didn't* discuss this. Maybe she won't think of it."

"Jesus," Henry said under his breath.

Shaking his head, Dr. Stoddard stepped toward Henry, his gray brows coming together. "Henry, how long've you been a cop? Thirty years? Forty? You big ape, you're bleeding inside, aren't you? You'd like to stomp the sonofabitch yourself." And when Henry didn't answer: "Proves you're human. Not many of us left. G'night Henry. Nurse is finishing the forms."

Slowly then Henry went out and down the corridor to Emergency Reception. Rolfe Jensen was at the counter, writing.

His wife was standing behind him. Standing very straight, staring off—at nothing. She reminded him again of a little girl. A child. Her husband had given her age as twenty-eight.

He hesitated to move. His throat was dry and clotted.

Then she must have caught sight of him somehow. She came toward him at once, walking as if her legs were stiff, head high. When she reached him, she asked, "You wanted to talk to me?" She was looking up into his face. Her brows looked natural and thick, and very dark.

No. She'd had enough. *No!*

But he nodded instead of shaking his head and then led her into the office where he'd interrogated her husband. He held the chair for her and then resumed his seat behind the desk. Although she did not cross her legs, he saw the edge of bandages on both knees below the hem of her skirt.

"Mrs. Jensen," he said, hearing the quiet in his deep voice, "I'm sorry but I have only a few questions." He took out his notebook and ballpoint pen again. "This is what they call a first, or preliminary, report by the investigating officer. It's routine." She nodded. Her hair was vivid black, with a shine in it. "It won't take long and then you can go home and go to bed."

He asked her first about the hours of the afternoon before she stopped to go into the woods. She was a little vague in her answers. "I can't seem to remember things," she said at one point. And toward the end: "I stopped the car on impulse, I guess you'd say. I've always loved sumac."

"And about what time was this? You said it was almost dark."

"Five twenty-three. I looked at my watch. Odd, I remember that. Now that's odd, isn't it?"

Now he had an exact time. It could help. "There'll be other things, Mrs. Jensen. And if you remember anything, just dial nine-one-one anytime, day or night. Whatever you recall. Your husband told me you never actually saw your assailant—"

She moved her head from side to side. Then she went on answering questions, every question, in a low, controlled voice, never losing the drift of the conversation. During the episode of the attack itself he was careful not to ask for too many details and he never mentioned her breast. But with her moist brown eyes meeting his in a direct stare, she asked, "Didn't Dr. Stoddard tell you about my breast?"

"I have that information, yes. Now, afterwards—"

"No. *During.* Or just before. You realize I couldn't fight after a certain point, don't you? I wanted to go on but I couldn't. The pain was so awful, I blacked out."

"Mrs. Jensen," he said, "there's no shame in that. Or blame."

"I was kicking before that but—" Her face and voice hardened. "I could have killed him." And then she added: "I wanted to kill him." Then in a whisper, "I still do."

So do I, he thought. But he said, "You leave the punishing part to us. Now. Would you mind telling me how you got the blanket off your head, after he was gone?"

By the time he'd led her, question by slow painful question, through that and then her visit with the man who owned the land and the house—she was sorry she couldn't remember his name, only that he had some sort of accent and a dark-reddish beard—and then through her return home, he himself was spent and drained and tired to the bone. And a vast stillness had settled through his enormous body.

"You understand," he said, closing the notebook,

"there'll be more questions and you'll have to sign the official complaint. Tomorrow, if you feel up to it. On Monday morning if you don't."

She didn't answer at first, staring at a point over his head. Then that flint he'd seen before returned to her eyes and her voice sharpened: "I wouldn't be here if I didn't want you to catch the sonofabitch and send him to prison forever. Or worse. Much worse. Thank you, sir."

A few minutes later Henry stood watching as she and her husband moved through the emergency room toward the sliding glass doors. The armor she was wearing would wear thin. Then what?

Rolfe Jensen left his wife standing under the portico with the light from above on her and disappeared into the parking area. Mrs. Jensen was joined almost at once by another man—a short slight fellow who looked vaguely familiar. Henry could not hear what they were saying but he saw Mrs. Jensen draw away after a brief exchange and then he saw the small man (he wore no hat and had curly bright red hair) start to follow.

Mrs. Jensen whirled, took two steps toward him and then, swinging wide, she struck him across the face with the palm of her hand. Then she turned and began to run.

Astonished, Henry started toward the doors when they slid open and the small man came inside.

Henry recognized him then: Joel White, a jaunty little fellow in his thirties with a sharp-featured face—which always seemed to wear a friendly sneer. Police reporter on the *Sudbury News-Chronicle.* He started toward the reception counter. But then he must have seen Henry because now, brown eyes brightening, he came toward him. "Chief Lindheim! How are you?" Then he stopped and lowered his voice: "So Carole Jensen's the one who was raped in Sheffield tonight, was she?"

"Don't jump to conclusions, kid. Mrs. Jensen's car's been stolen."

"So?" He tilted his head to one side. "So she comes to a hospital?"

"You know Mrs. Jensen, do you?"

"Sure. She works part-time for the paper. We're old buddies."

"Anyone could see that."

The print of the young woman's palm was just beginning to fade on Joel White's sallow face.

"God's truth, man. She does art work at home for the advertising department. Special arrangement, she's the old man's favorite." He stepped closer and lowered his voice again. "The police bulletin reads suspicion of sexual assault and grand theft auto. White Volvo wagon—"

Henry took one long stolid step, aware of his towering size and the ugly menace of his own face—which had proved useful many times before. "Mister White . . . sir . . . you know as well as I do your paper won't print the name of a sexual assault victim, no matter how many wild guesses you make. But . . . get this. Mrs. Jensen lives in Sheffield, that's my turf, and I *can* keep you from harassing her like you just did." He got a perverse stab of pleasure from the expression that had come into the small face beneath his gaze. The narrow glittering eyes had lost their glitter.

"Gotcha, Chief." Joel White lifted one hand to salute, but the mockery he'd intended failed him. He retreated, all jauntiness gone, to the doors, trying not to break into a trot.

Henry heard a snickering and turned his head to look at the nurses' counter. The young nurse with the frizzled blond hair winked. He relaxed then. He even grinned.

Then he went out the glass doors to his vehicle, which he still thought of as a squad car, although up here police officers never worked in teams.

He heard an ambulance siren approaching in the distance.

The night promised to be a long one. Once he stopped to buy some cigars, he might be able to get a charge out of it.

It'd been a long time since he'd gotten a charge out of . . . well, much of anything.

"I've heard you mention Joel White, sure." Rolfe was speaking while he drove through the dark side streets of Sudbury. "I remember you had everybody laughing at some party. How he puts women down with sexist gags. To prove how macho he maybe really *isn't*, you said. Still doesn't explain why you whacked him back there."

The shoulder harness was digging into her breast. She didn't want to talk. Or think. Or listen to anybody else talk. But she knew that if she didn't answer . . .

"He wanted to interview me," she said. Her voice was as weak as she felt all over. "When I refused, he said everyone knows all women really want to be raped at least once in their lifetime."

"What a prick."

"And . . . and did I really dig it when it finally happened?"

"I've got half a notion to go back and really deck the bastard myself."

"Please," she said, unfastening the harness, "please, oh, please, darling, just take me home." Why was he so far away? Why wasn't his arm around her?

"I shouldn't have let them do this to you. Not him, or that Chief Lindheim. Another asshole. A man that age with a gray brush cut! Head looks like it's been cut out of stone. Was *he* in the examining room?"

The car seemed chilled. When she spoke, the rawness in her throat caught fire: "Oh Rolfe, please. No more questions. No, only the nurse and Dr. Stoddard were in the room."

Then there was silence, her mind blurring. The nurse had given her a shot for the pain . . . maybe it made her sleepy, too.

She heard a sound. The cigarette lighter. Was Rolfe smoking again? He'd stopped, he'd sworn off—

"I think we'd better phone your folks when we get home."

"No, Rolfe, please." The lighter snapped out. "I can't face that tonight." Maybe never. Why tell them? They'd never given a damn.

The only one who had ever really loved her was Rolfe. Rolfe and, of course, and . . .

"Sandy," she said aloud. "Drive faster, darling. I want to see Sandy."

Smoke filled the car. She wanted a cigarette herself now.

"Sandy's not home, dear," Rolfe said. "Don't you remember? She's at Allison's for the night."

Now she remembered. But she *had* forgotten. Why, all of a sudden, couldn't she remember things?

"Not tonight," Rolfe said, "but sometime tomorrow, we'll have to really talk. Decide what we're going to tell Sandy."

Five years, almost six, only five years old—how can you tell her her mother's been raped? *What's rape mean, Mommy?*

Rolfe, hold me. Hold me!

She opened her eyes. They were on the highway now.

"What about the doctor? Did he tell you anything?"

More questions. But natural, logical questions. She had to answer natural logical questions, didn't she? "He . . . Dr. Stoddard said there was no serious damage, except he wants more tests on the breast."

"Breast! What'd the bastard do to your breast?" Rolfe's voice filled the whole car. "Why didn't you tell me, Carole? You couldn't have forgotten *that.*" His voice was tense, but not angry now, just on the edge. "Carole?"

"He squeezed it. He twisted it to make me stop yelling, and fighting—"

"To make you let him screw you, that's what you mean, isn't it?"

Her voice was a faint whisper: "I blanked out."

The car turned off the highway onto the narrow winding road to The Village. She glanced at Rolfe's shadowy profile. He was hunched over the wheel, staring ahead, eyes slitted.

Now they were passing through Sheffield Center. She saw the Congregational church, its steeple lighted, and the Village Store, its windows dark, and the police station with the blue globe-light over its entrance.

"What else did he do to you, Carole?"

"Nothing. What do you mean?"

"Sometimes I think you don't live in the real world. You know what I mean."

"No, I don't." But by then she did know. Her stomach tightened.

"What else did he do to you, or force you to do to him?"

"Nothing." She heard her voice rise. "He screwed me, as you put it. Isn't that enough? He raped me. Isn't that enough?"

The car was climbing Obtuse Hill.

Rolfe did not speak again until it reached the Four Corners and started down toward the bridge. Then he said, grimly: "Jerry was right."

"Jerry was wrong." Her firm tone surprised her. *"Both* Dr. Stoddard and Chief Lindheim . . . they couldn't have been nicer."

"What if it gets into the papers? On TV?"

"It won't. Dr. Stoddard explained—"

"You think Jerry and David and Allison, especially Esther—you think they won't talk? These things get around."

"Maybe. I don't know. Maybe."

"Why didn't we just assume some stranger did it and got away? Why didn't we just forget it, put it in back of us?"

Why hadn't they? Because . . . because, she had it now, because the animal had to be captured, had to be put in a cage, had to be made to suffer the way she . . .

There was another long silence. A blessed silence. Only the purr of the motor, the hum of tires . . .

They went down the hill between cliffs, into the clear, then across the long narrow steel bridge. LAKE LILLINONAH: the sign flashed by.

What now? When they arrived home, what?

"It's too late now," Rolfe said, still distant, lost in his own thought, not touching her. "It'll be the talk of . . . hell, everybody. Parties, bars, Jesus. Every time you go out of the house, take work in to the paper, movies, restaurants, every goddamn male'll be licking his chops and wondering how he can get it on with you."

More silence. Around curves. Then the car turned onto Harrow Road. Their road. But it was like driving home with a stranger. She slid lower in the seat and closed her eyes again. She didn't believe what he'd just said. *All* men weren't like that. If she believed that, if that was the way the world really was . . .

She felt the car turning. Into the driveway. Through her lids she saw the glow of the lights in the trees. And heard the familiar crunch of wheels on the gravel.

"Don't you even care who *I* think did it?" Rolfe said. And before she could answer: "The limey. Mr. Duncan Clive."

"Who?"

"Oh come on, Carole. The red-bearded bastard you had drinks with afterward."

Then she remembered. So that was his name. Duncan Clive. He, too, had been kind. Or—

Or had that been *after* he'd—

Then who stole the station wagon?

Or had he lied about that? To make the police think—

It was too much, it was all too much, too much, *too much!*

Then, as the car came to a stop by the big oak, she opened her door and heard herself shouting: "I didn't *have drinks* with anybody, so screw you, mister, screw you!"

Leaving the door open, she ran up the walk to the veranda, passing Cass's old maroon Corvette parked on the grass as usual, her knees stiff and hurting, the air balmy, lights in windows, she had to see Sandy, no, she had to call her, it was too late, was Cass in the house or in the cottage in back, she didn't want to see anybody, she didn't want to talk, she wanted to clean the filth off, finally, at last.

She was in the hall. Moving toward the stairway. Maybe it was all a dream, after all. And tomorrow they'd wake up, the sun shining, and it would be Sunday and she'd fix a big breakfast—

"Carole." Rolfe's voice stopped her. It sounded low and miserable, in pain. When she turned to look at him, he came toward her from the door.

And then he was holding her, at last, against his chest, at last.

Into her ear, a whisper: "Carole, I feel so shitty seeing you like this. So . . . helpless. I'm sorry. I don't want to make anything worse."

"Kiss me," she said. "Don't you *want* to kiss me, Rolfe?"

He kissed her then. On the lips.

But it was not Rolfe's kiss.

It was not *their* kiss.

And all of a sudden a wild grief went through her. She knew that her whole life had changed, was changing, and nothing would ever, could ever, be the same again.

When he released her, he stepped back. Away. Unclean, unclean—

She saw the torment in his eyes. Falteringly he said, "It's not exactly easy for me either, you know."

She knew. As she turned to go, slowly, up the stairs, she knew, but . . .

"You want me to carry you, darling?" he asked behind her.

But she didn't stop. If she stopped, she might fall back down the stairs.

Then she heard: "If only you hadn't gone into those damn woods by yourself—"

She did stop then. Near the top. But she didn't turn to look down. She had heard the anguish in his voice.

His anguish—which was not for her.

"Carole, listen. I want you to know this—I don't blame you." Blame? What had *she* done? "I don't blame you for anything and I'll stick with you and I'll do whatever you want me to do, okay? Okay, Carole?"

She nodded her head, tried to speak, couldn't, and then mounted a few more steps to reach the upstairs hall. Which was dim.

Had she ever been so alone?

And she hadn't cried. When was she going to cry?

On the way to have his own look at the crime site, smoking one of the cigars he'd bought on the way, Henry Lindheim realized something very strange. The juices in him were running again. *I wouldn't be here if I didn't want you to catch the sonofabitch and send him to prison forever. Or worse. Much worse.* A new excitement was coursing through his veins now, moving all through his legs and arms, in places of the ache he usually felt by this time of night.

Even before he reached the woods, he saw the lights. Reds flashing on and off, blues revolving, headlights burning. Closer now, he could hear the radios crackling and, as he climbed down from the cruiser, the mutter of heavy voices, filtered and indistinct. A white van was parked off the pavement, alongside a low fieldstone fence, which people around here called a wall; on its side the words CONN. STATE POLICE CRIMINALISTICS. Among the trees beyond it, shadows moved, flashlights probing. The whole scene had a nightmarish familiarity that roused something deep and dark in him.

He climbed heavily over the wall and, then, hearing his own footsteps on the brittle leaves, he stalked into the woods. A portable floodlight had been set up, glaring over a small area that had been cordoned off with yellow tape on stakes, a clearing among the trees.

"Evening, Chief." It was Duane Jessup, in uniform, one of the four officers on patrol duty in Sheffield tonight—a lanky middle-aged southerner, who, like Henry, was an outsider in these parts. "Trooper Dworsky," Duane drawled, "he practically told me to butt my ass out. Them're all his men and he don't want our help, Ah reckon."

Henry knew Brad Dworsky and had tried to steer clear of the man. To Henry one of the peculiarities of the police system up here in the country was that each town had, in addition to its own town police, a resident state trooper who lived within the town limits. And "town" up here did not refer to a village but to a township, which usually included several villages. The property here, although four miles from the *village* of Sheffield, was nevertheless in the *Town* of Sheffield. All lay within Fairfield County, which spanned an enormous area.

Dworsky, a wide-shouldered but slim young man who stood almost as tall as Henry, was wiping the sweatband of his wide-brimmed brown hat with his handkerchief, his totally bald dome of a head shining damp in the harsh light. "That's the works, Chief. We're still searching, but so far, what you see on the tarp—Indian blanket, belt, panties—that's about it. You onto anything?"

"I have the victim's statement, and her husband's. Also a preliminary medical."

The trooper's beady dark eyes, set deep in a smooth simian face, narrowed. "I was going to speak with the victim next."

Henry decided to ignore that. "I'd like to examine the belt."

"No can do. If we don't get prints on some of that stuff —and the belt's our best bet—we won't have any till we get the car. By then we'll have him anyway, fuck the fingerprints."

"Will we?" Henry was not so damn sure. He lowered himself to his knees and leaned over the tarpaulin.

From above, Dworsky said, "Just an ordinary man's belt. Only it doesn't have the size printed inside it."

The belt was *not* ordinary. In the first place it was not horsehide or cowhide but black snakeskin, and in the second place it had a slide buckle, the sort issued by the military, usually brass, but this one was silver. No holes in the leather, no prongs on the buckle. The belt slid behind the plate and was adjusted to comfort; then secured by a small roller mechanism on the back of the plate. Not many men wore such belts today. He stood up.

"I'd like to see the two statements as soon as they're typed up," Dworsky said, his eyes level with Henry's. "Before morning."

"Brad," Henry said, using the officer's name for the first time, "Brad, I don't have your secretarial resources."

Dworsky nodded and put on his stiff-brimmed hat and set it at an angle and spread his long legs. "Damn good reason why I should take the statements. If you don't intend to comply, I'll go from here to the Jensen house and get her statement myself."

"I sent the young woman home to bed," Henry said. "Brad, she's had plenty for one day."

Dworsky shrugged. "She's gonna *get* plenty if she takes a walk in the woods by herself. Almost dark. What's she expect?"

Something exploded inside. Henry said, "If you bother her tonight—" But he didn't finish.

The young man was grinning. A patronizing grin. "What, Chief? What'll you do? In the investigation of a first-degree felony, the State Police officer in charge takes precedence. You don't know the rules yet?"

Henry was remembering the way Carole Jensen had looked when she left the hospital. Now, only five or six hours after she'd been assaulted, now to be awakened by a State Police car coming down her driveway—

Henry knew when he was licked. The battle, but not the war. So he said, "I'll drive to the Ridgewood Barracks and dictate it to whoever's on duty."

"Good thinking, Chief. Got a fancy new recording system. Be my guest."

Every muscle and nerve rigid, Henry returned to his car, aware of a flash bulb flaring as he stepped over the stone fence, his hip joint catching. He saw a glint of red hair after the flash.

"Thanks, Chief," Joel White's voice again, and to hell with him. "Monday morning edition, Chief."

"Mr. White," he called, "could you spare me a minute of your time? In my car, please."

"Sure, Chief," the reporter said. And when they were in the seat together: "You don't want your picture in the paper, Chief, no sweat, I'll kill it."

"Mr. White, I'm in a hurry, so answer me short and quick. Where'd you spend the afternoon?"

"Chief, hey, man, you don't think—"

"Short and quick," Henry said again.

"Today's my day off. No Sunday edition."

The kid was giving himself time to think. "Cut the preamble. Where were you between five and six P.M.?"

"Lime Rock."

"What?"

"Lime Rock Racetrack. Sports cars. It's only an hour away."

"You go alone?"

"Usually. Say, Chief, you don't really—"

"Why'd Mrs. Jensen swat you a good one at the hospital a while ago?" Henry was keeping the kid off-balance.

"I . . . I guess I got a little outta line. But—"

"When does the last race end?"

"Four-thirty or so, five, but you know, you stay and

have a few beers with . . . you know, friends. Race fans're a friendly crowd, like a club."

"Anyone in particular?"

"You can't be serious."

"Anyone in particular? Names?"

"Chief, I honestly don't think I have to take this."

"What time'd you get back to Sudbury?"

"Late. I had to eat and I phoned the city room, routine."

"You got a belt on?"

"Belt?"

"The thing that holds up your britches."

"I wear suspenders." Joel White uttered a nervous laugh and opened his jacket. The suspenders were red. "I always say a man who wears a belt and braces has got to be pretty insecure inside, right?" He giggled. "I know someone who does."

Henry flipped on his headlights and reached for the key. "Stay away from Mrs. Jensen," he said.

Joel White opened the door and got out. "I'll do my job, Chief. Just the way you're doing yours. No hard feelings, right?"

To hell with him. *And* with Trooper Dworsky. What bothered Henry was that belt he'd seen on the tarpaulin. Something *wrong* about it. Something *not right.* But what? He couldn't get it into focus.

He realized that he was approaching a driveway. In the headlight beams he saw a carved wooden figure—was it supposed to be a nude woman?—holding a postbox in her outstretched hands. He saw the single word *CLIVE* carved on the side of the large wooden box and made a sharp turn, the car climbing up a grade to an old gray barn that, he knew, was now a house. Might as well dictate four statements as three—the victim's, her husband's, Joel White's, and now, since he was in the neighborhood, Duncan Clive's.

It wouldn't be the first time in his career that the suspicions voiced by a victim's spouse had led to the actual arrest. Nothing was unimaginable in Henry's book. Nothing.

And when he was seated in a huge leather chair in the enormous room with polished beams high above, the walls covered with strange, bright paintings, the word came back to him: unimaginable. The shoulder-high cubicles he'd seen when he came in were converted animal stalls. Above, the lofts running lengthwise had become narrow balconies with doors opening off them, probably bedrooms. Henry had begun to wish he hadn't acted on impulse. He felt ill at ease, and out of place, and awkward. And then of course he felt obliged to make an awkward comment: "What they call a studio, is it?"

"I don't have a studio," Duncan Clive said, in his odd accent, and stiffly. "My workshop's the other half of the barn."

Not a friendly, or promising, opening. This man Clive—dark red beard, cool gray eyes, maybe just a little wary, about forty years old—the man wasn't going to make it any easier. "I'd like to talk to you about what happened earlier this evening." Henry did not take out his notebook. "When Mrs. Jensen asked you for help."

Duncan Clive was wearing bedroom slippers and a black Oriental bathrobe that had seen better days, and was smoking a Sherlock Holmes pipe. He was now pouring himself a Scotch on the pass-through counter between the living room and the stall that was now a bar. "Whisky? Brandy?" His tone was polite, but far from cordial.

"Not while I'm on duty," Henry said, thinking of his bottle of ale waiting for him at home and wishing he'd brought a cigar inside with him. "I guess Mrs. Jensen was hysterical when you saw her."

"I'd say she was in shock, a wee bit hysterical, yes." Duncan Clive sat down on the leather couch and threw one leg over its arm. "I heard her outside first." His eyes filled with a sort of self-mockery. "As a lad in Scotland, I always imagined how a banshee would sound."

"You're a Scotchman then, not English."

"A Scotsman—on my mother's side. My father was a proper English gentleman. I tried to lose the burr when I was in art school in London, then I said to myself: Ye're a mongrel, be a mongrel, devil take the ass end. My work'll speak for itself." He took a long swallow. "My scoolpture garden out there terrified her further, I think."

While Henry listened, trying to picture the scene, Duncan Clive told him that he'd carried her in bodily. He'd felt helpless trying to "quieten" her. He'd all but forced her to drink some brandy, he'd tried to "ring" her home, she'd turned on him once when he'd tried to touch her—"for some damned thoughtless reason"—and then he'd "fetched" her home in his car. He took another long swallow of Scotch and said, "I was bloody churlish and I've felt only regret ever since. I'm accustomed to being alone and I'm a peevish and bad-mannered blighter when I'm not *let* alonc."

Henry took the point but ignored it, saying: "I live alone, too. People get that way, don't they? You wouldn't mind telling me where you were just previous to Mrs. Jensen's . . . intrusion?"

Duncan Clive looked startled, then he took a few seconds to think that over before his beard twisted into another self-mocking smile. "I begin to comprehend," he said. "What a bizarre idea."

"Just answer the question, Mr. Clive."

A quick glare came into the man's eyes. His voice became a growl: "As I tried to tell Mrs. Jensen, I don't go about ravishing young women who happen to trespass on my property."

"Were you here in the house?"

"As a matter of fact, I'd come in just before I heard the screaming." He stood up. "I'd been to visit my daughter, who lives with my ex-wife in Cambridge. I often motor up there on Saturday or Sunday."

"That's all I wanted to know," Henry said then—knowing that what he had heard was, in some way, not the whole truth. "Has your ex-wife remarried?"

"She's married to a professor of Romance Languages." Duncan Clive had begun to prowl about the room, a bitter personal note creeping into his tone: "His name's Keith Sutton and my daughter's name is Francie, for Francine, and my ex is named Elaine." He was telling more than Henry had asked for—why? "Anything else, Chief?"

"I wish," Henry said, "everyone I questioned was so cooperative." He knew that Duncan Clive was lying, not flat out perhaps but he was sure as hell telling only part of the truth. "I'm sorry I barged in." Henry lifted his weight from the chair. "You're the one who discovered Mrs. Jensen's station wagon had been stolen, weren't you?"

"When I couldn't find it along the road, I rang her house. If you're going to tell me I should have notified the police, the answer is that I thought that decision was hers, not mine, to make."

Henry nodded and started toward the door. "Thank you for your time, sir."

"I have a question for you. Is that lass getting proper medical attention?"

"She's been examined. Medication has been prescribed."

But Duncan Clive shook his shaggy auburn head, made an impatient gesture, and snarled: "Not *that* kind of attention, *damn* it! She's heading for an emotional collapse if somebody—doesn't *anyone* recognize the symptoms?" His gray eyes had become sharp and bright. "Don't you even know what I'm talking about?"

Henry realized that he had not seriously considered this possibility, even after Herb Stoddard had suggested it. "I know what you're talking about," Henry said, grudgingly. "I'll explore the idea. Thanks."

"She's a bonny lass, that one."

After he'd left, Henry remembered the AA meetings, years ago. Stories he'd heard, confessions. Alcoholic amnesia. Whole spaces of time blanked out. During which a man could have done anything—

No doubt in his mind: this Duncan Clive was a boozer. How far along, no outsider could ever guess. Hell, a mate, no matter how close, could never really know. If the man, after visiting his ex-wife and daughter, had been in a bitter mood and drinking all the way home from Cambridge, Massachusetts—

Then if he happened to see a "bonny lass" go into his woods just before he reached home—

Henry decided to check out the artist's whole story and background. At the crossroads he turned in the direction of the Ridgewood Barracks and picked up the mike and gave the code numbers, thinking of his bed and ale waiting for him upstairs over the Village Store.

When he heard Worley Walker's voice, he asked, "Anything?"

"Plenty," the voice said, "but not urgent enough to beep you. The vehicle, the white Volvo wagon, New Jersey State Police got it. Spotted it on the New Jersey Turnpike, heading south. The perp panicked and tried to elude. Cracked up the vehicle somewhere south of Camden."

"What about him?"

"In custody, but in the Intensive Care Unit, Camden Hospital. Touch and go. Are you ready for this? He was so intoxicated, he was blind. They found two full gin bottles and an empty fifth of Courvoisier in the back of the vehicle."

"The subject has a name, doesn't he?"

"Manuel Mendoza, no permanent address. We got him, Chief."

"Maybe." Henry said. "Maybe." And then he began to give instructions. "Phone Jersey State Police. Tell them to take his clothes, skin out, all of them, and send Bill Schiller down there to get them tonight."

"Sorry, Chief. State Police've already sent someone for that."

"Shit," Henry said, and then remembered that his voice was on the police band. "Okay, try to get his blood type. And when you phone New Jersey, find out whether he was wearing a belt when apprehended. Also, I want his record, if any. And get a copy of his prints."

"Roger, Chief. Soonest. Out."

Henry flipped on the siren, and the blue light, and trounced on the gas pedal, at the same time tempted to turn around, go to the Jensen house and inform Carole Jensen. She'd be relieved to know they had the man in custody, disturbed, probably, to learn that her birthday present had been wrecked. Also, she needed a night's sleep and he was damned if he could tell her that apprehending the auto thief was not the same as having the rapist under arrest.

Duncan Clive . . . he may have been lying about himself but he was damn well telling the truth about her: she *could* crack up and no telling what would do it.

Very strange, the way he'd come to feel.

He cared again. He cared about a young woman named Carole Jensen.

Maybe he was rejoining the human race.

She was awake again. Or was she?

The big old house was very quiet. The bedroom was dim. She could see the white fireplace and the closed door. Darkness beyond the dormer windows.

She was alone in bed, her bed, their bed—where was Rolfe?

He had come in once, after she'd bathed in the tub and then showered, and he'd held her and kissed her, and told her again how sorry he was, he hoped she understood. His breath had smelled of bourbon, and when she'd touched his face, it had been wet with tears. She'd never known Rolfe to cry before. Not once, ever.

He'd be back, he said, and they'd sleep till noon if she wanted to, tomorrow was Sunday.

Then . . . where was he? How long ago had that been?

She'd taken the medicines, all three . . . one for pain, one for sleep and the third, a black-and-green capsule. . . . For quiet, for calm, for peace . . . and she remembered placing the prescription pages on the nightstand to remind her to go to the pharmacy in the morning. . . .

Should she get up and look in on Sandy? But. . . . Sandy was not home. So she didn't move.

. . . No pain. Was it possible? A miracle. No . . . pain . . . anywhere.

So she closed her eyes and let the darkness fold over her.

And now she could hear voices. Far off. Downstairs. Faint.

Two voices. Rolfe and Cass. Sitting up. Talking. The way they always did. And drinking. Rolfe drank too much on weekends when Cass was here. Had she ever mentioned that to him? *Borderline*—that was Rolfe's word. *Cass is a borderline alcoholic, but he's not there yet.* And what can anyone do? The affection between the two men, comrades—she liked that word—comrades was better than simply friends, the proper word, on the nose, she'd never had a comrade, when she was a child, in college—not ever really—lucky Rolfe, lucky Cass . . .

She drifted away again. Half-asleep, drowsing, dozing. Should she take another capsule?

As she felt herself slipping into unconsciousness then, she wondered: Had she taken the pill before breakfast?

So long ago now . . .

Had she taken it automatically, as she always did? Hopefully, even when she knew that Rolfe was not going to make love to her today—

Or now, tonight.

Or any other day or night.

How long had it been?

A week? Two weeks? Three?

Why, why, why?

Maybe she should get up and take it now—

Or was it too late?

Was it too late *afterward?* This many hours afterwards—

Oh God, how long before she'd know?

When was her next period?

Were there tests they could give her now? Tomorrow—

Or was it too soon?

Dr. Stoddard would have thought of that—

She couldn't remember what he'd said . . .

And then, out of nowhere, a memory returned. It had been midsummer then, a hot day, hotter than Indian summer, and she'd been working in the tower room on the third floor, which they'd turned into a work studio because of the light on three sides, she'd been working hard yet nothing had seemed to come right, she'd made a hundred sketches, all wrong, all wrong, so she'd decided to have a swim. Sandy was still at day-care, she had a couple more hours, so she'd gone downstairs, unbuttoning her damp shirt as she went out to change into her tank suit—

But before she reached the bath house, she became conscious of—what? She stopped along the edge of the pond and looked around. Then she saw him. On the dock. Watching her. She recognized him at once: the doctor's son, who lived on Still River Road. He was half-stretched out on the canvas chaise she used for sun bathing, a shirt on his lap, over his swim trunks, his chest and legs bare. Long-haired, brown-haired, about sixteen or seventeen—what was the kid's name? And what was he doing here? He didn't move when she discovered him, only smiled, smiled as if they were old friends—when she couldn't even think of his name!

Had she said anything? No, because before she could find the words, he stood up, not tall, thin but muscled and tanned, and threw the shirt up over one shoulder. He was still smiling.

He was not wearing swim trunks. He was not wearing

anything. He still stood with his eyes taunting her, daring her to react, his arms at his side . . . while she stared, unable to speak at first, unable to move.

Had she been frightened? No, because he was several long yards away, across the water, and she could run, she was a fast runner. But did that even go through her mind?

Scott—his name had come to her then. Scott Keller, Dr. Kenneth Keller's son.

While she stood there—it all happened in less than a minute's time—she saw his penis limp and boyish and still. It went through her mind that it was odd that it had not stiffened or lengthened while he stood there naked and staring at her unbuttoned shirt. . . .

She was sitting up in bed now. The image faded.

But she remembered, very clearly, what she'd said. She could even hear her own voice in her ears now, outraged, thin and harsh with anger: *You're trespassing, you little punk. If you don't get your ass out of here, I'm going to call the police and have you arrested!*

Had she really shouted that?

She'd been furious then. Now she felt no anger, only a vague revulsion, the sick disgust returning to her mind and body.

Should she call for Rolfe? She'd never told him about Scott Keller. Why? No telling, no predicting what Rolfe would have done—find the kid, punch him out, or go to his parents, or the police, or what?

The boy had left. He'd simply turned and walked, naked, off the small dock and across the lawn and into the woods. Without looking back.

She lay in the bed and turned onto her side. The pillow was damp against her cheek. Had she been crying after all? In her sleep? Or were those Rolfe's tears?

And if you remember anything, just dial nine-one-one, any time, day or night—

But no . . . too late to phone him now. She'd remember in the morning. She'd force herself to remember!

Scott Keller. That grinning, smirking little sonofa-bitch—

If he was the one, if he'd been the one who'd raped her—

But, without accepting, she knew the truth: It could be anyone. A stranger. Someone she'd never met, or even seen, some cruel, savage, wild beast prowling the jungle—

Her mind drifted into darkness. As the sickness came back in waves of nausea and loathing and fury and disgust.

Finally . . . finally she lost consciousness.

PART 2

CAROLE WOKE WITH THE sun in her face.

What time? She turned in the bed to look. After eleven.

When she stood up, her head rocked and she felt a bit dizzy. But there was only the faintest pain, a low-keyed throb in her breast, the sensation of rawness, soreness, in her vagina. Then it all came flooding back—the outrage, the fury, the sickening hate. The sonofabitch—he was going to get his. She was going to make sure he got his!

This brought her out of bed and she had taken off the pajamas when she caught sight of her breast in the mirror: bulbous and purple, unreal—*grotesque!* Oh, God, was he going to get his! A bitter, fetid taste rose in her throat.

But as she dressed—why was the house so quiet?—she realized that there was something else, something important, which she'd thought of during the night, which she had to remember. Had to . . .

But couldn't.

Wearing a striped collarless blouse, chinos, and Reeboks, she was about to leave the room—hungry, actually *hungry!*—when she glanced at the bed. And realized: Rolfe had not slept with her in the bed. Then where?

And why?

That word came into her mind again: unclean. A biblical word. From her childhood. Lepers hiding their ulcerated, wasted faces. . . .

Again she had the eerie, overwhelming feeling, or certainty, that everything was changing, everything, and would go on changing. Nothing would ever be the same again. A vague sense of loss, emptiness, and regret, passed through her.

Bewildered, hesitant, she went down the stairs, her knees stiff with pain. Sunday morning. Where was Sandy? She suddenly ached to hear her daughter's voice.

The front hall was deserted. The living room was in perfect order. After last night, how could that be? She glanced into the den. A mess. Where Rolfe and Cass had sat talking. And drinking. Had Rolfe slept here, on the leather couch?

Passing through the dining room, she glanced out the window. The pond glimmered in the sun. Another summer's day. In October.

Why the *hell* couldn't she remember what she'd thought of last night? Something she had to tell Chief Lindheim first thing this morning. Something important—did it have to do with the pond? Swimming? What, damn it, *what?*

Rolfe stood up, coffee mug in hand, from the round wooden table in the kitchen. He was barefoot and wearing a white terry cloth robe. The Sunday-thick *New York Times* lay unopened on the floor. The kitchen sparkled—every copper pot and pan in place, the wood counters cleared and gleaming, polished.

"You're going to say you're sorry you slept so late," Rolfe said. "Well, don't." But he did not step to her. "You like what Cass and I did? Barefoot, I want you to know. Scared we'd wake you." He did not step to her and take her into his arms. "I came up during the night," he said. He was reporting, she didn't want a *report.* "You were so sound asleep I came down and crashed in the TV room. *But—*" and he gestured to the table "—I saw the prescription forms on the night table, so I had them filled at the pharmacy." She glanced at the three plastic bottles on the table. "How do you feel?"

"Slightly hung." And it was *exactly* how she felt. "Too much medicine. Woozy."

"Us, too. Cass and me. Too much boozy."

She stepped toward him then. She had to. He had not shaved yet. "Good morning, darling."

He grinned and kissed her. On the cheek. "I hope it will be," he said. "For you."

So this was the way it was to be. So this was it.

Was he punishing her? For what? *If only you hadn't gone into those woods by yourself—*

She was moving toward the refrigerator when Cass came into the rear hall from outside and stopped to lean in the kitchen door. He was also barefoot, wearing faded jeans and a lightweight gray sweatshirt. And he did *not* have a glass in his hand. "You slept," he said, a statement, not a question.

"Hi," Carole heard herself say. "You didn't. You look like hell. As usual."

"I begin to come to life just in time for my nap. How about a Bloody Mary to pop the eyes open?"

"No, thanks. I have to have a clear mind today."

"Not too clear, kid. Dangerous to the psyche, hard on the soul." He disappeared.

Poor Cass—he was offering her *his* cure, his comfort.

Rolfe was sitting again and unfolding the *Times.* The table, she saw, had been set for three. "Isn't Sandy coming home?" she asked.

"She'll be by after a while," Rolfe said, glancing down the front page. "Allison's taking Sandy and her two into New York for the day. Damn good idea. Postpone the inevitable questions till we get ourselves squared away, right?"

"Sure," she said. "Just so I see her before they go."

Cass returned with a gin and tonic, which he set on the table. "Rolfe," he said. "Move your ass. You said you'd do the eggs if I did the leftover steaks." And as Rolfe dropped the paper to the floor and stood up: "You, Carole, you sit down and crack the whip." Cass disappeared again. The screen on the back door slammed.

"Soft scrambled, right?" Rolfe asked, bustling, whistling under his breath.

She poured the orange juice into a tumbler. She sat down. In a few moments Cass returned. The pleasant crisp aroma of charred steak and brewing coffee filled the big room. Carole began to eat and Rolfe sat down and Cass located the Book Section in the *Times* and began to page it as he ate. It was just like any other Sunday. No, it was not. And perhaps those Sundays would never be again. Or Mondays or Tuesdays—

"Didn't Chief Lindheim call?" she demanded, out of nowhere. "What are the police doing? Isn't anyone *doing* anything to *catch* the sonofabitch?"

She saw Rolfe and Cass exchange a glance. Then Cass said, "I took one message. Mr. Duncan Clive called."

"Yes?" She did remember his name this time.

"Funny damned thing—he told me to tell you he was sorry for the way he behaved last evening."

"Behaved?" Rolfe said. "What the hell does *that* mean?"

"He seems to think he was rude. Gruff bastard, but he sounded damn sincere to me."

"Why," Rolfe asked, "why didn't you tell *me* this, Cass?"

"You were at the drugstore. And the message was for Carole. Oh, to hell with it."

Carole heard a horn beep in the driveway, then the sound of a car door slamming.

"Oh for Christ'sake," Rolfe muttered.

Cass stood up to go, then stopped in the doorway. "Listen, both of you—my two cents. You lighten up, hear? If you let this thing . . . if anything happens to you two, I fucking well wouldn't want to live."

When he was gone, Carole heard the back door close and then, from the opposite direction, the front door open and shut. And a voice: "Anyone home?"

"Esther," Rolfe said, "gush-gush." He stood up, reaching for *The New York Times* and calling: "We're out here, Esther!" Then in a whisper: "I'll be in the den. But I want to know more about the limey with the Scotch accent." He disappeared. "What the hell's he calling here for?"

Carole, still hungry, the confusion returning, cut another bite of steak. Odd, she thought, Rolfe always said he liked Esther Morse and David Slade although privately he'd say: *If they're going to live together that many years, why not get married like the rest of us?*

Now, from the hall she heard him greet her: "Hi, Esther. She's in the kitchen. I'm on my way to the john. How's Dave?"

Esther—brass earrings dangling, peasant skirt swishing, sandals clapping, bracelets jangling—seemed to burst into the kitchen. "No, *not* chicken soup," she said, moving to place a huge covered iron kettle on the counter. "Hungarian goulash, secret family recipe. So *you* won't have to cook!" She was staring down on Carole, dark eyes bright and concerned under black-lined, purplish-tinted lids. "You look terrific!" She stepped closer to place a wet red kiss on Carole's cheek. "That's a lie, of course." Then she sat down. "How're you making it, Carole? Level with me."

"I don't know," Carole said—the truth, suddenly near tears, the truth at last.

"You want to let go, don't you? Yowl. Howl down the universe."

"I don't think I ever knew what being really angry meant." And then, blurting: "It could be anybody, Esther. That's what's so terrible. *Anybody!* Some absolute stranger."

"It could be worse. It could be someone you know."

Esther stood up and waddled to the counter: "Thank you, I think I will have some coffee now that you've asked." And then, as she poured: "Anybody includes my David, doesn't it?"

"David?" In her mind she pictured the big soft bearlike man with his bushy dark beard and gentle eyes, always somewhat withdrawn. The idea was preposterous. "Dave's one of the sweetest, dearest guys I know."

"You haven't noticed the way he's been acting lately?" She resumed her seat, steaming cup in front of her. "Mid-life crisis. Also known as the plateau, when a man knows he's gone as far as he'll ever go. All those dreams of glory he had. Oh hell, I've been so worried, I've researched it. After eleven years the man's an enigma. A stranger to me. And he won't open up, he won't share."

"He's not that much of a stranger, Esther. You don't really mean that you think—"

"I don't know. I don't know anything anymore. Just before Christmas he learned that IKL Pharmaceuticals also supplies nerve gas and does germ warfare research for the Pentagon. Somehow that makes *him* an accessory. Like owning stock in Dow Chemical when they were getting rich on Agent Orange. Oh, some of us broken-down peaceniks still believe, you know. And he's so *angry* lately. Inside angry. Deep."

"Poor David."

"Easy for you to say. On the way home last night he said maybe we're all making too much of what's happened. Look at the world. Rape's endemic. Central and South America, Africa, the Mideast—every place there's a war, or revolution. And people in prisons everywhere, torture. Oh Christ, was I pissed! So what's Carole supposed to do, I asked him—pretend it didn't happen? He's so hypersensitive he gets into a sweat and so damned *down* just reading the headlines."

"Where is he now?"

"You won't believe this! Out in a rowboat on Lake Lillinonah. Says he's fishing. That's where he says he was yesterday, that's the reason we were late getting here. Oh, you didn't know that, did you?" She sipped her coffee and stared off, her eyes troubled. This was an Esther that Carole had never seen before. Or been allowed to see . . .

"I'm sorry," Carole heard herself say.

"*You're* sorry? Not that I'm all that desirable, but I'm getting tired of sleeping with a Jewish monk." Esther set down her cup. "He can't sleep and when he does he has nightmares. I know he's not on drugs, I can tell, then why's he so zapped out?" She leaned closer to whisper: "Forget screw, he doesn't even want to go down on me anymore. *That* doesn't take energy, does it?"

But Carole's mind was remembering. It had happened at a Christmas party at Jerald and Karen's house on the edge of Lake Candlewood. Very modern, all slants and angles and glass and cement. She had come out of the bathroom and she had stopped a moment in the hall, alone, trying to decide which group to join, when she'd felt an arm around her and then, before she could move, she'd felt herself being engulfed in an embrace. The lips on hers were framed in a beard and as she wriggled free she found herself looking into David Slade's teasing, almost taunting dark eyes. *You were under the mistletoe,* he said, and then, with a strange, baffled, almost abject expression, he'd turned away and moved into the crowd on the enclosed deck. Later, he had stammered horribly when he'd said good night so she'd decided he was just smashed. Holiday spirit. Drunken impulse. So she had not even mentioned it to Rolfe and she had forgotten it herself. Until now.

"Look at you!" Esther cried. "What kind of friend am I? Unloading on you now at a time like this with my—it's just that I don't know what's going on in his mind and it *scares* me." She rose heavily from the chair. "Oh God, Carole, I'm sorry. Why didn't you stop me?" She stooped to kiss Carole's cheek again. "Forgive, forgive." She was hurrying toward the hall when Carole's voice stopped her.

"You don't really think David raped me."

Esther didn't turn. "*Did* rape you, or *might have?*"

"Did."

"I don't know. He's always had a kind of yen—"

"Might have?"

"Anything's possible, isn't it?"

"Whatever happened to the boy who raped *you* when you were a child?"

"Him?" Esther did turn then, smiling. "He's the most respected and probably the richest man in my hometown. *Ciao.*"

Carole found herself bracing for the slam of the front door. Then she rose to go pour herself another cup of coffee, remembering Esther's saying that she'd never forgiven her parents for refusing to report it.

She'd never forgiven them, Carole knew, because the boy had not been punished. So Esther had carried that bitterness, that sense of injustice, all her life. A grinding sense of purpose went through Carole's mind. Why should *she* have to suffer that, too? Wasn't being raped enough?

Carrying the mug, Carole went into the hall and toward the den. Her head felt huge and empty and there was a faintness whirling in it, very slowly.

She stopped in the door. Rolfe was stretched out on his back on the couch, smoking a cigarette—so he *had* begun to smoke again—but he wasn't reading the paper. Or drinking. He was staring at the ceiling. And suddenly she felt that some vast depthless gulf lay between them. She couldn't let that happen. She remembered Cass's words a while ago.

So she said it: "Rolfe, I need you."

"I'm here," he said. But was he?

"I have no idea why Mr. Clive would call, darling."

"He called," Rolfe said, without moving, "because he's

trying to cover up. How could he guess you'd come to *his* house afterward?"

"Rolfe, you might be right." Not a lie, she couldn't be sure, she could barely remember what Duncan Clive looked like. But she couldn't resist asking: "Then who stole my car?"

"Oh, yeah." Rolfe sat up, reaching to stub out his cigarette in a tray on the desk. "Chief Lindheim called. I didn't forget, I thought I'd give you a chance to have breakfast without thinking about any of this. The police got the guy who stole the wagon. But I get the idea that Godzilla doesn't think he's the one who—" He broke off.

"Who raped me," she said, "that's the word, Rolfe. Rape."

Rolfe jumped to his feet. "I know the word! I still can't believe it, that's all. The police want to see you again at one o'clock. State Police Barracks. Ridgewood! And he told me to remind you to bring in all the clothes you were wearing yesterday."

She moved to the only chair and sank into it. "Anything else?"

"Jesus, I hate to tell you. It's wild. The guy who stole it also totaled the Volvo."

After a moment, Carole said, "Everything's being totaled, isn't it?"

After a second's pause, Rolfe said: "His name is Manuel Mendoza and he might not live."

"Then"—she couldn't believe it—"then it'd be over, wouldn't it? If he dies."

"Maybe. I hope so. Maybe he'll confess. Even then, I don't know whether that Cro-Magnon'll close the case. He doesn't believe anything or anybody." Rolfe stood up. "Last night, remember, he suspected *me.*"

She felt helpless now. An object. Charmless. Not female, not even sexual—a thing around which everything revolved. Not even human—as if she had been transformed in his eyes and in her own.

"Why," Rolfe asked, staring out the window, his back to her, "why would a man have to rape his own wife? It's never over. Once I picked up that phone and dialed nine-one-one—why didn't I listen to Jerry?" He turned to face her. "Listen. You haven't signed anything. Lindheim's still working on the case. He asked me whether anyone worked for us and I gave him the name of Janos Petofi."

"Who?"

"The guy who does the lawn. I couldn't think of anyone else. I make out the checks, but I wouldn't know him if I saw him. Did he ever make a pass at you? No, skip that. That Lindheim suspects everyone." He stepped toward her. "If you refuse to sign that complaint, Carole, it's all history."

"I can't do that." She refrained from saying, *I'm sorry.* But she was.

"Why not?"

She was shaking her head.

"I just can't."

"You're being stubborn. You're thinking of yourself. What about me? I have to go to work, face all those—"

"I'm the one who was raped!" It was not quite a shout. So she lowered her voice: "I am thinking of myself, yes, *yes!* If the police prove this man Mendoza did it, that's one thing. But if they can't, I won't walk away now. I'd be sorry the rest of my life and, can't you see, I'll never believe in anything ever again, don't you see?"

"No, I don't see, I'm damned if I do!"

"And if I give up now, *I'm* the one who's damned." She started toward the hall. "Any other messages?"

"Your boss, Mr. Fletcher. Pompous ass but a nice guy. Said he'd like to get his hands on the bastard personally. But he agrees with me—he also thinks it'd be easier on *you* if you didn't swear out a complaint."

"Anyone else?"

"Your other boss. Miriam Bishop." Rolfe sat down on the couch and avoided her eyes. "That little red-headed creep you clobbered last night—*he* called her first thing this morning to tell her the jolly news."

"And?"

"And she said you're to take tomorrow off, longer if you want to. She'll send someone out here in the morning to pick up whatever work you've finished. By the way, did *she* ever make a pass at you?"

"No," she heard herself answer, flatly. "And she's not the one who raped me, either."

Then she heard Allison's horn in the driveway, followed by the sound of children's voices.

Sandy!

Carole was running, actually running, through the hall to the front door.

Which burst open. Sandy rushed toward her. Carole crouched and braced herself as Sandy ran into her arms. Carole picked her up and held her tight. She could feel the whole small body against hers, quivering all over.

Sandy's hands rose to her mother's face, patted it, stroked it. Her small hands were childishly soft and smelled of soap, of sweat. Then Sandy held both cheeks between her palms and pursed her lips and kissed her mother exactly on the mouth, over and over and over again.

When finally, seeing Allison in the doorframe, Carole set her down, the child darted toward the stairs, calling back, without turning, "Hi, Daddy! I got to change." Then shouting as she climbed the stairs: "We're going to the Big Apple!"

Carole started to follow when Rolfe, in the hall now, said, "I'll take care of it, darling." The word echoed in her mind. Not dear. Darling.

"I hope you buy the idea," Allison said. Carole could hear the voices of Mike and Audrey outside, one shrill, one laughing. "Clear the decks for you here, I thought. Central Park Zoo, Museum of Natural History, maybe even the Metropolitan if we don't run out of time."

Suddenly, Carole was near tears again. "Thank you, Al." She went into the other woman's arms.

"As far as the kids know," Allison whispered into her ear. "FAO Schwarz is *not* open on Sunday. I'm such a liar."

Then the telephone rang. Carole shuddered. It shrilled again. She took three steps and took it up and spoke into it, hearing the reluctance, the dread, in her voice: "Ye-es?"

"Carole?" A male voice—she recognized it at once. "That you, Carole?"

"Yes, Jerry? Do you have some more legal advice?"

She heard his laugh. "Listen, you can't blame me if you didn't take it? Cops know: law of the jungle. They probably thought, what's all the fuss, you should have relaxed and enjoyed it, right?"

"Jerry, I'm in a hurry."

"So am I. But I wanted you to know: you've been on my mind all night."

"Well, thank you, Jerry. Is that all?"

His voice became a whisper. "I just thought that now that the dam's broken, as they say, we ought to get to know each other better."

"Are you drunk?"

"Not me. How about lunch some day—oh, not around here. Old Drover's Inn or Stonehenge."

"Screw you," she heard herself say.

Then he laughed again. "That's the general idea," he said. "And remember: no real man takes no for an answer."

"Oh, I know, Jerry. And all real men have always dreamed of raping a woman and all real women have always longed for it anyway, so what's the big deal?"

"You dig. Law of the jungle again. You want something, you take it, but cover your ass, right?"

After another moment, conscious that Allison was staring at her with her mouth open: "Thank you, Mr. Dixon, for your *legal* opinion. Mail me your bill and I'll send it back rolled up for your convenience. And give Karen my love."

"Karen? Hey, you really don't know what is going on, do you?"

She lowered the phone, tempted to slam it down. Hot fury was pumping through her but she was still stunned, as much at herself as at him. Had she really said those things? Her eyes met Allison's.

Then she heard Rolfe at the top of the stairs: "Who was that?"

"My *lawyer,*" Carole growled.

Sandy appeared beside Rolfe, wearing her best summer dress and daintily conscious of it. She came down, the picture of ladylike dignity, and then stopped and tilted her head for her mother's kiss on her cheek. "Don't muss my dress, please."

Allison moved quickly to open the door and Sandy passed Carole to go out. "Carole," Allison whispered, "you got my vote. Jerry amuses me, but I've been wanting to say something like that to him for years."

When the door closed, Carole whirled to go up the stairs.

Rolfe, a few steps above, blocked her way. "Jerry? What'd he have to say?"

She halted. "He came on to me for the first time. Isn't that flattering? My heart is going pitty-pat."

Rolfe's face had hardened, the muscles of his jaw vibrating. "I'll take care of that asshole."

"Please don't," she said, stepping up and around him on the stairs. "Don't deprive me of the pleasure."

"Where are you going?"

"One o'clock, you said. Police Barracks, Ridgewood, right?"

"I'm coming with you."

At the top of the stairs she stopped and turned. "I can drive," she said. "I'll take your car. I can manage very well by myself, thank you."

As she moved toward the bedroom, she heard him mutter, "Jesus Christ, what's happening to everybody?"

It was a good question. A damned good question.

Henry Lindheim felt completely and uncomfortably out of place in the State Police Barracks. All of his life he'd operated out of a precinct squad room, New York City—cluttered, shabby, olive green walls, windows looking out on an airshaft, water cooler, steel files, holding cell, bustle and flow of officers, suspects, witnesses. Now here he was in this clean, modern tan-colored brick building that reminded him of a Holiday Inn along the highway—everything neat, efficient, compartmentalized, computerized. Maybe even sterilized.

Behind the desk in one of the impersonal offices, Trooper Brad Dworsky, tall and imposing, was seated in a swivel chair, his stiff-brimmed hat tipped back on his bald head. Mr. Mark Rainer, the State's Attorney, was walking up and down and peering at Henry through horn-rimmed glasses. He seemed to be weighing every answer that Henry was giving to their questions.

"I have only seven men besides myself," Henry explained. "Four of them have to handle church traffic on Sunday morning. The other three have been canvassing two miles both ways from the scene, knocking on every door. So far, nothing."

"Waste motion now," Brad Dworsky said. "Perpetrator's in custody. No point in Mrs. Jensen even signing the complaint."

"Not so fast," the DA said. "Chief Lindheim may be right." Mr. Mark Rainer, a short youngish man, had a way of speaking that Henry had heard only on TV—as if he were clenching his teeth and forcing the words out between them. "To close the case, we have to get a confession or *some* evidence that this Mendoza committed the crime." Only his lips moved; the muscles of his jaw seemed locked.

"Stealing the wagon's not enough to *prove* he did sexual battery."

"We won't have to *prove* it if the wetback dies."

"Dworsky, what'd you do, sleep through the academy?" The DA removed his glasses and fixed his narrow blue-green eyes on Henry. "According to the woman's statement, she never saw her assailant, so we couldn't even ask her to ID the body. If he does die."

Henry squirmed in his chair. "I talked with the owner of the apple orchards where Manuel Mendoza's been employed. Good worker. A loner. No trouble, any kind. Mr. Woodall's hunch was that, since the apple season's over, the subject was broke and he probably snatched the wagon to get back to Florida for winter citrus or sugarcane season."

"You been a busy man this morning," the DA said, between his teeth. "To sum up then: We're going to have to assume the case is still wide open. You got any other suspects in mind?"

"Several," Henry said. "There'll be more if we don't wrap it up and walk away."

Trooper Dworsky stood up. "I say the spic was walking by, saw her go into the woods, his dong started bobbing, so he raped her, zipped off her car and off to the land of milk and honey."

Rage erupting in his gut, and spreading, Henry also stood up. He saw that look of challenge in the trooper's face and hated it, and the man. "Manuel Mendoza," he heard himself say, "is a human being, living or dead. Hispanic if you like, but not a *spic.*"

Trooper Dworsky grinned. "All you've been doing here is defending a drunken car thief—you got some kinda hang-up about spics?"

Very quietly then, hearing the word again, Henry said: "My wife was a Cuban-American. Also, my daughter." He was damned if he'd say more.

Mark Rainer said, "Sorry, Chief. I'm sure Trooper Dworsky didn't mean—"

"I'll tell you what I mean," Dworsky said. "We got nothing. The prints on the belt'll be the victim's, hers *only* if she had to fight to get it off. The blanket's hopeless. You said yourself, Chief, the examining doctor washed her breast. Zilch. No tire treads, or so many they have no meaning. Our only hope's a couple of shoeprints. If we don't hang it on the . . . Hispanic . . . we got a ball-busting case that could make us all look like fools."

Henry was thinking of what Carole Jensen had said last evening: *I wouldn't be here if I didn't want you to catch the sonofabitch and send him to prison forever.* "At least we'll have to wait till the belt—*and* the buckle—are run through the laser scanner. And especially Mrs. Jensen's clothes and the blanket—how do you know it won't turn up fibers from the perpetrator's clothes? Damn it, you don't close cases just because they look tough." He turned to Mark Rainer. "And you may as well know this: I'm not going to lie to the victim, who's depending on us."

"Might be easier on her," the State's Attorney said. "In the long haul."

Henry considered this. Relief through a lie? Her need for justice fulfilled by an injustice—injustice to a man who couldn't defend himself?

"I don't think that's what Mrs. Jensen would want," he said.

"What beats me," Mark Rainer said, glancing at his watch, "is why there are so many more rapes in the last few years. With all the sexual freedom around these days."

"Easy," the trooper said. "Man gets so much women's lib static at home, so he goes out to prove he's still in charge."

"If," Henry said, "a man has to prove he's a man by attacking a female who can't fight back, he's not a man, he's an animal, and he belongs in a cage."

The buzzer sounded on the intercom.

The trooper stepped to the desk to press a button with his thumb. "Yes?"

A female voice, slightly distorted, coldly efficient, said: "Mrs. Jensen's here."

Henry stepped to Mark Rainer. "You read her statement—ain't it complete?"

"Very thorough," the DA said. "Very professional. But Trooper Dworsky and I still have some questions."

"Yeah," Dworsky said, "you're slipping, Chief." Then into the intercom: "Tell her to wait."

Henry turned around, the hot lava still running, and was leaving the room when the DA spoke: "We'll be in the Interrogation Room."

When he saw Mrs. Jensen, sitting upright and stiff-backed in the waiting room, Henry was not prepared for the change in her. She wore pale tan slacks now, and a brown vest over a blouse with autumn-colored stripes. And she stared at him as if he were a stranger. She stood then and extended a paper-wrapped package.

"You wanted my clothes," she said. Even her voice seemed different—cooler, harder, all hesitancy gone—and her bearing, instead of reminding him of a trapped animal looking for escape, was composed and cautiously alert.

Taking the package, he said, for want of anything better: "Tough night, kid?" Not exactly his customary professional greeting.

"Dr. Stoddard gave me medicine."

"This way, please," he said, more formally, and as she fell into step beside him, they entered the maze of interlocking corridors. "Mr. Jensen didn't come?"

"He wanted to. I wouldn't let him."

At the closed door of the room, she spoke again: "I told you everything there is to tell. But during the night—almost a dream—I remembered something else. I haven't been able to get it back." She did *not* say, as she had several times last night, *I'm sorry.*

"Maybe you'll think of it now, whatever it is."

He opened the door and then stepped after her into the room, which looked like a corporate board room. "Mrs. Jensen, this is Mr. Rainer. He's the State's Attorney. And this is Trooper Dworsky."

She did not speak but nodded her head as if that was that, let's get on with it. Yep, she was different this morning.

"Mrs. Jensen," Mark Rainer said, "you recognize these items on the table, don't you?"

Henry moved around to the opposite side of the long polished conference table, where he could see her face more clearly. Last night's pallor was gone. The tawny glow on her flesh had returned, almost a flush—excitement, anger, what?

She stared at the items on the table and said: "The blanket's mine—rather, my little girl's. Those are my underpants."

"And the belt?" Mark Rainer prompted.

"I never saw it. It was dark." She took a step. "May I pick it up?"

"Please don't," Henry said quickly.

She drew her hand back, staring at him.

"Why not?" the trooper demanded. "We took the prints off."

"The laser may find more," Henry said, "and other things as well."

"Mr. Rainer," the trooper said in a pained tone, "if the witness can ID a piece of evidence, let's take what we can get."

Without glancing at Henry, the State's Attorney said, "I don't think it'll jeopardize the case." He turned to the girl. "Examine it any way you like, Mrs. Jensen."

But she turned her brown eyes on Henry, not moving.

He felt, beneath his helplessness, a pang of sheer pleasure that puzzled him, and exhilarated him as well. "Please try not to touch the face of the buckle, Mrs. Jensen," he said. "There's a thumbprint on the silver that doesn't look like the rest to me." Then he nodded, his eye catching the glance that passed between the other two men. "Go ahead, Mrs. Jensen. Please."

He saw her reach, with no trace of hesitation now, and take the black snakeskin belt into her two hands. She ran one hand over the surface of the leather and then, studying it, she slid the plain end of the belt, which had no holes in it, into the silver buckle at the other end. As if making an experiment, she drew the leather through the buckle and pulled it until she was holding a small loop in her hands. Then, looking across the table into Henry's face, she said, "That's the one."

"How do you know, miss?" Trooper Dworsky asked. Even *his* voice was subdued.

She didn't glance over her shoulder at him but tossed the belt onto the table. "It had to be that kind of buckle. The other kind, a regular kind with a prong that goes through holes, wouldn't have worked."

It was the attorney who spoke this time, and also gently. "Would you mind explaining that, Mrs. Jensen?"

This time she turned to him. "If it'd been an ordinary belt, he would have had to hold it around my neck the whole time because the holes would be at the other end. With this kind, all he had to do was clamp the buckle shut when he had it tight enough. That's why I had such an awful time—it took forever—to find the combination. To get it off."

"Very good," Mark Rainer said.

But Henry was not listening. Suddenly he knew why there was something about that damned belt that had kept nagging at his mind and now he had it in focus: There was no monogram on the buckle. Wouldn't a man with the money to afford a snakeskin belt with a silver buckle have his initial or initials engraved on the plate of the buckle?

"*My* fingerprints?" Carole Jensen was asking. "Mine?"

"Before you leave," the DA said. "Just routine."

She nodded. "Now what?" Was that a tremor in her

voice now, or did he imagine it? No, he didn't imagine it: she was still holding herself together with thin taut wires inside.

"Now," the DA said, "now I have here the statement you gave Chief Lindheim. Won't you sit down?"

He was holding the chair at the end of the long narrow table. Carole Jensen sat down on it, placing her hands flat on the surface.

Trooper Dworsky took a chair at the side of the table, leaving one vacant between himself and Carole Jensen at the end.

Mark Rainer began to pace again, slowly. "Chief Lindheim, you're excused."

Henry saw Carole Jensen lift her gaze in surprise to stare at him. Was that a plea in her brown eyes? Was she asking him *why,* or was she asking him to stay?

He was damned if he was going to take a chance. He strode down the length of the table and sat down facing her, but at the far end. He said nothing.

The DA shrugged his thin shoulders. "Suit yourself, Chief. If you don't have other duties—" He then stepped to the wall and threw on a switch. There was a low humming sound and three thin chrome-colored posts rose from the top of the table, slowly, about two feet apart, and stopped rising when they were a foot above the surface. Mikes. From now on every word spoken in the room would be recorded.

Instead of sitting down, the State's Attorney continued pacing. "Now," he said, his tone reassuring and friendly: "now, why don't you, Mrs. Jensen, start from the time you left the house and tell us in your own words what happened."

"I haven't thought of anything I didn't tell Chief Lindheim," Carole Jensen said.

"Well, maybe Trooper Dworsky and I will think of some questions Chief Lindheim didn't." His voice became a low purr. "You must think of me as *your* attorney, Carole. May I call you Carole? What was your first stop, Carole?"

She began to speak, using simple sentences, her whole manner cool and composed. Emotionless. She listed her stops, what she purchased at each—

"Excuse me," Mark Rainer broke in. "Did you see anyone you knew? Not the tradespeople but anyone you know personally?"

"Do *I* need witnesses?" she asked.

"Now Carole, no one doubts you, *or* that you've been . . . assaulted."

"You've seen the medical report, haven't you?"

The DA, Henry decided, had the same ice water in his veins that Dworsky had. He watched him cross to sit in the chair closest to her, at the corner of the table and diagonally across from the trooper. "Carole, relax. *Naturally* I've seen Dr. Stoddard's report. What interests us now is whether you saw anyone you knew or any stranger —male stranger—who might have . . . well, shown any special interest in you."

"No." She was looking directly at the DA now. "The only way to ignore such people is to ignore them. Perhaps I should have been more observant. But if I had, that might have been construed as a come-on, right?"

Mark Rainer cast a quick glance across to Dworsky, before he said, "Continue."

The next interruption came when she told of stopping the car—

"At that point, did you see anyone going by in a car, walking along the road, or possibly following you in another vehicle?"

"I wouldn't have gone into the woods if I had."

"You went pretty deep into the woods," Brad Dworsky said then.

She turned her attention to him. "It didn't seem far to me. It was almost dark by then."

"My point, Carole," the state trooper said, grinning.

"What's *your* first name?" she asked in reply.

"Brad. For Bradley."

"Well, *Brad,*" she said then, "that was my mistake. I guess I was asking for it, wasn't I? In that case, I've been punished, haven't I?"

Another glance was exchanged at the other end of the table. Henry blew smoke and held his tongue. He was beginning to feel better. He was beginning to feel a *lot* better.

"I was about to return to the car when I saw this blanket coming at me. He put it over my head, whoever he was, and then he did what he did."

"Did he say anything," the DA asked, "anything at all?"

"As I told Chief Lindheim, he whispered what they call sweet nothings. But he also called me a whore, a tramp, and a slut."

"During the act?" the DA asked.

"During the *rape,* yes."

"According to your statement," Dworsky said, "you didn't recognize the voice—"

Carole Jensen took a deep breath and said, "He was whispering, and in a hurry, growling like an animal. Through the blanket."

Henry relaxed slightly. Until he heard Trooper Dworsky ask: "That was during the act, you mean?"

"During the *rape,*" she said, again.

"Mrs. Jensen," Mark Rainer said then, "I'm afraid we're obliged to ask you questions of an intimate nature here. You realize that, of course."

"Chief Lindheim managed to do that without being offensive." Her tone somehow turned it into a warning.

The DA sat back in his chair and Brad Dworsky leaned forward to say: "You told Chief Lindheim your assailant held the blanket over your head with the belt. Was that after he ripped off your skirt and panties?"

She did not hesitate. "He did not rip off my skirt."

"Then you weren't naked?"

"No one said I was."

"If he didn't need his hands to hold the belt, where were they?"

Henry, by now, had stiffened. Very slowly, very carefully, he placed his cigar in the tray.

"Was his left hand over your mouth, Carole?" Mark Rainer asked.

"That would have been impossible."

"Then where?"

"I don't know."

"And his right hand?"

Carole Jensen opened her mouth to answer, then shut it and stared down the table.

"That's covered in the statement I took," Henry said. "*And* in the medical report."

"Where was his right hand?" Brad Dworsky's elbows were on the table and he was staring steadily at Carole Jensen.

And, Henry realized, the atmosphere in the room had changed. It was no longer the impersonal questioning of a crime victim, but three men were sitting in a room talking to a lone woman, who was the focus of their attention and at their mercy. A slow rage was moving in his massive frame, climbing toward his throat.

"For the record, Carole," the DA whispered. "Answer the officer's question."

"Gentlemen," Henry said, stifling the impulse to stand up, "you both know—"

But Carole Jensen's voice shrilled in the room. "His right hand was on my left breast, that's how he made me quit yelling, that's how he made me give in, he was squeezing my left breast, you hear the word, you scumbags? Breast, *breast, BREAST!*"

Mark Rainer stood up. "That's all we wanted to hear," he said softly. "For the record."

"Shit."

At first Henry was not sure he'd heard her say the word. Her eyes were not shut, they were glaring at Brad Dworsky, hot brown fire. "Exactly the right word," Henry said and now he did stand up.

The DA was pacing again. "I realize, Carole, this may be painful—"

"You *know* it's painful," Carole Jensen said, between tight, thin lips. "You know it because that's what you enjoy. *Both* of you. That's how you get it on!"

The DA stopped pacing and said: "I'm going to ignore that, Carole."

"Please don't," she said.

"One or two more questions, Carole." It was Dworsky again, sitting tall and straight in his chair. "Where were *your* hands during all this?"

"I don't know."

Then the DA spoke: "The officer is trying to establish that you fought back, resisted."

"When you stopped struggling," the trooper said, "did you decide to lay back and sort of relax?"

As if to cut off this line of questioning, Rainer asked: "Was there any oral sex involved?"

"Mr. Rainer," Henry said, "there's never been any—"

"Answer my question, please," the DA said to Carole Jensen.

"No," she said. "He spared me that."

"Don't knock it," the trooper said, and sat back.

Henry took two or three dangerous steps down the table. He was glowering down on Brad when he spoke to the DA. "Rainer, that's it. Interrogation closed. And I want a typed transcript of every word. Today. Including Dworsky's last remark."

Brad Dworsky turned his head to look up at Henry over his shoulder. "Who the hell do you think you are, Lindheim?"

"I know who *I* am," Henry said. "And Mrs. Jensen just told you *what* you are." He looked across to Rainer. "I demand a typed copy of this so-called interrogation. If you think I don't know correct police procedure, you'll learn different."

"I want to ask her," Dworsky said, "why she waited almost two hours to report the crime!"

"Because," Carole said in a low, tight voice, "because I'd been warned I'd be treated just the way I have been treated."

Rainer returned to the table and sat down by Carole, and spoke in an apologetic whisper: "Mrs. Jensen, it's sometimes, in the interest of justice, necessary to—"

Carole leaped to her feet. "Justice?" she said. Her voice was trembling and her whole body had lost its rigidity. She was shuddering. "Justice?" Then, fists on the table, she was leaning on her stiff arms when she hissed: "You ask one more question and I'm going to walk out of here and get my husband's gun and find the sonofabitch myself and *kill* him. *Then* you'll have a *right* to talk to me like this and I won't give a damn then because I'll already have done your job for you. That's justice!"

She straightened then and walked to the door, fast, limping slightly but apparently in control again.

Brad rose to his feet, pushing back the chair. "You want me to bring her back?"

But the DA shook his head. "She's too emotional to answer questions intelligently."

"She's too *intelligent,*" Henry snarled, "to answer *emotional* questions. If you two perverts think I don't know what's been going on here, put your hands in your pockets and feel your pricks." He turned and left the room.

By running, which he had not done in years, Henry was able to reach Carole's car before she could get the motor started.

She was twisting the ignition key over and over, the motor of the blue Saab was whirring and then roaring and then dying in spurts. At her shoulder he could see her trouncing viciously on the accelerator, urgent, desperate, *demanding* that the engine start. He also saw the tears on her face. He resisted his urge to reach through the open window and place a hand on her shoulder. She gave up, let go of the key, lowered her head to the steering wheel, and then her body was racked by sobs. She seemed to go limp all over.

Henry forced himself to stand there, helpless and silent, until the sobbing subsided into a small pitiful whimper. Something inside him turned over.

Then he spoke her name. "Mrs. Jensen."

She did not start, or draw away. She simply lifted her forlorn, wet face, totally composed, empty, and stared at him, waiting.

"Let me drive you home," he said.

She did not move, not even to shake her head, but said, in a tangled whisper: "It's . . . not my car. I . . . something's wrong with it."

"I'll take care of that later." He opened the door. "Mine's right here."

Careful not to touch her, he led her to the black Ford with the insignia on the door and the round blue light on the top. She walked submissively, blindly, as if it didn't really matter. He noticed that she walked stiffly and then he remembered her bandaged knees.

When they were out on Route 7, she sat slumped against the door, eyes open but unseeing, blank.

Those bastards, Henry thought. Those two bastards, somehow he'd see that they got theirs. After this was all over, he'd take the interrogation tape to Hartford himself. They'd get what was coming to them if he had to risk his goddamn job to do it.

Two or three miles along the road—the traffic was heavy because of the sunshine and the foliage and the certainty that after Indian summer winter is inevitable—she spoke without moving: "I forgot. Do we have to go back? I didn't let them take my fingerprints."

"I can do that in Sheffield. If not today, tomorrow morning."

"I didn't do anything. Why do they try to make me feel I did? Why do they want *my* fingerprints?"

"Because they want to match yours with others on the belt. If any."

"Then what?"

Relieved that she was talking at all, he explained: "Then they take the others and check them out by the computer. Against those of every convicted felon in the country, beginning with sex offenders, of course."

"But that . . . that'll take forever, won't it?"

"Almost." He didn't tell her that it would also be a waste of time if the perpetrator was a first offender with no police record. As, by now, he had begun to suspect.

When she spoke again, her voice was like a child's, quiet and uncertain: "If they match Mr. Mendoza's, then it'll be over, won't it? He's already being punished, isn't he?"

So then, speaking as softly as he could, he had to tell her: Manuel Mendoza, who stole her car, was not the man who raped her. Call it hunch, call it experience: He had somehow known this since early morning. He hadn't been able to explain it to the trooper or the DA and he couldn't explain it to her. "It's hardly ever that simple," he said.

It was then that Carole Jensen said something that he was to remember later, not because it had any true bearing on the ongoing investigation, but because it somehow intensified the strange, live feeling that he'd come to have for this girl. "Then," she said, "then . . . all he did was steal my car. And now he could die. For doing that." She turned her head to face him, her eyes troubled and searching. "I left the keys in the wagon. That's what tempted him—"

"Look," Henry said then, an edge coming into his voice, "look, Mrs. Jensen, none of this is your fault. Get that idea out of your mind. None of it, see?"

He was remembering how he'd felt, all those years ago: What did *I* do that led to this, what did I do or fail to do?

"Where are we going?" Carole Jensen asked then. "This isn't the road to Sheffield."

"Mrs. Jensen," Henry said, "I'm taking you to see a friend of mine. A doctor."

"Doctor? All I want to do is go home. I've got medicine. I can sleep. That's all I want."

"This is a different kind of doctor." He heard the plea in his tone. "Her name's Kahn. Judith Kahn." And then he added: "She helped *me* once."

But Carole Jensen was shaking her head, her dark hair moving. "All I want to do is sleep. *You* get the man who did it and you punish him. Then I'll be okay again. Once he's punished—the right one, the one who made me like this—then I won't *be* like this. I'll be free. I don't know how I know this, but I do."

But Henry was remembering again. He had known that feeling, too. But the killers had never been apprehended. Or punished. He had *had* to live with that. If you could call it living.

"We'll get him," he said—a promise, a pledge. "We'll get *him* but, meanwhile, look at what's happening to *you.*"

There was a long silence then.

Into which, after a time, Carole Jensen spoke: "How—" she was twisted in the seat, facing him—"how did Dr. Kahn help you?"

So then he told her. Aware that he was using the truth to convince her, knowing—or hoping—that he was manipulating her into accepting his decision. "I had a daughter who was gang-raped on the streets of New York." He was keeping his voice flat and speaking bluntly, knowing that he was hoping to shock. "She was fifteen years old. That was twenty years ago." He paused, on purpose, letting it sink in. "The police never caught them."

"And . . . and how is she now, your daughter?"

"She's dead." Another pause, but briefer. "After the animals raped her, they killed her."

Then, with satisfaction mixed with shame, he heard a small gasp.

Finally Carole Jensen said, in a whisper: "I'm sorry."

"I didn't tell you to make you sorry," Henry said. "Or any sadder than you already are."

"Your wife?" she asked, in a whisper.

"Also dead."

Another gasp.

He waited a second and then went on: "My wife, whose name was Luisa, died two years afterward. Of grief." And then he added: "And *because* they were never caught and punished, I think." It was a thought he'd tried to bury, because Luisa had tried so hard to make him accept what, inside herself—he knew, he knew—*she* had not accepted: that it had been the will of God, and that, later, God would punish all evil. There had to be a final justice.

"You said Dr. Kahn helped you—"

"When I first came here a police psychiatrist in New York gave me her name, and when things got rough, I called her. We're friends now."

"Then," she said, after a pause, "I think I'd like to meet her." And she added, "I really don't want to go back to sleep."

Dr. Kahn's office was an extension, with a separate entrance, of her small white clapboard house on a tree-lined side street near the college campus. There was a sofa facing the red brick fireplace, with an abstract oil painting above, two upholstered wingchairs in which she and Carole were both seated, facing each other across a small round table, a desk in one corner and no patient's couch, thank God.

Reluctant now, and somewhat edgy, Carole asked, "Well, where do we start?"

Dr. Judith Kahn was an extremely tall woman, and spare, with black eyes and black hair going gray, parted in the center, and drawn back tightly over a strong handsome skull, and she was almost overpowering in her self-contained way. "Where would *you* like to start, Carole?" The doctor's voice was low-pitched with a certain soft but detached tenderness in it. "What's troubling you, Carole? Right this second. What's on your mind?"

"I know this is an intrusion," Carole said then. "I'm sorry to bother you on Sunday, Doctor."

"The students call me Dr. Judith." She was wearing a long dark skirt and a loose-fitting tunic, with a paisley pattern. "I'm consulting clinical psychologist at the college, in case Henry didn't tell you. And, Carole, you'd be astonished at the number of rape cases that come my way. Date rape has become a big thing. Most go unreported and in some the emotional damage, believe it or not, is minimal. In others—well, I try to limit the consequences."

"If they go unreported, how can the rapist be punished?"

"I'd like to explore that idea with you a little later, but I asked you what's bothering *you,* right now."

"I . . . I forget things. I remembered this morning that something had come to me during the night, in bed, almost like a dream, something important, and I made up my mind to remember. But this morning I couldn't think of what it was. I still can't."

"That's fairly common in the circumstances. Some victims have total amnesia, the mind suppressing what's too painful to handle. Some memory losses are fragmented and temporary. I wouldn't fret about it unless it's something that could help Henry solve the case. Because that's what's important to *you,* isn't it?" So she knew—how did she know? "Henry told me you work for the *Sudbury News-Chronicle.* What sort of work?"

"In the advertising department. Part-time only. But I enjoy it, even the deadlines. Mother and Daddy would never let me take a job."

"You work for Vincent Fletcher then?"

"He's the editor. My boss is Miriam Bishop. Do you know Mr. Fletcher?"

"Indirectly. He's a pretty well-known, and highly respected, citizen in town. You like him?"

"He's always been very sweet to me. Like the kind of father a girl always wishes she had."

"Did you ever wish you hadn't been born, Carole?"

Startled, Carole said, "Yes. When I was very young—"

"I'd like to hear about that."

So then Carole told her of her childhood—the apartments, always on New York's Upper East Side, the convent boarding school and Manhattanville College, and art school in the city.

"A happy childhood?"

Carole shook her head. She seemed, to herself, to become impatient all of a sudden. "Not very and not very dramatic, either," she said. "Just a polite hell. If you can think of hell as cold, not hot."

"But you escaped it—"

"I escaped it when I married Rolfe. I don't see my parents often. What's all this got to do with *now?* I didn't come here to be psychoanalyzed. I'm not sick. *He* is. When they catch him, analyze *him,* find some excuse for his doing what he did, so he won't have to go to prison. What did *I* do?"

"You did nothing," Dr. Judith said. "Hang on to that."

"That's what people keep telling me, but it's not the way they make me feel. I'm hanging on." But was she? If she was hanging on, why was she here, why did she need a shrink?

"Tell me a little about Ralph."

"Not Ralph—Rolfe. He's in electronics and he's scared of losing his job and he *saved* me, he married me and I got away from all that, and I love him."

Dr. Judith allowed a long moment to pass before she went on: "Do you have any children?"

"One. Alexandria. Sandy. She's almost six. What difference does all this make? We're wasting time. The question is: will I ever be the same again?"

"That," Dr. Judith said, "and hard as it might be for you to accept it, that depends on you."

Carole stared at the branches and brown leaves out the window beyond Dr. Judith's head. She felt a collapsing inside. "I'm sorry," she said.

"Let's begin," Dr. Judith said, "let's begin by dropping that *I'm sorry* bullshit, shall we? Bury it. You have nothing to be sorry about. Nothing. That's the first thing that happens—you were right—they, everybody, even without knowing it, they manage to make *you* feel guilty."

"I was brought up to be polite," Carole said, meekly.

"You've apologized to me three times since you came in here. Let's knock it off, shall we?"

Something happened inside Carole then. She sat back and crossed her legs, ignoring the pain in her knees, and a small smile began on her lips.

Bullshit. Let's knock it off—what kind of shrink was this? "You said it, Doctor. I do feel guilty and I'm damned if I know why."

"Little girls in our society are brought up to be polite—to *please*. Especially to please men. But only a fool goes around being sorry for something she *didn't* do." Then she stood up. "It may take a while, Carole, but you'll do."

"So will you, I think." Then, in spite of herself, Carole experienced a suffusion of pleasure, and relaxed for the first time since yesterday afternoon.

"Now," Dr. Judith said, "now I'm going to prepare some lunch and you, *you* are going to sit here and *think*." She was drawing heavy curtains over the windows, dimming the room.

"Can't I help?"

"You can help yourself by doing what I tell you. The mind's a wonderful computer, dear, but you're in charge of it. Empty your mind of everything else and concentrate on last night—not what actually happened but what you remembered in bed. I'll lay odds you can do it." She went to the door leading into the rest of the house. "Feel free to use the phone if it comes to you. Coffee or iced tea?"

"Iced tea, I think."

"Probably the last of the season," Dr. Judith said and left her alone.

Returning to Sheffield, window open, the summerlike air on his face, smoking a cigar, Henry was remembering: *Why are you so nice to me?* Carole had asked just before they got out of the cruiser in front of Dr. Judith's house. *Is it because of what happened to Teresa?* How many years since he'd heard Teresa's name on anyone's lips? And then, inside, after he'd introduced her to Dr. Judith, he'd been almost certain there, for just a split second, that Carole was going to kiss him. She even seemed, impulsively, to rise up on her toes. But then her face sort of clouded over and instead, she said, *May I call you Henry? My friends call me Carole.* And then she'd reached out to shake his hand. Awkward kind of moment in front of the doctor, but hell, if anyone understood, Dr. Judith did. Damn woman understood everything.

Then, leaving Sudbury, he'd called in to learn from Bill Schiller, who was always on duty Sunday, that the suspect, Manuel Mendoza, had not been wearing a belt when arrested. *Pants held up by a length of dirty old rope, Chief. Men like that, working men, they can't afford snakeskin belts.*

Janos Petofi?

Sorry, Chief. I been doing nothing but answer the phone. Nothing on the news but the tom-toms're sounding. Those who know the victim's name want to know what we're doing about it and the others want to know her name.

Janos Petofi, Henry had said again, but in such a way that he knew he'd get action.

Right. Address: Long Meadow Hill Road, Sandy Hook.

Yellow sheet? Henry had asked, and then corrected himself for using a NYPD word: *Arrest record?*

One arrest before coming to area nine years ago. You ready for this? Suspicion of child molestation. Three years ago. Hackensack, New Jersey. Case dismissed for lack of evidence. The parents of the little girl decided they didn't want to have her testify.

Get me the inside on all this—names, exact dates, so forth. Who knows? Thanks, Bill.

Who knows indeed? Jesus, it happens every time. You start probing and pretty soon you're into a cesspool, smelling the stench, poking around in the . . . what was the Yiddish word he'd heard in New York? The *chozzerai.*

Now another weirdo. The woods were full of them. He had never really been able to get used to it. To anticipate it and then take it for granted: This is the way of the world, these are the people who make up the world.

As the squad car passed the sign reading SHEFFIELD TOWN LINE, Henry had to make a decision. He was tempted to drive directly to Duncan Clive's barn-house. Because he didn't like being lied to. He'd been lied to three times now, by three different men, all suspects: by Rolfe Jensen, the husband, by Joel White, who worked with Carole on the paper, and by Duncan Clive.

The sculptor sure as hell had an accent and Carole had said her attacker hadn't. But at a time like that, if the man was growling into her ear, voice muffled by a blanket—

When he'd placed the call to Cambridge, Massachusetts, earlier in the day, Mrs. Elaine Sutton had said, in a very cold, very precise voice: *I have not seen or spoken with Duncan for at least three years. Nor has my daughter, insofar as I know.* And then: *Why do you wish to know this, if I may ask?* He had thanked her without answering her question.

But the matter of Duncan Clive could wait, Henry decided now. Let him feel safe for a while. Henry was curious about this Janos Petofi. Any character capable of molesting a child . . .

Instead of continuing into Sheffield Center, Henry

turned at the next crossroad in the direction of Sandy Hook.

Ten minutes later he was slowing to a stop. J. PETOFI. The name was lettered on a rusted mailbox on a post alongside the country road. A beat-up old red truck was parked in the rutted driveway, a small yellow lawn tractor on its bed. Set behind a brown-grass yard was a weather-beaten trailer, up on cinder blocks. It needed a coat of paint, and a hell of a lot more. From the open door and windows country-and-western music throbbed and whined and blared.

The man who came to the screen door was short and muscular, wearing a dirty T-shirt, faded jeans and cowboy boots. He had tattooed arms and short, stiff, dark hair, and a hard, pockmarked face that showed nothing. Not even curiosity.

Henry decided to flash his tin this time. But Janos Petofi hardly glanced at the badge—so what?

"I'd like to talk to you," Henry said, conscious of his own height and weight and his very deep, very polite, but demanding voice over the deafening clamor from the radio.

"Sure."

Jan Petofi turned without opening the screen door. His stroll was slow and casual, not quite arrogant in its nonchalance.

When Henry was inside and aware of the man's flat, expressionless eyes on him, he glanced around. First at Petofi's belt: western type, wide and studded, its buckle suggesting a buffalo head. Then at the room, which was the mess he'd expected. Full ashtrays, empty beer cans, bottles everywhere. At the far end, a plastic-looking booth for eating, table littered, the serve-through counter stacked high with dirty dishes.

"How about knocking off the music?" Henry said.

"Sure." Jan Petofi took a step, touched the radio. The

silence was startling, but welcome. He spoke in a thin nasal voice: "Anything else?"

Henry moved to the tattered lounge chair in front of the TV. When he sat down broken springs attacked his backside.

"Make yourself to home," Jan Petofi said. No accent, although Henry took the name to be Hungarian. Still standing, the young man—not yet forty, closer to thirty—said, "It's about Mrs. Jensen, isn't it?"

"Mrs. Jensen? What makes you say that?"

The thin lips curled very slightly—with disgust, or contempt, amusement anyway. "It was on the morning news. Not her name, but who else drives a white Volvo wagon? Two plus two."

"How often do you work there, Mr. Petofi?"

"Once a week, Mondays. Other times if Mrs. Jensen calls me."

"For what?"

"Anything in the yard her old man's too lazy to do hisself."

"Do you have a contract?"

"Do you mean can she fire me any time?" The man's eyeballs seemed to have no bulge to them, like in a picture painted by a child. "Sure, she can fire me. And probably will since she sent you here."

"She never mentioned your name, Mr. Petofi. I'm checking out everybody."

"So?"

It was then that, searching for any clue or hint, Henry saw the pictures. They'd been clipped from magazines and thumbtacked at random, three or four at least on every wall. Not *Playboy* or *Penthouse* nudes, which he'd half-expected, but photographs of children. All little girls, no boys. Fully dressed. Some playing, some laughing, some posing for cereal and vitamin ads.

Jan Petofi waited. Then he said, in that same thin voice, without inflection: "No crime in that, is there? I like kids."

"So," Henry said, "so our records show," and waited.

"No dice," Jan Petofi said then. "I been hassled enough on that one. Case closed. Even the kid admitted nothing happened. So fuck off."

Henry stood up. "Have I hassled you, Mr. Petofi? All I did was ask you about your employment." Again he waited.

"Fuck off," the suspect said again.

Henry shrugged. "That's twice. I'll do that as soon as you tell me what you were doing and where you were between five and six P.M. yesterday."

Without hesitation—usually people have to think a second or two—the suspect said: "Merlin's Bar and Grill. Route 6. I don't work Saturdays. I drink. And that's not against the law, either."

"Thank you." He went to the door. "You'll have a lot of leaves to rake this week, won't you?"

Janos Petofi said nothing. Nor did he follow him to the door.

Climbing into his cruiser and driving, Henry was thinking: he's sick, he's not evil, there's no evil anymore, he's sick and the ones driving drunk and killing other citizens at random on the roads, they're sick, too. And the muggers and the druggies willing to kill, or maim, anything to get their fix. Nobody's guilty, everybody's sick. So anybody can do anything.

No, by God, whoever raped Carole Jensen was *guilty*. And if he, Henry Lindheim, could see that man punished, it might, it just might, set him a little more straight with the order of things, the order that every man has to impose because, if it's not in the sky, even if it's only in his mind, *that's* what has to be lived up to, that's what he has to impose by the way *he* behaves and by the way he insists others behave, without that there is nothing, only chaos, chaos and emptiness.

Merlin's Bar and Grill on Route 6 had once been a white farmhouse along the side of the highway. Now its interior was dim and filled with stale smoke and beer-and-whiskey fumes. A football game was playing on the TV screen behind the bar, the sound drowned out by the voices, especially of the players at the pool table behind the customers sitting at the long side of the L-shaped bar.

Although he'd left his cap in the car and was wearing a suit, Henry felt almost as conspicuous as if he were wearing a full uniform: the dress here was that of laboring men on a summer's day off work—short-sleeved sport shirts, summer slacks but mostly jeans, plenty of T-shirts, not a tie in sight. Only a few women, one or two in shorts, the rest wearing slacks, no dresses. Except the one behind the bar. Whose name, he learned right away because it was shouted so often, was Debbie: a smallish girl, late teens, early twenties, with short blond hair that bounced around her face when she moved. And she seemed to be always moving. Debbie wore a very short, very tight silk skirt and a pink shirt with the tails tied in a knot well above her navel and buttoned so low that when she leaned across the bar she exposed soft, youthful breasts to the edge of the nipples. Her dark blue eyes seemed always knowing, challenging, and slyly amused at what she knew any man was thinking.

When he ordered his pastrami sandwich and ale (leaving himself only one for the evening to come), Henry asked, casually, whether Jan had come in yet.

"Janos Petofi?" Debbie said. "He was in here when we opened at noon, but no, I ain't seen him for a while."

So Henry let it rest, sipping the bitter ale. When she served him he said: "I was looking for Jan yesterday at his trailer around five. I'll bet he was here, wasn't he?"

"Saturday? Man, on Saturday this place is so jammed—yeah, though, I remember. He was. Playing pool and so stinking he could see two balls for every one. He pro'ly won't even remember. Another Heineken?"

Henry shook his head and put on a grin and picked up half of the bulging sandwich with both hands. Either good ole Jan Petofi had been telling him the truth or . . . *or* he'd phoned ahead as soon as Henry left the trailer and told little Debbie to lie for him. Dear little Debbie would most likely be very obliging in that direction. As well as in others.

Henry let his eyes drift down the faces at the bar. Until he arrived at a vaguely familiar one. Male, about forty years old, thin brown hair, blunt features, thick lips, wearing a blue knit polo shirt. He'd seen the man around Sheffield at one time or another. The man took a pair of gold-rimmed spectacles out of his shirt pocket, put them on his broad nose, and peered back at him. Then he stood up—average height, big soft shoulders, but not a laboring man—and came down along the backs of the others to slide into the empty stool at Henry's elbow.

"Chief Lindheim? I thought that was you. How are you, sir? I'm Jerald Dixon. My wife and I live in Sheffield but over on the Lake Candlewood side."

I have a friend, Carole Jensen had said last night. *He's a lawyer. He warned me. He . . . he was wrong. He didn't think I should come.*

Henry nodded as if he recognized Dixon. "Mrs. Jensen mentioned you."

"Right, *right.* That's why I came down. How is she today? I called her this morning. She sounded . . . well, *distraught.*"

"What she's been through does that," Henry said, careful not to use the word.

"I'm an attorney, so I know it won't do any good to ask how the investigation is going. Buy you a drink, sir?"

Henry drained his glass, set it on the bar, and shook his head. "No, thank you. If you're asking whether we've made an arrest, the answer's no."

"TV said you have the man in custody, the one who stole the car."

"We do." Henry said. "He's under arrest for grand-theft-auto and fleeing to elude. Nothing else. Yet."

"Circumstantial," Jerald Dixon said, as if agreeing to something Henry had not needed to say. "Seems to me it'd hold up, though. If you run into a dead end and want to show you've solved the Jensen case, right?"

Reminded of Trooper Dworsky, Henry was about to say he wasn't in the habit of using patsies—especially ones with Hispanic names, no money, and no family—to solve cases that hadn't really been solved, but Jerald Dixon set down his glass and stared into it. "When I think that I was sitting right here when that was happening to Carole. All I could think of was that I didn't want to be too late for her dinner party. I mentioned it to Debbie a while ago. Christ, just thinking about it gives me goose pimples."

Debbie had returned and she was facing Henry from behind the bar, blond head tilted, her eyes teasing. "Another, sir?"

Henry shook his head and put a ten-spot down on the bar, hearing Dixon say, "We were just discussing the Jensen case a while ago, weren't we, Debbie?"

"Yeah," the girl said. "You said it gave you goose bumps thinking about you sitting here smashed while she was getting the business. Tough shit." She reached for the bill.

But Jerald Dixon placed his hand over hers. "I'm buying," he said.

"I'm not in the habit," Henry said, "of letting lawyers buy me lunch." He could as easily have said suspects. "But thanks, anyway, counselor."

"I'm not in criminal law," Jerald Dixon said, grinning. "You won't owe me anything."

Debbie yanked her hand away and stepped back with the bill in it. "*You* want another, I guess, Jerry." When he winked at her, she turned away.

"Some piece," Dixon said, his pale blue eyes on the girl's bare midriff as she worked the cash register. "She doesn't belong in a place like this."

"You're some distance from home yourself," Henry said, watching Jerald Dixon in the mirror behind the bar.

He heard the younger man laugh and observed him doing it. "A man has to let down somewhere. I never see anyone I know here and I can get as loaded as I like. Then, too, there's Debbie. By the third drink I've got a hard-on you wouldn't believe."

Debbie was back, placing his change on the bar, although around the L a huge bearded man wearing a trucker's cap was beginning to pound on the bar for attention. "You a friend of Jan's?" she asked Henry.

"More of an acquaintance. Why?"

"Well, maybe you should warn him. The boss is getting to where he's going to refuse to serve him. That dude's losing it."

"Losing it? Maybe you ought to translate for an old man." He picked up the five, leaving the single and the coins.

"You're not so old." Debbie's eyes were taunting him. "What I mean: that Hunkie's going bonkers or something. Wacko. What's he so mad about all the time? And what's he got against women? Boss thinks the guy's about ready for that Newtown bughouse. You tell him."

"I'll do that," Henry said, "when I see him." He swiveled around to stand up. And at that moment the beeper on his belt began to sound.

"Good luck, sir," Jerald Dixon said, turning his head. His knit shirt was not tucked in and it covered his belt.

"Thanks." Henry clicked off the beeper and was on his way to the door when he heard Jerald Dixon's voice speaking to the girl: "You get off the same time?"

And Debbie's answer: "Five o'clock, same as always. But only if you eat something and slow down on the booze. Anything I hate, it's a limp one."

In the row of vehicles outside—pickups and beat-up older cars—Henry saw a silver-colored four-door Audi sedan. It looked as out of place here as Jerald Dixon did in there.

Getting back into his squad car Henry was wondering if

he'd ever seen Jerald Dixon's wife. Since they lived on Lake Candlewood, they probably shopped over there. Well, considering that Jerald Dixon had tried to talk Carole out of reporting the crime last night . . . and considering also that Jerald Dixon had ID'd himself just now and had exhibited such *casual* curiosity as to how the investigation was proceeding . . . *and* he'd suggested how to close the case by pinning it on Manuel Mendoza . . . and considering as well that he'd *volunteered* the information that he was in Merlin's drinking and tomcatting at the almost exact time of the crime . . . considering everything, Henry made up his mind to find out just a little bit more about Jerald Dixon, his comings and goings and doings. And also to get Carole's point of view. How do people get to be friends anyway?

He radioed the station house and learned that Carole had phoned in from Dr. Judith's office and asked him to return the call.

Which meant that he had to find a public phone. Damn the Board of Selectmen anyway! He'd never been able to convince them that at least the Chief's car should be equipped with a telephone. Always the same answer: budget and taxes. Hadn't the beeper system done the job all these years?

Cursing, he turned on the blue light but not the siren, and gave it the gas. Had Carole found out what he'd learned this morning? What would it mean to her if she ever did? Henry had taken a little trip out to Dyer Electronics and the place had been closed tight, the chain-link fence locked, the guardhouse empty. When he'd finally roused the uniformed security guard, he'd learned that no one—repeat, *no one*—was ever allowed on the premises on Saturday or Sunday and that Mr. Rolfe Jensen had not tried to break that rule yesterday or any other day.

Another lie. And now, if little Debbie had been lying for Janos Petofi and if Jerald Dixon had *not* been in Merlin's at five-thirty yesterday because Debbie got off at five, well, maybe he should add two more liars to his list. It was always the same. Once you get into a complicated case, you learn fast what you've always really known in your gut: that the world is made up of millions of people who will tell a lie as quickly and convincingly as the truth, and without hesitation or any tinge of self-reproach.

Which, on the other hand, did not make all of them criminal rapists, of course.

He spotted an outdoor phone next to a Texaco station and swung the vehicle in to a stop. When he'd tapped out Judith's number, Carole herself answered.

There was a new note of life in her voice, a trembling rush of excitement. "Henry, listen!"

"I'm listening."

"I told you I'd remembered something last night in bed. And I couldn't get it back this morning. Something that happened last summer, by the pond. I've never told anyone before. Listen!"

"I'm listening," he said, again.

"Scott Keller. He's just a teenager. They live in that big Tudor house on Still River Road. His father's a doctor, he has his office here in Sudbury and—"

"Slow down, kid. What about him?"

"I'm telling you. One day last summer . . ."

PART 3

DURING LUNCH IN THE breakfast nook off Dr. Judith's kitchen—an exquisite summer lunch, shrimp-stuffed avocado, Melba toast, tart endive salad and iced tea—Carole had thanked the doctor for somehow forcing her to remember. Because now she had told Henry and Henry would investigate Scott Keller and if the kid admitted it, everything, this whole nightmare, might be over. "It could be over today!" she cried. "Oh, I can't thank you enough!"

But Dr. Judith remained quiet, strangely quiet, not responding, her eyes dark and narrowed as they studied Carole. Then she said, "Shall we take the fruit and cookies into the office? Don't forget your tea."

Following and seating herself in the same chair as before, Carole was puzzled. Bewildered. Why couldn't Dr. Judith understand?

"You phoned your husband, too," Dr. Judith said, sitting behind the desk now and putting on large, round, black-rimmed glasses. "Was he relieved?"

It had been Cass who had answered the phone: *Rolfe's roaming around outside. He's been climbing the wall. Wait a minute, he must have heard the ring.*

"I should have called him earlier," Carole said, "as soon as I knew." Dr. Judith did not reply.

A shrink? Rolfe had said. *You don't need a shrink.*

They've ruined more good marriages than lawyers, and they don't know shit.

So she hadn't told him about Scott Keller after all.

"Was he angry?" Dr. Judith asked.

"Angry? Well, at Cass, I think. Not me."

Cass is looped as usual, Rolfe had said, *and he's listing all my husbandly faults and failures. Look who's talking!*

"You mentioned a while ago," Dr. Judith said, "that you weren't sure that Rolfe really approves your working. But you'd know if it angered him, wouldn't you?"

"Maybe not. Or . . . maybe I just ignore it."

Listen, Rolfe, please—don't spend the afternoon arguing with Cass. Tune in a football game and stop drinking, both of you. "He's sore at Cass right now and he was really steamed last night. He thinks Henry suspects him of raping me."

"And you?"

"Are you serious? That's about the wildest idea—"

"Did that thought never occur to you?"

Carole leaped to her feet, feeling the stiff soreness in her knees. "No! Not once! What are you getting at?"

"Carole, I'm only trying to help."

"Well, you're not helping by attacking my husband!" She moved to stand looking out the picture window into the small garden. "I don't want to talk about that now. Why would Rolfe rape me? The whole idea's off the wall and I resent it. I told you: Rolfe loves me."

"How's your sex life?"

Carole whirled around. "Do you ask that of every woman who's been raped?" She saw the doctor smile, faintly. "My sex life's just terrific, how's yours?"

Then Dr. Judith laughed out loud. "Not very, thank you. Why don't you want to talk about Rolfe? You'd be amazed if you knew the intimate details of private lives that are discussed in this room."

Carole turned to the window again. Her breast had begun to throb with pain. "I lied," she said softly. "About my so-called sex life."

"So?"

"I'm . . . I'm a very passionate woman. Maybe too passionate. I love making love. Sometimes . . . sometimes, if we're coming home from a party, on a country road and it's night, I just take off my clothes while he's driving—all of them. . . ." She let the sound of her voice drift away, remembering. How long ago that seemed—

"Sounds healthy enough to me," Dr. Judith said. "I'd say he's a fortunate young man."

"Tell *him.*"

"I beg your pardon?"

The pain in her breast was becoming intense. "I said: tell Rolfe. Sometimes. . . . I often wonder if he doesn't resent it, afterwards."

"Because you took the initiative? Usurped the male prerogative?"

"We haven't made love in over two weeks." She stepped to the desk. "I have to take some medicine." She turned away and reached into the pocket of her vest and brought out several of the pills and capsules from the prescriptions Rolfe had had filled that morning—had she thanked him?

Careful not to take the sleeping pill or tranquilizer capsule, she swallowed the analgesic tablet, washing it down with the tea. The pain was acute and she could feel the hand twisting her breast again. Then she sat down in the chair at the small table and stared ahead.

"You'd rather talk about something else, wouldn't you?" Dr. Judith rose gracefully and came to sit opposite her again. "All right, tell me about your work. Do you enjoy it?"

"Yes. But not as much as I enjoy Sandy. That makes me a freak today, doesn't it?"

"Not at all. An individual, I'd say."

But Carole barely heard her. "Why," she heard herself demand, and surprised, "why does Rolfe always have to be *right?* Always. It infuriates him even if he's *mistaken* . . . and he'll never admit he's wrong, never. About *anything*."

Dr. Judith crossed her long legs and asked, "What makes me think there's more?"

"More?"

"It might help to talk about it. Have you, ever?"

"No, never. Not to anyone—" And then, suddenly: "I feel so disloyal. Rolfe always says sex is something you do, you don't *talk* about it. Even between the two of us."

Dr. Judith removed her glasses. "What is it you do that makes Rolfe angry?"

"I never said that. But it's true. Only in reverse. It's what he *wants* me to do that I . . . I *can't* do."

"Won't do?"

"No. Can't do. Can't, cannot, *can't*. I get sick to my stomach. I've tried, but every time I get physically sick. I have to run into the bathroom and throw up. Oh, I know what goes on all around me, that doesn't bother me, what other people do, but it's me. I can't. I just want to make love because we love each other. Maybe that's dull. It never is to me. Maybe I'm puritanical, I don't know. I love having sex. I really *love* it! Only . . . only not that way."

"And that makes him angry, too?"

"I don't know. Ask him. Why're you asking all these questions?"

"Because I have to know as much as possible. In order to find ways to help you."

"Well, I've already told you: you won't help me by accusing my husband."

"I haven't accused anyone, Carole. Nor has Henry, I'm sure." She stood up then, to stand behind the wing chair. "But there is something I think you should know. Carole, the current accepted theory is that rape is not really a sex crime."

"Not a sex crime?" The words brought her out of her seat. "If I hear that theory one more time—" She stepped toward the doctor: "What kind of *weapon* did he use? He also tried to twist my breast off at the same time! What the hell are you talking about, lady?"

Then, the fury quivering inside and shuddering along her flesh, she was taken by surprise when Dr. Judith did not ask her to sit down again, but went on with a small shrug: "Rape is *always* an act of rage. It's a crime of hate, aggression, seething fury that erupts into violence. What a rapist wants is to debase, degrade, subjugate—put a woman under *his* power. He has a sick, terrible need for absolute mastery. His victim is often only a symbol for all the things or people in the world who have hurt him. Or who he *imagines* have hurt him."

"I don't give a damn about the causes or reasons—"

"One theory as to why rape's becoming epidemic is that men are having a hard time adapting to the recent changes. On the surface they try to go along, but somewhere deeper they can't really accept women's new freedom. Sexual attack's one way, the ultimate way, to prove he's still the boss."

Carole heard the growl in her voice: "Doctor, speaking from *experience*—take it from me, lady, it's *still* a sex crime." She spun away, body shaking, mind ablaze.

Dr. Judith moved to the windows. "It so happens, Carole, that I agree with you."

Carole whirled around. "What?" she demanded. *"What?!"*

"I agree. Oh, there's some validity in what I said. It *is* an act of rage but it's also a sex crime, of course."

"Then why? Why did you try to convince me?"

"Because, my dear, when I see you this way, outraged and alive all over, then I get the satisfaction of thinking that you're going to make it."

"You bitch," Carole said, in a whisper, her body going limp.

"You should hear what some of my patients call me."

"I didn't mean that—"

"Don't say you're sorry, don't." She moved toward

where Carole stood, that small smile hovering on her lips. "Outrage goes a long way, Carole. Don't lose it. And don't apologize for it."

"Who's apologizing?"

Dr. Judith laughed again and turned to resume her seat. "Tell me, Carole, have you ever had what they call an extramarital affair?"

"I never even thought of it."

"And Rolfe?"

"Ditto." She moved closer. "Listen, Rolfe and I agreed on that. It was the one thing he *would* discuss. I even told him about my father—*his* affairs. No, thank God, that's something I've never had to think about and you can believe that or not."

"In this day and age I'm delighted to believe it. Now why don't you sit down and tell me about Cass?"

So then Carole returned to the chair, sat down, and told Dr. Judith what little, she thought, there was to tell: That Cass was Rolfe's oldest and closest friend, that he was now almost part of the family, that he'd written a novel based on his experience in Nam, published before she and Rolfe were married, and therefore before she knew him, and that now, presumably, he was writing another book but she doubted it. "And I've become as fond of him as Rolfe is. That's about it."

"Fond?" Dr. Judith asked. "That's not a very strong word, is it?"

"All right," Carole said. "Love. Sure I love him. He's a battered, lonely guy and I pity him and I love him. There ought to be another word. I don't love him the way I love Rolfe, it's a different way, but it's love."

"Isn't it a shame there's not another word! I hear what you're saying, dear. And him?"

"I don't understand?"

"Oh, I think you do. Does he love you in that *different* way?"

"Of course," she said, quickly. Too quickly. Because,

until now, she'd never given that idea a chance to come into focus. But she'd sensed, yes, she'd sensed that, although Cass was hesitant—no, careful—not to let their bodies touch when they kissed hello or good-bye, he probably did love her in the way Rolfe loved her, in a way she could never love *him.*

"Of course, but?" Dr. Judith prompted, sipping her tea.

"Damn you," Carole said, softly. "How do you do it, *how?*"

"You don't have to tell me, Carole. Just so you look at the truth, straight and hard, in your own mind." Then she changed the subject slightly: "I remember reading his book—*Flashbacks,* wasn't that the title?—and thinking: I hope this represents catharsis because this was written by a very disturbed mind, but with acute psychological perceptions, insights, in spite of his wrath."

"Cass told me once when we were alone—I even remember his words: *It was an insane situation and it made all of us insane.* And the world, he said, still wanted to think of it as a John Wayne movie."

"Is he still terribly bitter?"

"Not bitter. It goes a long way past bitterness. Deeper. I sometimes think he's filled with a kind of burnt-out despair. I don't think of it if I can help it. And damn you again."

Dr. Judith smiled. "You're really free to love him, you know. In *your* way. Whether that's his way or not. How does Rolfe feel about all this?"

"He's jealous. I never admitted that before, either." Then, the thought knifing into her mind: "But Cass could never hurt me. I know what you're thinking. No way, no way." Then she rested her head back and accepted something that she'd always refused to accept: "He's drinking himself to death and nobody's doing anything about it." She heard the muted anguish in her voice. "I guess Rolfe and I love him so much that we don't want to risk our friendship with him by trying. Isn't that . . . that's awful, isn't it?"

"Perhaps it's not too late, Carole." Then, without shifting her body in her chair, Dr. Judith said: "Perhaps you'd rather discuss your daughter. Did you say her name was Sandy?"

And then Carole heard herself say something else that she never thought she'd ever say aloud: "Rolfe loves Sandy, really loves her, but sometimes I think he's jealous of her. *Because* he thinks maybe I love her *too* much."

"And that makes him angry—"

"Stop saying that. I know why you keep using that word. Well, Rolfe couldn't rape me, and neither could Cass. If it wasn't the man who stole my car, then it must have been Scott Keller. I told you what I told Henry—don't you *listen?*"

"I try to listen with what someone called my third ear. It's very important to you, isn't it—that whoever it is, he be punished?"

Meeting the older woman's eyes, Carole said, "If he's not made to pay, the world makes absolutely no sense."

"Sometimes," Dr. Judith said, her own dark eyes not wavering, "sometimes it's necessary to accept that idea. To find a way to live with it."

"I could never do that," Carole said, in a whisper, knowing. "Never."

"Then it could destroy *you,* Carole."

"If that's the way the world really is," Carole heard herself say, "I wouldn't want to live anyway."

"I see," Dr. Judith said, very softly, frowning now. "Let's explore the idea of justice, shall we? And its relationship to order and reason and sanity in the world. And its relationship to personal vengeance. . . ."

"Fuck off," Dr. Kenneth Keller said.

"That," Henry said, "is the third time today that I've been told to perform that particular act."

"Discussion's over. You want my son, go find him. This way, Lindheim."

The tall, square-shouldered man wearing tennis trunks led the way out of the den, or library, and through the enormous cathedral-ceilinged, deep-carpeted living room, all the while grumbling under his breath: "I've got house-guests from the city, goddamn it. I've also got friends—including Mark Rainer, State's Attorney. We both belong to the Lake Club where I keep my boat. You goddamn New Yorkers, you come up here and take over. Damned if I know why a nice town like this'd hire a cop off the streets of New York." In the slate-floored foyer, he opened the huge arched door and stood back. "A seventeen-year-old kid taking pictures, that's not rape."

Striding to his car, Henry heard Mrs. Keller—a small slight woman with years of resentments in her bleak, narrow eyes and the leathery washed-out skin of the steady drinker—calling after him: "If something's happened to that bitch, it's her own doing. Posing for pictures like that. She's been leading the poor kid on for months."

The squad car was parked between a gray Mercedes sedan, the doctor's, and a shining tan Cadillac Eldorado with MD plates, New York, probably belonging to the doctor's guests. Did any MDs drive ordinary cars these days?

Leaving the formally landscaped and manicured grounds, driving between thin Italian cypresses, Henry could hear the plop of tennis balls and voices from the court behind the trees. Doctors always argued in the press that they had to charge such outrageous fees in order to pay malpractice insurance premiums. *And,* of course, to live like this.

When he'd questioned Dr. Keller earlier, the father had shaken his almost-bald head: *Don't ask me. About that or anything else. All I know is that I can't talk to him and he won't talk to me. Just flies into one of his insane rages. Couldn't hold a job even if he could get one, looking like a*

Jesus-freak. Sleeps in the woods more'n he uses his own bedroom. . . .

Well, Henry couldn't waste what was left of the afternoon prowling every road in Sheffield. Scott Keller was probably camping in the woods somewhere, and there were too many goddamn woods around!

He lit another cigar and glanced at the dashboard clock. Time for one more stop before returning to Dr. Judith's to pick up Carole at five-thirty. He could drive to the Jensen house and confront Rolfe Jensen with *his* lie while Carole wasn't there. Maybe have a chat with Mr. A. L. Cassady as well. Or he could go to Duncan Clive's house-barn and confront him with *his* phony story. Or . . . or he could continue into Sudbury to the offices and printing plant of the *News-Chronicle* and lean on the little red-haired reporter, another liar, Joel White. Which is what he decided to do because the newspaper building was only minutes from Dr. Judith's house-and-office.

He hadn't gone three miles when another vehicle—red Ford Bronco, four-wheel drive, Connecticut plates—charged around his squad car, doing at least seventy on a two-lane highway. "Damn fool," he muttered, flipping on the siren and blue flasher, giving chase almost automatically. The Bronco didn't have a chance against his souped-up engine.

Most drivers, approaching from behind, slowed down, reluctant to pass a marked police vehicle. He didn't need this now, he didn't want this, goddamn it, he didn't have time for it now, but he couldn't look the other way—whoever was driving that Bronco was breaking the law and saying *up yours* to the police at the same time.

But it didn't slow as he came closer. It passed a pickup and dared him to follow. The driver—was it a female, blond hair flying?—*had* to hear the goddamn siren by now, *had* to see the blue light in his, or her, rearview mirror.

What happened then made him snarl an incoherent obscenity against his training, his principles: the Bronco swerved left again, across a solid yellow line down the middle of the road, into the oncoming lane, no vehicle approaching, just luck, and from the left lane it made a sweeping, looping turn to the right, crossing the lane and plunging off the road to come to a sudden stop at a right angle to it, its nose inches from a low stone fence, or wall.

Henry, still furious, but by now cautious, braked onto the shoulder behind the rear of the Bronco, blocking it, and climbed out, much faster than he normally would. His .38 was in his shoulder holster under his suitcoat, which he automatically unbuttoned as he approached the other vehicle.

Then, before he reached it, the driver climbed down without being asked. *Not* a female, male, young kid, wearing dark shades, hair to his shoulders, short blond beard, handsome enough face—with a challenging sneer all over it. "I been looking for you, Chief," the kid said, leaning against the side of the Bronco. "I hear you been looking for me, too."

"Well," Henry said, relaxing, the anger still there, "in a sort of loose way I have been, Scott. You always drive like that?"

"Only when I want to get someone's attention. At least, that's what the psychology books say, right?"

"Speeding, reckless endangerment, crossing yellow line —you *got* my attention, Mister Keller."

Scott Keller snickered. "I been following you since you left the house."

Which meant that his mother, whiskey glass in hand, cigarette dangling, had lied—*He's out with the young people having a good time*—and his father had gone along with it. More fine, upstanding, respectable citizens.

"You got something to say to me?" Henry demanded, closing his coat over the gun.

"Just wanted t'tell you: Your idea sucks."

This sort of badgering Henry had dealt with all his life.

How to deal with it depended on the who and where and how far it went. "Does it? Why?"

Scott Keller frowned then, a sudden shift of mood. "Because I couldn't do that, anything like that, to *her.*"

Henry was startled—not only by the words, but by the simple sincerity with which they were uttered. "No? Why not?"

" 'Cause, you can believe it or not: I think I'm in love with her. Only she doesn't know it."

Rape? his father had scoffed. *You're in the wrong tree, Chief. Kid hasn't got the balls.* And he'd almost chuckled: *Besides, his goddamn hair'd get in the way.*

"That the only reason you're so sure? Or is it because you're always so loaded with junk, you know you couldn't get it up if you wanted to?" Or, Henry thought but did not say, because doing it that way, forcibly, was the only way he *could* get it up.

"Dad's idea, right? He thinks he's got the only balls and bat that work. You're wrong again. I couldn't do it to *her* that way."

"Unless she wanted you to—that what you mean?"

"She never would." Desolation in his eyes, his voice, he turned away. "I'm not dumb. I know that."

So did Henry. But he glanced around. Two other cars had stopped. Faces in the windows. Staring. "Just drive on, folks," he said. "This is a police matter, and private. I mean now." And when they were gone: "If you know she never would, son, why'd you expose yourself to her last summer?"

"She said that?" He had not turned.

"Was she lying?"

Scott Keller took a long moment to answer, facing Henry now, his face contorting slightly. Finally he asked: "The truth?"

"Why not?" Henry said. "Just for the novelty."

"The truth is: I can't remember."

"Don't try to con me, kid."

The boy was shaking his head, hair moving. He removed the sunglasses. His pale eyes were direct but troubled. "God's truth," he said. "I was so blitzed all summer, I can't remember. Not a lost weekend, a whole fucking summer. Just bits and pieces. Ask the almighty M.D. He'll swear I'm faking it."

Now Henry had to weigh the earnest candor in the boy's face and tone against his knowledge of the sly guile of the guilty mind, invariably finding new ways to evade consequences. He'd already been lied to exactly seven times now in the last twenty-four hours and he was damned tired of it. "You have these blackouts often?" he asked, his voice hard. "Or only when they come in handy?"

"I know you won't believe me. Mom's the only one ever does."

"Maybe I ought to have a look at your pockets. Or search the vehicle—"

"Be my guest. I'm clean, man."

"Since when?"

"Since," the boy said, angry now, glaring like his father, "since I realized what the crack was doing to my mind, that's when, around Labor Day. When I realized it was fall and the summer, almost all of it, was a *blank.* Don't you fuzz know anything? *Jesus.* Why do you all have to be so terminally *dumb?*"

"Then," Henry said, ignoring that, "then if you've been clean since Labor Day, you can tell me where you were yesterday afternoon about this time, can't you?"

Scott Keller turned and slammed his fist into the door of the Bronco. "That's not the way it works! I'm not on anything, nothing, now, but I still get the blackouts. They come. I don't know *where* I was yesterday. Go ahead, bust me. I don't care. They'll send me back to the snake pit, and I'll get out again somehow and then hit the stuff again, why not, why not, why not?"

Henry considered this. The whole sad pattern was clear, *too* clear: the alcoholic mother fighting for her kid's love, any love, the macho father filled with frustration and anger, self-righteous, hating what his son has become—and the disturbed kid also a victim, and hurting, and seething with fury *because* he was hurting. Unless . . .

Unless he was putting on a very clever act—

"If," Henry said, trying it on for size, "if you can't remember, maybe you did rape Mrs. Jensen—"

Scott Keller turned to face him. "If she said that, she's lying."

"How do you know?"

His boyish voice held a kind of awe. "I don't think I could ever forget that."

"Why not?"

" 'Cause . . . 'cause I couldn't. She's about the most terrific woman I've ever seen."

"I saw the photographs," Henry told him, and waited.

Scott Keller, looking helpless and furious and very young, leaned against the red door again, shaking his head, closing his eyes, his slim boyish body slack. "You're going to lay it on me, aren't you. All of you. Mom showed you the photos, right? Well, maybe it'd serve them right, both of them. Pictures in the paper, disgrace, scandal." He turned away again, shoulders slumped, silent now, in pain.

"Your mother showed me the pictures because she claims Mrs. Jensen posed for them."

In each of the photographs Carole was wearing a bathing suit, a black tank suit in two and a one-piece flowered job in the others. She was diving off the dock in one. She was in a canoe with a little blond girl in one. In another she was running across the lawn, slim and graceful toward the house from the pond. In another she was stretched out on her back on a chaise, relaxed and apparently asleep.

Something inside Henry relented. He stepped to where the boy stood. "They were taken with a telephoto lens at long distance. Where were you, up in a tree?"

Scott Keller faced him again, frowning. "If you know that, you know she didn't pose, don't you?"

"Way I read them, she was on her own property and had no idea she was being spied on. That's trespass, maybe invasion of privacy, and sure as hell voyeurism."

"You want me to confess, Chief? Okay. Bring out the handcuffs. I confess."

Having dealt with sociopaths who were capable of any kind of con game, who were so damned wily and sly and cunning and convincing that they could and often did deceive experts, Henry was considering taking the kid in, charging him with malicious trespass and the traffic offenses just to hold him.

"I know what you're thinking," Scott Keller said, his tone mocking, a taunting grin curling his lips now. "My old man'll bail me out in an hour."

Wrong, kid, wrong—not what he'd been thinking at all. But nevertheless, true. "I'm going to give you a speeding ticket, boy. Just to make sure you stay in the area."

The grin changed from mocking to triumphant. "You know I didn't rape her, don't you?"

"I don't *know* anything," Henry said. "Except this. If you go around exposing your genitals to women, they *are* going to remember."

"Goddamn her," the boy said, low in his throat. He had changed again. "How could she do this to me?"

"Watch your mouth and let me see your driver's license and registration. And lift up your sweat shirt—where's your belt?"

The boy was wearing gray jogging pants, with a drawstring.

"I don't like belts," he said. And then he said, "That bitch."

"I told you to watch your mouth," Henry said, "and where's your license?"

Scott turned, opened the door and reached up onto the seat. "Bitch, bitch, bitch, they're all alike!"

Henry's restraint gave way. While he wrote out the ticket, he growled, "Watch your mouth, I said. I don't take lip from snot-nose, wise-ass rich kids and I don't do diapers. Why the hell don't you grow up? It ain't easy, kid, nobody ever said it was. You got your whole life in front of you. Why blow it to get even with your old man?"

"What's that?" Scott snorted, "pop paperback psychology?" His eyes were hostile. "Sermons come with every summons?"

Hopeless, hopeless. Too late, too little. He handed the boy his copy of the ticket. "Next time I'll throw the book at you. Whatever the reason, you got no right to jeopardize other lives 'cause you don't give a shit about your own. That ain't psychology, kid, that's a warning."

"Well, I got a warning for you, too. You don't know what it's like, the way they treat you in that loony bin. Funny farm, they call it—well, there's nothing *funny* about it. You're not even a person in there. Not a human being at all. You're *nothing.* I'd rather be dead than go back to that hellhole." He took a couple of steps and stood peering up into Henry's eyes. "And I'm not going back just when I'm beginning to get my shit together. I'm not going back just because that bitch lied to you that I raped her."

"I told you, goddamn it. Mrs. Jensen didn't accuse you and don't call her a bitch one more time."

Scott Keller was climbing into the seat. "And I told *you:* I didn't do it and I'm not gonna pay for it, so fuck off."

The *fourth* time in less than three hours. Henry returned to his vehicle, remembering a time, not so long ago, when even the most hardened criminal, even in the most desperate circumstances, would hesitate to say anything like that to an officer of the law. And to a man old enough to be his grandfather on top of it!

Henry was beginning to feel old again.

The room was almost dark. Dusk gray and heavy outside the windows.

Before she went to get the coffee, Dr. Judith had told Carole something that, she said, she had found helpful with alcoholic patients—something about how we all respond to whatever stimulus. *In psych. one-oh-one there's only this: the stimulus and the reaction to it. But there's more to it than a simple reaction, or should be. The Third Step, I've come to call it. The human step which comes after the impulse and before the reaction. A sort of cognitive hesitation during which the mind considers and weighs and projects the potential results of the response. If and when he uses that Third Step, it's what separates man from the other animals. Then, when he does react, he's doing it as a rational, responsible human being rather than as an automaton.*

And before that, Dr. Judith had caused her to reveal things, not only to the doctor but to herself, that she wished now she had never had to consider, or think about, or admit. By now all the humiliation and tension of the long day had accumulated like a black cloud in her mind. Huddled on the sofa in front of the unlit fireplace, Carole was feeling defeated and depressed and depleted. Lifeless. She was feeling worse, not better, *worse,* more confused. What was she doing here and what had been accomplished?

When Dr. Judith came in with the silver coffeepot, she turned on a lamp over the desk in the corner. A pleasant golden glow came over the room.

"You're crying," she said.

And it was true. Carole was weeping. But silently, unmoving. And the pain in her breast had become a low-keyed aching knot.

Dr. Judith sank to her knees to pour coffee. "Letting go's probably good for you, dear."

"How can Henry be so kind, after all he's been through?"

"Possibly *because* of what he's been through." She stood up, cup and saucer in hand. "He told you then? I'm really astonished."

"And I was wrong: Rolfe *is* angry with me."

"It's natural for him to be troubled."

"What have I done? What have I really done?"

"Nothing, Carole." Dr. Judith sank into the only lounge chair in the room, facing Carole at a right angle. "That's what makes it so hellish."

"And Cass, he's a total mystery to me. And he does love me—the way you said. I guess I've always known that."

"And?"

"He did say . . . he said everyone who got out alive was at least a little crazy." She reached for her cup and lifted it to her lips. The coffee was hot and black and bitter. "It's a lousy world, isn't it? Rotten. Cruel. Who cares? What does it matter, who wants to live in a world like this?"

"Most of us," Dr. Judith said. "Including you, or you wouldn't be here."

"Maybe it's stupid to go on struggling. Dumb."

"That's the worm in the wheat, Carole. The good old existential angst and despair. No God, no reason, no point —grains of sand and what does it matter? Accident, chance, insignificance. You think you're the only one who ever went through it? And you don't have to be female . . . *a tale told by an idiot, full of sound and fury, signifying nothing.* Poor old Macbeth, and all the millions who've understood Lear's howling on the heath. Did you ever read Sartre, Camus, Kierkegaard?"

"Like most people, I guess I always meant to." Her voice seemed to come from a long way off.

"Well, don't run home and do it now."

"My mother would say: *God has His mysterious ways.* I wish I could believe that now. Of course, she'd also tell me to examine my own conscience. As if . . . as if this couldn't have happened if I hadn't done something to deserve it."

"*I* didn't deserve what happened to me. Nor did Henry. That's a very destructive idea—your mother's."

Startled now, drawn out of herself for a moment, Carole

said, "Should I tell you: *Physician, heal thyself?*" A quote. From the Bible. Long ago.

Dr. Judith's face was in shadow. Very softly her voice said "We've all been down those dark roads, Carole. Oh, not rape. There are many dark roads, my dear. But the darkest of all is not suicide, as I once thought. That's final. The blackest of all is a complete emotional and mental breakdown. When everything, inside and out, goes haywire. When you're alive but you've lost yourself, your reason, and sometimes you know it. Knowing's the worst torture of all."

After a second or two, Carole said, "You're warning me, aren't you?"

"I am. Because I know. I've been there."

"What if I don't care? What if it doesn't matter?"

"If not to you—what about Alexandra?"

Sandy. What time would she be back from the city? Was she already home?

"What time is it?" she asked.

"Not quite four-thirty. We have more than an hour." Dr. Judith stood up. "Relax, my dear. Henry won't forget you. Or forsake you." She was at the end of the sofa now. "Nor will I."

Their eyes met, and held. And all of a sudden Carole felt ashamed and contrite. "Let's get back to work," she said.

Dr. Judith smiled, faintly. "Oh, we've been working, as you call it, all along. But now there's one more thing I'd like to do before Henry comes—"

"What?"

"It's time for you to tell me what actually happened in the woods. Do you feel up to it?"

"No, but I'll do it."

"Have you ever been hypnotized, Carole?"

"No," she said, very uncertainly.

"Would you be willing to?"

"Why?"

"You might remember something, under hypnosis, that

you've forgotten or that your mind has shut out. Also, not so incidentally, it might help you to accept what's happened by reliving it one more time."

"I don't want to relive it and I'll never accept it. But if it'll help identify the sadist who did it to me so he can be punished—lay on, Macduff."

Judith laughed again. "Good," she said and crossed behind the sofa to the chair at the small round table. "Odd you should choose *Macbeth,* too—one of the greatest studies of evil ever written." She sat down. "In those dear dead days when the world really believed in evil."

Carole rose, her knees protesting with pain, and took a few stiff steps to the chair facing Dr. Judith. "I believe in it," she said.

When she was seated, the other woman said, "I'll be all three witches rolled into one. *Double, double, toil and trouble; fire burn and cauldron bubble.*"

When Henry took off his felt hat in the cavernous lobby of the *Sudbury News-Chronicle* Building and asked to see Joel White, the girl (she couldn't be more than eighteen) behind the curved counter picked up one of the phones and asked for the city room, then asked his name.

"Lindheim," he said, leaving out the Henry and the Chief, knowing that would be enough.

While he waited, he turned to stare out the plate glass windows at the scattered Sunday traffic in the dusk. He was thinking of Carole again. What was there about her that kept him going like this? He'd begun to feel downright possessive, as if she had become his responsibility—the kind of burden that a man accepted when he fell in love. As if he wanted to do whatever he could do, not because he wanted or expected anything whatever in return. Not even gratitude. It was more like the selfless love he'd felt for Teresa, rather the kind of love he'd felt for Luisa. With his wife he *had* expected something for himself. Like, he supposed, all husbands, all lovers. But he had not moved out of himself—there, that was it. A man can't move out of himself when he loves romantically. But with a child . . .

"Chief, you got a story for me?" And as Henry turned to face Joel White, the little red-haired reporter asked, faking the mockery now. "You get your man, Chief? Plenty of time for the morning edition."

Henry decided to get on with it. "You go up to Lime Rock often, do you?"

"I told you last night, Chief. I'm a racing freak." He strolled away from the counter and Henry followed. "Hell, I even go to stock car races."

"What kinda race'd you see yesterday?"

"Kind?"

"Formula One?"

"Not at Lime Rock. It was an IMSA-GT."

"Translate that, would you? I'm ignorant."

"International Motor Sports Association."

"You don't happen to recall who won, do you?"

"No name you'd know. These are rich amateurs, own their own cars."

"What make car, y'remember that?"

"Hey, man, what is this?"

"Keep your voice down, Joel."

"Maybe we ought to find an empty office upstairs. This way. My desk's in the city room with everybody else's."

Joel White, Henry knew, was giving himself time to think while they walked.

After they'd gone into a central corridor, they climbed a flight of carpeted stairs. Newspaper offices didn't *feel* the way they used to, or *sound* the same, or even smell the same—they'd all been computerized, sanitized, modernized like everything else. No smoking, no noise, no character.

Joel White led him into a large vacant room with big windows and high drafting tables with advertisement clipouts and proofs and sketches pinned to the corkboards on the walls. Troughs of fluorescent lights threw a soft blue glow over the room.

After he'd closed the door, he turned to Henry. "You don't really think I did that to Carole Jensen, do you? Did she send you here?"

"Why should she?"

"Well, I get on people's nerves. I . . . tease a lot."

"We were discussing racing, weren't we?"

"Yeh. Well, I can't remember who won, his name, no name you'd know, like Andretti, or Rick Mears. I think it was Murphy or Scanlon. Irish, I think."

Henry shook his head. "Yesterday it was SCCA Races, Sports Car Club of America. Amateur, all right, but not your average Porsche, like today's race. Winner yesterday was named Richard Palumba. Irish name if I ever heard one."

Joel White took a deep breath, dug a crumpled package of Camels out of the pocket of his knit shirt and said, "So I lied."

"That's all right, Joel." He was thinking of Carole's husband, and of Duncan Clive, and Dr. Keller and his son. "Whenever I'm on a case, people for some strange reason start lying to me."

Joel went to the steel-framed windows and looked out, lighting a cigarette. "If I tell you the truth, would it be privileged? Like talking to a lawyer—"

"Or a priest in confession? No, Joel, it wouldn't." And then he added: "I don't absolve sins, kid—I just root 'em out."

The reporter ran one hand over his curly red hair and turned. "I've got nothing to *confess,* Chief. Because I haven't done anything, see. But my private life's my own." He stepped toward Henry, narrowing his eyes, looking up into his face. "And if you don't believe me, tough shit. You don't have probable cause to arrest me, and you know it. Worst you could do would be to haul me out of here in handcuffs—I lose my job."

"You're used to that, aren't you?"

That got to him for a second or two. "You know, so you know. I lost a few, yeah. But not for rape, not for rape, mister."

The door opened and a tallish woman wearing a dark blue pantsuit came in. "Rape?" she said, her dark eyes darting from one to the other, sharp with questions. "Is that all you can think about, Joel? Sorry, gentlemen, but this *is* my department." She moved closer to Henry, eyes studying him, shrewd and direct. "I know you. Carole's husband, on the phone this morning, said you were on the case." She spoke the way she moved—brusque voice, brisk steps. In her mid-forties. A no-nonsense lady. "This is where Carole works. Or delivers her work. I'm Miriam Bishop." She stretched out her hand.

"Henry Lindheim," he said, taking it, a firm hand, a quick strong shake.

"I guess," Joel White said, "I assume I'm free to go, Chief?"

"Just keep yourself available," Henry told him. "Maybe your memory will improve."

Crossing to the door, Joel White said, "My memory's fine, thanks." Some of the bounce and confidence had returned to his step. And voice: "It's just that I know my rights."

"Obstructing justice is not one of them," Henry said. "This ain't Washington."

Blowing smoke, Joel White went out the door. Under a sign which read: POSITIVELY NO SMOKING.

After the door closed, Miriam Bishop looked him up and down before she said, "When a person says *take the weight off* to you, he's got to mean it, doesn't he? Well, do it, sit."

"Are you and Mrs. Jensen friends?" he prompted.

"Well, we ain't lovers!" Again that hearty, deep-throated laugh. She climbed onto one of the drawing-table stools and produced her own pack of cigarettes. "Is little Joel a suspect?"

Henry went to sit on a straight chair at one of the tables, which had been lowered to desk height and was covered with odds and ends of pen sketches, mostly of women's clothes. "At this point," he said wearily, "every male within a radius of a hundred miles is a suspect."

Miriam Bishop lit a cigarette and blew smoke. "You have any idea what he's going through?"

"Not if you're going to tell me—"

The woman's heavy brows came together over her pretty and very feminine nose and she uttered a pleasant guttural laugh. "Denial, they call it," she said. "While, in his heart, he's aching to kick down the closet door."

"All I really know," Henry said, "is that he has an unhealthy contempt for women. You're suggesting he's queer, aren't you?"

With the cigarette dangling between her wide sensuous lips, Miriam Bishop laughed—a husky but very merry sound. "Queer? Ohmigod, how long since I've heard *that* word? You not only *look* antediluvian, you *think* antediluvian, don't you?"

Henry smiled, relaxing. "Just a fossil left over from the ice age." He was wishing he hadn't left his cigars in the squad car. "The word today is gay, isn't it?"

"Doesn't queer mean strange, unnatural?"

"Doesn't gay mean cheerful, full of fun?"

"Touché, you big bastard. Joel's hardly that, is he? But *I'm* cheerful. *I* have a lot of fun."

Not even startled, but amazed at the good feeling that had come over him, Henry nevertheless said, "No offense intended, Miss Bishop."

"Somehow," she said, smiling now, "somehow I knew that. None taken, Chief." She blew smoke again and mocked him pleasantly with her eyes. "And it's Mrs. Bishop. It took me seven years of marriage—and of hell—before *I* battered down the closet door."

"Are you suggesting I should take Mr. White's name off my list?"

She shook her head. "The opposite. I'm saying Joel *might* be trying to prove to himself that he's something he secretly knows he's not."

Now she was the one who waited.

"Raping a woman'd be kinda going to extremes, wouldn't it?"

"I don't know." Her face was sober now, her eyes grave. "I slept with every one of my husband's friends, one by one, when *he* got suspicious of where I was really coming from. I became the whore of Babylon in Tarrytown, New York. *Anything* to keep from admitting." She turned her head to look out the steel-framed windows into the dusk. "I'm not trying to hurt Joel, Chief. Honest." Then she turned her eyes on him again. "But I'm thinking of Carole. I know what this has to be doing to her." She leaned forward. "And you know, too, don't you? Or you wouldn't be ere. Correct?"

"Correct," Henry said.

"Good man," she said. "Christ, how long's it been since I met a really good man?"

Embarrassed, Henry stood up, his right hip joint catching, as it often did, especially toward evening. "I'm meeting her in about half an hour. Tell me, does Mr. Fletcher know what you suspect about Joel?"

Miriam Bishop snorted a laugh. "If he did, it'd be Joel's ass for sure. Don't you read Vincent Fletcher's editorials?"

"Sometimes. I always kinda mistrust a newspaper that blames the courts and the police for the crime rate."

Miriam Bishop laughed again. "Poor man still believes every myth and every so-called principle he learned at his sainted mother's knee. Or breast. But, hell, he treats Carole as if she were made of blown glass, so he can't be all bad. *Is* she?"

"Is she what?"

"Is Carole made of blown glass?" Miriam Bishop was

leaning forward, blowing smoke, frowning. "How's she taking what's happened? I keep hoping it won't change her. Dim her. She's always had such a quick easy laugh. Bright, bright. If she loses that—"

There was a knock on the glass-paneled door. The man who entered wore a bow tie and was of medium height, pushing fifty, well-built but fleshy, with a distinct bulge at his midsection which was even more noticeable because the jacket of his suit was open and his suspenders were taut over the soft-looking belly. No belt, Henry noted—Christ, he was becoming a belt nut!

Quickly then, in that ironic way she had, Miriam Bishop said, "Chief Lindheim—Mr. Vincent Fletcher, our editor-in-chief, owner and all-around Simon Legree." She put out her cigarette. "We were just taking your name in vain, Mr. Fletcher."

Henry stood to shake hands. Vincent Fletcher, jovial and smiling, nevertheless left no doubt as to who was in charge. "Sit down, Chief, sit down. We don't stand on ceremony around here." He had a deep resonant voice, like an actor's. He glanced around and then perched himself, a little awkwardly, on one of the stools, one foot on the floor. "No way to keep secrets around this place. I trust Joel White was able to be helpful." His hair, a reddish brown color, showed no gray and was thick and wavy, and Henry realized, after a moment, that the man was wearing a toupee.

"Mr. White was very cooperative," Henry lied.

"It's about Carole, isn't it?" And when Henry blinked his eyes once, in answer: "Damnable thing. Horrible. I hope you've got some sort of lead—"

"Several," Henry said. None really worth much of a damn yet, but no need to admit that to a newspaper editor.

"Well, you'll get him. And when you do, I hope they throw the book at him. But you know how courts are. Degenerate pervert. What about the vagrant who snatched her car?"

"We've ruled that out," Henry said. "Or at least I have."

"I know, I know. I talked with Mark Rainer at lunch. Well, you fellows know what you're doing. But what I barged in here to tell you is that our resources are at your disposal. Even if you'd want to plant a false story. We've never done that. And I'm here to tell you my mother'd turn over in her grave if she could hear me. But we think a lot of Carole around here. And besides, it's war on the streets these days, isn't it? Anything goes." His whole face was red now. "Carole's like a daughter to me. Miriam'll tell you." The flush was fading from his soft cheeks, his high forehead. "How's she bearing up, Chief? Mark Rainer said she was a difficult witness. I just can't imagine that somehow—"

Miriam Bishop came down off her stool. "Well, Allah be praised! *I'm* relieved. I've been afraid she might curl up and roll over. If she doesn't get balls now, she's sunk."

"Chief Lindheim," Vincent Fletcher said, looking uncomfortable, but trying to smile as he stood up, "let's go down to my office."

He went into the corridor. Henry glanced at Miriam Bishop, who winked, then said: "Queen Victoria is alive and well in Sudbury."

Henry smiled, nodded, and followed Fletcher, who was walking briskly along the hall, heels clicking. Henry looked at the man's shoes: built-up leather heels that made him look taller. He stopped at another door and waited. Walking, Henry felt another catch in his right hip, a single sharp stab of pain this time.

As he held the door for Henry to enter his office, Vincent Fletcher said, under his breath, "It beats me why a lady like Miss Bishop wants to talk like some hussy on the street."

The phone on the desk began to ring. "Sit down, Chief, and excuse me, will you?"

Fletcher's office was large but modest, agreeably untidy, with one wall of glass looking over the city room. Henry could hear the smooth click and hum of word processors—instead of the clackety-clack of typewriters. On the floor in one corner was an old-fashioned rowing machine.

While Fletcher spoke on the phone, Henry looked at the huge oil painting on the wall above the editor's head: a formidable woman, elderly, imperious—the mother who was, presumably, turning over in her grave? Henry studied the room, trying not to listen: "Of course she's excited, Joyce, but I do have a paper to get out. Tell her that she's going to rehearsal with *me* or not at all. *Period.*"

Henry was staring at a photograph on the wall when Fletcher sat back and apologized. A group shot, outside, against a baseball backstop: Vincent Fletcher with his staff on both sides, all wearing shorts or sport togs and sneakers, under a banner reading: NEWS-CHRONICLE ANNUAL PICNIC. Joel White was in the picture, and Miriam Bishop, and then he picked out Carole Jensen. Her face was radiant with a smile, her dark hair held in a sweatband, and she was wearing very short shorts and a tight tank top and was holding a softball bat over her shoulder.

"Sit down, Chief," Vincent Fletcher said. "Damned rehearsals take every evening. That's where I was when the city desk here phoned to tell me what had happened to Carole."

Henry lowered his bulk into one of the straight-back chairs and discovered that he was already tired, physically tired.

Fletcher jabbed a button on the phone and spoke into it: "When my daughter arrives, send her up." Then he replaced the phone, his genial face becoming grave, his stare direct. "What I want to speak to you about is very serious and, well, upsetting. Chief, I hate saying this but I'm glad to have the opportunity. I think you're on the right track. I've been on the verge of letting that young man go more than once—"

"Joel White?"

"Precisely. Exactly. He's a good reporter, excellent, but

behind that devil-may-care manner, I think he's a very disturbed young man. Angry at the world. Don't ask me why. All I know is that he makes life miserable for some of the girls—and *I* think it's because he really wants to get into their pants." He stopped then, as if his own words surprised or embarrassed him. He tapped his neat manicured nails on top of the mahogany desk. "That little S.O.B. hates Carole. Ask her." Then he leaned forward in the chair. "Now I'm going to be presumptuous. I'm thinking of Carole, Chief. Mendoza did steal the car. Wouldn't it be easier on *her* if you could close the case as quickly as possible?"

Henry had to think his answer through. The single-word answer was obviously *yes.* Slowly he said, as much for his own benefit as for Fletcher's: "I'm working on the assumption that Carole wants the truth. If I allowed the DA to close the case, without proof, and even if Carole never knew that Mendoza was not the one, it'd be a kind of betrayal. I'd feel I'd let her down, whether she knew it or not. Also, this Mendoza character's in a coma, can't even defend himself. It's hard to put into words, Mr. Fletcher."

"I admire that, Chief. You're my kind of man." He shook his head. "I did some research today because of this thing. Would you believe that in one poll fifty percent of the males said yes, they'd commit rape if they felt there was no chance of getting caught? Fifty percent, imagine!"

But an idea had been taking shape in Henry's mind. So he said: "Mr. Fletcher, you made an offer a few minutes ago—is it still open?"

"To publish anything you'd consider helpful? I'll do it, but if it's disinformation, it's against my principles." He drew a yellow legal pad toward him and took a yellow pencil from the container in front of him. "I'm doing this for Carole's sake, you understand."

Henry, with a new excitement beginning inside, said: "Not disinformation, Mr. Fletcher. If that makes you feel better. The opposite. Mr. Rainer doesn't have all the facts himself."

"What facts?"

"First of all, fingerprints. We have one clear print, besides Carole's, which will be put through the laser process first thing in the morning." The truth. "We have the perpetrator's belt, the one used in the attack—"

Fletcher looked up from his scribbling. "He beat her?"

"No. He almost strangled her."

"The sonofabitch."

"We have shoeprints we think are his." He was moving away from the truth now, and knew it, and went on: "By noon tomorrow I'll have a profile of the man—height, weight, plenty more."

"Why didn't Mark tell me all this?"

"Normally, it's not good policy to release these details to the public—"

"Anything else?"

"Yes." Henry then took the plunge—into the fabrication of fiction. "We have tire tread prints that we *know* are those of the perpetrator's vehicle. There are a limited number of suspects, so the kind of car he was driving is important."

"My God."

"And, best of all, we have an eyewitness—"

"To the attack?"

Henry's excitement—no hesitation, no reluctance, no qualms—was running high now. "Someone driving by at the time, around five-thirty yesterday P.M., saw a man stop his car behind hers, get out and follow her into the woods."

"You want to name the witness?"

"Not yet. They didn't think anything of it at the time."

"They?"

"Two of them. A couple on the way home from Lake Lillinonah."

"This'll be a front page story. It'd be better journalism, though, if we could use names—"

"If the rapist is someone local," Henry said, "no telling what he might do to silence actual witnesses. We don't want to endanger any innocent people."

"True, true. My God, Chief, you're really close, aren't you?"

"Damn close," Henry said. "One thing more . . ." Another outright lie—was it worth the risk? "In her statement, Carole said that she was not sure, but she thought she recognized the man's voice."

"You want me to print that?"

"Why not?"

"She mention the name?"

"Not yet." Then he added: "She's with Dr. Judith Kahn now. I'm hoping she might recall more."

Fletcher tossed the pencil to his desk. "You sure you want all this in the paper? Why?"

Henry stood up. "If he reads this, and he will if he's local, it might flush him out. Cause him to do something reckless—maybe make a run for it, leave the area. Who knows, who knows? Shot in the dark, Mr. Fletcher."

"Dr. Judith Kahn? Is that the psychologist out by the college?" And when Henry nodded: "She's a good doctor. Fine reputation in her field." He stood up with the yellow pad in one hand. "Quid pro quo?" he asked. "I run your story for you, you guarantee my paper breaks the arrest story—"

"Tit for tat," Henry said. The ache was in the hip joint, but he didn't give a damn now. He had just committed the most unorthodox and possibly the most unethical act of his professional career, and he didn't give a damn about that, either.

There was a quick tap on the glass-paneled door and a young girl opened it and came in—kid, fifteen or sixteen, wearing white shorts and a T-shirt with printing on it: CIVIC THEATRE. "Daddy, we're going to be late for rehearsal." Then she saw Henry and her blue eyes rose to meet his. "Excuse me," she said, suddenly shy.

"My daughter, Madilyn," Fletcher said. And then to her, a fond rebuke: "Impulsive as usual, my dear."

"I'm sorry, Daddy," the girl said, "but you know how Miss Brewer gets whenever we're late or miss a rehearsal."

"Mady," Fletcher said, "is assistant stage manager at the local community theatre."

"And Daddy's playing one of the leads." Mady held a thin paperback book with *Barefoot in the Park* by Neil Simon printed on its cover and a loose-leaf ring binder in her hand—cute kid, fair hair, not pretty, but a lively glitter in her eye. "He has the funniest accent and he's going to steal the show!"

"My not-so-secret vice," her father said. "Strictly amateur. Good for the old ego." He came around the desk. "Mady, this is Mr. Henry Lindheim. He lives in Sheffield and we've just become friends."

"Hi," Mady said.

Henry nodded down at the girl, then reached to shake her father's thick, soft hand, their eyes meeting.

Fletcher's looked troubled and impatient, or annoyed, but he winked as he said, "Co-conspirators, you might say." Then to the girl: "I have something to do, Mady, while you go home and change."

"Change?" Mady cried. "Daddy, I *am* changed. It's Indian summer, all the other girls'll be wearing shorts."

"It won't take long," her father said, gently but firmly.

As Henry turned to leave, he caught the expression on the girl's small face: disappointment, crushed-down rebellion, but something more. What?

"That's my good girl, now," Vincent Fletcher said to his daughter.

"Oh, all right, Daddy," she said. "But we're going to be late and Miss Brewer's already mad at both of us because of last night." She brushed past Henry. "Nice to meet you, sir." Her eyes met his, fleetingly. They were filmed with tears now.

As Henry stepped out the door, he saw her trotting down the corridor, then breaking into a run, her bare legs flashing, before she disappeared under the EXIT sign at the stairway.

"Don't forget our deal," Fletcher called after him as Henry headed down the hall. "And if you see Carole, give her our love, everyone here."

Climbing into the squad car, Henry realized that a familiar soreness had returned to his right hip joint. He knew that, in time, it would turn into a nagging pain. Whatever the hell was wrong in there, Henry didn't want to find out. No more hospitals and doctors, thank you; he'd outlast the pain and if he didn't, what the hell, he'd suffer it.

Driving, he radioed the Sheffield station.

"Officer Schiller, remember me? I asked for a rundown on Scott Keller, Still River Road, Sheffield. If you couldn't reach me by radio, you could have beeped me."

"Not much in our files. Maybe you better come in so we can talk. Every shortwave in the area is probably tuned in today."

"Officer Schiller," Henry said, "digest it and spit it out."

"Well, one: The subject's seventeen now. Two arrests. Both drug-related. Sudbury police raid, a house on Lake Candlewood. Subject blew his cool and attacked a police officer with a broken oar. Two: subject wandered into a house in Bridgewater. Stoned to the gills. No burglary. He just passed out on the couch. Nothing on him, trespass only. Charges dropped when the owner discovered subject was the son of the surgeon who'd taken out his prostate."

"Convictions?"

"None." Just as Henry suspected. "But—"

"But what?"

"Possible arson. In New Milford. Some girl he was going with threw him over. Later that night her family's car caught fire in the driveway. Nothing proved. No arrest. But more important—"

"Go on—"

"Three stays in the Fairfield Hills State Hospital in Newtown. Committed as a juvenile by his parents, walked away once, twice signed out by his mother against psychiatrist's advice. I spoke with a Dr. Monash there. All he could say was that officially the kid's not considered a threat to himself or society."

We'll see, Henry thought, but he said, "Nice work, Bill. Except for a few minutes at Dr. Judith Kahn's office, I'll be available. Out."

When he went into the tiny waiting room a few minutes later, Carole and Dr. Judith were seated next to each other on the couch. Carole stood up at once, bent down to kiss Dr. Judith on the cheek, which was a good sign, but then she scurried outside without looking at him, which was not.

When he asked "How'd it go?" all Dr. Judith said was: "I'm not sure. It'd be better if she told you, I think." Then she stepped closer and lowered her voice: "Henry, I shouldn't even talk to you about this. I'm on a spot. I have a serious ethical problem. One I've never had before." She shook her dark head from side to side and went on in a breathless rush: "It's terrible, Henry. Because I know something—and not through Carole—no, I don't mean I know, I mean I *suspect* something. I might know the name of the man you're looking for."

"Someone who's a patient of yours?"

"The rules of confidentiality won't let me tell you even that."

"I'm out of my depth," Henry said. "I know the court wouldn't subpoena your files, but what if I asked you for a list of your patients?"

"You can't. All of this falls under the rules of confidentiality. And if I told you even a name and the court found out and if you were asked under oath later, they wouldn't allow any evidence springing from it. Not to mention that I'd probably lose my license."

"I'd never let that happen, kid." He turned to the door. "Forget it. I'll get to him on my own."

"But . . . in time, Henry?"

"In time?" He was standing with the door half-open.

"What if he does something else? Something worse? *Before* you—"

He shut the door and said, "To Carole?"

"To anyone. If he's who I think he is—I really shouldn't say this much. People like him are walking volcanoes. They themselves don't know when they'll erupt again."

Undecided, torn, Henry said, "If I could arrest him on some other charge. Or at least put him under surveillance, we might be able to prevent—"

"We can't, that's all, we can't."

He heaved a long sigh. "Judith, we all have to do what we have to do. I can't ask you to break your rules."

"But . . . but what if we're both making a mistake, right now, a mistake that later we'll look back on and regret, maybe the rest of our lives?"

He was remembering what he'd asked Vincent Fletcher to print—part truth, part lie—in the hope of spooking the perpetrator into giving himself away. What if he gave himself away by committing another crime?

"If it carries on too long, Judith, what about Carole? Will she last? Can you answer that?"

She came toward him, smiling a sad, somber smile. "Henry, dear Henry, no one can answer that. We all have our emotional Plimsoll Lines." Then she went around him to the door. "Sorry, Henry, but right now I can't prognosticate." She opened the door and he went out without pausing.

The dusk was almost darkness now. When he was behind the wheel, turning on the headlights, seeing her in the passenger seat, he knew that, Carole being Carole, she would not ask what had taken so long, so he said, "Sorry for the delay, kid." He'd always called Teresa kid. *Teresa is such a beautiful name,* Luisa had always said. *Why do you call our daughter keed?*

"It doesn't matter." Carole was not slumped, not stiff—she was sitting normally, and seemed to be looking out the windshield at the quiet streets as they passed the college. A few students were walking, shadowy under the lights on the campus walks.

Henry was damned if he knew what to say. But he had to know. "Did you like Dr. Kahn?"

"I love her."

Just like that. As simple as that.

"Come to think of it," Henry said, "I think I do, too."

"It's so strange, isn't it? That it takes something like this to find two new friends. In less than twenty-four hours—no, almost *exactly* twenty-four hours. It's five-thirty."

A silence. In a few minutes they'd be on White Street. Should he drive through town or take the ramp onto the interstate? He wanted time, needed time with her because he had to find out some things before they reached the Barracks on Route 7.

"Maybe I should drive you home," he said. "I could bring your husband back to get the Saab."

"No." And then she added, "Please?"

When she returned to her silence—which seemed both thoughtful and gloomy—he wondered whether he could bring her round by reporting on his afternoon. Oh, hell, yes, tell her about Duncan Clive, who'd claimed he was in Cambridge, Massachusetts, yesterday afternoon. Or Petofi: tell her he's mad at the world, a heavy boozer and a child molester, unconvicted. Or her lawyer friend Jerald Dixon, doublecrossing his wife with a nymphet barmaid. Anything to make her feel good. Such as: maybe she didn't have to suspect Joel White after all because he was probably a homo who might or might not be trying to prove he's not.

They were on White Street, turning left on Main, which had been the old Route 7 through town before the interstate was completed the year he'd moved up here.

Better yet, just to complete the job, no stone unturned, tell her that her husband did *not* go to work on Saturday afternoons. And that, therefore, he might well be her attacker, after all. Go ahead, tell her, see what happens.

Instead, aware of evading, he asked: "Did Dr. Judith mention anything about her own life?"

"Nothing," Carole said, "except that we all have to travel down dark roads."

Go ahead now, make her cheerful, tell her what you know about Judith's life: that one day when she was waiting to meet a plane at Kennedy International, a voice had announced that there would be a delay on the arrival of Flight So-and-so. The delay turned out to be caused by the crash of Flight So-and-so over the mountains in Pennsylvania. Judith's husband and both of her young children had been strewn in pieces over those mountains that she had never ever seen. *That was when I had to find a way to live with the idea that accident and happenstance are the only gods there are,* Judith had told him, when he was no longer a patient but a friend. *That's when I had my breakdown—it was a beaut—that's how I decided to get into this profession, if you can call it that.*

He was helpless. He didn't have the words and he was not certain whether he had the right to probe, or demand to know why Carole had left the doctor's apparently in worse shape than when he'd dropped her off.

"What about Scott Keller?" she asked, suddenly.

Still evading, he said, "I spoke with him—"

"And?"

Go ahead—tell her that you'd doubted her then but now

you don't. Tell her about the photographs and Fairfield Hills State Hospital and the kid's police record, arson, battery against a police officer, violence—

"I'm not sure of anything now," he heard himself say, at once wishing that he hadn't said it.

"Neither am I," she said. "That's what's so awful." And then she went on: "And I hate what I am sure of."

"Which is?"

"Henry, have you ever been hypnotized?"

"No," he said, startled but relieved. "Have you?"

She was looking out on Main Street, almost deserted on Sunday, a few buses. "I wish I hadn't let her do it."

"Why?"

"I had to live through it again, that's why. No, that's not why. This time," she said, "I remembered *everything.*"

Reluctant, hands gripping the wheel, he asked, very softly: "Such as?"

"I remembered—I even heard it just like it was happening again—I remembered what he said, what he kept saying, over and over."

When her voice drifted away, he whispered: "Words of endearment, and then obscenities—?"

She turned her head. "That, too, but, Henry, he used my name."

There was a silence.

The professional part of his mind went over the list. This eliminated only Manuel Mendoza. No, it also narrowed everything down to the list in his mind.

Then the other part of his mind, flooding with guilt, realized that this could only be more terrible for her.

"So," he said, feeling foolish, "he's not a stranger."

She was shaking her head again. "He's someone I know. He used my name over and over. How could I have forgotten that? Someone who knows me and thinks he loves me but must really hate me, too. I vomited up everything. It was supposed to cleanse me, purge me, I know the theories, but it didn't, Henry, it makes me sick. It—" She broke off and her head went down onto her knees. Her black hair fell forward. Her voice was low and muffled. "It's worse, it's much worse now, it's too much. I never felt so dirty, filthy. I hate the world. Everything. I wish I was dead."

He was driving very slowly. They were out of town, in the country now. He reached with his right hand and placed it on the back of her bare neck. "*I* don't," he heard himself say. "I'm glad you're not dead, Carole."

She moved then. She straightened and threw herself against him, her head against his upper arm. Was she crying?

No.

Don't cry, Carole, Please don't cry.

"Dr. Judith said—she wasn't surprised—she said that more than eighty percent of the victims know their . . . their attackers . . . knew them before it happens. Isn't that awful, Henry? Isn't that . . . horrendous?"

Both hands on the wheel now, confused but deeply moved, Henry waited before he said: "Tomorrow we'll have to talk about all your friends." He carefully did not say male friends.

"No. Now. Tonight. I don't even want to think about tomorrow."

Henry prompted: "You have many?"

"Not really. Oh, the one or two Rolfe works with, but I just know them by name. And the ones I work with; you know Joel White."

"And I just met Vincent Fletcher—"

"Isn't he the dearest man?" Then, her head hard against his arm: "The *second* sweetest man I know."

With a glow in his blood—a glow he had not known for many years—Henry said, "And I met Mr. Dixon this afternoon, too."

Her head moved then, drew away. "Oh? How come?"

"By accident, really. We had lunch the same place." He did not mention that the lawyer, being a lawyer, had taken advantage of the coincidence to give himself an alibi. Nor did Henry remind Carole now that, last night, it had been Jerald Dixon who had advised her *not* to report the crime. To spare her or—

"I think," Carole said now, "that I'd better tell you: Jerry phoned me this morning and . . . and he came on to me." Her tone had become cold. "Just thinking about what happened turned him on—oh, what a shit he's turned out to be!"

It was not the first time she had shocked him by her language. He himself had used every swear word and obscenity in the book, and often, but when a young lady who looked and acted like Carole Jensen uttered them—well, he guessed he was more like Vincent Fletcher than he wanted to admit.

"If it's Jerry," she said then, "if it's him, I'll kill him myself."

"Don't talk like that," Henry said before he could stop himself. "And don't ever say you wish you were dead again. That's an order, kid."

A moment passed. It was dark now, winter-dark, and there was rain in the air. His bet was that the weather would change overnight. He was waiting for her to reply—

Then he felt her head against his arm again. "The only other close friend is David Slade. I don't think it means anything, but Esther—she's one of my closest friends, they live together—she told me she's worried he might be having some kind of emotional crack-up. They don't make love anymore. And . . . and there's something else I haven't told you. . . .

Then he listened while she described an incident that had occurred during the Christmas holidays. David Slade had kissed her when she was unknowingly standing under a sprig of mistletoe at a party in the Dixon house. "There are different *kinds* of kisses, right? This was . . . it was a different kind of kiss. He tried to put his tongue in my mouth." And then: "I only told you because I had to. I know Dave . . . and . . . well, what you're thinking isn't so, that's all."

"Tell me about Mr. A. L. Cassady," Henry said. "We're almost there."

"Cass? Look, forget it. Don't even *think* it."

"Spends almost every weekend with you. Viet vet. Novelist. One book in ten years. A book that some critic said: *. . . passionately reveals the outrage and wrath of a generation mortally betrayed, mortally wounded—*"

"How," Carole demanded, sitting up straight, "how the *hell* do you know all this?"

"Nothing mysterious. I know the Sheffield librarian. Linda Powell opened the library for me instead of going to church."

"Listen! To even suspect Cass would be like thinking Rolfe could have done it. Oh, you're *disgusting.*"

Disgusting. The word was like an arrow, sharp and hurtful, and Henry was again amazed at himself. "I've often thought I couldn't do my job if I wasn't a bastard," he said. "Here we are."

He turned the cruiser into the state police parking area in front of the building.

"Now," Carole said, not touching the door handle when the car came to a stop alongside the blue Saab, "now I've hurt you, haven't I? Oh God, Henry, I don't want to hurt you, you're my dearest friend!"

"If I'm your friend," Henry said, turning off the ignition, "do me a favor. Let me drive you home."

But she was shaking her head as she opened the door. "I can't. Don't make me, please."

He got out and joined her on the driver's side of the Saab, stood watching while she turned the key in the lock and opened the door. A floodlight on a pole threw a glare over them. Her face looked ravaged, contrite, dismayed—and very sad.

"I really don't think it's safe for you to drive."

"Henry, you heard me. Dr. Judith tells me I should stop saying I'm sorry, but, damn it, I *am.* I know you're wrong about Cass. I love him like a brother but, damnit, I love you like a father! So you *have* to forgive me!"

Staring down into her angry, lovely little-girl face, Henry found himself grinning. "I already have," he said.

"Then stop grinning at me. Rolfe has to have his wheels to go to work tomorrow, and if you knew how he loves this car! Oh, Henry—" She stepped to him and rose on her toes and kissed him on the cheek. He heard her whisper: "I'll never be able to thank you. Never!" Then she stepped back. And her voice took on a teasing bitterness. "What does that make me, Henry? If Trooper Dworsky's inside there watching, he'll swear I'm a little tramp who asked to be raped, won't he?"

"There're ways of taking care of Trooper Dworsky," Henry said.

She was in the seat, the window humming down between them. "I'm all right," she said. "I can drive and I want to think." Then almost playfully: "Henry, you're going to have to stop worrying about me." She twisted the key. The engine surged to life immediately. The drive home—and whatever was to follow—seemed to hold no terror for her now.

By the time Carole, safety harness buckled, driving Rolfe's Saab 9000, passed the Sheffield Town Line sign, she was in full control. Some of the shock had worn off, thanks to Henry, and she was able to think, thanks to Dr. Judith. At least her mind was no longer fighting and denying Dr. Judith's conclusion after she'd brought Carole out of the hypnotic trance, or whatever it was called: *Well, now we know that much, don't we? If he used your name as often as that, your attacker was certainly someone who knows you.*

Accepted. Granted. But not Rolfe! And not Cass!

Thinking of Cass, his bittersweet, quiet, ironic manner, his sad smile and sadder eyes, she wondered whether Sandy had returned from New York. (Odd that Cass should remind her of Sandy—Cass, not Rolfe. Very odd.)

Sandy, Sandy—was it possible that she'd been so drowned in her own confusions and concerns that she hadn't really thought of the child all day? Except when Dr. Judith had asked her, very directly, explicitly. *I didn't know what having a baby really meant till it happened. It was like a sort of explosion in my life. So indescribable, so beautiful! Not like anything else that ever happened to me. I can't explain it. Maybe all mothers feel this way. No, I know better. Mine didn't.*

At Hawleyville now, which was little more than a Y in the road with a small antique store in the notch and a few houses and barns on both sides, she had to make a decision: whether to continue on Route 25, which curved left up Whisconier Hill and in a mile or two passed through The Village or take the unnumbered Obtuse Road to Route 133. Whichever was quicker. She chose Obtuse. Which wriggled and snaked in the headlight beams, narrow and treacherous.

In the few places where the blacktop straightened, she could see the sky in the west: a dark wine-red glow, streaked with purplish low clouds. A winter sky. Glowering, menacing.

Sandy, Sandy, Sandy—why hadn't she phoned to see whether Allison and Sandy had returned from the city?

She was telling herself to slow down, she was remembering Rolfe's warnings—*You always drive too fast, Carole*—when she saw the lights in the rearview mirror.

Headlights. Behind her. And coming fast.

So she slowed the car without using the brakes. Let him pass. She *had* been going too fast and the car behind was coming even faster. No headlights approaching, no yellow line here, why didn't he pass?

But the car behind did not come closer. Still some distance behind, it also slowed down.

Dear Henry—still concerned, still trying to take care of her. Just when she was beginning to be sure that she could take care of herself. How had she been so lucky as to meet such a man when she needed him most? And what could she ever give in return? A slow, strange warmth passed through her. She remembered how secure and calm she had felt with her head against his thick, hard arm a while ago . . .

The Saab passed over a small bridge, Merwin Brook, and she followed the road into a sharp curve, braking carefully, seeing the red glow of the Saab's taillights in the rearview mirror mounted outside her open window. Now the glare of the other headlights had disappeared.

She passed a high white Colonial house on her left: all windows lit, an outdoor floodlight illuminating the cars in the driveway and on the lawn, the sound of rock throbbing and blaring—

Then the headlights from behind stabbed the darkness again and flooded the black pavement behind her.

Without slowing now, she looked into the mirror again. The car behind was silhouetted in the lights from the house.

There was no dome light on its roof.

The warmth seeped from her body.

Instantly then, she remembered that moment of helpless terror in the woods.

And what had followed.

Without further thought, she plunged the accelerator to the floor.

The powerful engine responded with a low satisfying bellow of sound and the Saab charged forward.

She did not glance into the mirror now. She knew.

The car behind had also escalated its speed.

She tried to picture the road ahead, before it reached the

highway where she would turn right toward the bridge. Toward home.

She passed a few houses. But she was going too fast to swing left or right into a driveway—

If she slowed to do so at the next house with lighted windows, would she be able to turn in, leap out, reach the door before—

Once she turned right at the crossroads, there would be a few houses, some very close to the road, and there'd be more traffic on Route 133—

She saw a farmhouse on the corner, at the highway ahead.

No lights. Dark windows. No cars in the driveway.

Now the headlights behind were closer. He didn't care now, whoever he was, he was reckless now, and determined.

Her body felt hollow, empty.

Why hadn't she let Henry drive her home?

At the corner she swung right, ignoring the low painted sign reading STOP, gunning the engine on the turn, tires skidding and whining.

Lights on her right now. The shapes of houses—

A truck went by, going in the opposite direction, fast.

She pressed on the horn, driving with one hand and keeping the heel of her hand on the horn—

The truck went on, sounding its horn angrily or playfully in reply—

In the mirror above the windshield, she saw the car behind make the turn at the corner, its rear wheels slithering sideways so that, for a second, she thought, hoped, it might turn over, or go off the road, smash up—

Trying to breathe, both hands gripping the wheel, she bore down on the accelerator pedal again—

At the first house on her right, its lights burning, she slowed. Should she risk turning in at this speed? Should she stop the car on the shoulder of the road, leap out and make a run for it?

Then she felt a terrible jolt and heard the thudding of bumpers from behind and now the Saab was rolling, out of control for a second, continuing toward the decline that led down to the bridge—

Breaking the impulse to slam on brakes, seeing the lights of the other car swing as it came alongside—should she risk another collision?—she leaned over the wheel, clutching it, the seat harness digging into her left breast, stirring pain, and drove, fast, the car plunging down the hill in a narrow canyon between flat walls of stone on both sides. She knew where she was. She knew the road ahead, the bridge at the bottom of the hill, over the damned-up Housatonic River, Lake Lillinonah, no more houses, she knew this road well, her only chance was to get across the long steel bridge, no houses then for a while, her only chance was to reach the next crossroad, turn right and make it home.

But, hunched over the wheel, she knew this would not be possible—

Because the car was alongside now. On her left. In the other lane.

A tan car. Big. It was all she could see, its hood—

No approaching lights in the other lane.

Who drove a tan car, who?

Whoever had raped her, that's who!

If she went any faster, she might lose control, might not be able to shoot the car into the bridge opening, which she could see now, the shadow of the high steel frame, a dark glimmer of water far below on both sides—

The other car was inches away, alongside, on her left. But not gaining, not passing, not quite touching—

She risked a quick glance. The driver was only a shadow—

Then she heard, or imagined she heard over the hollow thunder of the two engines, the sound of a siren.

Was it possible?

Then she realized that both cars, charging side by side

downhill, were going to enter the bridge at the same time—

No! Oh my God, *no!*

Did she scream? She couldn't hear it in her ears, only in her mind.

If both cars entered the bridge side by side, he had her. On the narrow two-lane span he could wreck them both.

And if any vehicle entered from the other end—

But then she heard another sound—crunching metal—and this time her body, in spite of the harness, was thrown sideways against the door, and she felt the Saab being pushed toward the edge of the road on her right—

She fought the wheel to keep it on the pavement.

Ahead, on both sides, no walls of stone now, the road ran down to the bridge between sloping bare shoulders of dirt and gravel—

If she hit the gravel at this rate of speed—

Hands rigid on the wheel, she refused to let the front wheels turn.

Pain climbed her arms to both shoulders and her palms were wet.

If her hands slipped—

The tan car was still against the side of hers, scraping, metal clashing against metal, bearing against the door, against the fenders.

She could no longer hear the siren. Only the metallic grinding. And the deafening bellow of the two engines—

There was no siren. She'd imagined it.

She was alone in this. Completely alone.

And she was being forced off the road, inexorably—

If she gave in now, or panicked, the Saab would most certainly careen down the sloping gravel bank, its own momentum plunging it into the water on the right side of the bridge.

Which was his intent, damn him!

Whoever he was, now he was trying to kill her.

Her teeth ground together.

The sonofabitch, sonofabitch, sonofabitch!

She could see the water glittering ahead, on both sides.

It was then that she made her decision.

It erupted in her, a fury of emotion, not a thought, a savage instinct of self-preservation: she was not going to die, she didn't want to die, Henry was right, she didn't want to die, she wanted to live!

Sandy's face flashed vivid and terrible in her mind: small and soft, her loving blue eyes—

She had to live, *had* to!

The opening onto the bridge loomed ahead—the concrete abutments, the high steel frame, the impossibly narrow gaping hole.

At this speed could both cars enter the two-lane bridge side by side?

What if another car entered from the other end?

Taking her eyes off the dark strip of downhill pavement ahead, she risked a quick sideways glance.

She saw a shadow hunched stiffly over the steering wheel of the other car. Only a shadow—

Her own jaws were clenched so hard that an ache climbed both sides of her face. Her whole body rigid, she felt a shudder of fear and hopelessness pass through her. Her mind blanked for a split second, but she gripped the wheel harder, pain exploding all through her chest and arms and shoulders, her left breast a huge hard knot of agony, burning and pulsating.

The huge tan car seemed now to be a part of the Saab—two savage, furious, roaring animals rushing downhill, locked in mortal combat.

Once on the bridge she'd be trapped between the other car and the steel guardrail on her right.

No!

Without conscious decision, but acting fast, she took her foot from the fuel pedal and placed it on the brake, bearing down as slowly as she could.

The screeching of scraping metal was more shrill and loud and nerve-shattering now—

The seat belt against her breast caused her to utter a scream as her body was thrown forward.

Then the Saab was free, slowing, shuddering, and it threatened to swing right, but she fought it.

She saw the other car shoot ahead.

Now she bore down harder on the brakes, slowing even more.

Ahead, the huge tan car was charging toward the bridge. She saw its brake lights flash red. She saw the frame swerve left wildly. It hit the shoulder of the road, swaying and rocking, its wheels spitting gravel—

And as she passed, she saw it plunge, out of control, at a wild angle down the slope, its headlights sweeping over the dark shimmering surface of the water ahead of it—

This was her chance. *NOW!*

As she entered the bridge, she returned her foot to the accelerator and heard, or imagined she heard, the explosive sound of a splash off to her left—

Her rigid body was beginning to tremble all over, threatening to go slack.

She did not look back.

It went through her mind that she should stop—only a vague misty distant thought, gone before it could take shape. She continued over the bridge.

Then—was it possible?—she heard the sound of a siren again.

As she drove off the bridge, she glanced into the mirror. In the distance, framed by the steel girders, she saw a blue light revolving slowly in the darkness. And the wailing of the siren died away.

Henry?

Had he been following after all?

Her body stopped quivering and she felt a great enveloping sense of serenity come over her. Henry would know what to do.

Now . . . now it was really over.

Whoever had been driving that car, whoever he was, he had to be the one. Whether he was dead or not, he still had to be the bastard who'd raped her.

At Harrow Road she made a right turn between dark trees, conscious of the incredible relief settling in. She did not need to hurry now. In less than three minutes she would be home.

PART 4

HAVING BEEN BORN IN the Bronx, lived in Brooklyn, and worked most of his life for the NYPD in Manhattan, Henry Lindheim had never learned how to swim.

This fact alone removed the necessity for decision as he stood in the glare of his headlights, staring at the water that was closing over the roof of the tan vehicle as it sank.

With his eyes still on the water's surface, he stepped alongside the squad car and radioed for state police assistance, an ambulance and a fire-rescue vehicle with divers.

The surface of the lake was very calm now. Very still and dark.

Then he heard and saw other vehicles begin to stop, drivers attracted by the blue light revolving—two or three on the bridge, blocking it, others along the sides of the road, doors opening, voices. . . .

So he decided to cordon off the area, using the small sledge hammer and painted stakes and the yellow strip of plastic—POLICE LINE DO NOT CROSS—which he always kept in the trunk of his squad car.

Two men and a woman started down the gravel embankment. Henry barked them back. Then, as he was pounding in the last stake, he heard the first siren on the far side of the bridge, and coming fast.

The officer who appeared was a town constable from

Bridgewater, who introduced himself as Otto Pegler—a wide-eyed kid, no uniform except for a cap. "I wasn't more'n a mile away, sir," he said. "What's up?"

Quickly and succinctly Henry told him that he personally had witnessed the entire incident. He carefully did not mention that the driver whose vehicle was in the drink had tried, intentionally and with malice, to force the other vehicle off the road but that the driver of the other vehicle had refused to give an inch.

"Driver still down there?"

Another siren came across the bridge, red lights flashing.

"What're you doing?" Henry asked the constable, who had taken off his shirt.

"I'm going down to get him." He was undressing, fast. "Why didn't you, sir?"

"I can't swim," Henry growled.

"Why didn't you apprehend the driver who left the scene?" the constable asked, down to his shorts and trotting toward the water.

"That's where I'm going now," Henry snarled. Seeing the young constable wading in, he called out: "If he's alive, have him examined at New Milford Hospital, then put him under arrest."

"What charges, sir?"

"Speeding, reckless endangerment, attempted homicide. I'll be back."

The constable, looking startled, took a deep breath, nodding, and disappeared under the water.

After Henry had driven up the gravel slope to the road, then using his siren in low, short, urgent spurts—*wow-wow-wow*—to clear his way through the growing crowd—where the hell had everyone come from all of a sudden?—he drove over the bridge and passed Harrow Road, tempted to turn, and drove on to the village of Bridgewater. To hell with the radio. He had to speak *privately,* on the telephone, with Judith before he tried to talk with Carole. Help. That's what he needed now.

The booth stood in front of a grocery on the edge of the pavement where the road became a street. "Judith. It's me."

"Yes, Henry?"

Then he told her what he'd seen and where he now was and what he now faced.

"If there are any legal difficulties," Judith said—

"Not legal," Henry said. "Her. Carole. How much more can the kid take?"

"Well, Henry, as I said to you a while ago, everyone has his or her Plimsoll Line—"

"Whatever the hell *that* is," Henry said, irascibly.

"That's the line on a ship, above which, if you stow more cargo, you put the whole ship at risk."

"Got you, and she's got to be near it. So?"

"Do you know whose body is in the lake?"

"I think so. I can't be sure."

"When she finds out—is it someone she loves, Henry? That's what's been on my mind ever since she left here."

"Not if it's who I think it is. But if I'm right, it'll be troubling for other reasons."

"Such as?"

"Such as—" he was almost shouting and his body was stiff and tense "—such as: if I'm right he's not the one who raped her!"

There was a long silence on the wire. Outside the booth, an ambulance passed, claxon sounding, lights flashing.

"Have you told me everything, Henry?" Judith's gentle, soft voice asked in his ear.

"No."

"Perhaps you'd better."

"He was trying to kill her. She outfoxed him and he lost control of his car. So she'll probably blame herself if he's dead."

"Oh God," the doctor said after a moment. "I'm coming up there."

"No."

"Why?"

"She's got her husband to deal with. And they have a guest. And I may be able to keep Dworsky and his kind off till morning but"—he reached a decision in his mind—"I'll handle it, Judith. If she didn't recognize him, she won't have to know who's in the lake till morning anyway."

"Risky, Henry. She trusts you. If you lie to her—"

"Everything's risky," Henry growled. "I really *don't* know for sure."

"Call me later. No matter how late."

He returned to the cruiser. Slowly.

What had occurred to him, what he had not said, was that if the man in the lake died, it might be possible to close the case. It would mean placing the guilt on a dead man, but at least Carole could feel that justice had been done—whether that was the truth of the matter or not.

Would that free her, in her own mind? Not if she ever learned that the dead man was *not* the rapist.

Then Henry realized that he had arrived at a decision that he had never thought he could even consider. But did he have the right, the moral right, against all the assumptions and training and thrust of his whole life, willfully to obstruct justice and let the actual perpetrator—whoever, *whoever*—go free without punishment?

Goddamn it, hadn't Carole had enough?

Yes, but who was he to judge? Who was *he* to make that decision?

Carole was in the bathtub. She felt clean again. Finally.

By the time she had arrived home, a sort of quiet, secret elation had been running serene and healing in her blood. Strange, very strange.

At the front door, where Rolfe had met her after hearing

the car in the driveway, she had gone naturally, without hesitation or thought, into his arms. And Rolfe had placed his fist under her chin and tilted back her head, the way he always used to do, and he had kissed her on the lips. *I've needed that,* he'd said, leading her inside. *Hey, you even look better. If the shrink did this, I take back what I said on the phone.*

In the living room she had gone to the sofa to stretch out, on her back, kicking off the moccasins. Where was Cass?

Rolfe had lifted her legs, to sit down under them and to massage her feet. *If you knew the things I've been imagining,* he'd said. *I been running scared, darling. About us. You and me. You look—Carole, I can't get over it. What's happened to you?*

It's over, she had said. *It's all over now.*

You mean the police know—

Not yet, but very soon. Very soon now. And then it'll all be history

Except the goddamn trial—

No trial. Over.

I can't believe it!

Where's Sandy?

At Allison's. She called. All three kids went to sleep in the car coming home from the city, so she took them to her house for the night—

Carole had lifted her legs, placed her feet, socks only, no shoes, on the floor and walked, as if floating, toward the hall.

You act like you've had a couple of drinks, Rolfe had said —not a question, not accusing or jealous, just admiring and relieved.

It was the way she had felt, too. (Still felt now, lolling in the lukewarm water.) As if she'd had two or three drinks or had just finished the first reefer, her head pleasantly unfocused, no reason to focus, no need now—

I'll go over to Route 7 and get some pizza, Rolfe had

called after her. *Take your time, darling. And Carole—if I acted like an asshole, it was only because I was scared, right?*

How long ago had that been? How long had she been lying here?

She stood up and reached for the terry cloth robe. She had to remember in future to take tubs, not showers. She had never felt cleaner. Really clean. Inside and out.

Purged.

She dried her body and then took two or three swipes at her damp hair with a brush, glancing at herself in the mirror. Her deep-set brown eyes peered back at her, red-rimmed but clear and untroubled.

Then she caught sight of her breast. And stood with the robe hanging open. Her breast was no longer the lavendar color it had been: it was a deep purple, and swollen, misshapen and ugly and not a part of her body, of any human body, the nipple almost black.

Revolted, she closed the robe and tied the sash. To her surprise, no anger followed. Tomorrow Dr. Stoddard would call to tell her where to go for further examination. Only a detail. Only one more small thing to get through. What's a little pain? A little *more* pain?

She was going barefoot down the stairway, the edge of the robe tickling her heels and ankles, when she saw Rolfe coming in the front door, carrying three pizza boxes.

"What the *hell* happened to my car?" he asked, scowling up at her now.

She didn't want to talk about it. Or think about it. But she had to say, "I had a little accident."

"Little? Jesus, the whole left side of the car!"

"Someone tried to run me off the road."

"Who?"

"We'll know soon. Henry'll be calling."

"Henry?" Rolfe disappeared down the center hall, going toward the kitchen. "So you call him Henry now. And what does Mr. Cro-Magnon call *you?"*

At the foot of the stairs, she was about to follow and explain—*Henry's my friend, Rolfe, you'll have to accept that!*—when she heard: "Accident? Are you okay, Carole?"

Cass had come out of the den. Trusty glass in hand.

"Don't I look okay?"

"You look terrific!"

"Thank you, Cass." She started toward the rear of the house. "Let's eat! I had a *great* lunch but I'm starving."

In the kitchen Rolfe was sliding the pies onto three plates. "Your father phoned. Twice. He wants you to call him back."

And Carole felt the blissful sense of euphoria beginning to seep away. "Not until I have the whole answer," she said.

And behind her Cass asked, "Mix you a drink, Carole?"

"I'd love a weak scotch and soda," Carole said. And then to Rolfe when Cass disappeared: "How long's it been since Daddy's called me? *Before* tonight."

"I don't know. How long since you called *them?*" His tone was gentle again. "They *are* your parents, you know."

Carole sat down at the table. "Biological accident. I've spent too much time feeling guilty for what I *don't* feel."

"Biological accident! Shrink gibberish. Who is this Dr. Kahn anyway?"

"Henry's friend. And now mine."

"Henry again—anything Henry says, she does."

"Anything *Rolfe* says, she does." And then, unable to stop herself, she added: "Or did."

Rolfe was seated across the table from her, beginning to eat. "What's that supposed to mean?"

Before she could answer—she didn't need this now!—Cass came in and set a glass before her, then turned and placed another one, also full, next to Rolfe's plate. "Let's drop it, whatever it is—what're we celebrating?"

She picked up her glass. "Freedom," she said, *"Liberté,*

égalité, fraternité." She lifted her glass and took a long swallow.

Instead of sitting down, Cass roamed to the other end of the kitchen to stare out the window. "Esther phoned. And Karen. We didn't know what to tell them. David, too—I think David is more deeply shaken up than anyone. As he was last night. Did you ever hear him stammer that much before?"

"It could have been anyone," Carole said then. She took another long swallow. Her head, already faint, was swimming now. "Most rapes are committed by someone the woman knows. And this doesn't include the date rapes that are not reported. Or the spousal rapes—"

"Spousal?" Rolfe said.

Cass returned to sit down at the table, not touching the food. "Let's scrub that. Carole, are you saying it might be one of us? David? Jerry? Me?"

"I'm only quoting my *shrink,*" Carole said, realizing that she was already feeling the drink and that the anger was returning, like poison, threatening the composure and serenity she'd been feeling since she came home. "No, *not* you. Or Rolfe. You're both ex. . . exonerated. You're both here and alive. Thank God. Whoever did it's at the bottom of the lake."

Rolfe was leaning across the table. "Carole, are you sitting there and calmly telling us that there's a dead body in Lake Lillinonah?"

"I told you some one tried to run me off the road. Well, I didn't let him do it. And that's where the sonofabitch is, at the bottom of the lake, and I'm not sorry. He raped me yesterday and tonight he tried to kill me. When they fish him out, we'll know who he is and that'll be the end of the whole thing."

"Jesus," Rolfe said, a whisper.

Cass reached across the table and placed his hand over hers. His small, knobby, homely face looked helpless and tormented. "We know how you feel, Carole."

"Well *I* don't," Rolfe said, standing up. "How can you be so cool, so *detached?* Weird. You're sitting there like a total stranger. It's scary."

Was he *blaming* her? She couldn't believe it. "I told you — didn't you hear me?—he was trying to *kill* me."

Then the telephone in the hall shrilled.

Carole withdrew her hand and stood up. "Now we'll know," she said as she went into the hall.

But it was not Henry's voice that asked, "Carole? Is that you, Carole?"

She recognized that voice at once. "Yes, Daddy, it's Carole."

"Didn't Rolfe tell you? This is my third call."

"He told me."

"Carole, your mother and I are most upset." She couldn't imagine Stanley Vance ever being upset. "Now, I want you to do me a favor. Have I ever asked you to do me a favor before?"

"Never, Daddy," she said. And then: "I'm fine. You didn't ask but I'm just fine, Daddy."

A silence. Then: "Rolfe told me you had no ill effects."

"None, Daddy. Absolutely none, thank you."

"I can see we're not going to get very far—"

"What favor can I do for *you,* Daddy?"

"This is my proposition. I want you and Rolfe to decide where you'd like to go. Write this thing off, these things happen, put it behind you. Winter's here now. How about the Riviera? Or the Caribbean? Soak up some sun. Take a small villa on the water. Sandy would love it."

Then he waited.

"Sandy's in preschool. And she's fine, too, Daddy."

"Carole, I can't talk to you when you're in this mood. I'm making you an offer, my treat."

"Why?" Carole asked. The odd chill in the house had reached her bones. She was holding the phone too tight. Waiting. "Was it in the paper? Or did you hear your name on the news?"

"One thing damn sure: *you* didn't phone to tell me."

"I didn't want to *upset* you, Daddy."

"I should have known you'd throw that back in my face."

"That's what you're thinking of, isn't it?"

"What?"

"Your face."

After a moment he said: "Perhaps I am." And then in a steady stream of words: "No, it hasn't been in any papers that I can lay my hands on here. They wouldn't print a rape-victim's name anyway. But some reporter from one of those unscrupulous, trashy, grocery-store scandal rags did phone me. Wanted to know whether the Mrs. Carole Vance Jensen who lived in Sheffield, Connecticut, was my daughter. And when I said yes, he wanted me to comment on what I thought should be done to her *rapist* if he's apprehended. Don't ask me how those slimebags get their information. It's an underground network of filth and slander. Reporters all over the country feed them what the respectable papers won't print." He seemed to run out of words. But she did not speak. "Carole, excuse me, I'm sorry, you hit a nerve. Are . . . are you still on?"

"I'm on," she said. And then, in spite of herself, she added: "There's nothing to be ashamed of, Daddy. If you knew the statistics on rape in this country—"

"Are you saying you won't do me this favor?"

Carole was leaning against the wall now, remembering what Dr. Judith had said: *People who can't love, can't. They're crippled. It's their loss, so why go on resenting them the rest of your life? That makes you a loser, too.*

"You may as well answer me, Carole. Your mother and I are a different generation. We feel shame, as you call it, over things that perhaps you wouldn't."

Then, startled at hearing anything so personal and revealing from Stanley Vance, Carole was tempted to explain —her job, Rolfe's, their friends, Sandy's school. How could they possibly leave now? But she said, realizing that it was even closer to the truth: "I *am* putting it behind me, Daddy. The sonofabitch who did it—he got what was coming to him."

After a moment, Stanley Vance said, "Well, that doesn't happen very often. Every grown person knows there's no such thing as justice. Your mother wants to talk to you. Goodbye. And talk it over with Rolfe."

Waiting, expecting her teeth to start chattering, or grinding, Carole heard the echo of Dr. Judith's words in her mind: *Maybe love was just left out. It's sad and if you could be sad about it, instead of bitter and angry . . .*

"Hello, Carole."

"How are you, Mother?"

"Have you seen a doctor?"

Carole almost smiled. Anna-Maria Vance (née Russo) placed a great deal of faith in doctors. Until they could find nothing wrong with her. "Several doctors, Mother."

"Well . . ." her voice was so weak and muted that Carole had to strain to make out the words, "well, I trust they gave you something for your . . . nerves."

"I have a tablet in my hand right now, Mother," she lied.

"That's good." The faint voice trailed away and now Carole knew that Mrs. Stanley Vance had downed a few pills or capsules herself during the evening. "Well, just remember: God has his own way of punishing those who've offended Him. Examine your own conscience, dear, examine your conscience."

Carole heard the connection being cut, very gently. A gentle woman, her mother—lovely and withdrawn and, yes, sad. But also cruel. Carole stepped to the thermostat on the wall. The house was suddenly downright *cold*. She adjusted the control and heard the oil furnace thump on in the cellar. In all the years she'd lived with her parents, nothing had ever happened to her for which she was not to blame. Well, *this* time she was not about to examine her goddamn conscience!

She drifted into the parlor. No longer hungry. If Anna-Maria Vance had religion and chemicals to get her through life, what of Stanley Vance? She knew. She had known since she was twelve or so: Stanley Vance's escape was women. As many women as he could afford. And he could always afford whatever he desired. Would she ever be able to accept that? Even now, of all times, sinking down onto a sofa, she felt a cool familiar contempt as she remembered the shrieking headlines she'd read when she was thirteen: FINANCIER'S LOVE NEST SPARKED BY PASSION? And the photograph of a charred, once-elegant, chaotic bedroom with a firehose draped across the circular bed. The caption beneath (she still remembered the exact words): WALL STREET'S STANLEY VANCE HAS NO COMMENT, FEMALE COMPANION (UNIDENTIFIED) DENIES SMOKING IN BED.

"Well," Rolfe said, coming in from the hall, glass in hand, "well, what did *Henry* have to report?"

"It wasn't Henry. It was my parents." She lowered her head. "Daddy wants us to take a vacation. On him. The Riviera, the West Indies."

"The Riviera, wow!" He drained his glass. "I hope you took him up on it."

"No. No, I didn't," she said.

"God, Carole, I've never understood why you're so tough on your folks."

And suddenly she was exhausted. Suddenly all she wanted to do was to go up the stairs and take the medicine and sleep. As she had done last night.

What was Henry doing?

Where was he? Why didn't he call?

"I thought it might be Duncan Clive again," Rolfe said, moving into the hall, empty glass in hand. "He also called twice. I told him all I knew, but he wanted to talk to you, *personally.*" He turned in the door of the den. "You want to know who's in the lake? I'll tell you."

She was shaking her head. "Maybe. I don't think so."

"No? Why not?"

Her breast was throbbing again. She was suddenly very tired.

Rolfe returned, crossing the hall to stand in the opening, "I suppose you don't think a famous artist like that is capable of doing such a thing, right?" He took several long steps toward her, head tilted. "How well do you really know that guy, Carole? *Before* last night?"

It took a long moment for the shock to take hold. And the anger. "Go to hell," she said then, and stood up. She stepped around him and went to the stairs. Wondering if her legs would hold her upright, whether she could make it to the top—

Behind her she heard Rolfe go into the den.

When she reached the top of the stairs, she heard another voice from below: "Carole, listen. Don't blame him." Cass's voice. "He didn't mean that. He's on his way to getting really smashed."

"He thinks I'm terrible, doesn't he? Because I don't *care.* Well, maybe I am. But I just can't, Cass. I wish I could. I *know* I should, but—"

"Shock, Carole. I tried to write about it. Savagery spawns savagery. Perhaps that's the most vicious circle of all."

"You sound like Dr. Judith." She was wondering where that calm sense of well-being and elation had gone. Had that been a kind of savagery, too?

"What can I say?" Cass asked, his voice filled with helplessness and misery. "Writers never have the words when they need them, do they?"

After Henry had taken a squint at the Saab in the driveway — its left side mangled, scraped to raw metal, the front fender caved in—he walked to the wide veranda, stepped up and knocked on the door. Aloysius Leo Cassady opened it. Small body, once hard, now going soft, short dark hair, oddly misshapen face, age thirty-seven, looking sixty. The writer invited him in, introducing himself and adding: "Cass will do." He led Henry into a big, square, high-ceilinged living room off the hall, conventionally furnished, pleasantly cluttered, comfortable.

"You know there was an automobile accident, don't you?" And when Cassady nodded, head tilted, slate-blue eyes waiting: "I'm here to get an official statement from Mrs. Jensen."

"She's resting, I hope. It couldn't wait till morning?"

"Afraid not. I'd like to close it out tonight. And I'm sure she would."

"Right," Cassady said. "Want a drink while you wait?"

"No, thanks." How long ago since he'd had that single ale in Merlin's Bar? With Jerald Dixon at his elbow. One more ale to sip very slowly just before he turned in—if that time ever came.

"I'll tell Carole you're here." He walked, Henry noticed, on the balls of his feet as he went to the hall—no stagger to match the red in his eyes—calling back, "Sit down, Chief."

Good idea. Henry chose a large upholstered chair, tempted to use the footstool. He was really tired now, the catching pain in his hip joint had been coming and going for hours, and he was hungry, too. But it was the dread inside that he hated. And the haunting confusion: could he —*should* he—try to wrap it up tonight? Did he have that right?

He heard a tapping on a door, then Cassady's soft thin whisper from upstairs, not the words—then footsteps coming down the stairway.

From where he sat he could see Cassady go into a room across the hall. When he came out, he was carrying a full glass of clear liquid—gin? vodka?—and in his other hand a cigar.

Henry lifted his voice slightly: "Why don't you keep me company while we wait, Mr. Cassady?"

"Why not?" He strolled into the room and offered Henry the cigar. "Rolfe's in the game room downstairs—watching some cop show on TV—justice every hour on the hour. Did they ever hang the bastard who invented TV, do you know?"

Henry said, "Thanks," as he removed the cellophane wrapping from the cigar. Then: "Did they ever put your book on TV, Mr. Cassady?"

"They wouldn't dare." He grunted a laugh and then stretched out on his back on the sofa, his glass balanced in one hand on the very small bulge of his belly, ankles crossed. His old, once-white sneakers looked dirty and frayed. "I'd like to think you read my book, Chief, but you wouldn't have believed it. No one else did."

Lighting the cigar, Henry said, "I had to be satisfied with a few words from a couple of reviews."

Cassady laughed again. "I'm pretty tanked so my defenses are down. You want to know where I was around five, five-thirty, right? Well, I was sleeping out there in the guest room. And, alas, alone, as usual, so I can't prove it. Opportunity, sure. Motive? Isn't that the way it goes? Motive—you tell me, Chief."

"How long've you known Mrs. Jensen?"

"Eight years. Since Rolfe married her. And I've known Rolfe since high school. You mean was I in love with her *before* he married her? No, and I'm not *in* love with her now. I love them both."

"Were you in Vietnam long?"

"Anyone who was in Nam was there forever. It was an eternity tour. Me, I just didn't want to miss the fundamental experience of my generation." His face crinkled into a small smile. "Afraid I'd end up like F. Scott Fitzgerald."

Henry had no idea what he meant by that. "Way I understand it, rape was pretty common over there."

"Nam was one big rape scene. Individually and physically and metaphorically. Casualty count still coming in. And unto the next generation—the Dioxin orphans, the Dow Chemical monstrosity babies. If you'd owned the right stock, Chief, you'd be rich and retired by now."

Hearing the quiet bitter rage in Cassady's voice, Henry

recalled the book review that Linda Powell had glued inside the library copy of *Flashbacks—A Novel by A. L. Cassady: ". . . a gritty, honest yet poetic odyssey . . . naked romantic sensibility exposed to the appalling barbarism of reality . . ."* He was about to ask whether Cassady had undergone any medical, meaning psychological, treatment when he heard a sound and turned his head—

To see Rolfe Jensen standing in the wide opening into the hall. "What the hell's going on up here?" He peered into the room: empty glass in hand, tall body loose and off-center, blue eyes slightly blurred. Then his face tightened. "Listen, for your information, Chief, Mr. Cassady is my oldest friend. He is also a guest in my house and I'm damned if—"

Cassady interrupted: "Get yourself a drink, Rolfe. I'll be down in a few minutes, after I fail to convince him I didn't rape your wife."

Rolfe Jensen came into the room, shaking his head. "Oh no, oh no. No more questions. Carole's asleep and she's going to stay asleep and—" He broke off, frowning down into Henry's face. "You just can't stay away from her, can you?"

The man's drunk, Henry reminded himself before he said, "There's been an accident, Mr. Jensen. Your wife left the scene. I thought it'd be better if *I* took her statement before some other officer filed a charge. Okay?"

Rolfe Jensen's eyes were blinking. "Okay," he said. "What'd you expect her to do, dive in after him after he tried to kill her? Who was it?"

"We don't know yet."

"Yeah? Well, you go over to Duncan Clive's house, ask *him* your goddamn questions—"

"Oh shit," Cassady said and stood up. "Look, Rolfe, Carole doesn't need a big scene. Will you for god's sake split? I'll come down to the game room and watch any phony fairy tale you want to see as soon as Carole comes downstairs."

"Deal?" the other man asked, blinking and scowling at the same time.

"Deal," Cassady grunted.

"Okay." He was moving, uncertain and off-balance, into the hall. "Goddamn cops. *I* could have had the body up by now with my bare hands."

After he disappeared into the room across the wide hall, Cassady shrugged and uttered a sound under his breath.

It came to Henry then that, solicitous of Carole as the writer might be, he might have an altogether different motive for raping her—to get back at her husband. To get back at him for what? Some childhood offense that only *he* remembered the pain of? Some hurt, or imagined hurt, that he'd nursed all his life? Or because he'd been in Nam and his friend hadn't. In his time Henry had dealt with motives far more improbable. Or how about envy? Miserable himself, lonely, seeing the happy life close-up and firsthand, maybe even harboring a lust for the wife— "Have you ever been married, Mr. Cassady?"

"Once. For two years. Until I realized she loved me because, at that time, I was a celebrity. And until *she* realized, and damn smart of her, that I was also hopeless. We formed a kind of mutual deterioration society." The writer seemed to savor the words, smiling faintly.

Henry heaved a deep sigh. The weariness in his muscles and in his gut had become an ache, worse, a general and debilitating soreness all through him.

"Chief," he heard Cassady say as he took a step to glance into the hall—

Henry twisted his head. Rolfe Jensen was going toward the rear of the house, carrying a fresh drink, walking stiffly.

Cassady waited another moment or two before he began to roam the room, saying: "Suppose, Chief, just suppose each of us has an invisible but perfectly balanced set of scales built into that part of us that makes us human. Listen, Chief, bear with me now, man. And when something happens to us—Nam with me, rape with Carole—something to throw those scales out of whack—" He took several steps towards Henry's chair. "And after that we *know,* we just *know* that unless we can do *something* to put those goddamn scales in balance again, in our soul, life won't be worth living. You following me?"

Henry didn't say that he was about twenty-four hours ahead. Because this was exactly what he'd sensed in Carole last night at the hospital. She had even tried to express it herself, in her own way. "I'm following," Henry said, tempted to glance at his watch.

Cassady's eyes, suddenly tense and dark, were boring into his. "When Carole came home a while ago, even knowing she might have caused someone to *die,* she was relieved. She was at peace inside because she had the idea the scales were somehow being balanced. That sounds far out, I know, but I understand it. Do *you?"*

"Why the hell do you think I came here instead of letting someone else handle this?" Henry heard the gruff irritation in his own voice now. "No one wishes this was over any more than I do."

"But it's not, is it?"

"It might be," Henry said, carefully. "It could be."

Cassady was shaking his head. "If the bastard who raped her was dead at the bottom of the lake, you wouldn't have spent the last fifteen minutes trying to decide whether I might have done the rape." He came closer. "You know whose body's in the car, don't you?"

Before Henry could answer he heard another voice: "Is that what you've come to tell me, Henry?"

Carole stood in the opening. How long had she been there?

Long enough. Because then she said, "You know who it is and you know he, whoever he is, is not the one."

Henry stood up. Heavily. His hip catching, sharp pain this time.

She was wearing a long flowered bathrobe over pajamas

and her face looked pale and stricken and very frail. "Who is it, Henry?" The demand was a plea. "Tell me."

Torn, a writhing all through him, Henry said, "I can't tell you that, Carole, until I'm positive."

"If he's not the one, why did he try to kill me?" Her voice was faint, but the question had an iron logic and this logic was what he was depending on. "Henry?"

"I didn't say he wasn't the man who raped you, Carole. Mr. Cassady did."

"If he is, then I'm not sorry he's dead."

Henry felt a stab of relief. "Carole, I do need to have a statement—about the accident. Think you're up to it?"

"I'm up to it if you'll tell me who it is. Bargain?"

"It'd be a guess till they get a positive ID on the body."

"Then no statement," she said.

For the first time Henry was annoyed. Damn such stubbornness. "It's only a formality anyway," he said. "I saw the whole thing."

Her face went whiter still. Her brown eyes opened wider. "You . . . you *were* following me, weren't you?" And when Henry nodded: "I thought I saw a blue light . . ." She took a few uncertain steps toward the sofa.

Cassady stepped in and took her elbow in one hand, placing his arm around her back. He spoke to Henry in a whisper. "Can't all this wait till morning?"

Then another voice broke in: "What hell's goin' on here?" Rolfe Jensen was back, glowering drunkenly into the room. "Leave her alone, Cass. Take your goddamn hands off her."

The other man ignored this and stood by as Carole lowered herself to the sofa. Then he turned to her husband: "Let's you and I go downstairs and talk of worms and epitaphs and tell sad stories of the death of kings."

"Screw you," Rolfe Jensen said, quietly. "An' don't ever let me see you touch my wife again. Tha's final, buddy."

"Shut up," Carole said. "Both of you." She had not

taken her eyes from Henry. "I have to know who he is and that he's the one, and that he's dead."

Henry was tempted then. He could tell her that while he was following he had noted the license. But what if he was wrong? "I'll go confirm my information, Carole. If you want me to, I'll come back or phone you later tonight. Fair enough?"

"No," Carole said, sharply. Her eyes, withdrawn and fearful a few minutes ago, now glinted brown and hot again. "You know now, Henry, and you won't tell me. Why?"

"It wouldn't be proper procedure when I—"

But now she was shaking her head from side to side. And there was an angry certainty in her face and tone: "Cass is right. You won't tell me, Henry, because you don't think he's the one who raped me. Then why did he try to kill me? You said you saw it. *Why?*"

"I don't have the answer to that, Carole. Yet."

"Then you admit it!" Carole leaped to her feet. "It's crazy. It's wild. It makes no sense. Nothing makes any sense whatever!" And then she was running from the room.

Christ, Henry thought, you blew it. He glanced at the other two men, his anger at himself mounting while he heard Carole's footsteps skittering up the stairs.

Cassady waited a second or two before he moved into the hall.

"You're not planning to leave the area, are you, Mr. Cassady?" Henry said, as he followed.

The writer had stopped and turned at the foot of the stairs. "I usually drive back to New York on Monday morning."

"Make it Monday afternoon. Late. And let me know where you'll be."

"Anything you say, Sarge." He made a mocking salute and started up the stairs.

"Where y'think y're going?" Rolfe Jensen asked.

Cassady didn't break stride. "I'm going to make sure she takes her medicine and goes to sleep, *goddamn it!*"

Rolfe Jensen, for the first time, looked embarrassed and at a loss. He was shaking his head, not moving. "Every male comes within her . . . orbit." Eyes on Henry: "Any age, too."

The pent-up frustration erupted inside Henry. "I talked to the security guard at Dyer Electronics," he said. "Nobody works on weekends. Nobody."

"Wha's that supposed t'mean?"

"It means I still want to know where you were five-thirty yesterday and I don't want any more bullshit."

"Oh? We're back to that, are we? Well—" and he moved to stand closer— "well, what I do with my time, that's none of *your* goddamn business, *mister.*"

Henry, almost reaching, broke the impulse, and said, "It's my business if the case is still open." He went into the hall.

Striding to the front door, Henry had to choke down the fury that was threatening to take over. The bastard—he knew now, was positive—the bastard was two-timing his wife.

Outside, a sharp wind had begun to blow. Hate was gripping his gut as he lifted himself into the cruiser in the circular driveway, a new foreboding closing over his mind: what would happen to Carole if she ever learned?

Why did she have to know?

Only if her husband had raped her, only then—

And then of course it wouldn't matter.

He was about to turn the ignition key when he saw the red signal light on the radio. He picked up the mike and barked: "Give it to me."

A woman's voice, deep and businesslike, answered: "Yes, sir. On the accident at the Lake Lillinonah Bridge: we don't have an ID on the vehicle yet, but—"

"To hell with the vehicle. What about the driver?"

"Yes, sir. Name: Scott M. Keller. Address: Still River Road, Sheffield. Age: seventeen."

Henry discovered he could not take a deep breath. He'd known, or had been almost certain, ever since he'd seen the tan Eldorado Caddy charge past him to get behind Carole's car—that it was the same car he'd seen earlier in the parking area at Dr. Keller's estate. "Dead?"

"No, sir. Constable Otto Pegler, Bridgewater, saved him. Sheffield Rescue Squad resuscitated the boy."

"And? And?"

"He's under arrest. Various charges—"

"Where?"

"State Police Barracks, Ridgewood."

Henry uttered a curse and snarled: "With information like this, why didn't you beep me? Who's this on duty?"

"Officer Charlotte Greer, sir. I had no instructions when I came on—"

"You don't *need* instructions. That's what you *do*, Officer Greer."

"Yes, sir. Sorry, sir."

"Anything else, you beep me. I want to see you in my office tomorrow morning. Out!"

He slammed down the mike and sat there a moment, reluctance pulling at every muscle, every nerve in his body.

Then he climbed out, ignoring the sharp twinge in the joint, and strode over the crisp grass toward the house. Knowing he should return to the scene, but first now—and even more important, God forgive him—he had to give Carole the news. He, himself, no one else. He should have told her when she asked. Even then, he'd been almost certain.

When he knocked, the door was half-opened by Rolfe Jensen.

"I have to see your wife," Henry said.

"She's gone to bed. Sorry."

Henry reached and pushed the door all the way open and stepped in. "Official business," he said.

* * *

Lying in bed in the dark room, still wearing the robe over her pajamas, still cold, Carole heard the front door close, and voices in the front hall. The medicine Cass had insisted she take was not doing its job. Her breast was still clenched in pain. And she was still wide awake.

Rolfe's voice: ". . . my house and unless you have a warrant—hey, where you think you're going?"

Footsteps on the stairs, heavy, determined. "Carole, it's me."

"She's in bed, you big gorilla!"

"I'm in here, Henry," Carole said.

Then the door of the bedroom opened, a huge shadow filled the space with the hall light behind, and from below Rolfe's voice shouted: "Invasion of privacy, goddamn it!"

The door closed. The room was dark.

She was not frightened. She suddenly felt very calm. Reaching to switch on the bedside lamp, she discovered that she was eager to see his face.

He still stood by the door. "Carole, I have to have your statement now."

"Why? You said you saw it all—"

"I have to have it officially." Because he knew that Scott Keller, or his lawyer, would soon have a distorted version, if they hadn't already concocted one for the State Police.

He moved to pick up the chair at her vanity. He stepped closer to set the chair down by the bed. "Remember your telling me about that kid, Scott Keller?"

She remembered. She nodded.

He sat down. "He's the one who tried to run you off the road."

"Then he's the one who—"

"He's under arrest, Carole."

"For what? Raping me?"

"Not yet."

"Why not? If he's the one who tried to kill me . . ."

Henry was shaking his head, his eyes reluctant, as if he

hated what he had to say: "It doesn't necessarily follow, Carole. Logically, maybe. But not legally. And not, in this case, in actual fact. I'm sorry, Carole." He flipped open his notebook and took a pen from the breast pocket of his brown suit. And then, eyes on hers: "Now let's begin at the time you left me at State Police Barracks in your car."

It came to him then that Scott Keller must have been following the cruiser from the time he'd given the kid a ticket—no, that wasn't possible. Scott Keller had been driving a red Bronco at that time.

"Henry, listen. If you're so convinced that whoever tried to kill me wasn't the one who raped me, then who, who? And why did Scott Keller—"

"I wish I could answer that," he said, remembering Scott Keller's fury on the roadside when he'd cried: *Damn her, goddamn the bitch!* And he was remembering the father saying: *He goes into these insane rages—*

Wondering then whether he himself had not helped drive the boy into one of those murderous furies, which could have resulted in Carole's death, Henry said, "Scott Keller was, or is, in love with you, Carole. In his own twisted way. He felt you'd betrayed him in some weird way."

"That's terrible, isn't it?" She spoke in a small faint voice. "Terrible. He could be dead now, couldn't he?"

Henry heaved a silent sigh and closed the notebook. "Now don't start blaming yourself, kid. You want me to report you to Dr. Judith?"

For the first time Carole smiled, very faintly, before she said, "But how did you know? Why were you so sure?"

"Call it hunch. Or experience." Still seated upright on the spindly chair, he heard himself say: "Think of it this way. Let's say Scott Keller had been arrested and tried for rape and was convicted—where would that leave you? Maybe you'd be convinced then that justice had been done. But since he was in fact innocent, even if you didn't know that, you'd have your satisfaction, your whatever-you-want-to-call-it, emotional release, all that, you'd have it on a false basis. Not a lie, but not the truth. Would you really want that, Carole? Even if you never really knew the truth. Would you want to feel whole and healthy again that way?"

She sat up in bed and threw back the sheet and blanket, sat facing him, her bare feet on the carpet. "Oh, you dear man, you dear, sweet man—how do you know me so well?"

He didn't say—because he never could say this—that he'd come to feel, in the last thirty hours or so, that he had known her for years. Forever.

He stood up then, towering over her. "I got to tell you this, though. No one wants to close this case as much as I do, except you, but I gotta warn you. Whoever he really is, we might never really know. And he may never be punished."

Her eyes on his, her head uplifted, she said, "Dr. Judith warned me, too."

"It ain't gonna go that way if I can help it."

"I know that, Henry. I *know.*" Then she heard herself laugh—how long since she'd laughed out loud? "Henry, Henry, we're always so serious. I hope, I hope someday we'll be able to, oh, I don't know, just have fun. And laugh. I'd love to hear you laugh, Henry!"

Henry tilted his massive head sideways, and smiled. "It's been a long time," he admitted. "Let's try that sometime, huh?" But his huge square face was grave again when he said, "You know, don't you, that you could be in for more pain if and when I do nab him."

She nodded, but without taking her eyes from his leathery ugly-handsome face. "Because it might—probably will—turn out to be someone I know. Or even love. I know." She stood up then. "But even that, even that would be better than never knowing."

"Good God," was what she thought she heard him say,

low in his throat, as if he were amazed. Then he said it again: "Good God Almighty."

And she laughed again. "Don't call for help, Henry," she said. "I don't think there's anyone there."

"Where's Trooper Dworsky?" Henry asked—as if he gave a damn. He had to shout over the grinding and growling of the red tow truck that was struggling to bring the sunken vehicle up from the bottom of the lake.

"Dworsky's off duty today," Mark Rainer said, also shouting, but still in that lockjaw way of his.

Thank God for small favors, Henry thought but was careful not to say.

Above and off to their right, several uniformed officers were using flashlights to keep the traffic moving on the bridge. Standing on the bank, in the garish glare of police vehicle headlights, were several officers and the two divers, wearing gleaming wet suits, who had probably gone down to hook the tow cable to the Caddy—everyone waiting for the submerged vehicle to appear. The tow truck driver was twisted in the seat, looking out the rear window of the cab as he eased the red truck forward, its huge wheels digging into the gravel.

Henry, wondering why the State's Attorney would be here, and on Sunday night, now recalled Dr. Keller threatening: *Mark Rainer's a good friend of mine.* So, what the hell, Henry decided to ask: "You always take such a personal interest in traffic accidents, Mr. Rainer?"

The younger man, who was wearing a green windbreaker over an open button-down shirt and chinos, touched his mustache and peered up into Henry's face, as if amused. Then he motioned for Henry to follow and walked a few yards farther away from the noise and action. Turning, he said: "Seems to me you're taking a sort of personal interest yourself, Chief. I've got a few questions for you, too."

"Such as?"

"Such as why you didn't stay on the job here after the dunking."

"I had to get a statement from the driver of the other vehicle," Henry said, flatly.

"Did you also issue her a summons?"

"How do you know it was a *her?*"

"Scott told the arresting officer, Constable Pegler of Bridgewater. He said Mrs. Jensen forced him off the highway. Also, of course, she left the scene of an accident resulting in bodily injury—although she might have intended more than that. That, in case you don't know, is a third-degree felony in this state. Punishable, incidentally, by up to five years in prison and a five-thousand-dollar fine."

"Scott Keller's a liar." Henry was tasting bile. "Didn't the constable tell you that I witnessed the incident?"

"And that brings up other questions. What'd you do to prevent it?"

"What would you do if you were following two cars going downhill at fifty-sixty miles per hour, side by side?"

Mark Rainer smiled his mocking lopsided smile. "She threatened to go out and find her attacker and take justice into her own hands, didn't she? You remember. If you don't, we got it all on tape."

Henry was glowering down into the DA's face. "I remember what preceded that statement of hers. She ain't gonna be arrested."

"That *ain't* for you to say, Chief."

"It's for me to say." He almost added: *How much more do you think that child can take?* But, knowing it would do no good, he went on: "It's for me to say if you don't want that so-called interrogation tape played for the State Attorney General in Hartford."

Mark Rainer was squinting at him, something like hate replacing the amusement in his eyes now. "They call that blackmail, don't they?"

"Call it anything you goddamn like, Counselor. You go near Mrs. Jensen with a summons *or* warrant, it'll happen." He took one step closer, seeing out the corner of his eye the tan roof of the sunken vehicle emerging from the water. "And if your friend Vincent Fletcher doesn't print it, I'll see it's printed in the New York *Daily News* verbatim. And, just to ice the cake, I'll see your wife gets a personal copy of the transcript."

Mark Rainer tried his little smile again, but it didn't come off. "You play hardball, don't you? Well, Chief, so do I. Like why did you leave the scene when you knew that kid was in the car? That's what we call dereliction of duty around here."

"Because," Henry said, "there was another officer here who knew how to swim. If I went into that water, it'd be suicide and I ain't gonna commit a crime like that because people like you'd want to punish me for it."

Now it was Henry's turn to grin. His empty, intimidating gargoyle grin that he hadn't had occasion to use for years. Then he turned away to start up the slope leading up to the road.

He was moving heavily, his hip catching, his heart beginning to pump, hard. But the taste of bile was no longer poisoning his mouth. As he made his way through the tangle of vehicles, police and civilian, parked at all kinds of angles off the road, he heard a cheer go up. The Caddy was out of the lake. He didn't turn around.

The wind was sharper now. And colder. He climbed into his squad car. If it came to a showdown, and he hoped it wouldn't, he could add another charge to whatever charges had been filed against Scott Keller: attempted homicide. With himself as witness. At least he could threaten it. Much as he'd hate doing even this. But . . . but he'd do anything, anything, to keep the hounds off Carole's heels. Christ, they were going to try to make the victim the criminal. Again. Well, they weren't going to get away with it.

As he drove, he relit the stub of the cigar that Cassady

had snitched off Rolfe Jensen's desk for him. Oh Jesus, he was tired.

And he still had to write up his official report on the "accident" while the details were still fresh in his mind.

He hoped that Carole was finally sleeping. He hoped the telephone and that drunken husband of hers would let her sleep.

Tomorrow, somehow, he'd find out where Rolfe Jensen spent yesterday afternoon. Then what? What about the goddamn Plimsoll Line then?

While Henry had been in the room, Carole had felt composed, in control, and even confident. But once he had gone, after he'd carefully put a glass of fresh water on the nightstand next to the three plastic bottles of medicine which Cass had placed there, the torment had returned, focused now, and intense: if Scott Keller hadn't raped her, then who had? Both Henry and Dr. Judith had said that she might never know. Could she live with that?

No.

Regardless of Henry, regardless of Dr. Judith, the answer was no, she could *not*—

She threw back the covers violently, the pillow falling to the floor. The air was cold. Freezing!

She stood up, legs weak, knees stiff and hurting. Her heels hitting the floor sent pain stabbing into her crotch, reaching upwards.

Into the hall. No light. Opening a closet door. Where was everybody?

She took a down-filled comforter from a shelf. Towels and sheets tumbled to the floor. Ignore them, forget them. What was happening to her? If Scott Keller hadn't raped her, then who?

Who, *who,* WHO?

She returned to the dim bedroom. She'd forgotten to turn up the thermostat. Again? When had she—

Into the hall again. Turn on light. Turn control on wall, all the way, right to left, up or down?

The phone started to ring.

She stepped. Snatched it up on the second ring. "Henry?" she heard herself shouting into it. "Henry, where are you, what are you doing, what's *anyone* doing?"

"Carole? Is that you, C-C-Carole?"

She recognized the voice. Not Henry's. "It's me. David."

"What do you want?"

A silence. His face in her mind: soft, dark-bearded, the shock of hair, friendly hesitant eyes. She remembered: his mouth on hers, Christmas music, his lips demanding, tongue probing. Not so hesitant. Not so friendly. Arms powerful, hugging—

"What, David, *what?"* She was shivering now.

"I know Esther talked with you this m-morning. . . ."

"She did. How's the fishing, David?"

"F-f-fishing?"

"Isn't that what you do? Isn't that where you said you were yesterday?"

"Carole, please, you w-w-worry me. I just heard it on FM—about the Keller kid. How they fished him out of the l-l-lake. He's under arrest. But he's out on bail already. The . . . the newscaster gave a description of the other c-car. It sounded like Rolfe's Saab, so naturally I-I-I—"

"So naturally you *what,* David?" Her teeth were chattering. "What, *what?"*

"So of c-c-course I wanted to know how you are. Carole, listen, we're your fr-fr-friends, we—"

She was locked in his bearlike grip again, his mouth over hers, beard harsh, his tongue—

She slammed down the phone. Lifted her hand to her mouth, placed her knuckles between her teeth to stop the chattering. Into the bedroom. The pain farther down had come back. Her flesh was quivering all over.

She got into bed, chilled all through, pulled the blanket

and comforter up to her chin, her whole body shaking, brass bed trembling.

You haven't noticed the way he's been acting lately? No, Esther, I haven't. Not till now. *He can't sleep and when he does he has nightmares. A stranger to me—*

She reached to turn on the lamp. Would another sleeping pill do the trick?

She realized that she'd uttered a low moan. Oh no, no, not David, please God, don't let it be David.

She couldn't go on like this, her mind skittering and leaping around like this all night. Not with everything she had to do tomorrow. Read her testimony, sign the complaint, give Henry her statement on the accident, tell him about David's call, more questions, the results of the other tests, VD, AIDS, more examinations, more questions, if she took another sleeping pill and maybe two tranquilizers, which kind, which was which . . .

She heard steps on the stairs.

Then a voice.

Rolfe's.

"I know you're not asleep, Carole. I heard you on the phone—"

She reached blindly for the glass, the one Henry had placed here for her, and the vials, any one would do, pain, sleep—

Rolfe appeared in the door. "Also, the light's on." He had a half-filled highball glass in his hand and he was almost, but not quite, slurring his words. "Lissen, I been thinking. I'm tired-a waiting for the ax to fall. At work, I mean. Why don't you call your father back?"

She washed one tab and one cap down with the water, emptying the glass. Then waited—

"Why don't you tell your ole man we accept his offer?"

She returned the glass to the table. It fell to the floor.

Rolfe came in to pick it up. "Or . . . if you don't want to do it that way"—he placed the glass on the table—"since the case is all wrapped up now—"

"It's not wrapped up."

He was frowning down on her. "You mean . . . y'mean the guy in the other car's not dead?"

She had stopped shivering. "I mean he's alive, but he's not the one."

"Oh shit. How do you know?"

"I don't. But Henry does."

"So." He picked up the chair Henry had used. Turned it around in one hand and sat down, straddling the back of it. "Henry knows all evil, sees all evil."

Should she tell Rolfe about David's call? About last Christmas? Rolfe would laugh. Or he'd call up David. Or, in this mood, worse—would he want to kill him? No, no he wouldn't. . . .

"Whah I was thinking, Carole: mebbe if you called your father back, he'd be willing to advance us enough to cover a few months anyway. Split this whole scene."

"Advance us?"

"From what we'll have coming. You know what I mean."

"When they die." Suddenly she did know what he meant. "When they *die.*"

He shifted his body in the chair. "Why do you have to put it that . . . like that? You always have to spell out everything, don't you?" He took a long swallow. "You're saying no."

"Yes," she said. Why wasn't she getting sleepy, how long would it take? "Yes. I'm saying no."

"You really want to go on with all this, don't you? Well, all r-i-i-i—it's your bullgame, all r-i-i-ight. What's the name of the guy you say now didn't—"

"Rolfe," she said, "I'm so tired. And cold. I don't want to go over all this." She wanted to close her eyes, but didn't. "What makes you think my father's going to leave me his money?"

"We both know that, don't we? Christ, if I didn't have that to look forward to—" He finished his drink, set the glass on the table, and lowered his forehead to his knuckles on the back of the chair.

"If?" she heard herself ask—

"I've had it with that damn job. An' *then* where's it coming from? We can sell our stocks but—" He lifted his head. His eyes looked bloodshot, and bleak. "Now this. Is it ever going to be over?"

She did close her eyes then. "Not until—" But she didn't say it. She'd said it so often. Why didn't he understand? The savagery inside had returned. The awful, aching need, the familiar fury, like hunger . . .

"Eye for an eye, you mean?" His tone roughened. "That's weird, Car'le."

"Weird? The whole thing is weird. But that's it, Rolfe." She opened her eyes: he was staring at her. "That's the deal, as Daddy would say."

Rolfe's face looked baffled now, faintly accusing. "You can't set the rules like that, Carole. And then . . . then expect the world to—" He stood up abruptly. "It's *scary.*"

"You," she said, "*you* don't know what scary is."

Rolfe moved away, his back to her, tall and stiff. "Even if they arrest someone—depositions, postponements, the trial itself. It could go on forever." His tone was bewildered. "For everybody. Not just you. All of us. And crimes like this aren't always solved, y'know—" Then he drew back the curtain at the dormer window and the night came in. "Cass has been saying—" he turned, framed in the outside darkness, "—Cass knew you felt this way. How come I *dint?*"

"Maybe he guessed." And maybe, she thought, maybe he just sensed it. Maybe that was the reason he was a writer. Or . . . maybe it was because he loved her—which she knew now, which she admitted now.

"By the way," Rolfe said, "just by the way, I don't like other men to be in our bedroom, Carole. Cass or that asshole cop."

She refused to answer. To speak at all. She waited. No sleepiness in her, only tiredness, and the pain . . .

"Doesn't anyone give a damn how *I* feel?" Rolfe asked. "It's not easy, you know. Even Cass knows that."

She did speak then. "I'm sorry," she said, remembering Dr. Judith. But it was true: she *was* sorry.

"What about tomorrow? I hate the idea of going to work. Knowing what everybody's thinking. Feeling sorry for me. Picturing it in their filthy goddamn minds!" He stepped to the end of the bed, took hold of the brass foot-piece. "And you, how's it going to be for you, Carole?"

"You told me Miriam is going to have someone pick up my work. I won't have to go in." Suddenly she hated herself for saying it. More evasions, more ways of saying *I'm sorry!* "People are going to think what they want to think and to hell with them."

"I'll tell you what they're going to think." The bed shuddered from his grip on the brass frame. "Every male who looks at you's going to wonder how it felt. They're going to strip you naked with their eyes. Worse! And can you imagine the jokes?"

"You're making me feel great," she warned, her body stiff, her mind theatening to ignite again.

"That Joel White you walloped last night—you *know* what he's going to be thinking. And your boss—did Vincent Fletcher ever try to get it on with you?"

"No. Never. Why are you asking these questions?" Her hands were tight fists under the covers. "Rolfe, you've been drinking all day—"

"And that Attila the Hun. Since when do you call cops by their first name?"

A scream began to gather in her throat. "Please, Rolfe, let me go to sleep now. Please, *please.*"

"Did he come on to you in his car? Any time. Answer me, did he?"

The scream was a knot beginning to unravel. "You have

no right to do this to me, Rolfe. I'm sorry for what you're going through. I'm sorry, sorry, sorry, but—"

"You ought to be sorry. Going into that woods, almost dark—what the hell did you expect?"

"Not what I got, Rolfe—and not *this!*"

"Listen, Carole, things've got to get back to normal around here. I mean it." In one quick movement he pulled his knit shirt over his head. "And I know how we can do that right now."

The scream was threatening, her throat clogged. No, this was not happening, she didn't believe it, no—

"Just because you've had someone else doesn't mean I don't still want you." He stepped out of his chinos—

"I didn't *have* anyone," she heard herself say. "*He* had me!"

Rolfe was pulling his briefs down over his hips. "You ought to be glad I still want you, Carole. And I do, damn it, I do."

She was tempted to tell him of the pain inside, the torn tissue, the insistent throbbing in her breast, the explosions going off in her skull—

But seeing him stepping naked around the bed to come to her, she couldn't tell him, he should know, she refused to tell him what he should *know!*

"You're still mine," she heard him say, his voice husky, standing close now, his penis extended and quivering only inches from her face. "You're mine, goddamn it."

She was *not* his, goddamnit! She belonged to herself, not anyone else!

He leaned down and ripped the covers back.

"Don't you want me, Carole?" he demanded. "Don't you love me?"

Then she heard a sound.

A scream.

Which went on and on, filling the house.

And then she realized, feeling the tightness in her open

jaws, seeing his naked body step back, that it was the scream in her own throat which had finally erupted.

It had begun to rain.

The windshield wipers were clacking and the narrow road glinted wet and dark in the headlight beams. Henry passed the familiar sign: SHEFFIELD CENTER 1792—not referring to the population, he had learned, but to the date the town had been founded.

In The Village the lights were going off in the Congregational Church. Sunday evening services were over; Reverend Carpenter was closing up. The storefronts were dark but there were a few other lights burning in windows here and there through the falling rain.

He parked alongside the station house and got out and ran through the cold downpour, the pain in his joint piercing down the length of his leg.

He did not go to his office, but checked at the front counter, routinely, and learned that Scott Keller had been charged only with failure to use due care in the operation of a motor vehicle—and had been released. No surprise, only a quick sharp stab of anger. Well, a night in jail wouldn't teach kids like Scott Keller anything, anyway. If anything would. Since his troubles were inside and probably too complex and deeply rooted to be reached by punishment. Also, of course, highly respected citizens like Dr. Keller and his friend Mark Rainer, those upstanding types knew how to finagle things for spoiled little rich boys who give in to their savage impulses and think they have the God-given right to try to take another human life. Justice. But since he hadn't really succeeded in harming Carole, to hell with it. Unless . . . unless Mark Rainer tried to carry out his threat to arrest Carole—

"Anything else?" Henry asked.

Elderly, arthritic Tim Stevens, on duty five nights a week, lifted his shaggy white brows. "Like what, Chief?"

"Like the blood and semen tests that the New Jersey authorities were going to have run on Manuel Mendoza."

"Nothing yet, sir. But since it's Sunday and the labs don't—"

"I know what the labs do, everywhere. Thanks, Tim."

Henry went out into the rain again and crossed the narrow street between the station house and the Village Store and climbed the outdoor stairway to his flat. He was chilled to the bone, and wet.

But when, having changed into his old flannel bathrobe, bottle of cold ale in hand now—he allowed himself only one tonight because he'd had the other one with his pastrami sandwich in Merlin's Bar and Grill—Henry stepped to flick on the TV set in the corner, making sure to turn the volume off. Then he sank down onto the old broken-down couch, picked up the phone, and dialed. Mr. Jerald Dixon, Attorney-at-Law, who'd tried to buy Henry's lunch, was another one who, whether he knew it or not, was going to have some questions to answer tomorrow.

While he waited for Judith to answer, Henry watched the picture fade in: a cop show, guns going off, fusillades, bad guys falling, handsome police officers firing away grimly, speeding away, cars rolling, bursting into flames. Henry sighed. If only it were so simple. Or so exciting. Instead of so damned tedious, grueling—and heartbreaking.

"Henry! I'd almost given up on you," Judith said.

Without preliminaries, Henry said: "The driver of the other car was a kid named Scott Keller, father a physician—"

"Carole told me about him. Did he drown?"

"He survived. But he's not the rapist, Judith."

"And Carole?"

"Did she phone you tonight?"

"No. I suspect she's decided to tough it out. Possibly all for the best. Now tell me: how are *you,* Henry?"

"Tired," he admitted. "Goddamn good and tired."

"You told me you were convinced the driver of the other car wasn't the rapist anyway—"

Henry yawned, aloud. And he heard Judith laugh, "What else do you know, Henry?"

"I know that there may come a time, and it may be soon, you're going to have to tell me what or who you suspect."

"You know that's impossible, Henry."

"I know that if the stakes are high enough, there are ways of getting around the impossible."

"Not in this instance. And I may be very wrong."

"Tell me this much, Judith. Is one of your patients a friend of Carole's?"

"Damn it, you're making me mad!"

All the accumulated frustrations, vexations and unfamiliar emotions of the long day exploded in his gut. "There's already been one attempt to kill Carole. I'm not asking for myself."

"I know that, Henry, and please don't shout."

"I'm not shouting," he shouted. "You're the one who warned *me*. Are you going to risk Carole's going off the deep end when you could—"

"Henry, you're making me very angry."

"Well, be angry, goddamn it! I'm angry, too. You could at least give me a clue, anything—"

"Goodnight, Henry."

He heard the click, definite and final, and loud in his ear. Damn her. *Goddamn* her!

When he replaced the phone, he did not turn up the volume on the TV. He sat glaring at it. He was furious and confused and, yeah, he knew he was being unreasonable. But there had to be a way to change Judith's mind. They both knew this couldn't go on much longer.

Then . . . another thought occurred to him: the one *certain* way for Carole to be destroyed, emotionally devastated, would be for her to learn that the animal who'd attacked her was her husband. *What I do with my time—that's none of your goddamn business, mister!*

Henry listened to the rain beating in loud windy gusts against the windows. End of Indian summer. The printed credits were rolling on an otherwise blank screen. He took a final long swig of ale and was glad he couldn't hear the loud raucous blare that was called music these days.

He didn't even want to stand up to go to the bedroom.

He hadn't been this dead on his feet for many years. And the pain from the hip joint was shooting up and down his right leg. His mind was almost blank with fatigue.

Yet . . . yet somewhere in him, mind and body, a heady sort of excitement streamed, feverish and vital.

He had not felt so *alive* in over twenty years.

Carole was in bed. The room was warm. The bed was warm. She was still cold.

She had taken more medicine, one of each. For pain, for sleep, for nerves. Too many? Too many, too soon after taking the others?

After Rolfe had gone downstairs and after she'd stopped screaming, she had not been able to think of anything else to do but drug herself to sleep. All she needed was oblivion for a while, a few hours anyway. . . .

You're still mine. What had she answered? *Don't you want me, Carole?*

Whatever she had answered, she knew what she had been thinking: Rolfe, her husband—whom she *did* love, yes—he had been turned on by thinking of her having sex with another man. Just the way Jerald Dixon had.

But Rolfe wasn't himself tonight. He was sloshed out of his skull. When she'd stopped screaming, she'd heard Cass, at the foot of the stairway, asking Rolfe: *What the hell did you say to her?*

And Rolfe's voice: *None of your goddamn business. This is my house! That's what really bugs you, isn't it, Cass? That twists your gut, doesn't it?*

Then, their voices farther away, fainter but still audible, because they were getting louder and louder as they moved toward the den.

You've been jealous of me for years, Cass. 'Fess up, 'fess up, you bastard.

In vino veritas, Cass had said, *and screw you, pal.*

After that she'd heard only an occasional mumble through the sound of the falling rain. If only Cass hadn't come. He'd been drinking himself to death for years now. And what could she, or anyone, do? Even the people who loved him—possibly the only two in the world who did love him . . .

Her body was without pain now. But, even as her mind blurred, reaching for sleep, there was an ache in it. For Sandy. She needed Sandy. But thank God Sandy was *not* here now.

Listen, Carole, things've got to get back to normal around here. Would anything ever get back to normal? That was what she wanted now, too—longed for, needed. Cass and Rolfe chatting, reminiscing, joking and laughing together . . . watching football on TV . . . the clink of billiard balls from the game room . . . passing a softball back and forth on the rear lawn . . .

Softball. Last summer. The banner on the backstop: ANNUAL PICNIC SUDBURY NEWS-CHRONICLE. *And your boss, Vincent Fletcher—did he ever try to get it on with you?* Rolfe had always been jealous. Without reason, without any reason whatever—ever, ever, *ever.*

She was remembering, as if from a distance, the fun and laughter of that August day, and what she had been wearing, and her discomfort. The very brief running shorts she sometimes wore around the house on hot days, tight tank top—Rolfe's idea. *Let 'em look,* he'd said when she'd wanted to change into slacks. And on the way home: *Can you imagine a company picnic without beer? Hey, you were the star of the day! And I don't mean because you can swat a three-base hit. I can't wait till we get home so I can peel'em off you.*

But Vincent Fletcher had not been pleased. A few days later, his sun-reddened face had worn a nervous apologetic but reproachful expression in his office: *Carole, I don't know precisely how to say this, especially to you. But I do feel obliged to tell you that next year . . . would you dress a bit more modestly? The way you do when you come into the office here. Just as a favor to me. You are a good girl, Carole. Not one of those harlots on the street. Ponder this, my dear. It's a wicked, wicked world. Evil.*

She knew that now. If nothing else, she'd learned that.

How long had she been lying here? How many minutes, hours? Then she heard footsteps below and voices in the hall again.

"Whatever it is, it can wait till morning!"

"Can' wait." Rolfe's words were slurring together now. "Got t'go upstairs and tell her . . . how much I love her an' . . . an' that I forgive her."

"Forgive her? For what? Pal, you're bombed. Let the poor girl sleep."

"Don't tell me whut t'do—y'been lecturing me all day. She's *my* wife—get that straight. Not yours—got it, pal?"

"Rolfe—" and Cass's voice turned into an angry whisper—"I'm not gonna let you—"

"*Let* me? Y'think I don't know what you been thinking? Every time she walks inta room—"

"If you want me to say I love her—"

"Say it!"

"All right! I love her. And I see what's happening to her even if you don't. Are you blind, you sonofabitch, or do you just not give a damn?"

"You may love her . . . but you can' have her. She's mine, buddy. Not yours—*mine!*"

"No one *belongs* to anybody else. If she's crazy enough to love you—"

"Or maybe you already *have* had her—"

"You're wiped out—"

"Yeah, maybe I . . . maybe you're the one threw that blanket over her head 'cause it's the only way you *could* have her."

Oh no. Carole found herself praying silently. Oh God, make them stop, please. Rolfe doesn't mean that, please God—

After a long silence, Cass's voice again: "If you can think that, screw you."

Carole reached a decision. She got out of bed. The air in the room was hot now. It had stopped raining.

From a distance—in the den—Rolfe was saying: "You been on my case all day. What're ya tryin' t'say?"

She heard ice clink into an empty glass.

"All right," Cass said. "You want it straight? You don't deserve her."

"And you do, I guess. Big shot has-been author. Big fart war hero—"

"I'm not a war hero, I'm a war *criminal.* Like everybody else."

Carole had moved into the upstairs hall.

"How many women'd you rape in Nam?"

Legs weak, heart fluttering, Carole was going down the stairs in her bare feet, holding onto the banister. They had to stop this. Even if they were both plastered, *because* they were plastered—stop, stop . . .

"Y'always held that against me, dint ya, Cass? I dint go an I dint protest, march up'n down, burn my draft card . . ."

She was moving toward the open door of the den.

"What I held against you, pal, is that you didn't care! *Care!* Then or now. *Me* first, get outta my way, let'em die over there then, let'em starve on the streets here now, or freeze to death. Just so it's them, not me! *Me, me, me*—the new religion, back to the jungle, me, *me,* the theme song of the 1980s!"

Carole stopped in the doorway. Rolfe was standing behind his desk, eyes red and blurred and burning, breathing hard. Cass was pouring at the bar, his back to her, stiff and straight.

"Please," she said, her throat catching. "Please, both of you!"

Rolfe stood blinking at her as if trying to get her into focus. Cass turned, slowly; his face looked stricken. White. Sick.

"Don't do this to each other," she begged in a small whisper. "Please don't do this because of me."

Cass opened his mouth to speak, but Rolfe moved around the end of the desk to come to her. "God, darling, I'm sorry," he said. His blue eyes looked wretched now. "Lemme—"

Before she knew what was happening, he had picked her up in his arms and was going into the hall toward the stairs.

It suddenly occurred to her that he might not be able to carry her up the stairs. His face was close, the stench of his breath sickening, but in his arms she felt her body relax slightly.

Over Rolfe's shoulder she saw Cass down below, staring up at them. "Carole," he said, in a strangled voice, "I'm sorry."

And then Rolfe, breathing hard, turned into the dim bedroom, and she heard Cass's voice from below: *"But one man loved the pilgrim soul in you, and loved the sorrows on your changing face."*

As Rolfe lowered her to the bed and was pulling the covers over her, she heard the back door open and close.

Rolfe stood looking down on her. His tall, slim body was weaving slightly in the light from the hallway. Was he going to bend down and kiss her?

"Carole," he said, "there's something important, somethin' I got to ask you. But not now." He did lean down then and he did kiss her, very softly, on the forehead.

The first time he'd ever kissed her, she remembered, the

first time he'd taken her out, he'd kissed her first on the forehead and then, boyishly, on the lips.

He did not kiss her on the lips now.

"Sleep tight," he said quietly. "You need it. Christ, it's hot up here!"

Then he went into the hall, fast, and shut the door, very softly. "My God, this thermostat's up to ninety-five! You'll burn the goddamn house down!"

The room was dark.

Why hadn't he stayed?

And then she felt sleepiness close over her at last. Her body was limp, her mind a blessed blank, beginning to drift again—

She closed her eyes and turned onto her side, one arm under the pillow when she heard: "Cass! Where the hell are you?"

The void into which her mind had been moving was suddenly filled with hurtful blazing light, filled with sharp shards of glitter and dazzle, a blinding kaleidoscope behind her eyelids—

She was fully awake again, the loss and regret merging into a slow-burning anger.

She heard the rain blowing in wintry gusts against the windows.

She heard the back door open and close again. Hard.

The anger sharpened. And the fear—

Then from the rear lawn she heard their voices again, but not the words—

Oh please God, no.

Their voices were very loud now, through the closed windows. Rolfe was yelling, demanding to know where Cass thought he was going, and Cass was saying fuck it, he was going back to New York. "If it's any of your goddamn business!"

She rolled out of bed and went to the windows.

"What'll Carole think if you leave now?"

"Who the hell do you think I'm doing it for?"

She drew back the curtain. The rear lawn was dark, but there was a light in the window of the bathhouse-bedroom where Cass slept.

"Well, that suits me fine. Farther you stay away from Carole, better I'll like it."

As her eyes adjusted, she could see two shadows, both moving on the wet grass, a few feet apart. Toward the bath house. The pond shimmering in the light from the guest room window—

Then the smaller of the two shadowy figures turned and waited for the other to reach him.

Cass, as drunk and angry as Rolfe, or drunker and angrier now, shouted: "I'll say it again. *You don't deserve her!*"

Then there was a long silence. She waited, every nerve taut.

"The only way *you* could ever have her is to *rape* her!"

Another silence. Before Cass spoke, very precisely, shouting: "I've got just one last thing to say to you, pal."

"Spit it out."

"You don't love Carole or you wouldn't be fucking that goddamn ice queen!"

Then Carole saw a sudden movement. Even at this distance, she heard an ugly flat wooden sound and, seeing Cass stagger backwards, realized that Rolfe had hit him in the face with his fist.

Tempted to turn away, helpless with shock—she couldn't handle this, she couldn't handle it now—Carole discovered that her body was locked, she couldn't move.

Cass was crouched now, low to the ground, like a jungle animal ready to pounce. "Man," he said in a low snarl, "I could tear you apart. I been taught by experts."

"Stand up and try it!" Rolfe bellowed. "Come on, *come on!*"

Cass turned his head and spit something out onto the grass. Blood?

Carole was too weak to move. And sick, her stomach turning—

Rolfe stepped in closer and, leaning down, struck again, the blow landing on Cass's face, with that same flat wooden sound she'd never heard until tonight.

Cass dropped from the crouching position onto his knees. "I won't fight you, Rolfe," he said, not shouting. "I can't."

"Why not, why not?"

"I just can't, that's all. I can't."

And Rolfe swung again, hard and fast. Cass's figure toppled sideways to the ground.

No, this was not happening. She'd fallen asleep after all, she was dreaming this, it was not real. . . .

The figure on the ground did not move.

The tall shadow waited a second or two and then turned to stagger, almost losing its balance, toward the house.

Then Cass managed to stand, wobbling, lurching toward the bathhouse.

She let go of the curtain and slid slowly down to the carpet.

It was not a dream. It was very real and it had happened.

Then a terrible sense of loss engulfed her mind. And guilt: *she* had caused this. It was her fault.

Could she make it back to the bed?

Would she have to crawl?

Part 5

She was aware that her mind was fighting consciousness.

Dull gray light in the windows. And silence. A vast unnatural quiet, everywhere. As if a shutter had come down over her mind. As if she couldn't get time or place into focus, although she knew where she was, of course; she was in her own bed and it must be early, very early.

But where was Rolfe?

Her body heavy and sluggish, she had to force herself to roll over. The red lights on the nightstand clock, blurred as if she were peering at them underwater, read 8:47.

Then she was up and running, the carpet warm and soft under her bare feet, until she reached the hall. Where the hard cold of the wood floor stabbed through her feet and up her legs and into her groin, and her head rocked.

It was not until she was in Sandy's room, staring at the huge, big-eyed stuffed panda on the neat and otherwise empty bed, that she stopped, startled at first, disoriented; then, her breath leaving her body in a rush, she felt her mind clear and it all came flooding back—*everything*—and she was left leaning against the doorframe, dazed and bloodless, already spent, the long, impossible day stretching endlessly before her, all the things she had to do, important things—but what? Rolfe was already at work, of course, of course, and Sandy was at Allison's, but Carole knew she was forgetting something else, too. What?

She turned and retraced her steps across the hall to the telephone on the table. The air was warm but she was shivering as she sat on the chair, placing her bare feet on its rung while she tapped out Allison's number. Then she waited, hearing the phone buzzing at the other end of the line and remembering that Rolfe had come upstairs to sit on the bed (how long ago? hours, or only minutes?) to whisper: *I can't begin to tell you how sorry I am, darling. I'm so goddamn ashamed I just can't tell you.* How miserable his lean, handsome face had looked, how contrite and sincere, while she had recalled those two shadowy figures on the rear lawn last night. *Where's Cass?* she had asked. And Rolfe's whisper had become so faint that she was not certain she heard: *I hope he made it back to New York, polluted as he was. Lenny Arnstein is picking me up in about two minutes, so you'll have my wheels for the day.* And then, leaving, he had added, *I still have something important to ask you. . . .*

There was no answer on the phone. By now they'd be on their way to preschool. And now Sandy's face filled her mind, small and soft and eager, her blue eyes intense and bright. And an ache began in Carole's depths. Followed by a bewildered anger: How, oh God, how do you tell a five-year-old her mother's been raped? *Raped, Mommy? What does that mean?* How do you even explain the meaning of the word?

By now Carole had begun to dread the day. And she was still forgetting something—something she had to do, now, first thing this morning.

She broke the connection and touched Cass's number, remembering to insert the 1 and the area code 212. *You don't love Carole or you wouldn't be fucking that goddamn ice queen!* The nightmare returned, vivid and violent in her mind—that odd, terrible, wooden sound, the two unreal figures in the rain.

There was no answer. Strange. Had Cass had the good sense to turn in at some motel rather than try to drive the seventy miles? Ice queen, ice queen, ice queen—Cass wouldn't tell her anyway. Not because he was a man protecting another man but because he was Cass, who loved her, who also probably still loved Rolfe.

But . . . but why hadn't Rolfe denied it? Why had it driven him to violence?

Hey, you really don't know what's going on, do you?

Who'd said that? When?

She started toward the bedroom.

Jerry. On the phone. Yesterday, when he'd called to ask her to lunch—no, when he'd really asked her to fuck him. After she'd said, *Give my love to Karen.*

In the open bedroom door Carole turned, returned to the table, took up her personal phone directory, leather-covered, her name embossed, a gift from her father.

Dixon and Doyle, Attorneys. She jabbed out the numbers.

What the hell was she doing? And why?

When Jerald's voice came on—"Carole, wow, did you change your mind?"—she said, "Who's the ice queen?"

"Ice queen?"

"Answer me." Her hand was clutching the phone so hard that pain was beginning to climb her arm.

She heard his familiar mocking laugh. "Don't you know? That's what Cass calls Karen. Even to her face. Didn't you ever hear him? And does she get pissed off—hey, wait a minute, what's this, why do you—"

"And Rolfe's fucking her, right?"

Silence. And she was certain.

Then: "Carole, I'm due over at the jail in—"

"And you know. Everyone knows." And she added, "Except me."

"Carole, baby, listen. Karen and I have our own arrangement. We—hey, look, why do you think I suggested what I did? Goose and gander, baby. How about it?"

She discovered that she couldn't move. Or speak.

She heard, but from a distance, his lubricious whisper: "You're wising up. Rape's not my style, but I do have a style, Carole."

Slowly she began to lower the phone when he lifted his voice: "Don't hang up, Carole. I heard about what happened last night at the bridge, the good doctor's hippie son—"

She brought the phone up to her face. "He didn't rape me!" Almost a scream. "And you know it!"

Then she slammed down the telephone and went into the bedroom, taking off her pajama top. Why had she swallowed so many damn pills last night? She'd slept but hadn't rested. And now her head felt swollen and empty and blurred. She'd have to remember to tell Henry about Jerry. And she'd forgotten to tell him about David Slade's phone call last night. Her body longed to return to the bed, the warmth, the oblivion. But no, no, she had to shower, to put something in her stomach, anything.

She stepped into the tub, slid shut the glass door and was reaching for the mixer knob on the shower when she remembered she'd taken a bath late last night.

It was then that she heard a sound.

From outside, and familiar, yet for a moment she couldn't identify it.

She tensed, listening.

Then she slid open the door and stepped out of the tub and went to the window overlooking the rear lawn. She looked out over the half-curtain and down to the wide, sloping, leaf-covered grass. Parked beside the pond was the familiar battered red truck. Even at this distance, she could make out the lettering on the door: J. PETOFI, LANDSCAPING YARD MAINTENANCE.

Then she saw him. He was kneeling in the leaves working on an attachment on the rear of the small yellow tractor. She recognized it at once—the vacuum apparatus that sucked leaves into a canvas bag. He was wearing jeans and a red plaid flannel shirt, its tails hanging out. Even if he turned to look, he couldn't see more than her head, but slowly she became aware of her nakedness.

She took down the towel-robe from its brass hook.

Lindheim asked me whether anyone worked for us. I gave him the name of Janos Petofi, Rolfe had said.

It was not until she was back in the bedroom—uncertain, trying to decide—that the terror took hold.

What was he doing here today?

And . . . and it had rained last night. The leaves would still be wet—

As she was putting on the robe, a shiver passed down her body. Should she dress quickly and sneak quietly downstairs and out the front door? The shiver turned into a shudder.

Was this the man whose penis had been in her, who had called her by name, who had called her darling and sweet and a bitch and a whore? Had Henry ever mentioned him?

Tying the white belt at her waist, she stepped into the hall and lifted the phone again. Did Henry suspect Janos Petofi? She damn well wasn't going to start running like a scared animal from every male who appeared on the horizon.

It went through her mind, but only fleetingly then, that it could not possibly have been Janos Petofi if it had really been David Slade or Jerald Dixon.

But even before she was informed by a female officer that Chief Lindheim was not in at the moment but would return her call shortly, Carole thought of the lightweight revolver Rolfe kept in the drawer of the nightstand by the bed.

So she made up her mind. "I'll be at home for only a few minutes," she said into the phone, hung up, and went into the bedroom to get the gun.

At nine-thirty Henry had checked to make sure that Rolfe Jensen was in his office at Dyer Electronics. What Rolfe

Jensen did with his time was, as he had said last night, his own business, and he may have just been so enraged to have been caught in a lie, or so boozed up that he was being stubborn like a Swede, but the worst thing that could happen to Carole now would be to learn that her husband was the one who had raped her. If it turned out that way, Henry wanted to be the first to know it. Judith would know how to tell her.

Now Henry was in the lab in the basement of the Sudbury police station, which also housed the jail on the third floor. He had just learned that both Manuel Mendoza's and Carole's clothes had been sent to Hartford this morning to be put through the laser ID process. A preliminary examination had revealed there were no semen stains on the suspect's and only traces on the victim's—which was about what he expected anyway. A semen sample wasn't like a fingerprint; it could only be used to eliminate suspects who didn't fall into that blood type. He had also learned that the thumbprint lifted from the perpetrator's belt buckle had not yet been put through the ID processor—same old familiar excuses: too much work, not enough personnel, and too many priorities. Hell of a way to start a day! But he had demanded and now had in his pocket his own personal copy of the print. Which, of course, was of no use to him unless he could match it against the print of every suspect. Which of course he did not have and could not legally obtain without first making an arrest.

In the parking area behind the station house, OFFICIAL VEHICLES ONLY, he was striding, feeling the new cold, toward his car when he saw a metallic gray Audi Quattro pull in and park. So he stopped and waited, watching Jerald Dixon get out and walk toward him.

Dixon wore the attorney's uniform: a three-piece suit with a topcoat over it, both tan, and he was grinning. "We've just got to stop meeting like this, Chief," he said, extending a hand.

Which Henry ignored. "You know somebody upstairs, Mr. Dixon?"

"Prelim hearing at ten at the courthouse," Jerald Dixon said. "Hand-holding time. Makes the guilty feel innocent." He tilted his head. "I just talked with Carole a while ago."

"So?"

"Didn't she tell you? She suspects *me*. How does that grab you, Chief?"

Before he could answer, the beeper on his belt began to make its familiar demanding sound. Reaching to flip it off, Henry asked, "Would you mind unbuttoning your vest, Counselor?"

"I think I would, yes."

"Well, change your mind, fast. I want to take a squint at the belt you're wearing."

"Chief, I've got legitimate business here. That'd be in the nature of an illegal search, wouldn't it? Even *you've* heard of probable cause."

Jerald Dixon stepped to one side, as if to pass. And Henry planted himself in his path. They were very close now, face to face, toe to toe.

Whatever the lawyer saw in Henry's face caused him to take a backward step, glowering now. "I don't have anything to hide," he said. He was unbuttoning his vest from the bottom. "Mark Rainer told me your tactics leave something to be desired." He threw open the vest. "Read 'em and weep, Chief."

Henry was staring at the trousers. There was no belt. Or belt loops. None required. The flap of the waistband extended and buttoned over the center closure on the young man's thickening midsection.

"Tough shit, old man." Jerald Dixon was grinning again, not quite taunting. "Now if you'll excuse me, I have to instruct my client to plead not guilty to all charges." Buttoning his vest, he moved around Henry's frame and toward the rear door of the station house "This isn't New York, y'know."

In his squad car Henry radioed headquarters. To learn of Carole's call. Now, thanks to the tightfisted Board of Selectman, he had to find a public phone again.

So he returned to the old gray stone building and placed the call from a phone on the wall, ignoring the bustle and noise from the lunchstand now serving breakfast.

She answered almost at once. Her voice was a whisper fluttering with terror. When he learned Janos Petofi was on the premises, he said, instantly recalling the man's yellow sheet, "Where's your daughter?"

"At school. Why?"

"Because Mr. Petofi may or may not be dangerous to you, but—"

"He's still working down by the pond." He heard the panic in her voice. "I'm leaving now."

"Lock the doors!" he shouted, seeing heads turn. "Wait till I get there. Where's Mr. Cassady?"

"He's gone back to New York."

"Carole, I'm on my way!"

"I won't be here," she said, in a rush. "But don't worry, I've got a gun." And then he heard the click and the humming on the line.

Jesus, what now?

He returned to his car on the double, breathing hard, and switched on the siren and blue lights before he was out onto the street.

If she was leaving, where the hell did she think she was going?

Better to make sure, gun or no gun. Christ, did the girl even know how to use a weapon? And if she did, *could* she use it?

Yes. By now he'd begun to think she could.

Had he written off Janos Petofi in his own mind? No. He had not written off anyone, not yet.

But if Petofi was guilty, would he show up this morning to work at her house? Was he cunning enough to think that pretending it was an ordinary day would prove his innocence? Would he have the chutzpah to risk it?

Or was he there for another purpose altogether? Knowing he was under suspicion or even thinking he was going to be arrested, was he there now to make *sure* that Carole could not testify against him?

Every muscle and nerve stiff, suddenly very cold, Henry drove faster, hearing the urgent howl of the siren, cursing himself for having wasted time. He radioed the Sheffield station, and dispatched a car to the Jensen house: "No siren, routine inquiry, why hasn't Mrs. Jensen come in to sign the complaint? But extreme caution on approach. And at once, damn it, *now!*"

Hurrying, skipping the shower, her hands fumbling, Carole had dressed—whipcord slacks, tan bucks, yellow turtleneck—and now she was coming down the stairway, her tweed car coat over one arm, the large flat portfolio containing her sketches in the other hand. Very organized, very much under control, but still in the grip of fear, straining to hear every sound outside.

The car coat did not seem heavy, even though she'd placed the gun in its pocket. When Rolfe had shown her how to use it, he'd said: *It's a Smith and Wesson .38—but called an airweight, it's so light. I hope we never have to fire it, but we're really isolated out here.* He'd warned her it would always be loaded. *No safety catch. All you have to do to shoot is to take aim and squeeze the trigger.* In the strangely quiet and empty house, she could hear the tractor engine and the whooshing suction sound of the vacuum mechanism, closer now, not on the rear lawn but on the north side of the house.

By now, though, she had begun to wonder whether she had any real cause for alarm, although her stomach was still tight and hard, almost queasy, with dread. Would Janos Petofi have come to work just as if it were an ordinary Monday if he'd been the one who'd raped her? Still, she had to get out the front door unnoticed, unobserved, and into the blue Saab before his work brought him to the front lawn—

At the foot of the stairway she put on the car coat as she stepped to the front door. Immediately after trying to reach Henry on the phone earlier, she had hurried downstairs in her robe to lock and bolt both front and rear doors.

Now, deciding to leave the portfolio on the veranda, she was twisting the lock release when the telephone behind her began to ring.

The sound seemed closer than usual, and harsh, and insistent. Henry again? He was *not* going to stop her, *nothing* was going to stop her, *nothing!*

She turned and stepped to the table. She lifted the phone and then, instead of answering, she waited, quivering inside.

"Hello, hello. May I please speak with Mrs. Jensen please?"

She did not recognize the voice. Nevertheless, she said, in a whisper: "This is Mrs. Jensen."

"Carole? It's Vincent Fletcher. How are you, my dear?"

She overcame the impulse to growl: *Couldn't be better, Mr. Fletcher, except there's a man in the yard who wants to rape me again. Or kill me.*

But, instead, she heard herself say, "I'm just going out the door, Mr. Fletcher. But I'll leave the sketches on the porch."

"No, no, no, I'm not concerned about that, nor is Miriam. What we *are* concerned about, Carole, is what all this is doing to you. To you as a person." And then he added: "Just between us, wouldn't it be better for you to stay home and rest now?"

"I'd like to, Mr. Fletcher—there's nothing I'd like better."

The sound of the tractor and the vacuum outside stopped.

"Precisely. Exactly. And there's no reason now to do anything else. The State's Attorney himself is convinced that the man who harmed you is already under arrest in New Jersey."

The silence outside was more nerve-racking, more ominous, than the sound had been.

". . . the vagrant who stole your car, he'll be punished for both crimes now."

"Mr. Fletcher, I appreciate your thinking of me, but I do have papers to sign, things like that." A lie, a lie—that's not where she was going.

Where was Janos Petofi now, where had he gone?

"None of that's as important as you are, my dear. And not even necessary now." He cleared his throat, and then his deep resonant voice continued: "Now, Carole, it's not my place to tell you what to do—"

There was no sound whatsoever outside now.

". . . but if you were my daughter—"

Had she bolted the rear door?

". . . I'd advise her that the sooner she put it all behind her, the sooner you'll—"

"I'm sorry, sir, I know you're trying to be kind—"

The tractor's motor whirred suddenly and then growled to life on the side lawn. She stopped talking to listen.

"You're a smart girl, my dear. Sooner or later you'll have to accept that it happened and it's over."

The sound of the motor seemed to be moving toward the front lawn.

She had to move.

Fast.

Into the phone she said, "Chief Lindheim doesn't believe that, and neither do I."

Then she heard a loud, grating, clattering sound and the motor died.

And then she heard the note of frenzy in her own voice: "You're very kind but I know what I have to do, I *know!*"

She set down the phone and ran into the living room to

look out the front windows. She saw the tractor. On the front lawn. Only a few yards from the car—

But the man was not in sight.

A wild terror shot through her.

Then there was a knocking on the front door.

The blood seemed to stop flowing in her body—

The knocking was repeated. Louder now.

And then a voice. "Mrs. Jensen." *His* voice: "Could I use your phone, please?"

She shoved her right hand into the pocket of the car coat.

A shriek rose in her throat. She placed her knuckles between her teeth.

She was standing rigid, panic shimmering in her mind.

"Mrs. Jensen, I know you're in there. I can't finish the—I can't move my tractor." The whine in Janos Petofi's voice became a plea, with anger in it. "I'm not going to hurt you, Mrs. Jensen."

If she ran up the stairs and he broke the door in, or a window, she'd be trapped.

She edged into the hall, toward the telephone table, slowly. Every muscle ached and her left breast had begun to pulse and quiver with pain.

She knew now. She knew. He was the one, not David, not Jerry, *him,* he was the man who'd raped her—

Her hand closed over the gun. Her finger found the trigger.

Then she heard the man snarl: "Goddamn it, Mrs. Jensen, why'd you tell the police I did that to you? *Why?*"

With her left hand she lifted the phone off its cradle and placed it on the table. "I'm calling the police!" she shouted.

"I don't give a shit! I didn't do it and I don't give a shit!"

She was pressing the buttons with the forefinger of her left hand, taking her eyes from the closed front door for only a second: 911. "I've got a gun!" she called, her tone cold now, her mind remembering—the blanket over her head, gasping for breath, knowing she was going to die, the pain in her breast, choking, then the terrible pain when he entered her—

Abruptly then she was moving. "I'll open the door!" she heard herself scream. She was rushing to it, taking the gun from her pocket. *"I'll open the goddamn door!"*

She threw it wide.

She lifted the gun, holding it in both hands, arms extended.

He stood staring at her.

At her face.

Then his startled dark eyes went down to the gun.

His mouth opened, wide. His whole face contorted, eyes blurring with amazement, and then fear.

Then his small, muscular body went into a crouch, and he backed away across the veranda, hands rising, palms perpendicular, as if to stop a bullet he knew was coming.

Her finger was damp and trembling on the trigger.

The guy in the gunshop said never fire it unless you intend to kill.

But the man was turning on the porch steps, trying to run, stumbling, almost falling, scrambling to stay erect. "You're nuts, lady," his voice was saying, "loony, loony, loony—"

He did not stop running until he reached the tractor. He hurled himself behind it, flattening his body on the brown leaves, out of sight.

Out of range.

Slowly then she lowered the gun.

She should have killed him.

She knew, she was positive now—why hadn't she shot him dead?

Would she be sorry later that she hadn't?

Could she risk running to the car?

Gun in hand, lifted again, she stepped outside, eyes on the tractor. He was out of sight.

If he moved, she'd do it.

When she was down the two steps off the veranda, she still did not run. With the gun directed at the tractor, her finger tight on the trigger, she arrived at the car and opened the door with one hand.

"The nine-eleven call that wasn't completed, Chief." Officer Benita Hendryx's voice on the radio was clipped, cool, precise. "It originated in the Jensen residence all right, and the phone's still off the hook there."

"I'm almost there—crossing the Lake Lillinonah Bridge now. Out."

He didn't even glance to see whether the area below was still cordoned off.

Seconds later, without slowing, tires screaming, Henry swung the car onto Harrow Road, then turned off the light and siren. In another few moments he was braking and turning the cruiser's nose into the driveway.

A Town of Sheffield police car was parked in the area where the pavement curved to circle a huge old oak tree. Car 7. Recalling the day's schedule which he had set up at 6:00 A.M., Henry realized, with a silent groan, that Duane Jessup would be on duty here.

On the lawn the truck, which he recognized instantly as Janos Petofi's, was standing with the small yellow tractor behind it, two long wooden planks angled from the tractor's front wheels up to the bed of the truck. And beside it Duane Jessup was standing facing Janos Petofi, who was slumped in the seat of the tractor, head down over the wheel. In the same instant that he climbed out of his car, Henry saw the front door of the house standing open and the officer's hand hovering above his weapon.

"Where's Mrs. Jensen?" Henry asked, approaching the two men over the damp leaves.

"The missus left before I got heah," Jessup drawled. "This chac'tuh was jist sittin' heah like this." A note of awe crept into his slow nasal drone: "He wants me to 'rest him, he *says.*"

"Did you search the house?" Henry asked.

"No, sir. I don't have no warrant tuh—"

"Search the house!" Henry barked. "Look in all the closets." And then, as the officer shambled away on his long spindly legs, Henry turned his attention to Janos Petofi. "You want to be arrested? Why?" And when there was no answer: "What'd you do to her, Petofi?" From where he was standing Henry could see the end of the long pond beyond the house, and felt his balls tighten with dread. "Janos," he said, in a different, friendlier tone, "if you've got anything to say, now's the time to say it." He stepped closer. Very softly, very gently, he asked, "Where's Mrs. Jensen?"

Slowly the man lifted his head from the wheel. His pockmarked face was bleak with a kind of stunned resignation. "Damned if I know," he said, his voice blurred. "That woman's out of her fuckin' mind. Man, she's bonkers."

"You want to explain that?" Henry asked, exerting rigid control, but aware the dark-haired man had said *is,* not *was.* "You want to confess to the rape, right? What else?"

This caused Petofi's dark eyes to go black and flat. "What *else?*"

"Today. Here. What else?"

"Her car's gone, ain't it? I told him, the other one. She got in and peeled out of here like she was in orbit."

"Don't shit me," Henry said. To hell with rules, he was on the street again. "Now climb down here, turn around and put your hands on the hood." He waited for the young man to get off the tractor. "Turn around and spread your feet apart. You been searched before."

He had not touched the .38 in his holster. He did a body search. Rougher than usual. Rougher than necessary. Petofi was clean.

Then, tensing to hear Duane Jessup's voice from the house, he said, "Now look at me. Not that way, look me in the eye. Now, why did Mrs. Jensen call the police and not wait for an answer?"

"Because she's nuts."

Then something that Petofi saw in Chief Lindheim's eyes caused him to take a single step to one side.

Henry's hand went to the .38 and Petofi changed his mind. His body froze. Henry lifted the gun from its holster nevertheless.

"Oh God," Petofi groaned. "How'd I get into this?" He turned sullen then. "All I tried t'ask her was t'use her phone. My fuckin' tractor broke down."

"So she dialed the police; make sense, Petofi."

"I told the Southern guy, I'll tell you. She came to the door with a revolver in her hand." Then he groaned again. "She thinks I raped her. I seen it in her eyes." A whining came into his voice. "You both think I did it. That bitch was going to kill me! I wish she had; I ain't got a chance. I know how things work." He closed his eyes and leaned against the tractor. "Why me? Why me?"

"You tell me, Janos. And if you call Mrs. Jensen a bitch one more time, I'm going to break your jaw. You tell me why we were summoned here."

Petofi opened his eyes. "That kid in Hackensack, right? One mistake. Only thing I did was put my hand on her leg. Maybe I wanted to do more but I didn't. Her old lady started running and screaming. Cops dropped the case, I was only in jail one night—Christ, they gonna hound me all my life 'cause that's in their goddamn computers?"

Henry had heard this story before in various forms. To a degree, he understood. "Mr. Petofi," he said, formal again, "I'm going to ask you one more time—"

"I didn't touch her!" Petofi's face was twisting, and his voice screeched: "I didn't rape Mrs. Jensen but by Jesus I wish I had now! I had every chance, lotsa times. I wish I'd gone in there this morning and tore off her clothes and shoved it to her. At least I'd a got *something* out of this!"

Tempted to lift the gun in his right hand and smash it

across the man's face, Henry swung with his left instead. It happened so fast he didn't realize he'd moved till he felt the blow jarring up his arm, heard the ugly bone-on-bone sound, saw blood, and then stood, legs apart, watching the man's body sliding down the hood of the tractor.

Then he heard another voice. "Jee-sus, Chief," Officer Jessup said, coming fast, staring. "Jesus."

Henry saw the handcuffs in the officer's hand as he stepped toward the fallen man. He saw Janos Petofi staring up at him, blood between his lips, his eyes hopeless, no longer furious, shaking his head, the resignation returning.

"What's the charge?" Officer Jessup asked.

"Suspicion of sexual battery on a female," Henry growled, already ashamed, already regretful. "Don't book him till I get there, just mug shots and prints."

Henry stalked toward the house, cursing Jessup, cursing Petofi, cursing himself, and went in through the front door.

First, he picked up the humming telephone, which Jessup, of course, had not even noticed, and placed it in its cradle.

Then he made a thorough search of the big house, by now convinced it was a waste of time. As he had been last night, he was again impressed by its pleasing atmosphere of comfort and casual living, in spite of its size and spaciousness. On the top of the desk in the den was a photograph of Mr. and Mrs. Rolfe Jensen: not a close shot, a boat behind them, both wearing sailing whites, smiling and happy. Without hesitation he removed the picture from its frame and slid it into the side pocket of his uniform.

When he'd gone through the whole house, noticing that Carole's three vials of medicine were still on the nightstand —wouldn't she need them, wherever she was?—he went outside and walked to the bathhouse.

Mr. A. L. Cassady had left the guest room a mess. The portable typewriter on the desk was not covered, a half-filled quart of gin beside it, the floor was littered with crunched-up wads of typing paper. Why had he left so abruptly? And when? And after he'd been warned not to leave the area, *goddamn it!* All Carole had said on the phone was: *He's gone back to New York.* Well, his photograph had been on the dust jacket of his book in the Sheffield Library and since he'd served in Nam, his prints would also be available. Just because Cassady was in love with Carole, as any fool could see, it did not preclude the possibility that he may have raped her. Maybe the opposite: it could be the *motive.*

When he was back in the squad car he radioed the station even though he was only minutes away.

"Has Officer Jessup come in with a Janos Petofi yet?"

"Just two or three minutes ago, Chief."

"Get his photograph and fingerprints," Henry told her, "then release him."

"Release him?"

"You heard me, Officer Hendryx. He's not our man. Out."

Then he realized he had finally eliminated his third suspect. Or had he really done that, without being aware of it, even before he'd ordered him taken into custody? He could tell himself now that he had to have the photograph and prints, just in case. But why snooker himself? He'd arrested him for the same reason he'd decked him—because of what he'd said about Carole. Damned unprofessional, Henry—but a man's already dead when he can't feel outrage anymore.

All along, he had realized that even someone as plain stupid as Petofi wouldn't rape and/or murder a woman and then sit waiting for the police.

Forget Petofi—one less possibility to deal with. The question now was where Carole had gone. And why.

Another fear began then to seep through his mind. Carole had told him, and Petofi had confirmed it, that she had a gun, and that she was either out of control, or on the verge of it.

Christ, the whole case was turning into some complex and potentially tragic pattern so interwoven and tangled that even if the perpetrator was finally apprehended, convicted, and imprisoned, the girl's whole life—and how many others?—would be changed. Even if she didn't collapse emotionally, no matter what, her life would never be the same again. Nor would she.

He was remembering Luisa again as he turned into the small parking lot alongside the Sheffield station: she had never recovered from what had happened to Teresa. It had destroyed her.

Entering the waiting room, he did not, at first, recognize the bearded, heavyset youngish man who stood up from the bench and said, "Chief Lindheim, r-r-remember me? David Slade?"

Henry nodded then—David Slade was on his list, had been from the beginning: lived with a young woman named Esther Morse in the saltbox on Merwyn Brook Road, not married, scientist of some sort. Carole had scoffed at the idea that David Slade could possibly have raped her.

"Thanks for coming in, Mr. Slade," Henry said. "I have to make one phone call, then I'll be with you. Sit down."

Henry took his message slips from the desk officer, then stood at the counter and scribbled the name *Aloysius Leo Cassady* on the back of one of them. "I want this man's address and phone number in New York City. Try the library across the street; they should have a Manhattan phone directory or a *Who's Who.* And tell Miss Powell I want to borrow the copy of this man's novel with a photograph on the jacket."

In his office, he went behind his desk and discovered the front page of the *Sudbury News-Chronicle* lying open there. The headline, bold and black, ran all the way across the page: HOUSEWIFE ASSAULTED IN SHEFFIELD WOODS. He let his eyes scan the first few paragraphs, noting the by-line: Joel White. The victim was carefully not identified by name, description, age, or address. Then he saw the photograph—not, thank God, of Carole but of him, goddamn Joel White and all his rights and freedoms! The caption below read: *Sheffield Police Chief Henry Lindheim leaving the scene of crime late Saturday night.*

What went through his mind then was that the newspaper probably had a photo of its employee Mr. Joel White in its files. Vincent Fletcher, he knew, would be more than delighted to provide it. But since the two "eyewitnesses" had been part of the fiction Henry himself had created and since Carole had never seen her attacker, what possible use could he make of the pictures he'd begun to collect? You never know, you never know. . . .

Sitting down quickly then, Henry read the story with swift care. Vincent Fletcher had been as good as his word . . . *Investigation progressing . . . Police have fingerprints . . . footprints . . . other unspecified but tangible evidence . . . leading Chief Lindheim to predict an early arrest . . . two unnamed witnesses have come forward and have provided authorities with a description of a suspect who was seen following the victim into the woods—*

Another long shot, but if reading this caused the perpetrator to take action—such as A. L. Cassady's leaving the area—this disinformation could be Henry's single most important maneuver so far. Although, to himself, he admitted qualms. Which, to squelch, all he had to do was to remember Carole's face when she'd laughed last night, sitting on the edge of the bed. *Henry, Henry . . . I hope someday we'll be able to, I don't know, just have fun . . . I'd love to hear you laugh, Henry!*

He shoved the newspaper to one side and began to leaf through his messages. One read: *Negative on investigation clothing stores Sudbury and New Milford. Canvassing continuing.* Since nine this morning he'd had more men than he could spare asking questions in every men's clothing store within a fifteen-mile radius—every mall, every street, all stores large and small. Beginning, he had instructed, with the more expensive shops. Damned few stores would stock snakeskin belts *or* silver slide buckles. *Another* long shot.

He made a note for himself to check the police lab in Hartford in the early afternoon. Now that he had a copy of the single thumbprint—one goddamn print!—he'd have it matched with the ones he hoped to obtain soon from at least some of the suspects. Those with prints on record and those who'd be willing to have them taken voluntarily. Without a suspect already under arrest, it was next to impossible to obtain evidence like that, prints and semen and/or blood type samples, so forth—the very evidence that could provide "probable cause" to justify the goddamn arrest!

It was a Catch-22 he'd faced before, but this time, when he lit a cigar, he tasted only a bitter sour frustration.

He reached for his private line phone and tilted back in his swivel chair, feeling a painful catch in his hip joint and realizing for the first time that it was not yet noon and he was already physically tired. Getting old, Henry, getting old . . .

He tapped out Judith's number, hoping that Carole had gone there, or possibly phoned.

Waiting, he began to think of ways to get photographs of the remaining suspects—just in case his men got lucky and came up with a store that stocked those belts.

"This is Dr. Kahn's office," Judith's voice, distorted somewhat by the answering mechanism, said into his ear. "I'm sorry I'm not available to talk now, but if you'll leave your name and number—"

Feeling a bit foolish to be speaking into a machine instead of to a person, he gritted his teeth and reported what little he knew: the incident Janos Petofi had related, her leaving the house with a gun in hand, *like she was in orbit,* and Henry's own conviction that she had had no good reason to threaten the yardman. And, to end it, he barked: "She's in no condition to be running around with a lethal weapon in her possession. If you see her, get it away from her!"

Her left breast had begun to pulsate again but the turbulence inside had subsided somewhat. In its place now was a cold, fierce determination, fixed and numbing. Beyond question, beyond reason.

She was driving south along the east side of the lake, which she could see only in flashes between the houses on her right. On her left, every few yards or so, were high, jutting stone bluffs that caused the narrow road to twist at such sharp dangerous angles that she had to grip the steering wheel with both hands, hard, to stay on the road instead of plowing into the jagged cliffs.

Liar, liar, liar—

Rolfe had always been a liar. She'd accepted that years ago. He had his faults, she had hers, *c'est la vie.* But . . . but sometimes she'd wondered whether he even knew the difference between a lie and the truth. *Sorry we're late, we had a flat. . . . Carole and I love Bermuda*—where they'd never been . . . *My father*—whom he hated for his violent abuse—*was the gentlest, sweetest man who ever lived.* Why had she accepted his lies so easily, why? Because he'd told them to others, not to her.

How long had he been lying to *her,* how long?

Carole was dimly aware, in a sort of distant way, that she was being foolish, even reckless—*stupid,* perhaps—but her mind had moved into a weird world in which she was powerless to fight the compulsion that, excluding everything else, was driving her on. It was as if that shutter had come down over her senses again and her mind was not a part of her actions, only a helpless watcher in the shadows. Shock? Duncan Clive's word. In his house. Saturday night. How long ago had that been?

And why should she think of him now? Of all people, why?

The Dixon house was a stark pattern of redwood slants

and angles on the road side and, she knew, almost completely glass, with overhanging decks on the lake side—two stories high with an enclosed boat house forming one end and a two-car garage attached to the other. Karen's familiar brown Jaguar sports car, its top in place today, was parked in the very short driveway. Carole turned in and brought the Saab to a stop beside it. When she opened the door, the air was knifelike cold and there was a steady but soundless wind, chilling and damp off the water.

On the small slate-floored stoop, Carole was remembering the genially bitter argument that periodically erupted between Jerry and Cass. *Sure we want it all,* Jerry would say. *And we want it all now—why not, why the hell not?* And afterward once Cass had said on the way home: *You two have some of the damnedest friends.*

When she touched the button, wishing she'd worn gloves, Carole heard chimes sounding through the house, in sequence, room after room, so that even when Karen opened the door, the chiming could be heard behind her.

Karen was wearing a pale blue body stocking, skintight, and nothing else. Her face was damp with sweat, a towel wrapped around her blond hair. Her blue-green eyes sharp with surprise, or trepidation, she stared. "Since when do you ring my doorbell?" She turned away. "I've been expecting you."

So it was true. Then why should she go inside, as she found herself doing? Why should she follow Karen into the long wood-paneled living room, toward the enormous fieldstone fireplace, where a log was smoldering? Why, when she knew now what she'd come to—

"Coffee, tea, a drink?" Karen asked, reminding Carole that Jerry had met Karen on a flight when she had been an airline hostess. *It started that same night—wham!* Jerry had once said. "I've been working out in the torture chamber and I need a shower, but this is more important, right? Scotch?"

"Nothing," Carole said, hating her own politeness, hating Karen and Rolfe and Jerry and all the parties she'd enjoyed here. She saw Karen shrug her slender shoulders, her full breasts high and full and moving as she walked. To drape her exquisite figure over one of the built-in divans. With the wall of full-length windows behind her, the overhanging deck and lake beyond. What was it Cass loved to quote? Something about sitting on the ground and telling sad stories of the death of kings. Carole moved toward the fireplace, watching herself as if she were an actor on a stage—what next, what now? How about the death of love? Friendship? *If you loved Carole, you wouldn't be fucking that goddamn ice queen.* Standing with her back to the dying fire, Carole let her eyes rove over the other woman's body. So this was the body that Rolfe had chosen over hers. But she was amazed: there was no fury in her. By now she had begun to have the feeling that she was in a dream, a quiet nightmare—spooky, unreal.

"I sort of expected to see your picture in the paper this morning. Don't you hate being called a housewife?"

Karen's a cool drink of water, Cass had said once. *But I guess there has to be a person there. Behind all those clichés she keeps spitting at you.*

"Do the police know?" Karen asked.

Startled, Carole stared. "The police?"

"Oh, I knew *you'd* get wise sooner or later. Well, no more suspense, let's have it. What are the police going to do to Jerry?"

"Jerry?" Her voice sounded foolish. "What're you talking about?"

"It'd be the end of his career, you know. If you press charges. Oh, we had a beautiful row on the way home from your place Saturday night. All the time he was trying to get you not to call in the police, he knew I suspected him."

Carole's head had gone faint and giddy. Astonished, she heard herself ask: "Wasn't he with you?"

"We came in separate cars. He was late." Karen suddenly leaped to her feet. "I want a drink if you don't."

Carole watched her move, lithe and lovely, down the length of the room to the bar built into the wall. "Then when we got home, he pressed one of those little buttons in his mind, turned on all that smooth shyster charm. Mellowed down with some grass on top of all that booze and tried to convince me he couldn't have raped you—get this for the legal mind at play—he couldn't have done it because he'd been in the sack all afternoon with some teenage hooker named Debbie. Works in some crummy bar on Route 6. How's that for an alibi?"

Hey, you really don't know what's going on, do you? Again remembering Jerry's voice on the phone, Carole strode along the wall of glass, seeing the sky dull and glowering over the far shore of the narrow gray lake. "Karen, let's cut the bullshit. If Jerry raped me, he'll get his, I'll see to that. I came here to talk about Rolfe. You and Rolfe."

She waited. Knowing. But she had to hear it. Why? If she already knew, *why?* Didn't she believe it, even now?

Karen turned from the bar, glass in hand—scotch and soda, Carole knew. She knew what all her friends drank. "So," Karen said, her pale thin brows arched, "so Rolfe spilled the beans, did he?"

"How long?" Carole heard herself ask, wondering why, what did it matter? "How long, Karen?" It was not a plea but a harsh demand. *"How long has my husband been fucking the ice queen?"*

"Don't *you* start calling me that. That shithead Cass. Not long. Since Christmas." She shrugged again. "Off and on." She took a long swallow. "Our Christmas party here, remember? What difference does it make, Carole? What's the big deal?" She drifted closer. "It's just one of those things. Just sex. It doesn't mean anything."

"You bitch," Carole said. It was, she realized now, what she had come to say. Only that really. So she said it again. "Cass was right—you really are a bitch."

A cold glint entered Carole's eyes, but she spoke quietly, a sly smile hovering on her lips. "Sweet, innocent Carole.

When all you had to do was open your mouth and go with it. How do you know if you won't try it?"

Rolfe had told her. It was certainty, not shock. Rolfe had discussed the most intimate part of their life with this —with this *bitch, bitch, bitch!*

The hate was there now, inside, hard and cold—but where was the anger? She thought of the gun in her pocket. She had not the slightest inclination to touch it.

"Oh Carole, relax. Come on, have a drink. You're forgetting what Jerry calls the pleasure principle."

"Jerald," Carole said then, "Jerald's the one who told me." Then she added, "When he tried to come on to me yesterday morning."

"After he'd raped you the night before." Karen nodded and strolled to gaze out at the lake through the glass wall. "Sounds like Jerry all right."

"You don't even care, do you?" But why was she asking, what could it possibly matter now?

"I care that he's gone too far this time. If he had to rape someone, really rape, not play-rape—why the hell didn't he pick on a stranger? I care one hell of a lot that he's going to be exposed. Disbarred. Or worse. I'll probably have to divorce him."

Mind reeling, Carole turned and started toward the front door—

But Karen's voice, no longer polite and light, stopped her: "You want to know about my nice, charming, respectable husband, Carole?" Karen had turned from the lake. And now her face had taken on a haggard expression, eyes bright and hard but still mocking. She looked suddenly older, the flesh of her face tight, features thin. "Jerry's always been a charter member of the knothole gang. One cunt like any other. You think I wasn't jealous once?" She drained the glass. "And you think I didn't hate it when he got into that kinky stuff? You want to see the handcuffs, the riding crop? Massages that make me howl with pain. That's what he really gets off on. And more. Making me sunbathe nude on the deck out there. Or on the deck of our boat. Making sure I can be seen by every male on every boat going by. The more miserable it makes me, the more he enjoys it. You ought to see our real video library. Strictly triple-X. All the SM numbers." Suddenly she hurled the empty glass at the stone fireplace. It shattered. "You want proof?"

No, Carole thought, no, no—

But she did not move.

Karen squirmed and shrugged and then she was half-naked, her breasts plopping out of the body stocking, that same cruel smile distorting her lips, eyes furious and defiant and demanding. She turned her body to face the deck.

And Carole stood staring at her back. Which was a mass of crisscrossed welts, dark red and purple and revoltingly ugly.

"Don't," Carole heard herself say, still unable to move. "Please, Karen—"

"Even last night," Karen said, not turning. "Look, you may as well know what he *might* have done to you. You were lucky he didn't. Look."

Her hands were peeling the tight clinging cloth down over her hips—

"No!" Carole cried and ran to the door.

"You don't want to know, do you?" And then when Carole stopped, turned to see Karen facing her: "A Ping-Pong paddle. The sandpaper kind." Then she growled: "He says he loves the *sound.* It drives him *wild.*" Her face twisted. "Most of all what he loves is hearing me cry, begging him to stop—"

For only an instant Carole was afraid that she was going to be sick to her stomach.

Or worse.

"You think I should divorce him, Carole?" Karen shrugged her bare white shoulders, breasts swinging. "I always told myself I loved my Jaguar too much." A light, teasing tone entered her voice: "Now when he's arrested,

I'll have my excuse and no one will know, will they? Except you. You and Rolfe, of course." She strolled closer. "Just think, Carole—if Jerry hadn't raped you, you'd never have known, would you? About Jerry, or about me and Rolfe."

CRACK! Not the click of a camera shutter this time. An explosion in her head, in her mind, which left her faint and dizzy—sick, *sick.*

She tore her eyes from the half-naked figure and turned to run to the door.

The cold outside struck, taking her breath, but she made it, stumbling, to the car.

Driving fast, too fast, north on the lake road, she tried to fight the sickening disgust that was engulfing her, body and mind. *You shall know the truth and the truth shall make you free.*

And then everything came surging back, roaring back, gushing—rage and horror and that sick, hot, chaotic intensity that she could not control, that wild shuddering inside that terrified her *because* she couldn't control it, she couldn't—

"You still don't believe me, do you, Chief?"

Henry leaned back in his swivel chair and peered at the dark-bearded younger man. "Mr. Slade, it's in your favor that you came in here on your own." Which of course was not totally accurate. How many times had police officers been taken in by a guilty suspect with the chutzpah to try that ploy? "By the way, you wouldn't have a photograph of yourself on you, would you?"

"Just my ID card for IKL Pharmaceuticals—no, hold on a sec—" He unbuttoned his tan cardigan sweater and reached behind his considerable girth to take a wallet from his hip pocket, "Just a snapshot, and Esther's on it, but—"

Henry leaned forward and took the small photo, glanced at it and slid it into the side pocket of his uniform.

"Thanks." And then he asked: "You always wear that kind of belt, Mr. Slade?"

"Belt?"

"I noticed just now. That slide buckle—you told me you weren't in service."

"Not me, just the opposite. Peacenik from way back, man." He rose heavily to his feet and his beard twisted into the first genuine smile Henry had seen all morning. "I go for that kind of buckle 'cause I keep losing weight, then regaining it." His hazel-colored eyes sparkled—a very disarming fellow, ingenuous, even charming—a quality that Henry had unfortunately come to distrust. "Belt's just some kind of nylon but you're right, that kind of buckle's not easy to find."

"I could use one myself," Henry said, also standing up. "Get it here in town?"

"I'll have to ask Esther. She buys my clothes from mail-order catalogs." He extended his big soft hand. "I guess I really bent your ear, didn't I? Told you more than you really wanted to know, didn't I?" David Slade's handshake was surprisingly strong. "But you want to know something else? This'll blow your mind, Chief. Talking to you, l-l-letting it all out like this—I've come to a decision. Money's not worth what that job's doing to my head. Nobody's going to stop the Armageddon, it's in the cards. Sometimes I think people really *want* it to happen. But still, I can't go on working for a c-company that manufactures nerve gas, germs for warfare. Hell, all my l-l-life, all my training—I thought we were *fighting* germs so people could *live*. Well, goodbye, sir, and thanks for l-l-listening to me. I really let it all hang out, didn't I?"

"One thing more, Mr. Slade. Since you're here. You're under no legal obligation, you understand, but it might help our investigation if we could get a set of your fingerprints."

"F-f-fingerprints, sir?"

"Takes three minutes."

David Slade's bushy brows came down over his eyes. "W-w-well, it's not the time element, I took the d-day off, but there *is* a principle involved. If you s-s-see what I mean."

"It's a little out of the ordinary," Henry said, making it very casual. "And I have no legal way to compel you." Which was putting it mildly. "Let's just say I hoped you'd volunteer."

David Slade was shaking his head. "Sorry, sir. Oh, I know how that probably strikes you, b-b-but I told you: I'm still lost in the sixties and—well, the answer's no. S-sorry, sir, that's just my moral conviction."

Henry was struggling with his goddamn anger again. The scientist was well within his right, but . . . "If you were fishing until almost six on Saturday, I'd suggest you try to find somebody who saw you at the lake. And don't wander too far from home."

At the door, his light brown eyes resentful for the first time, David Slade said, "The reason I came in was because Carole seemed to suspect me herself. On the phone. Now you've got the same idea, don't you?"

"Good morning, Mr. Slade."

After the door closed, Henry flipped one of the levers on the old-fashioned intercom and instructed Benita Hendryx at the dispatch desk to remind all the officers canvassing the men's clothing shops not to overlook the larger retail department stores, especially those with mail-order catalogs, such as Sears and Spiegel's and Penney's. Even while he spoke, he cursed himself for having to be reminded that more people than ever shopped by mail these days.

Officer Hendryx then informed him that Janos Petofi's prints, taken a short time ago, did not match the thumbprint in the Jensen case. So Henry had been justified in not holding Petofi and now he didn't need the mug shots.

Two solid days work and everything falling out negative, negative, negative—

"Chief Lindheim. Officer Greer—Charlotte Greer—she

phoned in from home to ask what time you want to see her this morning."

Henry swallowed his pride, a big gulp, and said, "Inform Officer Greer that I lost my temper last night and that I hope she'll accept my apology."

He flipped off the intercom and reminded himself again that he had to keep more rigid control of himself—had to if he was going to do Carole any good.

Then he picked up his private-line phone and tapped out Judith's number again, expecting and dreading the recorded voice on the answering machine. But, instead, she herself came on: "Dr. Kahn."

"Judith, nobody knows where Carole is and she's carrying a lethal weapon. Don't you listen to that goddamn machine of yours?"

"Don't bark at me, Henry Lindheim. I have your message and Carole has not come in or phoned."

"Well, she's accused a man already this morning, with a gun in her hand—a man who's definitely innocent. Listen, Judith, she's on the edge. We both know it and you're the one who can help me close out this case before she—"

"Henry, I've already come dangerously close to violating a patient's confidentiality. The information that I happen to have is secondhand, from another patient."

"All I want is a name, Judith."

"No way. No judge in the country would subpoena—"

"Then you might have to do it as a favor to me!"

"Not even for you, Henry. And stop growling."

"Then for *her,* goddamn it!"

He noted the long pause. Was she considering? Then: "You have your code, Henry. I have mine. I'll try to talk with her. Good-bye, Henry."

He set down the phone, remembering: *You go over to Duncan Clive's studio,* Rolfe Jensen had said last night. *Ask him your goddamn questions!*

Not a bad idea. Henry took down his uniform cap from the rack and went out the back door. Not a bad idea, but also, Henry knew, the guilty almost invariably try to place the blame on someone else.

It was getting colder by the minute. Winter was settling in again, fast.

He had driven out of the Village before he realized that he hadn't told anyone where he was heading. Another little slip of memory. But they were occurring too often lately. Much too often!

Could it be possible that, somehow, Carole had learned that her husband had not been working on Saturday? In her present state of mind, what would she conclude from that?

God, that'd be too much, that's all, too goddamn much!

Now he was warning himself again that he had reached an unprofessional level of involvement—was he as helpless in the grip of his own emotions as Carole might be in the grip of hers? He'd have to cool it. For *her* sake, he'd damned well have to cool it, that's all!

Frustration and a helpless urgency tugging at his mind, he flipped on the blue light and siren and plunged the accelerator to the floor. Then, for the first time, a thought came to him that brought that shot-away empty feeling back to his gut. What if . . . what if he'd outsmarted himself? What if the story in the paper, intended to flush out or cause the perpetrator to act . . . what if it had done just that and the man had, somehow, somehow, found a way to keep Carole from coming in to sign the official complaint this morning—

His mind was again in turmoil as he bent over the wheel.

Did Duncan Clive imagine that he'd gotten away with his lie?

And that bearded young scientist, he probably still thought of all police officers as pigs—did he imagine he was free and clear just because he'd put on a convincing act? Even tears in his eyes—*I swear, Chief, f-f-for almost a solid year n-n-now, I've been a stranger to m-m-m-myself, shaking inside, no sleep, busting into tears at the damnedest times*—if he thought a scam like that would work with Henry Lindheim, who had been conned by every sociopath and psychopath and streetwise junkie and wino and pervert in New York City. Only thing David Slade had established was that he was unstable as hell and *could* be capable of anything.

Do you do drugs yourself, Mr. Slade?

N-n-not me. I tried that route years ago. "Strawberry Fields Forever"—no m-m-more "Purple Haze" for this slob.

You forget things, though, don't you? Such as the way you kissed Mrs. Jensen last Christmastime—

Oh, she told you about that? Well, that was just some k-k-kind of drunken urge, I don't know—

You get these urges, do you?

Doesn't everybody? Every male, anyway. And Carole's such a lovely girl—

Well, Henry had enough hard-earned savvy not to be taken in. And if Slade thought a police officer was a priest, or minister, or rabbi, if he expected absolution, forgiveness, a ticket to heaven—

. . . beginning to think I might be c-c-cracking up . . . n-n-not that I can't have sex, but I don't w-w-want to . . . l-l-like I'm dead inside—

So . . . so just to make sure, just to prove you're not, how about following your friend, also your wife's friend, around in your car till she gives you a chance, then throw a blanket over her head and take her by force, like some animal?

Only two men off the hook, Slade. Two. Mendoza and Scott Keller. And now Janos Petofi, but not you, not you—

Or your friend, that smartass shyster Dixon. That bastard knew how an investigation worked: he'd be shrewd enough to wear beltless trousers today even if he had to dig out an old suit—

Henry saw the red light blinking and picked up the mike.

"Chief, more bad news. Footprint report from the State Police lab. I really hate to tell you—"

"Spit it out."

"It seems Trooper Dworsky had the idea to do the matchup. The prints fit Officer Duane Jessup's shoes exactly."

It figured. Oh holy God yes, it figured. Another fuck-up. And this time Trooper Dworsky had seen it coming!

By the time Carole arrived home, she was empty. The shuddering had stopped. Not, she realized vaguely, because she had been able to control it—possibly because the panic had been drained from her mind when she had had to stop alongside the road to open the door and lean out to throw up, emptying her stomach. A dry heaving, she'd had no breakfast, a chest-crushing series of convulsions, paroxysms. Which had left her drained, aching. At the same time she had begun to feel, if not relief, a strange composure anyway. No longer frantic, a deep quiet, even though she had never been more at sea, lost. She could see herself from above, drifting in a very small boat on a very calm but limitless gray sea.

In the driveway she saw the red truck and yellow tractor still parked on the lawn. Distantly she wondered why Janos Petofi had left them there. Then, for some unexplainable reason, this caused her to think of the gun in her pocket as she climbed out of the car.

When she was inside—why had she left the front door unlocked?—the house, her house, her home was like a strange, empty, silent tomb.

And she wondered what she was doing here. She found herself leaning against the door, staring blindly. Her body was weak and slack.

The phone was ringing. She heard the sound as if it were coming from her studio room up in the tower, or from the guest room by the pond, or from the woods even farther away. But she could see it while it went on ringing, only a few feet away.

What did its ringing have to do with her?

Still, still . . . she supposed she did have to stop its ringing, didn't she?

So she stepped to the table, her legs stiff.

If it was Henry, she had to tell him what she knew now. Not about Karen and Rolfe, no, she'd never tell anyone that, but about Jerald: his own wife was convinced he had raped her. The pleasure principle—

She picked up the phone. And listened.

"Carole?"

She knew that voice—not Henry's. The nausea threatened to come back.

"Carole, is that you? It's me—Rolfe."

"*Is* it?" she heard herself ask.

"Where've you been?"

"Visiting," she said, relieved that the rage and revulsion did not return. She was not even tempted to tell him where she'd been.

"Listen, have you heard from Cass?"

"No."

"There's no answer at his apartment in New York. I've been having my secretary call every half-hour."

"Susan, you mean?" The girl's face, young and lovely, flickered in Carole's mind. Distantly she realized that she probably should have been suspicious, or jealous. In that faraway time when she had never been suspicious or jealous . . .

"Sure, Susan, who else? Hey, Carole, you sound wiped out. I know you're pissed at me, but—"

"I'm not pissed at you," she said. "I hate you."

"I know, I know. But it was as much Cass's fault as mine."

"Who?" What was he saying? "Whose fault?"

"Cass. But he'll get over it. So will you. We were both bombed out of our skull last night."

"I always get over everything, don't I?"

"Listen, Carole, are you alone?"

"I've never been more alone," she said. And then: "Why?"

"I'm at a pay phone outside the plant. So we can talk privately. Remember, I said this morning: There's something I have to ask you. It's . . . well, it's something that's been on my mind. All day yesterday. And all last night. Now—don't get angry. Promise?"

Sandy's voice echoed in her mind: *Promise, Mommy? Promise?*

"Ask it," she said, but she could not use his name. "I'm listening."

"Well, I've been trying to think of a way to put it into words. I thought maybe on the phone—"

"I'm going to hang up."

"No, don't. Don't do that, darling. Please."

In the brief silence the word *darling* cut through her mind like the blade of a razor.

"What I've got to know, just *got* to because it's been driving me wacko . . . is this: Saturday, when that creep, whoever he is, when he did what he did to you . . . did you feel anything? I mean, it'd be natural, we're all human, right?"

"I don't feel human," she said, not certain she'd heard.

"What I'm asking: did you feel, you know, even a little of what . . . well, what you feel when you and I make love?"

It took a long moment for the meaning to reach her.

She kept waiting for the shock.

The rage.

But instead, what she felt was an awesome sense of inevitability. As if she should have expected this. She should have realized that the question had to occur to him. Not that she knew him, not that she had ever really known him—

"I loved it." She heard the words, her breast shriveling

with pain again, her vagina again feeling the painful thrusts, her body crushed under the body pumping on top of her while she fought for breath, choking with hate—

"What did you say, Carole?"

"I said I loved it. I loved every second of it."

There was a yawning silence. Vast. Empty.

Oddly satisfying.

Finally his voice: "Carole, I know you better than that. You . . . you told me you wanted to kill him—"

"Don't you?"

"What?"

"Don't you want to kill him?" Her tone was quiet and level—almost serene. "*Why* don't you?" As if she didn't know. "If you loved me, you would."

"Jesus, Carole."

"Don't you even want to know who?"

"I've got a meeting this afternoon, but I'm coming home."

Her hand reached into the pocket of her car coat. Her fingers touched the gun. "If you come home, I'll kill you."

Another silence. Not so long this time.

Then: "Are you telling me you know who raped you?"

"Law of the jungle," she heard herself quoting. "You want something, take it, just so you cover your ass."

"Carole, what the hell, *answer* me."

"Karen knows. Your ice queen knows. Jerry Dixon knows. And you're just like him." She replaced the phone, very quietly.

So this is the way the world ends.

Knowing also what she had to do now, she stepped and went up the stairs very slowly, her knees hurting.

Not with a bang but a whimper.

By the time she reached the upstairs hall the phone was ringing again. She moved to the table and picked it up and placed it on the table and continued along the hallway to the door of the stairway to the attic, where the luggage was stored.

* * *

"Where in the name of God do people get the notion that artists and writers do not really *work?*" Pouring himself a whiskey, which Henry had already refused as they came inside, Duncan Clive was grumbling in that odd English accent with the burr in it.

Henry had already apologized for interrupting when he'd found the sculptor on the outside deck built onto the rear end of the weathered old barn. Working in the cold, he had been using a small, humming, sanding tool on the life-size female figure of pale, raw wood. Now, inside, Henry was damned if he'd repeat the apology. Flat out he said: "You have not visited your ex-wife *or* your sixteen-year-old daughter in more than three years. I ain't here to play games, Mr. Clive." The word *ain't* echoed a warning in his mind, but he went on regardless: "And I ain't here to watch you get drunk before noon."

The burly, red-bearded, red-haired man smiled in a dour sort of way. "Ye've been talking with my ex, have you?" He took a long swallow of whiskey from the brown coffee mug and said no more. Arrogant sonofabitch. But Henry knew how to wait—he'd spent half a lifetime doing it.

They were now in the rear half of the big barn—which looked like a huge carpenter's shop, with workbenches along the walls, electric lathes and sanding wheels and saws fixed to their surfaces. Above, steel cables extended down from a metal track, holding an enormous log still covered with bark. There was the pleasant smell of raw wood and sawdust in the air.

But Henry was not in a pleasant mood. "Being lied to burns my gut," he warned.

It was as if he hadn't spoken. "How's Mrs. Jensen faring?" Duncan Clive demanded.

"Not well," Henry said, irked by the quick change of subject, hearing the hostile gruffness in his tone. He did not add: *She has a gun and I have reason to think she's coming apart at the seams.* Nor did he say, *I'm here to find out whether it's your fault, you cocky bastard.*

Duncan Clive set his mug on the bench and took his Irish fisherman's sweater off over his head. A tight black T-shirt covered his brawny chest and, instead of a belt, an old frayed necktie held up his rumpled and stained gray flannels. "I trust ye'll tell the lass I inquired." He picked up the mug and began to pace up and down in the sawdust on the plank floor. *She's a bonny lass,* the man had said on Saturday night, with admiration. Or possibly with something else as well. . . . "Chief, do ye by chance have a daughter yourself?"

"I had a daughter." It was an area of life he did not discuss. "We're talking about *your* daughter, goddamn it."

Duncan Clive stopped walking, his back to Henry. "I *was* in Cambridge day before yesterday and I *did* see my daughter. That was God's truth. But she did not see *me.*"

"Did anyone see you while you were there?"

Shaking his head, Duncan Clive turned to face him. Anger had entered his eyes. And possibly pain. "She did not see me because I made sure she wouldn't. I drive around the neighborhood. Sometimes I park down the street, or across it. I see her come out or go in. Sometimes I don't see her at all, so I drive home." His voice hardened: "You can believe that or not! I go up there when the loneliness and the longing get to be too much in my blood." His stare dared Henry to doubt him.

And Henry had to remind himself that the perpetrators of some of the worst crimes he'd ever investigated had tried (some had succeeded) in rousing his pity. And Mr. Duncan Clive had had plenty of time by now to concoct and rehearse his story. Because of which, Henry said: "I'll have to have more than that, Mr. Clive."

"According to the terms of the divorce—that was seven years ago—I was to have what they call, in this country, visitation rights." Duncan Clive had begun to move again, not pacing—prowling. "One bloody weekend a month.

This seemed to work for three years, but Francie was growing up—the child became more and more high-strung, and hostile, and depressed. Elaine of course concluded this was my fault, too. But she was not the one who decided. I did. For Francie's sake. Well, I've tried to live up to my bargain, as they say." He was now walking in long swift strides, but like a blind man, in an erratic pattern. "I *did* live up to it, too—" His voice was harsh and furious. "Don't ye see, man? I have to watch her grow into a woman even if I cannot share it."

In spite of himself, Henry suggested: "You had to eat somewhere. Someone must have seen you, Mr. Clive. Lunchroom, diner, restaurant—did you talk to anyone, charge gas on a credit card?"

"I don't use credit cards." He grunted an ugly laugh. "I have no credit—not with the bills my wife'd run up. An' the child support. An' the alimony." He shook his rust-red beard and grinned at Henry, moving toward him. "But you're not interested in all this, Chief."

"I'm interested in why your marriage didn't work," Henry said, hating the compassion he'd begun to feel, hating that ache in his mind that he knew could be his enemy.

Duncan was close now, head tilted again with just the suggestion of a taunt in his gray eyes. "You mean: did I rape someone and my wife found out about it?"

This, Henry had to admit, had not occurred to him. "Did you?"

"Elaine will tell you I'm a sex-mad swinger with a lust for every female who comes into my ken." He was speaking in a slow, bemused, self-mocking tone. "Sketching or clay-modeling from the human female form was tantamount to fornication in the woman's mind."

"All in her mind," Henry said—not quite a question, *or* an accusation.

"Chief Lindheim, I've always had nothing but contempt for men who discuss these things with other men, but I'll tell you to satisfy your professional curiosity and you may believe me or not, as you bloody well choose." He moved to the open door and stared outside. "My ex was and is neurotically, obsessively jealous. You have no idea the pity I felt for the ways she tormented herself in those years." An edge came into his voice and he turned to face Henry again. "But when that jealousy was turned on our own daughter, when she began to accuse me of loving Francie more than I loved *her*—and vice versa—well, I couldn't let the child grow into adolescence with that sickness in the house." He strode to the bench. "You won't mind if I have another, will you?"

It was Henry's turn to move. He stepped to the workbench where the man was pouring another drink. "Regardless of all you've told me," he said, "I have to ask you whether your fingerprints are on file anywhere."

"Ye know I don't have a criminal record because you've bloody well looked it up. But I'll drop by the station and ye can make a set—at *my* request—any time you'd like."

"How about two o'clock today?"

Duncan Clive was grinning again. "Two o'clock," he said.

"And one other thing. Do you have a photograph of yourself that I could borrow?"

"The morning paper said ye had a witness."

"Could be," Henry lied. "Do you have a picture?"

Promptly, glass in hand, Duncan Clive went to the door that led from the workshop into the living quarters of the barn. "Some of those ridiculous publicity shots around here somewhere."

While Duncan Clive was gone, Henry had to admit to himself that his suspicions had faded somewhat. Unless, of course, what he'd been listening to was a whole logical-sounding pack of lies.

When he returned, Duncan Clive handed him a plain nine-by-twelve manila envelope and then, his face grave and eyes strangely sad, said, "May I ask *you* a question, Chief?"

"I may not answer it," Henry warned him.

"Ye said ye had a daughter yourself—"

"She's been dead for twenty years," Henry said, flatly.

"I'm sorry," Duncan Clive said. "But I think I surmised. Christ, man, forgive me."

Then it was Henry who surmised: "You have also guessed how she died, haven't you?"

"Aye, I think I have. Aye."

Henry realized, astonishment moving through him, that after all these years he was finally free to talk about Teresa's death. First with Carole yesterday, now with this stranger. Except for Judith, seven years ago, when he himself was on the brink, he had never—

"Why," Duncan Clive asked in a whisper, "why should you be ashamed to admit that you love Carole Jensen?"

Still Henry could not find or force a word to his lips. Damn the cheeky bastard, *damn* him!

"I'm not ashamed to say it, " Duncan Clive said.

Startled, frowning, Henry said: "You just met her." Was the man trying to con him after all?

"I met her several hours before you did." And then, when Henry only grunted: "Damned if I thought it could happen to me. *Comfort me with apples for I am sick of love.* She broke my heart in here the other night. And damned if I've been able to get the lass off my mind since. And I have not slept more than twenty winks for two nights."

"Keep yourself available, Mr. Clive," Henry said, and then he went out into the cold air and along the deck, and down the steps, then along the side of the barn to get into his car.

To discover the radio light blinking red.

"Why didn't you beep me?" he demanded, his emotions chaotic.

"Nothing urgent," Benita Hendryx informed him. "Sergeant Dozier, Car Nine, just reported from Sudbury. He's located a small men's store that stocks the belt you're interested in, but the owner's not cooperating."

"Address?"

"One-eleven Elm Street, just off Main, Morgan's Men's Shop. Sergeant Dozier's standing by."

"Tell him to wait, and not press the owner. ETA: fifteen minutes. *Less.* And Officer Hendryx—hereafter—let *me* decide what's *urgent.*"

Automatically he lowered the accelerator, flipping on the blue light and siren as he turned onto Route 133 toward Route 7. And now he began to wonder whether his mistrust of Duncan Clive, which he could not throw off, remained with him because the man had said he had fallen in love with Carole Jensen.

Wily, wily. Sensing Henry's own feelings, the clever Scotsman had played on them. Had he also fed him a phony story about his daughter? Only to add the clincher: that he also loved Carole. Love at first sight—what the hell kind of an old fool did he think he was playing games with?

Hell, on Saturday night at the hospital Carole couldn't even remember the man's name. She didn't know the bastard existed.

Since she had no idea where she was going (not that she gave a damn) and since she was never coming back, Carole had decided that the two large leather suitcases and the canvas backpack that Sandy always claimed as hers would not hold enough. You can't give up everything, you can't leave *everything* behind. . . .

Calm at the core now, mind fixed, she was concentrating on the job at hand. Sitting on the floor in Sandy's room, she was trying to choose. How could a five-year-old have so many pairs of shoes? More important, which ones still fit?

Along the highway somewhere, whichever highway she chose to travel, whichever direction—she could call Henry from a payphone. To tell him about Mr. Jerald S. Dixon, Attorney-at-Law, sadist, all-American shithead, quoting his own wife who also thought he was a rapist! Henry would know how to get him to confess. If she didn't wait to call until she was out of the house, Henry would try to stop her. She'd probably have to come back to testify at the trial, but that was even further into the future.

But she had to hurry now. Just in case Rolfe did come, if he cared enough to come—if he dared to come!

She stood up, knees catching, and tossed two more pairs of colored sneakers and a red-lettered T-shirt to the bed, alongside the backpack that Sandy considered hers.

Her breast was throbbing, which reminded her that she must remember to pack the medicines in her cosmetic kit. So she crossed the hall to her bedroom—correction: *had* been hers, once upon a time, another century, another world, another planet—

Sadness hovered on the edges of her consciousness. And a Bob Seger song was playing in her head, the words she had never really understood till now: *I wish I didn't know now what I didn't know then—*

In the bathroom she opened the door of the towel cabinet and took her cosmetics case down from the top shelf.

If she phoned Henry now, as she knew she should, he'd only try to change her mind. He'd say she was in shock, or acting in panic. When there was no panic in her, none. She'd never felt so together, and calm, and certain.

She placed the case on the new marble surface alongside the old marble basin. Then she opened the door of the medicine cabinet over the basin, faced with more decisions—

Did it matter, to hell with it, she began to empty the contents into the cosmetics kit, jars and bottles, a jumbled clatter everything, his, hers, ours—take it all!

Without closing the lid, it wouldn't close, she carried the kit into the bedroom, placed it on the dressing table, and turned to the drawers to start packing her own suitcase on the bed.

But . . . but what was she doing in here? Had she finished in Sandy's room?

She'd forgotten Sandy's koala bear. Where was it? What else? She couldn't leave behind anything that Sandy would particularly miss, or some piece of clothing she loved.

She was in the hall again. She saw the phone. It was not in its cradle. How could that have happened? She lifted it into place. Then, instead of crossing into Sandy's room, she went along the wide hall and opened the door to the attic steps. Again.

Wondering what she was doing.

And why.

She was mounting the narrow musty-smelling stairway (she had it now: more suitcases for packing) when she heard the telephone ringing. Hadn't she taken it off the hook a while ago?

Well, let it ring!

Then why was she coming down again?

If it was Henry, she'd have to tell him. About Jerry. Karen and Jerry. Not about Rolfe. Not about her whole life, which had become a bleak black lie!

She was going along the upstairs hall.

Shame. She could never tell Henry, or anyone. She was like her parents after all: *Your mother and I are a different generation—we feel shame over things that perhaps you wouldn't.*

Shame. Passing Sandy's room, she wondered, again, what she'd ever be able to say to her. Ever, ever, ever. How could she *ever* explain till Sandy was old enough?

The phone would not stop ringing.

If it was Rolfe again—

She stopped and stood rigid at the small table.

If it was Rolfe, she would simply hang up and then leave the phone off the hook. Again.

She lifted the phone, bracing herself, saying nothing.

"Carole, is that you?" Not Rolfe's voice, Dr. Judith's,

low-pitched, strained, demanding. "Carole, I know you're on the line. I *insist* you talk to me."

"I don't have time." Had she really said that? To Dr. Judith? "I'm leaving, I don't have time."

"Would you wait for me if I came there right away?"

"No!" She couldn't handle that now. Dr. Judith would try to change her mind, too. Everyone was always telling her what to do. Rolfe, in particular. "I don't need you now," she heard herself saying. "I don't need anyone."

There was a silence.

She began to lower the phone. She couldn't explain—

"Don't hang up," Dr. Judith's voice said. "You're my patient, Carole, and I insist that you listen to me."

Slowly she placed the phone at her ear, and heard: "Henry's been worried, and so have I, Carole."

"Why's everyone making so much of a little old rape?" She heard the words and wondered who was speaking them. "The males of this world are always shoving their cocks into females they don't love. No one makes love anymore. Everyone thinks fucking and sucking and God knows what else is the same as making love. It's the national pastime in the jungle, Doctor. The pleasure principle. You and Henry are living in another world. And so was I, once."

In the silence then, out of breath, she was thinking of Rolfe stripping down in the bedroom last night, *his* cock extended and bulging and bobbing, excited by the idea of another man fucking his wife—

"Have you finished, Carole?"

"I'm perfectly fine, Doctor. I've been visiting one of my best friends, the ice queen herself, who's not so icy after all. Whose husband, she's certain, is the one who raped me."

But then she stopped herself. She was thinking of Rolfe's suspicions, his jealousy, his questions, even about Henry and Mr. Fletcher. Guilt, his own guilt—not love, not even possession, just guilt. And that last question, the one that had tormented him, the one that he'd had to have an answer to *(I loved it)*—now she knew why he really had to know! Oh, what a phony lying sonofabitch—

"I can't see why," she said into the phone, "I can't see why everyone's making so much of a single little rape. My husband's been raping me for eight years." She wasn't speaking the words, she was listening to them, and they were true, true. "He never loved me. He told me himself. He's been waiting for my father to die so he can be rich, so he can quit work."

"Carole. Dear girl, you're not *thinking* again. Listen to my words now, please. You're frightening me. Listen and *think*. You must do as I tell you—"

"You said that's what I've been doing all my life, what others expect me to do. *You* said it."

Dr. Judith's voice lifted. "Well, I'm saying it again. Whatever happens to you now is up to *you*. Only *you* can save yourself. There's a big wind blowing, a monsoon, and you're loaded to the danger line. Okay, what does a reasonable, *thinking* person do if she doesn't want the ship to go down?"

"She unloads some of the cargo. That's what I'm doing. I'm unloading my goddamn husband."

Another silence. Did Dr. Judith laugh, or did Carole imagine it? "All right, dear, your decision. But, *not* a decision to be reached while you're in this state."

"I never saw things more clearly in my life!"

"There's something else you've found out, isn't there?"

In a tone so low she could barely hear it, Carole said, "It's the same thing. It's all part of the same thing. My whole life is one big terrible lie."

"Somehow I doubt that, Carole. But not that you feel it. Now, more than ever, you have to see things the way they really are."

"I hate the way things really are. I do see it now, the way it really is, and I hate the world!"

"Sometimes we all do. But we have to get through it, don't we?"

Tears were burning her eyes. "Why? Why'd this happen to me? *Why, why, why?*"

Dr. Judith said then, very quietly, "No one can answer that question and probably no one ever will. When you accept the fact that there *is* no answer, you'll have *found* your answer. That's what all thinking people have to face sooner or later. You think you can do that? Do you have what it *takes* to do that?"

Carole's hand was moist, her curled fingers stiff, her hand like a claw on the telephone. "I don't know," she said, faintly. "I don't know. I doubt it. I don't know."

Then the voice changed, hardened: "Now listen to me, Carole. You're on very thin ice and you have to realize it. Will you stay where you are until I get there? Will you *think* about what I just said?" Then Dr. Judith's low voice dropped to a whisper: "Dear, you're very sick. It's not your fault—"

"I'm crazy." She felt the fury take over, gave in to it. "Is that what you're saying? I've lost it? I'm the one who's insane. *I'm* the one who's sick!"

"Carole, listen to me now. What happens to *you* depends on *you.* You can be well again. You can still *choose.* Your whole life now, Sandy's, both depend on *you.* No one else. It always comes to this in the end. The only human being who can save you . . . is you." She took a breath. "And if you go under, dear, if you sink, he'll win. Whoever did it, *he'll* win. Think about that. *Think!* I'm on my way."

There was a sound, not a click, a gentle muffled sound, and Carole was holding a humming telephone at her ear.

The throb in her breast had become so intense it threatened to explode. She went into the bedroom, examined the vials: *Four times a day for pain.* She picked up the glass and washed down two tablets with the stale water. Then she took one Librium, just one more. How many had she taken since morning? She couldn't remember. They didn't seem to be doing any good. *Nothing* seemed to be doing any good!

She returned to the job. She couldn't forget anything. She crossed the hall to Sandy's room, picked up the backpack, opened it, and began to pack from the drawers, no longer selecting, taking whatever her hands came across—

When, once more, the telephone shrilled in the hall.

She never wanted to hear his voice again. But . . . but what if it was Henry this time?

The telephone kept ringing, over and over.

Henry's been worried, and so have I.

She *couldn't* go without telling Henry.

She found herself at the table in the hall, and longing to hear Henry's deep gentle voice.

She lifted the phone. "Henry?"

No answer.

"Hello, hello. Who is it, what do you want?"

"Ah yess," said a voice she'd never heard before. "Missus Yensen, I haf tried to reach you before—" An odd accent—Swedish? German?

"Who is this? What do you want?"

"All in due course, dear lady." A man's deep voice, not quite distinct, muffled, but ingratiating in a strange way: "You may call me Mr. Deutsch. Although of course that iss not my name."

She was tempted to slam down the phone. Why didn't she?

"It vill not be to your advantage to hang-gup." A cool, knowing, amused menace had come into his tone. "You vould be *very* sorry. I am calling in regart to your daughter."

The impulse to replace the phone pulled at the muscles of her arm. Yet, she didn't move. Couldn't.

"Missus Yensen, you are a smart young voman. Nothing in this vorld could induce you to hang-gup now, and you know it." There was a silence. She could feel the impulse all the way into her shoulder and in her armpit. But she couldn't speak. "Ach, now I haf your full attention, no?

Alexandria." His voice seemed to caress the word. "Such a, such a bootiful name, vhy do you call her Sandy?"

Panic finally struck—a freezing hand clutching her heart. "Who are you?" she shouted. *"What do you want?"*

He disregarded this, his tone almost kindly. "Age fife years, nine monts. Such a luffly child. So lifely and charming. So sveet . . . She iss vit me now."

There was a knock at the front door. Carole barely heard it.

She was not breathing. She sank down onto the chair, body faint, mind reeling—

"She iss vorking vit crayons and she iss smiling at me so sveetly."

The knock at the door was repeated.

But Carole was helpless now, fury beginning, body suddenly scalding hot—

And then it came to her.

This was him.

This was the man.

How did she know?

She could hear his breathing. But he was not touching her now, his hand was not digging into, twisting her breast, he was not on top of her, penis inside, he was not whispering: *You sweet, adorable, darling, beautiful girl,* voice soft and urgent, then harsh, full of hate and anger: *You bitch, you whore, you tart—*

But she knew. Now she was positive. As she heard: "Now, you vill do precisely vhat I tell you. You vill not leaff the house. You vill telephone no one. You vill sit and—"

That voice, almost a whisper now, it was his. Only the accent was wrong, the man didn't have an accent—

"If you touch Sandy," she heard herself say—

"No threats, pleeze. *I* giff the orders. You vill sit and vait for my call." There was a brief silence. Then the voice, cool but pleasant, almost cajoling: "You vill speak to no one. You vill sit and ponder vhat can happen to such a sveet helpless little gurl who iss so bootiful and *desirable—"*

Click.

She was holding a humming telephone.

And someone was knocking at the door.

PART 6

FOR THE FIRST FIVE minutes in the men's shop *(Morgan's Fine Clothes for Gentlemen, Est. 1897)* Henry had been almost convinced that all the dull dreary canvassing by his officers since nine this morning was not going to pay off after all. Neither the owner, Lawrence Morgan, who was extremely tall, cadaverously thin, sedate, late middle age, nor his clerk, a short, clean-cut young man named Jeff Wilder with an eager-to-please smile hovering on his lips, had been able to recall having sold a belt such as the one Sergeant Dozier had been admiring—not ever, to anyone. But now Henry had begun to suspect they were stonewalling. Why? Because, like most upright, respectable law-and-order advocates, they didn't want to get involved? Or was there more to it than that?

So Henry shifted tactics and brought out the photographs, placing them one by one on the glass counter: the snapshot of David Slade (with live-in sex partner), Rolfe Jensen (and wife, with sailboat), A. L. Cassady's dust jacket, even the mug shot of Janos Petofi, just for the hell of it, and then the black-and-white glossy of Duncan Clive. Mr. Morgan's narrow, balding head shook, almost imperceptibly, and Jeff Wilder's boyish face looked disappointed, almost apologetic.

Henry was about to ask whether they had regular customers by the names of Joel White or Jerald Dixon, but Mr. Morgan spoke, in his own Yankee way: "I saw the morning paper, of course. And of course I'd hate to think of one of our belts being used for such a purpose."

"Of course," Henry said, as he gathered the pictures together and shoved them into Duncan Clive's nine-by-twelve manila envelope. Then he realized there was something else inside. So he slid it out—a small folded sheet of pale blue stationery with handwriting on it—and placed it in his shirt pocket while he spoke: "Maybe someone came in off the street and paid cash." He picked up the loosely coiled leather belt from the glass countertop. "Do you keep records of cash sales?"

"We keep records of *all* sales," Mr. Morgan said, as if he'd been insulted. "IRS sees to that."

"Then perhaps I could take a squint at the sales slips for, say, the last six months? Make that a year."

"We have only this month's records in the store." Mr. Morgan, who was wearing a three-piece gray suit, with bow tie and highly polished brown shoes, lost none of his polite disdain as he came from behind the counter. "But of course you may examine those. However, I can give you my word: no such item was purchased in the month of October."

Henry had to decide. Whatever else he might be, Mr. Lawrence Morgan didn't strike him as a man who'd take chances. "I take your word, Mr. Morgan," he said, in no mood to savor the irony. He had made up his mind: the man was a liar.

"Thank you," Mr. Morgan said, not smirking, no hint of satisfaction or relief.

"How much did you tell Sergeant Dozier a belt like this sells for?"

"Fifty-two dollars," Mr. Morgan said through his nostrils. "Anaconda snakeskin. You won't find anything like this anywhere else this side of Westport."

"And the silver buckle?"

"Ninety dollars. It's sterling, of course."

"Maybe you'd be kind enough to let me see the list of charge-account customers." He shrugged carelessly. "I just might recognize a name."

"I . . . I don't think that would be quite . . . ethical." Then, irascible for the first time: "Now look here, Officer—Sergeant Dozier, when he came in, gave no indication he was on duty. He said he was personally interested in buying a snakeskin belt, if we stocked them."

Henry turned his head to look across the large room at the short, squat, bland-faced officer, who was intently examining neckties on a circular rack. "Sergeant Dozier follows orders very well."

Mr. Morgan continued in a faintly hurt and accusing tone, as if he'd been betrayed: "He also asked to see our selection of slide buckles. But Sergeant Dozier was not being entirely truthful, was he?"

"Mr. Morgan," Henry said, flatly, "a felony has been committed, and a belt almost identical to this was used in its commission." Then, carefully, he added: "Wouldn't a man who bought a buckle worth ninety dollars—with a flat plate like this—wouldn't he normally have it monogrammed?"

Mr. Morgan stepped behind the counter, picked up the belt and began to roll it into a tighter circle. "Some do, some don't. Matter of personal taste."

Henry turned, with purposeful abruptness, to fix his eyes on the boy. "You keep a card file of customers who'll bring merchandise back to be monogrammed later?"

For the first time, Jeff Wilder glanced at his boss before answering, and now Henry was absolutely positive Mr. Morgan was protecting *someone.* The boy said: "Mr. Morgan handles the regular customers." His smile was apologetic and almost desperately intended to please. "I just work here," he finished, lamely.

Not the answer Henry had expected—but better in its

own way. So he continued to concentrate on the kid. "Get me that file, will you, Jeff?"

But it was Mr. Morgan, extending his arms and shooting his French cuffs, who answered: "Chief Lindheim, we're busy here and Jeff hasn't had his lunch break. We don't have such a list. I keep such things in my head." Then, abruptly, his attitude changed: his parched-looking lips curled into a smile, displaying brilliant, neat false teeth, and his voice dropped to a confidential whisper. "You know the way these young yuppies are today, Chief. Money means nothing to them, or maybe everything. Y'know, I actually saw a bumper sticker the other day that says it all: HE WHO DIES WITH THE MOST TOYS, WINS." He shook his head and another frosty smile appeared. "If one of them took it into his head he could use a belt like that in a rape—well, he'd probably want to do it in style, wouldn't he?"

The idea was as ludicrous as Mr. Morgan's camaraderie, but Henry acted surprised. You, Henry thought, you, Mr. Lawrence Morgan, are a gentleman and a scholar and a very *bad* liar. You've suspected since you read the paper that the belt described in the news was bought in your store, and you know who bought it. But all he asked was: "Do you belong to the Lake Club?" He was thinking of Jerald Dixon now and he was also fighting his own agitation. If Lawrence Morgan imagined they were playing some prep school game here . . .

"Well, yes, I am a member, as a matter of fact." Morgan's face was trying to keep from scowling. "But I don't see that that's any of your concern, Chief Lindheim. I really don't. Jeff here and I have been harassed enough."

There was that goddamned word again. Henry was admiring his own restraint. And the casual precision of his words: "I told you that a felony has been committed, now I want to give you both something to think about. Obstructing justice is also a felony, punishable by several years in prison. So is lying to a police officer." He heaved a sigh and swiveled his body to fix his eyes on Jeff Wilder. "Also punishable by a prison sentence." Although he tried to smile, the boy's face looked bleak and pale—terrified, if Henry was any judge. Exactly what he had hoped for. But for good measure he twisted the knife: "If the weapon used in such a crime was sold in this store and if either of you had knowledge of this fact"—he kept his gaze on Jeff Wilder—"and withheld that knowledge, well, a case might be made for accessory to sexual battery and attempted homicide." Like hell, but why should the lawbreakers have exclusive rights to lies and exaggeration? He turned to Morgan again. "Even if none of this could be made to stick, it wouldn't be the best advertisement for a solid old business founded in 1897, would it? Is the patronage of one customer worth it?"

He lumbered to the front door and went out.

The poison had been planted. Hell, it'd been fertilized with more bullshit than he'd had to spread around in years.

What kind of weeds would grow in it?

If any.

She knew she was driving, she had to keep her mind on that, she was driving, and too fast, much too fast for this narrow road. *You always drive too fast, Carole.* Stay away from me, Rolfe. Now and forever. Stay away, I hate you, I'll always hate you, it's over, over, over—stay the hell away from me forever.

The road was familiar, curves and twists and more curves, she took it every day, but it was not three o'clock, it was too early to pick up Sandy.

You vill not leaff the house . . . telephone no one . . . you vill sit and vait for my call—

Which she had not done. She was on her way to Pendleton Day-Care, where Sandy was, where Sandy had to be, had to be, had to be. . . .

The rear end of the car slid sideways on loose leaves. She

fought the wheel, she'd driven in enough ice and snow to know how to—

After she'd heard the click, after Mr. Deutsch had hung up, what had she done? She couldn't be sure. Had she called the school's number? Yes, because now she remembered how surprised she'd been that she could remember it, and the line had been busy. Oh no, God, oh God, then she'd punched out 911—had she really done this or had she only intended to do it? She remembered the knocking on the door, everything a blur, tears, and the man standing there: *Remember me, Mrs. Jensen? My name's Clive. Duncan Clive.* She'd remembered the beard, the accent, but what had she said, had she brushed past him without a word, her hand on the gun in her pocket, hearing: *Ye should not drive, upset as ye are, Mrs. Jensen—*

She couldn't remember what she'd said. Only his bulky figure, legs apart, in the rearview mirror, only a flash as the car charged up the driveway—

Now she was making the turn onto Hawleyville Road, she heard a horn blasting, she didn't glance—

To fight the pictures, vivid and cruel, flashing in her mind, she drove even faster, both hands clutching the wheel—

Eyes riveted on the road ahead, she saw, instead, Allison's station wagon arriving at the school this morning, how many hours ago, Audrey and Mike and Sandy tumbling out, another car parked along the road on the other side, a male voice calling Sandy's name, Allison not noticing, driving on to work, in a hurry, always in a hurry, Mike and Audrey running to the playground swings, Sandy crossing the road toward—

She wouldn't get into a strange car with a stranger, she'd been told too often, warned over and over and over—

Oh God, Carole knew she wasn't going to make it, she was almost there, one more curve, but she wasn't going to make it—

And then, rounding the curve, she saw the white clapboard building, once a farmhouse, white picket fence around the playground, and then she was trying to slow down, putting on the brakes, opening the door, almost going down on the blacktop as both knees, stiff with bandages, buckled, but only for a second, and then she was inside the wide front hall, children's drawings on the walls—

But not a sound. The hall was empty. No children's shouts, or cries, or laughter, no droning teacher's voice—

Stunned, amazed, she stood in the vast quiet trying to call out, unable to find her voice, or even to move—

"Oh, Mrs. Jensen, it's you." A loud whisper. She looked down the hall: TEACHERS ONLY over an open door, Mrs. Ferber coming toward her, raw-boned and tall and tweedy, eyes troubled, still whispering: "Mrs. Jensen, dear, what is it?"

Mrs. Ferber was close now, short white hair awry. And Carole found her voice at last: "Where's Sandy?" Almost a shout.

"Shhh. It's nap time. Sandy's asleep with the others in the art room." She placed her forefinger upright over her lips. "Mrs. Jensen, I must say, I didn't expect to see you. Although someone did phone to ask for you a few minutes ago. Extraordinary. A Mister Deutsch, he said. Do you want me to waken Sandy?"

Henry, who had been waiting with as much patience as he had left, stood up when Mark Rainer entered the small waiting room of his courthouse office. Already scowling, the DA took his messages from the middle-aged secretary, who had treated Henry like an intruder, and flipped through them, speaking at the same time in that lockjaw manner as he went into his office. "Come on in, Chief. And we don't have to go to bed together but at least leave us to be civilized, okay?"

When Henry came in, the State's Attorney was sitting,

chair tilted back, ankles crossed on the desk. He was loosening his tie and collar. "If this is about Scott Keller, you're out of your bailiwick. The kid's not right in the head, that's all. Dr. Keller and I reached a reasonable gentlemanly agreement. Kid was charged with failure to use due caution—traffic violation, nothing else. Couldn't have him bragging to his hippie-druggie friends, could we?"

Puzzled now, and disconcerted because he hadn't come here to discuss Scott Keller, Henry nevertheless asked: "Where's the boy now?"

"Where he belongs. Fairfield Hills."

"What?"

"Fairfield Hills State Hospital in Newtown. What's the matter with you? You look as if I just kicked you."

Snake pit. You're not even a person in there. I'd rather be dead than go back to that hellhole.

"He's been there before," Mark Rainer said. "His father was furious. He's the one who had him committed. Says maybe he'll learn not to steal cars from his father's houseguests."

"Is that what we use mental hospitals for these days?" Henry asked through tight lips. "I thought we had jails for punishment."

"Oh Christ," Mark Rainer groaned. "Look here. Chief. I'm on a fifteen-minute recess. What've you got in your craw today?"

So, knowing he'd never get it now, Henry made it brief: What he wanted, needed, was a court order allowing him to examine the business records of Morgan's Men's Shop, Elm Street, Sudbury.

"Yeah. Something about that in here." Puzzled, Mark Rainer riffled through the message slips again, read one with a frown, then looked up. "Larry Morgan claims you harassed him and his clerk in his store a while ago."

Henry was damned if he was going to defend himself. An explanation, yes: "I need the records to find out what

Mr. Morgan won't tell me—who bought a snakeskin belt and silver slide buckle in his store."

"Chief, did you really drop in from outer space?" Only his lips moved under his neat mustache. "Look, why are you trying to make a federal case out of this? Rape's as common as shoplifting. Look at that desk, will you? I've got all kinds of important cases to deal with. Drugs, million-dollar heists, frauds, two first-degree homicides. This isn't a murder case, you know."

"In some ways it's worse. The victim's still alive, still suffering. Are you going to get me that subpoena?"

"Not unless you can show probable cause that Larry Morgan's obstructing justice. Has the victim signed the official complaint?"

"How could she? I've been trying all morning to get the transcript of her statement so that when she does come in—"

"Oh, yeah. I thought Trooper Dworsky told you about that—"

Henry stood up and took a single long stride toward the desk. "Let me guess, Counselor." Knowing now, certain, he was choking down fury. "The recording device malfunctioned yesterday when you and that bastard trooper were interrogating the victim. The tape came out mangled, or blank— which?"

The DA smiled and touched his mustache. "You got it, Chief. Trooper Dworsky was with me when we tried to play it. The tape was both mangled *and* blank." He shrugged his narrow shoulders, his eyes mocking and innocent under arched brows. "These things happen." Then he put on his horn-rimmed glasses and began to shuffle through the folders on his desk. "Maybe Brad and I did get a little carried away, we're only human; the woman's a beauty. But it's your word and Mrs. Jensen's against the trooper's and mine. I doubt the Attorney General's office'll be interested in who's telling the truth, do you? I can show him the blank tape."

Henry straightened to his full height, shaking inside, and placed his hands, fists clenched now, behind his back. "When I arrest the actual perpetrator, with proof, the Attorney General will be interested that you closed the case peremptorily and *without* proof." He swung about and stalked to the door, his mind seething.

"You're learning big words up here in civilized country, *ain't* you, Chief?"

At the door Henry turned. "I'm learning," he said, "that the jungle's moved up here from the city, only up here it don't use words like *ain't.* Or *justice.* Or *suppression of evidence.* You don't even know the meaning of those words."

"You want to play rough?" Mark Rainer stood up and took off his glasses. "Let's play rough. You bring any charges like that—"

"Who are you protecting?"

"You bring any public charges like that, Chief, and I'll instigate a full investigation of that accident at the bridge. *Everything.* I'll issue a warrant for the arrest of Mrs. Carole Jensen—reckless endangerment, leaving the scene of a vehicular collision involving grave personal injury. Or worse. From the look of those two cars, attempted homicide. Maybe she decided the Keller kid raped her, so she took justice into her own hands. She warned us—you heard her yourself."

"If you send anyone near that girl today—"

"Don't threaten me again," Mark Rainer hissed. His eyes were dull and hard with anger. "Because you don't have anything to threaten me with." He turned to stare out the window. "The Jensen case is closed, as of now."

"Like hell."

"Hear me out for God's sake. Not Mendoza. Not Scott Keller." He pivoted to face Henry. "We've got a death on our hands this time. You should know about it by now—"

"Well, I *don't.*"

"It was on the TV news at noon."

"Who, goddamn it?"

"Aloysius Leo Cassady, Esquire."

This time Henry felt a blow to his midsection—a solid, massive blow which left him speechless, almost physically sick.

"He put a bullet through his head sometime during the night. With the service revolver he used in Vietnam. His body was found this morning in his New York apartment."

Finally, and with difficulty, Henry found his voice: "He left a note?"

"He left a note. It'll be headlines tomorrow."

"A confession?"

A smile appeared below Mark Rainer's mustache. "The note was very short. It read: *I was cleaning my gun.*"

"Just that?"

"According to the TV report, just that. Smartass literary type."

"Good God." Henry lowered himself into the chair. His mind was on Carole—how would she take this, did she know, would he have to be the one to tell her? But he said, "That's hardly a confession."

"Maybe so, maybe not," Mark Rainer said, slowly. "It could be interpreted that way. Oh come on, Chief, let's put the case away. We won't have to prove anything to anybody. Let 'em make up their own minds from the obvious. Forget it. I'm sick of the whole thing, aren't you? Just let it . . . sort of drift away—"

Henry found the strength to stand up then, the catch coming into his joint for the first time today. Yes, he'd have to be the one, he couldn't have anyone else telling her, what if she heard it on the news herself? But what he said was: "It won't drift away, Counselor."

"No? Why not?"

"Because what you're suggesting—Mrs. Jensen won't accept it. And neither will I."

"She'll have to." His tone sharpened. "And I'm afraid you will, too."

And then it came to Henry, bright and hard and sharp: suddenly he realized that this man had known this all along, yet he'd used every excuse not to ask some judge for the search warrant Henry had to have. Why? Henry thought he had the answer to that now, too. So he said, anger propelling him to recklessness: "I won't accept it. And you don't accept it yourself." Henry had watched lawyers half-convince themselves of what they had known was not true in order to argue it with such convincing sincerity that they were able to sway a jury or judge. He had the truth now, though. "You and your friend Lawrence Morgan—who are you trying to protect, Mr. Rainer?"

The beeper on his belt began to sound. Automatically he flipped it off.

Then Mark Rainer spoke: "Now listen, Chief—why do we always come to this? Remember what I said: let's be friends."

"You got too many friends, Rainer. And since you think rape's some kind of minor misdemeanor anyway, you and your *friend* Lawrence Morgan think you can protect one of them."

Mark Rainer's face hardened and then he spread his legs, like a brawler ready to bring up his fists. "Your handling of this whole case has been unethical and incredibly unprofessional and warped by your own feelings from the start. I warned you: I can have your badge."

"My badge ain't worth it if I have to polish it for bastards like you. You know, or suspect, who bought that belt because you know who wears that kind of belt, or because he asked your help. That amounts to suppressing evidence."

"That's a serious charge." The younger man's face had gone a vivid red. "I'll make you prove it." A shrill, shaking rage had come into his voice: "If you accuse me of *anything,* Mister, I'll see both you *and* Carole Jensen behind bars! So use your fucking brain if you've got one in that aboriginal skull of yours!"

Henry slammed the door behind him. The sound echoed through the courthouse.

All the concern and anguish and fear had turned to savage fury on the way from the school to The Village with Sandy next to her in the front seat. Even with the incredible relief still streaming through her blood, her mind was on fire. What a cruel, what a mean, sadistic, inhuman trick!

Probably just someone who had read about what happened in the paper, Mrs. Ferber had said, *and decided it was you. Poor dear—I'm so sorry. It had to be someone with a perverted sense of humor who thought it'd be . . . oh, I don't know . . . fun? Oh, Mrs. Jensen, it's a sick world, isn't it?*

Yes, sick. Worse! Vicious. A swamp, a jungle, a primeval forest with prowling monsters—

But Mrs. Ferber could have been right: the whole diabolical thing could have been a hoax, a fiendish game, a sadistic trick. Then he, whoever Mr. Deutsch was, had phoned the school in order to gloat, to wallow in his neurotic, secret glee—

No. No, no, Judith was right: she couldn't tell herself that because she wanted to believe it! No more of that. That voice on the phone, forget the accent, that was *his* voice and even the words, some of the phrases had sounded vaguely familiar—

But how could she be sure?

She couldn't afford to take chances. She'd made up her mind, she knew what she had to do—

Mommy, why do you keep looking in the mirror like that? Nobody's in back of us.

Paranoia, she had said. *Mommy has a bad case of paranoia. It's like a disease.*

Sort of like rape?

It had to come, that question; she'd been dreading it,

trying to brace herself for it. She heard herself ask: *Who . . . who told you about rape?*

Nobody told me. But I heard Allison talking on the phone with somebody. About me. She said: "Her mother's got rape."

But then Sandy had begun to talk about a fat boy named Jeremy who *scarfs down his food like a pygmy. Gross.*

Now, facing the young officer across the high counter in the Sheffield police station, where she'd never been before, she was saying, "You must be wrong. You've got to be wrong! Look, look for it, Chief Lindheim told me—"

"Sorry, Mrs. Jensen. Nothing here for you to sign."

"Where is he? What's he doing? He wanted my fingerprints, too."

But, turning away, snatching Sandy's hand, she also felt relief: she didn't want to see Henry, he'd insist she stay in town and she was not staying now, hoax or no hoax, she knew it wasn't a hoax!

When they emerged from the police station, Sandy was squirming— "You're hurting my hand"—so Carole loosened her grip, but held on. She had no intention of allowing Sandy out of her sight again, ever again. Sandy asked, "Was I good, Mommy? I didn't say a word, did I?"

"No mommy could ask for more."

"But you, Mommy, you weren't even polite. Why would they want *your* fingerprints? You didn't do anything bad, did you?"

And then suddenly, out of nowhere, Carole was near tears, the urgency still pulling at her mind, at her body, every muscle, every nerve—

In the car again, leaving Sheffield Center, Sandy asked, "Did you see the bars in the windows? Is that where they keep bad people?"

Carole almost answered by rote what she had always believed or had been taught to believe: that there were no bad people really, only people who sometimes did bad things. But, instead, she heard herself say, "That's one of the places. And, yes, there *are* bad people, Sandy. Evil people. And that's where they belong!"

After a long moment, Sandy asked, "You're not mad at me, are you, Mommy?"

"No, darling, not at you." At him, at all the *hims* in the world, at the world itself—

And that's when the question finally came, but not as she'd expected it: "That funny way you walk, Mommy, like your knees won't bend, is that because you've got rape?"

So then, knowing she couldn't handle it yet, if ever, she said: "Sandy, I want you to do me a favor. I'll tell you all about it, I swear I'll try to explain everything, but not now. When we get to Maine. Deal?"

"Maine? Where's Maine? Is that were we're going?"

"As soon as we can get packed. Okay?" She realized then that she had decided. "It's a lovely place, a sort of lodge all by itself on a lake with pine trees all around."

"Lodge? You mean log cabin?"

"A big log cabin. Yes, dear. You'll love it."

"And no school?"

"Not . . . not at least for a while."

"And Daddy?"

"No, not Daddy."

"He has to work, right?"

Oh God, she had her job cut out for her . . . rape . . . divorce . . . she'd have to tell Sandy about him, too, the man, the voice on the phone. Some way. Somehow. "Let's keep it our secret," she said, approaching Four Corners. "Let's not mention Maine at all."

"Like a plot? Just you and me? Deal, Mommy?"

"Deal. Now, first thing when we get home, you choose the toys you want to take, and don't forget those in the tree house—"

"I wish Cass could come."

Not Daddy—Cass. Poor Cass. She decided she'd have to

phone his apartment. But not till they were on their way— or from the motel tonight, so they could really talk.

Now, crossing the Lake Lillinonah Bridge, Carole felt a hurtful stab of nostalgia, followed by a pervasive sense of emptiness and loss and sadness. But no guilt about what had happened here last night. And no uncertainty as to what she was doing. Only sorrow that it had to be. Turning onto Harrow Road, she could feel tears burning her eyes, knowing that if she started to bawl, she'd never stop, never, never—

When they reached the familiar driveway, she saw through a blur the trailer and tractor still on the lawn and then two other cars she did not recognize: a tan Jeep Wagoneer and a gray Honda Accord. Her first reaction as she started to brake, touching the pocket of her car coat with one hand to make sure the gun was still there, was to plunge the pedal to the floor, circle the big oak tree, and shoot the car up the driveway and back to the road.

What stopped her was seeing Dr. Judith coming out the front door, crossing the veranda and coming down the steps.

She was wearing a gray capelike coat and she asked no questions as Carole stepped from the car, the pain in her knees so instantly sharp that for a split second she again thought she might go down.

Dr. Judith did say, as they approached the porch: "You promised to wait, Carole." But no reproach, no blame. And, thank God, no questions.

"Rolfe?" Carole asked.

And Dr. Judith shook her head.

"Mommy," Sandy said, in a hurt tone, holding the door open, "you're not being polite again."

And Dr. Judith laughed. "My name's Dr. Judith, Sandy. I've been looking forward to meeting you."

"How do you do, Dr. Judith." Sandy offered her hand. "I think your coat's neat."

Then they were in the hall, Dr. Judith taking off her

coat and Sandy moving to the back stairs leading down to the game room. "Only the best toys, Mommy, right?"

"I've sort of taken over, Carole," Dr. Judith said. "The door was unlocked. Lunch is ready, such as it is and late as it is, and, let's see—let's go out to the kitchen—Dr. Stafford's office phoned, to remind you to make an appointment—and your friend Miriam came by to pick up the portfolio"—they were in the kitchen now—"and, let's see, your father phoned from New York, he'll call back between two-thirty and three"—she placed a tray stacked with sandwiches on the table—"and that's your medicine beside your plate, and water, take it"—an order—"does Sandy drink milk?"

Carole had almost forgotten, or become accustomed to, the pain in her breast, but it was horrible now—how could she have forgotten it, or the medicine? So she sat down, both knees protesting, saying, "She loves milk," and swallowing two of the analgesic tablets, but not the Librium, she had a long drive in front of her, she had to have a clear head—

"You don't want to tell me where you're going, do you, dear?" Dr. Judith set three steaming mugs of coffee on the table—why three? "I saw the suitcases. I'll help you finish packing *after* you eat." She lowered her voice: "Before they come upstairs, I want to know only one thing. . . ."

"They? Who else is here? You shook your head—"

"No, not your husband," Dr. Judith said, knowing.

"I don't have a husband."

Sitting across from her at the round table, Dr. Judith asked: "You wouldn't like to tell me where you've been, would you?"

So then, quickly, lowering her voice in case Sandy appeared, Carole told Dr. Judith, not about her visit to Karen—she couldn't tell that, even to Judith—but about the phone call, forcing her mind to remember every detail . . . the strange accent . . . threats . . . the names he'd called her . . . the wild ride to school . . . the mind-boggling shock and vast incredible relief when she'd discovered Sandy unharmed . . . and then that "Mr. Deutsch" had phoned the school before she arrived—

"You don't remember Mr. Clive being here when you left?"

"Vaguely, yes. I think I was terribly rude to him."

"Well, he was still here when I arrived. He's been almost as concerned as I have, I think. And he seems to have something important to say to you." She was placing two sandwiches on a plate. "I suggest you take these down to him and listen to what he has to say before your father calls back."

Carole leaped up from the chair. "He's in the TV room with Sandy?" Panic was quivering all through her. "Damn you, Judith, oh no, damn you, he could be—"

She was trying to run now, on stiff legs, into the hall, to the narrow back staircase to what had once been the cellar, her heart hammering, her mind fluttering again, terror icy in her blood.

The television was not turned on. Sandy was seated on the couch facing it, no longer wearing her snowsuit, various stuffed animals around her ankles, and Duncan Clive was standing, leaning against the billiard table, smoking a pipe. His brawny body seemed to stiffen when he saw her. The rock-walled room was filled with the raw, savory fragrance of pipe smoke.

For a long moment, during which she began to feel foolish, they stood staring at each other.

Then Sandy twisted her head and saw her. "Mommy!" she cried, jumping up. "I met a new friend! He says he knows you. His name is Dunc."

"Dunc?" Carole heard her voice echo the word, stupidly. "Mr. Clive, dear."

"He said I should call him Dunc. He said that's what his friends call him. Mommy, I'm *starving!*"

"Dr. Judith has sandwiches in the kitchen," Carole said, stepping aside to let Sandy pass. Her eyes were still on the man—dark-red beard, gray eyes uncertain—and she had begun to feel damn foolish.

Going upstairs, Sandy spoke in a rush: "He's read Cass's book and I *love* the way he talks!" Then, out of sight, she called: "Bring the toys when you come, will you, Dunc?"

"With pleasure, princess," Duncan Clive called after her, an odd grin on his face, stepping to the fireplace to knock ashes from his pipe. And when he turned to face her, he said, no longer grinning: "I came more than an hour ago to say what I'll say now, then go. Mrs. Jensen, it's not my wish to add to your burden. I behaved like a bloody churlish boor Saturday night and I apologize. But . . . lest ye think that I'm the one who did harm to you as Chief Lindheim seems to suspect, I came here directly from the police station. Where my fingerprints were duly recorded. When I saw you come flyin' out the front door a while ago, I knew ye thought—" He broke off and took a deep breath, as if he were trying to remember the words he'd already arranged in his mind. "I told you night before last: I'm not a man who has to take a woman by force, nor can I have ye thinking that I could've done so."

Carole moved to the couch, sat, and began to gather up the stuffed animals and several dolls from the floor. "Mr. Clive," she said, "I'm the one who owes you an apology. While you were knocking at the door, I was on the phone." She was shaking her head in astonishment, although what she was saying frightened her. "Damned if I still didn't think you might be—how could you be on the porch and on the phone at the same time? It's my mixed-up mind. I guess I'll be suspecting everyone and everything until—" She stood up, her arms filled with the little animals and dolls. "You see, the man on the phone threatened my daughter. I guess I was sort of insane. Maybe I still am. I'm sorry." And then she smiled and hastily added: "Don't tell Dr. Judith. Saying I'm sorry, that's against the rules."

"Ye have my promise." His dark red beard was twisting

into a grin. "I'll not report ye to Judith if ye *will* report to Chief Lindheim that *ye* believe what I've just told you."

She realized that, standing, she was closer to him. "Are you afraid he'll arrest you?"

"Who gives a bloody damn about that? For some reason I can't explain, the man's *respect* is of some import to me."

Carole felt like smiling herself. She understood. And then she said something she could not recall having said before: "In some ways, not knowing is almost the worst part. It's really hell, you know."

He stepped closer, his eyes probing, but still hesitant under the bushy brows. "It'll pass. The bright hills and the dark valleys—what'd life be without 'em?"

Suddenly for some reason she dared not try to fathom, she believed what he'd said, just for the moment at least. And she felt a faint and distant healing all through her. An easing of the tautness. And also, now, a strange quivering awareness of his closeness, his masculinity. The vigor and vitality in his quietness.

Hope flared through her. And something else, something she had been afraid she might never feel again.

He sensed it in her, too, she was sure. As she sensed it in him. And she was not embarrassed. Nor was there any taint of guilt. A strange sense of *déjà vu* invaded her mind—as if she'd stood here before in this very room, with him.

"You," she said, "you look as if you want to kiss me."

"Aye." A whisper. "Aye."

Then, without hesitation, she said, hearing the words without surprise. "Then do it."

He took a single step and leaned forward, slowly, his beard touching her hand and a stuffed giraffe she held in her arms, and then she felt his lips on hers, the beard amazingly soft, the lips full and firm. He did not open his mouth.

It was a youthful, innocent kiss, more reverent than passionate—and incredibly tender. His arms remained alongside his strong bulky body, their two bodies not touching.

Then he straightened but did not step back, his face still so close that the tanned upper part of it looked like fine leather.

"I'm not so certain I understand," he said in a whisper.

"I know *I* don't," she said, but still not embarrassed. And then: "Maybe I had to prove to myself that I was still . . . kissable." And then: "Can you understand that?"

"Aye," he said, softly.

"Or maybe," she said, "maybe I wanted to prove to myself that I could still feel—" She broke off, glanced around the room and then finished the thought: "Feel what a woman ought to feel when a man kisses her."

"And did you?"

She met his gaze, shaking her head from side to side. "I'm sorry. No."

"No reason to feel sorry, lass. Too soon. Could be ye're rushing yourself. Feelings often come in a rush, but we can't rush them to come." His eyes were smiling. "Old Scottish proverb I just made up." Then he tilted his head to one side, eyes teasing but not taunting, bright and gentle, suggesting a gaiety she'd not seen in him before. "Well, whatever ye've proved to yourself, lass, the pleasure is mine."

Through the ceiling they heard a telephone ringing.

They were still staring at each other, soberly now, when they heard footsteps above, another ring, and then the indistinguishable mumble of a voice.

Then that same voice, lifted, definitely Judith's: "Carole, your father's on the line."

The moment faded away, and Carole was astonished at the reluctance she felt as she turned and went to the narrow stairway, and up the steps. In the hall she realized she was still carrying her collection of toys. Passing the kitchen door, she heard Sandy saying: "Grandad never comes here. I don't think he likes me."

Dropping the stuffed toys and picking up the phone, Carole realized that, she was moving again into still another world, backward in time, and after she spoke, she waited to hear Stanley Vance's cool executive voice, which said, "Now, Carole, please listen before you say no. Have you thought over the offer I made, your mother and I made, last night?"

Her instinctive response, which she choked down, was: *Yes, I'm feeling better, Daddy, and Sandy misses you.* But instead she asked, "Daddy, is anyone using Wildwood?"

A brief silence before: "At this time of year? No one ever uses Wildwood except me—you know that."

She knew—as she knew, always with bitterness, how he used it, and for what purpose, and with whom. It had always been the place where he took whichever young bitch he was involved with at the moment. "Sandy and I'd like to drive up."

"Sandy and you? What about Rolfe?"

Tempted suddenly to lie—*This is Rolfe's busy time of year at the plant*—she said: "Rolfe and I are no longer together."

"Carole!" His shocked tone seemed sincere. And then he said, "I see."

"Do you? What?"

"I always knew Rolfe wouldn't be able to handle—well, to cope with something like this. Your mother and I talked about it last night."

Startled, Carole asked, "How is she, Daddy?"

"Well, she's taking it better than I expected, that's the truth. One Valium at bedtime and one call to her pastor. We all have our crutches, don't we? Usually I can blot out whatever's bothering me by my work here at the office. Oh, I know you called it paper shuffling, but it's been my salvation. Or my damnation. Damned if I know." You're forgetting sex, Carole thought, the shadow of that old familiar bitterness touching her. "Do you know, your mother and I talked late into the night. First night we've spent in the same room for . . . oh, fifteen, twenty years."

Carole felt something collapse inside—a wall, a rampart,

a levee giving way. She could never recall her father talking to her at this length before, or in this human, person-to-person way. And, feeling cheated, deprived, shut out, what effort had *she* made to smash down the wall? She'd walked away, blaming him. Blaming both of them—and marrying Rolfe.

"I love you, Daddy," she heard herself say, fighting tears, the words strange in her throat.

"What? What'd you say, Carole?"

"You . . . you heard me," she said.

"Do you know, daughter, this is the first time you've ever asked for anything. Since art school. The first time."

"I'm asking now," she said, hoping Sandy would not come into the hall.

"You've got it, daughter. I'll phone up there now. Mr. and Mrs. Payne'll have the place shipshape before you get there, even if you decide to fly. Wood chopped for the fireplaces, furnace going, food on the shelves—"

"And Daddy—"

"What, dear?"

"No one's to know where we are. No one. Including Rolfe." And then she added, hearing Sandy's voice in her own: "Deal?"

"Of course you've got a deal, Carole!" Had she ever heard such hearty exuberance in his tone? "Now look don't be offended: how about money?"

Money! She hadn't thought of it since early morning. Why hadn't she stopped at the bank? Damn, damn, damn! "I've got credit cards, and probably enough cash for sandwiches on the way."

"Well, there's only one bank in town up there. It'll be waiting for you when you arrive—"

"And?" she prompted, never having heard him say it.

"And I love you, too, daughter. Maybe it takes something terrible like this to—listen, it'll be dark up there in a couple of hours, you know Maine. And don't try to drive straight through—this is your father talking. I . . . I'll give your love to your mother when I get home. No, I'll call her now."

She waited to hear the connection break before she lowered the phone. She could feel the tears wet on her face.

It was Judith, not Sandy, who came into the hall. Her head down, forehead on the top of the table, Carole felt a hand on her shoulder—

"I couldn't help but hear some of it, dear."

"Where's Sandy?"

"Duncan and she are in the tree house searching for her koala bear. Carole, I thought of something while you were talking to your father. Oscar Wilde, of all people, wrote it: 'Children begin by loving their parents. As they grow older, they judge them. Sometimes they forgive them.' "

Carole stood up, shaking tears from her face, saying, "Let's get the car packed; I hope we have room," when the phone jangled again.

She picked it up, "Hello," and then, when there was no answer, she said, "Hello," again, and abruptly she knew.

The voice was a rasping, savage whisper: "Missus Yensen, you haff done eggsactly vhat I told you *not* to do! You left the house, you were not there to get my call, you have spoken with the po-lice!" Then his fury exploded and she could hear his voice roaring: "You think you can defy me so? You bitch, whore, you slut harlot! *You vill do only vhat I tell you!*"

Carole glanced, made a gesture to the stairs, then snarled into the phone: "You sonofabitch!" She saw Dr. Judith rushing up the stairway. "You sadistic *bastard!* You enjoyed what you did to me, didn't you? You *loved* it! Well, I don't have to take any more of your—"

"You vill not get avay vith defying me!" His voice was rough and loud and strident with rage. She heard a faint sound on the line and knew that Judith was listening—did he hear it? "You vill hereafter follow my orders, Missus Yensen, or you vill regret it!"

"Not anymore." Her blood was streaming hot and wild. "Not anymore, Sandy's safe, you cruel—"

"I gafe you time. Vhatefer you imagined, it is *nothing* to vhat can happen to your daughter! Nothing to vhat I can *really* do!"

"You come near Sandy—"

"No threats, pleeze, *none!*"

"I have a gun, I'll—"

"You vill do nothing, nothing but vhat I say, *nothing!*" His voice sounded frantic—was he losing control?

So she said: "I know you raped me, I *know!*"

"Iff I am arrested, even if I go to prison—" He was breathing in great gasps of sound. And then his tone changed, became gentle, chiding: "You vere not a goot gurl, Carole." The caress had returned to his voice. "My sveet, lofely darling, you vill please listen carefully now. If your friend . . . that police chief . . . if he comes near me, or any police—"

"Shut up," she screamed. "Shut up, shut up, *shut up!*"

". . . you vill regret it all the days of your life."

"I have a gun, I said, I'll use it, I'll *kill* you!" Now she was struggling to control her own voice, her shaking body. "I *want* to kill you. I've wanted to kill you ever since—"

His voice barked: "You vill *listen,* I said!" Then it changed again, became a whisper again: "Carole, my darling gurl, I don't vant to do vhat I shall haff to do—"

Carole's own voice was now a low hiss: "You won't do anything, you sonofabitch, you'll be in prison, rotting with the rest of your kind—"

"And Sandy . . . dear sveet Sandy . . . vhere vill *she* be?" Then his voice, quivering, exploded again: "Dead, dead, raped and dead! *Now,* you are listening, are you not, Carole?" When she couldn't speak, he went on, gently, softly: "Answer me, my sveet darling. Are you listening?"

"I'm listening," Carole said, and sank back down onto the chair, too weak to stand. "I'm listening."

* * *

It had been Henry's idea when he left the courthouse—again furious, again frustrated—to drive out Route 6 to Merlin's Bar and Grill. To have a little chat with sweet little, flirty little Debbie. To ask and then to double-check with her boss what time she got off work on Saturday. Well, the attorney had made sure yesterday to tell Henry that he and Mark Rainer were friends. And he also wore the kind of clothes Lawrence Morgan sold in his store. And probably all three of these highly respected gentlemen belonged to the same yacht club or country club or poker club, as well as the Lions, the Elks, and the Moose, and probably the Masonic Camels—anything for a pal, what's a little sexual quirk between members, naughty, naughty, don't let the teacher catch you raping—

He was slowing as he approached Merlin's. No metallic gray Audi anywhere in sight. About to swing the wheel, he remembered his beeper had gone off while he was still in Mark Rainer's office. Damn.

He drove past the bar. Goddamn.

What was happening to his memory? In the last year or two he could go from one room to another and forget what the hell he'd intended to do there, or to get. Now, and this was serious, it was beginning to happen on the job.

Hating himself, hating old age and all that came with it, he picked up the mike and reported in, no apology or explanation.

"Another nine-eleven came in from the Jensen residence half an hour ago. A Dr. Judith Kahn. For you, Chief. She wouldn't speak with anyone but you. Said to tell you she'll wait there."

He reached to turn on the blue light and siren, not the wailer, the urgent one—***WOW-WOW-WOW-WOW***—then he lowered the gas pedal before he barked, "Anything else?"

"Officer Woodward on the front desk reported that a Mr. Duncan Clive came in at two to be fingerprinted."

"Match-up?"

"Negative, Chief."

But he already knew that. He'd known it for some time now.

"And we have a report from the New Jersey State Police: Manuel Mendoza's come out of the coma. He'll be okay. But . . . according to the Hartford Lab, the semen samples from the victim's clothes indicate perpetrator's blood-type is O positive. I phoned the Camden Hospital—forget Mendoza."

"What about Mrs. Jensen?"

"She came in to sign her statement, Woody said. And she was quite agitated (his words) when there was nothing to sign. She had her little girl with her. A knockout kid, Woody says."

"Anything else?"

"You know about Mr. A. L. Cassady?"

"I just learned," he said, as he turned the squad car off Route 6 onto the Old Hawleyville Road. *WOW-WOW-WOW-WOW.* "Now listen, get me the official time of death. Try the Manhattan coroner's office. Dr. I. Hoshito's the man I used to deal with there. Use my name. I want to know whether Cassady did it during the night or some time this morning. I'm en route to the Jensen residence. Out."

WOW-WOW-WOW-WOW.

Oh Jesus, what had he been thinking of? Had he been trying to evade the dirty job? Had his unconscious reluctance to tell Carole caused him to focus on Jerald Dixon's possible guilt? His dread of watching Carole's face when he told her that the man she called Cass, whom she loved, had put a bullet through his head—had his own cowardice, or pity, or love, taken control of his sense of duty?

And worse, worse, what if A. L. Cassady had still been in the area this morning, what if he'd seen the Sudbury paper? If he was guilty and became convinced the police were getting closer, if that front-page story spooked him, just as Henry had hoped it would spook whoever—

All he could do now was hope Carole was right. She'd never faltered in her conviction that Cassady could not have—

That poor beat-up, battle-scarred bastard—

WOW-WOW-WOW-WOW.

At that moment he discovered, fighting the wheel on the narrow curving road, that he was driving without headlights. Oh no, Christ, it was almost dark, winter-dark!

He flipped on the lights and saw he was at the top of Obtuse Hill.

And then, his mind veering suddenly, as it was beginning to do more and more often, Henry was remembering the letter scribbled on the blue stationery that Duncan Clive had placed in the envelope with his publicity photo: *Dear Dunc . . . hate to dump this on you. Mother's worse. Now she's accusing me of trying to come on to Keith. (I still can't call him Dad or Daddy—even if I do call you Dunc and you're really my father) . . . like she's got some demon inside . . . I see you almost every weekend, you know . . . always want to go running to the wagon . . . but she gets wild if she even suspects I'm THINKING about you . . . one year and seven months, I'll be eighteen—she can't stop me then . . .wherever you are . . . Maybe we could just wave sometime now that you know that I see you—*

Henry wished he'd never had to read that letter. He couldn't bear the way it made him feel.

WOW-WOW-WOW-WOW.

Once he'd read it, he'd removed another name from the list.

Leaving Joel White, David Slade, Jerald Dixon, A. L. Cassady, if Carole was wrong—and of course the unlikeliest of all by his reckoning, the husband.

Unless . . . unless it was none of these—

Unless the crime had been committed by someone he hadn't even thought of—

Or someone who didn't really know her, only her name maybe—

Then what'd happen to Carole Jensen, who swore she couldn't live if the bastard wasn't punished?

WOW-WOW-WOW-WOW—

"You can't go till you talk with Henry," Judith said. "You owe him that much."

Carole slammed shut the lid of the huge leather suitcase, then hoisted it off the bed with both hands and started toward the upstairs hall, grunting with each step: "To hell with Henry. Where's he been all day?" She dropped the suitcase at the top of the stairway. "What's he doing, what are the police doing?" She swung around to face Judith, who was in the doorway of Sandy's room. "And if you tell me one more time to *think* that's what I'm doing!"

"Where's my Indian blanket, Mommy?" Sandy asked from the foot of the stairs, looking up, wearing her snowsuit again. "Dunc and me . . . Dunc and *I* want to put all the toys in it and throw it in the backseat. The trunk's already full." But now she was frowning, realizing: "My Indian blanket's gone, too, isn't it?"

Yes. Gone. Like everything else. "Rip a blanket off one of the beds! Anything! Anything, for God's sake, *do it!*"

Then she saw Sandy's face—first the incredulity clouding her eyes, the bafflement, then a quivering in her chin, pain in her eyes, as if she'd been slapped and was fighting tears.

Her heart twisting, tempted to go running down the stairs, Carole was stopped by her daughter's voice: "Mommy, you're scary today. I *mean* it." Then the small face hardened, the jaw set, and her eyes flared blue and bright. "Well, all *right!* You don't have to *screech* at me!" And as she slammed out the front door: "What's the big hurry all of a goddamn sudden?"

Carole turned and went into the bedroom that had once been hers, glanced, picked up the cosmetics case with one hand, then crossed to Sandy's room to pick up the backpack and turned to see Judith standing in the door.

"You're leaving out that third step again, Carole, you're just reacting."

"You heard him," Carole said. "You heard the perverted sonofabitch!"

It iss nut a capital off-ense. Eefen iff they convict me, they cannot keep me in prison foreffer—

Carole passed Judith and went into the hall to place knapsack and kit alongside the suitcase on the floor, trying not to see the helpless appeal in Judith's dark eyes.

"Carole," Judith said, "I've put in a call to Henry and you're going to stay until he comes."

Carole's breast was not throbbing now, only a dull, steady, nerve-racking pain—which she could endure, she could endure *anything!* "All right," she said. "So you're against me, too."

"Careful, Carole. Dangerous ground."

Carole whirled, lifted her leg and kicked the suitcase, which tumbled and thudded down the carpeted stairway. Then she turned to face Judith. "You're against me, so is Henry, but you can't stop me. Either one of you, or *both!*"

Quietly then, Judith said, "I have the keys to your car, Carole." She moved to place herself between Carole and the stairs. "People in panic, hysterical people—"

"Go ahead!" Carole shouted. "Say it! *Patients.* Crazy people, insane people—*nuts!*"

"Unfortunately, dear, restraints are sometimes necessary," Judith said, but very gently.

No matter how long it iss, I vill someday be free. To do to Sandy vhat I did to you. But she vill not live to put me through the torment you are putting me through today—

Carole stooped to pick up the cosmetics kit. "Get out of my way," she snarled.

Then, at the same moment, they both heard the sound of the siren—distant, urgent *wow-wow-wow,* getting closer.

"He's not going to stop me, either," Carole said, gritting her teeth.

Softly Judith said, "He can't *stop* you. But he loves you. Carole. He might be able to help you."

Carole burst into tears then, dropped the case, heard it shatter on the floor, and then, her knees stiff and treacherous, she ran down the stairs, past the suitcases, to the front door. Where, seeing the darkness outside, she stopped and flipped a light switch on the wall before rushing out into the cold.

As Henry turned into the driveway, lights came on from the trees, illuminating the lawn and the front of the house. Quickly, automatically, he took in the scene as he began to brake: the tractor and truck, the blue Saab with one side scraped and bent (she had to be here now,) and two other vehicles. One he recognized, with surprise, as Duncan Clive's tan Jeep Wagoneer, the other a gray Honda Accord that he knew was Judith's.

Then, slowing to a stop, he saw Carole. She burst out the front door and came running, limping, toward his car, so that by the time he stepped out, she had reached him and she was holding him in her arms, kissing his cheek, her own face wet, her body quivering all over, her lips mumbling words he could not make out.

She stepped back then, her liquid brown eyes on him, anger in them, and love, and relief. "Where the *hell* have you been?" she demanded.

But before he could answer, Duncan Clive appeared from behind the Saab—which, Henry saw now, was packed to the gills, its trunk open—and came toward them.

"Carole," the man said, "would you forgive me for making a suggestion?" He nodded to Henry, but just a nod. "You and Dr. Judith and Chief Lindheim have matters to discuss, aye? Well, I could take Sandy to my place—"

"Sandy stays with me!" Carole cried, her voice loud and shrill and wild, body suddenly stiff.

Henry saw Duncan Clive glance at him. "Ye can trust me, lass," he said, very softly.

Then Carole changed again, quickly. "Yes, yes, I don't want Sandy to—" Then to Henry, dismissing him: "Judith's inside. She's the one who called you." And then back to Duncan Clive, lowering her voice: "There's something you have to know first. . . ."

Henry was moving along the flagstone path to the veranda, hearing Duncan Clive's voice from behind, speaking in a tone he'd never heard the man use before: "I have surmised more than ye think, Carole. She'll be safe w'me, as by now ye should well know."

"I'll pick her up at the barn as I leave." Then her voice dropped. "Now listen . . ."

Safe? The word echoed in Henry's mind as, on the veranda now, he saw a little girl, smaller than he'd somehow imagined, come through the front door and stop in front of him.

She looked up into his face with blue eyes squinting and asked, "Is your name Henry?"

"It is. And you're Sandy. And so's your hair."

Her head was tilted back, eyes looking up. "Well, all I can say is I'm glad you're here. Hi. No one told me you were a *giant.*"

And then she trotted down the steps toward the driveway, passing him, "You left your lights on."

He looked. It was true—no blue flasher but the headlights. "Would you turn them off for me, Sandy?"

The child stopped and turned at the front of the Saab. "Do you *mean* it?"

"Please," Henry said, and heard her voice behind him as he crossed the porch: "Wow! *Will* I?"

He went inside and closed the door. The hallway was empty.

"In here, Henry," Dr. Judith's voice called from the room where earlier he'd found and taken Carole's and her husband's picture from the desk. Dr. Judith was standing stiff and tall behind the desk, her dark eyes intense and troubled. "Sit down, Henry." She spoke in a clipped, precise rush of words. "A man with a strange accent has phoned Carole twice. On the second call I listened on the upstairs extension. He threatened to rape and kill Sandy. I have to get this said before Carole comes in. He says he'll do it even if he's arrested. No matter how long he has to stay in prison."

Startled, struggling to stifle the fury rising in him, Henry sank into the big leather chair. "And you think the man's capable of doing what he threatens?"

"He's capable of anything. I heard his voice, Henry. He's a sick and dangerous man. Carole imagines she can hide from him, but she knows better. She's terrified, and not entirely rational, no matter how she may seem. She told me just before you came in that she doesn't want him arrested."

"If he's capable of *anything,* he's got to be put behind bars." He was shaking his head. "No one on my list has an accent."

"Henry, it may be somcone you haven't even thought of."

In which case, Henry thought, he had struck out.

And then he heard a car's motor start outside.

"Mommy! Mommy, you should smell the nice smells in here. Like wood. Like a forest!"

Carole was standing at the driver's side of the Jeep. Sandy was clambering around in the back. And Duncan, behind the wheel, was saying: "Leave it to Chief Lindheim now, why not?"

Carole nodded, knowing this was exactly what she could not do. She reached to place her hand on Duncan's arm in the open window, surprised at its thick hardness, and at herself.

"It's boasting t'say," he said, "since there's little I do know. But one thing is how to make little girls happy."

Carole withdrew her hand and started toward the house, hearing, "Love you, Mommy," as the Jeep wagon moved up the driveway.

She dreaded what Henry would say, had to say, but her mind was fixed. Her hand reached inside the pocket of the car coat and closed around the gun.

"We're in here," Judith's voice called from the den just as Henry came into the hall from there.

"I have to use your telephone," he said.

"No." She moved quickly to the phone table.

"I have to have those two calls traced. It'll take time. Especially if they were dialed from within the 203 area code."

Iff your friend . . . that police chief . . . iff he comes near me, or any police—

"Henry," Carole said, "I'm withdrawing the charges."

He stepped toward her. "You don't mean that. The man has to be apprehended, he has to be stopped."

"Didn't Judith tell you? What about Sandy? Didn't she tell you, he means it. She *knows* he means it!"

"Then we can't have him loose in the streets."

"What about Sandy! God help me, that's all I care about now. Sandy comes first!"

Shaking his head, he said, quietly: "He may be some nut we never heard of—"

"I don't *care* who he is now. He wins, let him, he's won!"

Henry's face hardened. "Carole, I have a sworn duty as an officer of the law—"

"I won't testify! I'll swear I wasn't raped. I'll say I made it up to get back at my husband because he was having an affair. And he was, everyone knows it, everyone but me." Then she heard herself shouting: *"If I don't testify, then what can you do?"*

You will nefer have a moment's peace of mind for the rest of your life. You will nefer know when, or where—

"And you believe," Henry said, "you actually believe

he'll do nothing if he's *not* arrested? Do you want him to do this to somebody else?"

It was then that she said it. She asked, softly: "Would you ask yourself that if Sandy was Teresa and Teresa was still alive?"

The expression that came over Henry's face then filled her with sudden, terrible anguish and remorse, and the impulse to shut her eyes, to run and hide. But she did not move.

A long moment passed. In the silence she heard a movement in the den and, without taking her eyes from Henry, she realized that Judith had come to the door.

At last Henry said, "I can't do it, Carole." His voice was low, filled with dread and regret. He turned and walked heavily to the telephone table and, his back to her, tapped out some numbers.

Sandy vill be older then and I vill enjoy it more. But not so much as I enjoyed you—

"If you do this, Henry," Carole said, "I'll never forgive you and I'll never want to see you again."

She turned to go into the den. Judith stepped aside and let her pass. She moved to sit behind the desk, slowly lowering her burning forehead to the cool surface.

"And what about you, Carole?" Judith's voice asked. "You told me on Sunday you couldn't live a decent life if he wasn't punished."

"No one lives a decent life," she said. "They just pretend and fool themselves." She heard Henry's voice in the hall and then the door of the den closing.

Judith's voice came closer. "You told me you'd never be able to believe again. In anything."

"I never will anyway. But," she lifted her head to stare up into Judith's face, "I told you—that comes second now, damn it, everything else comes second!"

"And what will you teach Sandy?"

She heard the emptiness in her tone: "I'll tell her what I know. What she'll learn sooner or later anyway. There's no such thing as justice. Or meaning. Or truth. Or love. I wish . . . I wish to God somebody had taught *me.*"

Henry came into the den. Carole and Judith stared at him. "It may take several hours to find out where the calls originated. All I can say is: I'm sorry, Carole. All I can do is what I have to do. Now, let's go back. An accent—what kind of accent, what nationality?"

Judith said, "Weird. Not like any I ever heard before. A mixture. I've decided it was phony. Carole?" When Carole did not answer, she went on: "You should know, Henry, that he—this Mr. Deutsch—he also said that, even if he was in prison, he could hire someone to have it done."

Iff you haf the money, you can buy anything, anyone. Oh, it is a vicked vorld, Carole.

Then, having made up her mind, Carole asked, "You can't force me to testify, can you?"

"That," Henry said, "that's a legal matter. We don't have a sworn complaint, but we do have other corroborating evidence. Hospital records, so forth." Then, very gently, he reminded her: "I didn't invent the system, Carole."

"The system sucks," Carole said. "Like everything else." And then: "There's no way—that's what you're saying, isn't it?"

She saw the other two exchange glances.

"There's another possibility," Judith said. "I told you the man's sick. I heard the voice, I know the storm signals. If he himself should crack under this—"

"Then what?" Carole demanded, harshly. "A year or two in some hospital?" Then she snarled again: *"Read the newspapers!"*

Judith ignored that. She was beginning to pace. "Henry, she's right. In his mind, no matter what comes, Carole will be the one who caused it all. It's a twisted mind, with its own private logic—"

"Like mine, you mean?" Carole stood up behind the desk. "Well then, there's only one thing to do."

"Like what?" Henry asked.

"Find out who he is and kill him myself."

Carole saw another exchange of startled, disbelieving glances.

"Then," Henry said, "*you'd* be arrested."

"If no one even suspects him of raping me, who'd suspect me of putting a bullet through the bastard's head?"

"Carole," Judith said quickly, "Carole, I told you rape's always an act of rage. Now you're talking murder. Because of *your* rage."

"Cass said it!" Carole heard herself say. *"Savagery breeds savagery.* Eye for an eye; the Bible said it, too."

Henry spoke very softly: "You *will* be arrested, Carole. Because *I'll* know and that's what I'll have to do. *Then* what will happen to Sandy?"

"She'll be *alive!"* She was not quite screaming. "Don't you listen? She'll be *ALIVE!"* Then, moving around the desk, she said politely, "Excuse me."

"Where are you going?" Judith demanded.

In the doorway Carole turned. "I'm going to take your advice, Judith. I'm going to pretend I'm a thinking, civilized human being. I'm going to *think.* And if my husband comes, tell him I said: if he's the one, I'm going to kill *him."*

She turned and went along the hallway to the rear of the house and then down the narrow staircase into the TV room, where she sat down on the couch in the dark.

She had to do it herself. She had to be alone, so she could decide, herself, no one else, who the sonofabitch really was.

Until she could do that, she could not find out where he was and go there to kill him.

"I think she means it," Henry said when they were certain Carole had not gone out either the front or rear door.

"I know damn well she does," Judith said. "You notice, she hasn't taken off her coat since she came home. I'm sure that gun's in her pocket." Then she reached to turn on the light over the desk.

Henry was sitting upright in the leather chair. "You may as well know the whole thing," he said. "Or as much as I know. Her friend Mr. Cassady—"

"I heard it on the car radio. But there was no way to tell her. Not in the state she's in." Henry realized that Judith was taking short shallow breaths as she spoke. "That news will have to be broken to her very carefully, very gently." She sank to the leather couch and covered her face with her hands. "One more jolt and she's liable to blow. She has no idea how dark and wild it can get then."

Henry stood up abruptly. "Judith, the time has come. I have to know what you know."

Shaking her head, she lowered her hands from her face. "I can tell you this much. Mr. Deutsch is a vain man, and a cruel one. Right now he's terrified of being exposed, arrested, but he's even more terrified of losing control. He's taking an obscene pleasure in his power over her. But he also could shatter any second. No way to predict when or how. Or what could trigger it."

Henry shook his head. "You don't know all that from listening to his voice on the telephone. Judith, the goddamn chips are down." *Momento de verdad,* as Luisa used to say. "I don't want to know *what* he is, I want to know *who* he is. And *now.*"

Judith stood up. "Henry, we've been through this."

"Codes can be broken if a human life's at stake!"

Judith was facing him from behind the desk now, her dark eyes filled with torment, her face drawn. "Even then," she said.

Henry took a single long step. "Even if it means destroying Carole."

Suddenly Judith's voice was strident, as he'd never heard it before. "Henry, you stop this! You said you don't have enough tangible evidence to make an arrest. Well, anything I might know is privileged and wouldn't be admitted in any court, and you know it." She whirled to turn her back on him.

But a cool sort of excitement had begun deep inside him. "The man on the phone—is he one of your patients?"

"I *can* tell you that, yes. I mean *no,* he isn't."

"Then you have no reason not to tell me who you think, or even suspect, he is."

"I can't, Henry." She returned to sit behind the desk. He heard the anguished plea in her voice. "I can't *do* that."

"It *is* someone I haven't thought of, isn't it?" The thing he'd feared: "Someone who's not even on my list."

Her fingers were nervously examining the frame from which he'd removed the photograph. "Without regard to what I might know professionally, I can say this: I do doubt that you've considered him."

"Jesus," Henry said, under his breath. With only four names left—David Slade, Jerald Dixon, the husband and Joel White—now he had none. "Jesus Christ. Moment of truth, all right. I *am* getting old, Judith." The excitement had shriveled in him. "You mean I made the assumption that it had to be a friend? Because he used her name during the attack, and because Carole was so sure?"

"No," she said then, slowly. "Carole's assumption was probably right." She slammed her palm down on the desk. "Oh no, God, Henry, go out and find him yourself! I've already said more than I—"

Then she broke off and Henry turned to follow her gaze. Carole was standing in the doorway. She had changed again. Her face was pale and drawn, and her eyes looked stunned and dull, her body sagging against the door frame.

Judith stood up behind the desk. "Carole, dear, what's happened?"

"I've been following your advice," Carole said, in a lifeless voice. "I've been *thinking.*" And then: "I sat in the dark and I forced myself to go over everything Mr. Deutsch said on the phone. Both calls. Phrase by phrase, word for word." She came into the room and sat down limply on the couch, facing him, her eyes avoiding his, just staring. "Ponder. He told me to sit and ponder. Who is it who says ponder? . . . And he called me a slut and a whore and *harlot* . . . I'd only heard the word spoken once before. Once before the rape, I mean. Last summer when he made me feel so guilty because I wore the clothes Rolfe wanted me to wear, to the newspaper picnic. . . ." Her voice seemed to drift away.

Then: "I don't believe it. I still can't believe it."

"Go on," Judith prompted in a quiet professional tone.

Did she already know?

"Exactly. Precisely. Mr. Deutsch said that, too."

And then Henry knew. He remembered: *He treats Carole as if she were made of spun glass.*

He knew but still couldn't quite believe it.

"You were nott a goot gurl," Carole continued, her voice dull and lifeless. "He was always telling me I was a good girl, a smart girl. The accent—it fooled me."

Her brown eyes seemed to focus then, and they lifted to stare at Judith. "He said it himself. It *is* a wicked world, isn't it? Evil." And then she turned her gaze on Henry. "He knows doesn't he? Because he's so evil himself."

Henry took a deep breath and lifted himself to his feet, hearing Judith say, "No more riddles, Carole. Give Henry the name. I can't."

Henry took one long stride to the desk and leaned on it, his arms stiff, his fists tight on the surface. "Judith," he said, "Vincent Fletcher is not one of your patients, is he?"

"No," she said, her eyes fixed on his.

"His wife then?"

"No."

Henry turned away and was stepping to the door, cursing himself silently, when he remembered: the daughter, the high school kid wearing shorts and that quick shamed look in her eyes that puzzled him. He knew now what it was—fear.

He stopped and turned and spoke past Carole to Judith. "Mady. Is Madelyn Fletcher your patient?"

Softly then, her dark eyes meeting his, Judith said, "I can't answer that, Henry. And I don't know why I should have to now."

He went out into the hall.

"Henry!" Carole cried. "Where are you going?" He turned to see her rushing toward him. Her face still stricken, but her eyes bright and intense with alarm. "What are you going to do?"

"I'm sorry," he said. "I'm going to do my job."

"What about evidence?" Judith called from the den.

"I'll get it," he said, thinking: find it or manufacture it. And then to Carole: "For your sake, too, Carole. Whether you believe that or not."

He opened the front door and the cold air struck and by the time he had reached the squad car, the cold had reached into him, flesh and marrow and mind.

Helpless, Carole watched the door close and waited—because she couldn't risk leaving while he was still here.

Then she felt Judith's arm around her waist, and heard the whisper in her ear: "Henry'll handle it, dear."

Handle it? Was Judith crazy, too? Everyone had gone crazy all of a sudden! "You heard," Carole said. "You *know.* What's the matter with everyone?" She whirled around, shrugging free of Judith's arm, facing her. "Henry's against me and so are you!"

"Carole, stop this now. We both love you—"

"And you—you knew all along, didn't you? You let me go through that hell!"

"I couldn't tell you, dear. Shall I explain? I just couldn't. I'm sorry."

"I trusted you," Carole said in a whisper, the anguish of betrayal in it. "I trusted both of you." And she had trusted Mr. Fletcher, too. She had needed a father—*If you were my daughter and that's the way I think of you, Carole.* Oh God, she was going to be sick.

She heard a siren begin—*wow-wow-wow*—and knew Henry had reached the road.

"Henry has no choice now," Judith said.

"Well, *I* do," Carole muttered, and started toward the front door.

Judith moved quickly, and managed to place herself with her back to the door, facing Carole. They were very close. Eye-to-eye, both breathing hard.

"Carole," Judith warned, "I learned very early that there are times when physical restraint is justified." Then, in a low rush, "You're not well, dear. You're sick. Maybe all of us are by now—"

"Is it sick to love your daughter?"

Carole whirled and ran the length of the long hall—why wouldn't they understand, why wouldn't *anyone* understand?

When she reached the rear of the house she went through the dark pantry and threw open the back door and plunged into the cold darkness.

The night came back to her, that night in the woods, in pain, falling, shouting in the dark—

But now, reaching the front lawn, she had the lights from the trees flooding the driveway and she could see the two cars. She ran to the Saab, stumbling, both knees sharpening with pain, and then she had the door open—where was Judith, what was she doing?—and then she was in the seat, reaching for the key—

It was not there.

Only then did she remember.

Judith. Damn her, oh no, damn her, *she* had the key, God damn her, she hates me, everyone hates me and blames me—

She got out, fast, and moved to Judith's car.

She opened the door, she leaned inside, found the dashboard, no keyhole, ran her hands down along the steering column, her fingers found the round chrome frame of the ignition keyhole—

There was no key in Judith's car, either.

So she straightened and started walking up the incline of the driveway, the floodlights from the trees in her eyes. She'd hitch a ride, she'd risk it, she had the gun, she'd—

It was then that she saw, first, headlight beams on the road and then the shadowy profile of another car, slowing and turning in. It had a small yellow light on its roof.

She was walking straight toward it, the twin beams of its lights blinding her now, as it came to a halt a few yards away.

She did not stop walking, tempted only for a second to run across the lawn and into the woods, but then she made out the lettering on the yellow light above the windshield: TAXI.

Shadowy movements behind the glare, a door slamming, and then a voice, a familiar voice, which stopped her. "Keep the change and fuck off."

The voice she had hoped never to hear again—

A strange thought shot through her mind, a giddy thought: God's not against me. He's on my side—

"What're you doing out here?" Rolfe asked, his voice blurred. He came into the headlight glare, tie loose, jacket over one shoulder, vest unbuttoned. "Carole, what's happening?"

But she ignored him, walking again, passing close, smelling the stench of booze even in the cold crisp air, shouting, "You want a customer?"

And heard a voice: "Sure, lady, hop in."

And then Rolfe's voice: "Hey, look, I know I'm late and I knew you'd be in a mood, but—"

Mood? All of a sudden, reaching the side of the cab, she felt certain she was going to laugh out loud—

The driver's face was a roundish, shadowy shape behind the dark window. "Where you going, lady? I'm from Sudbury."

"She's not going anywhere, driver. I just got home—"

"Sudbury?" she heard herself saying as she opened the door. "That's just where I'm going."

Rolfe reached, grabbed the edge of the door, held it. "Karen called—we've got to talk." She had one foot on the gravel and one on the floor of the taxi. "Look, darling, I deserve everything you want to say, but let's go inside and have a drink and sit down like civilized—"

He was very close. "Don't call me *darling,*" she snarled. It was as if some stranger on the street had used the word. Or Vincent Fletcher while his body was on top of her, his penis inside her—

She had acted before she realized she'd moved. Her fist smashed into Rolfe's face, she felt the jarring sensation all the way up her arm and pain in her knuckles, she saw amazement and disbelief in his wide-open, startled eyes, she saw blood from his nose running over his upper lip, she lifted her leg and was inside the cab, sitting back, slamming the door—

"Where to in Sudbury, lady?"

And then, as the cab started forward, she saw Rolfe stumbling to stand in front of it, his arms extended, waving up and down, his face wild, his mouth moving with blood on it, she could hear a sound, but not the words as the taxi came to a jolting stop.

"Back up!" She screamed—was that her voice? *"Back up!"*

As the driver threw the cab into reverse, he twisted his head to look past her out the rear window. Chunky, middle-aged, bewildered face. "Is that guy nuts?"

"No," she said. "I am."

The taxi stopped momentarily astride the road, then shot forward, and in the dark she heard Rolfe's voice through the open window—furious, frustrated, shouting: "You better listen, goddamn you, I need you tonight! It's all your fault, anyway!" And then a bellow, filling the night: "Cass is dead! You hear me? *Cass killed himself!*"

PART 7

ALL THE WAY INTO Sudbury, siren wailing, Henry was giving himself hell. Why hadn't *he* seen it? Why hadn't he realized? *Him,* Henry Lindheim, not Carole! What the hell kind of police officer was he anyway?

He remembered now that first night, in the hospital emergency room after Carole had slapped Joel White: *She does art work . . . special arrangement . . . she's the old man's favorite.* And the bastard himself, the way he'd tried to shove his guilt onto the reporter: *He's a very angry young man . . . that little SOB hates Carole, ask her.* Why? Why hadn't he been listening?

Because Vincent Fletcher was such a highly respected pillar of society? Had he let himself be taken in by that? Or was it because Vincent Fletcher had reflected his own feelings when he'd said: *Carole's like a daughter to me.* And: *I'm thinking of Carole—Mendoza did steal the car—wouldn't it be easier on her if you could close the case as quickly as possible?* That's why the bastard phoned Carole, too—not to sympathize, but to convince her to close the case!

Jesus, it was all coming together now. Yet . . .

Yet his mind was still shadowed by doubt. Why?

Was it because he still resisted admitting the truth?

Which was that he had fallen down on the job. He'd botched it!

He's a vain man, and a cruel one, Judith had said. The barbershop manicure, the sharp-edged, built-up leather heels, the youthful toupee, the rowing machine—

But he still didn't have any tangible evidence, not a goddamn crumb! *None.* And if he placed Vincent Fletcher under arrest without probable cause, the bastard would be out on bail within hours. Mark Rainer would see to that, and then he'd demand Henry's badge, with damn good cause, and then the whole case would go down the tubes. And, without authority, he'd be helpless to do *anything* for Carole.

Well then, he'd have to find a way to do the job *without* evidence. Or maybe he could make the guilty man himself produce it.

An idea began to take shape in his mind. He stopped the car at the next public booth and placed a call to Miriam Bishop at the *Sudbury News-Chronicle.* After she listened, she said, "You don't ask much, do you, Henry? I'm not sure I can do it and I damned well *know* I can't do it before you get here. But if you're thinking what I think you are, I'll give it a go. Drive slowly."

He returned to the car and drove on, no siren. He considered dropping by Morgan's Men's Shop, then realized they'd be closed and that it was past his dinnertime and that he hadn't eaten since morning and to hell with his stomach, let it growl!

His oh-so-logical supposition as to whom Lawrence Morgan and Mark Rainer had been trying to protect—he'd been off-track there, too. If he'd had Vincent Fletcher on his list, he could have made a logical case against him instead of the one he'd built against Jerald Dixon. Morgan and Rainer and Fletcher and Dixon—probably they *all* belonged to the same clubs. But why hadn't this occurred to him! He knew why now: the failing was in *him.* Time to throw in the towel, Henry. Time to admit the obvious—

Approaching the cloverleaf where Route 7 joined the interstate, he radioed headquarters and demanded when they'd have a list of the incoming phone calls to the Jensen residence during the day, and added: "Also, get me a list of calls to the Pendleton Day–Care in Sheffield. If any numbers match up, get back to me at once."

"Sorry, sir," a male voice responded. "It takes time, even with all the computers they got—"

"We don't *have* time!" He heard his own shout in the closed car. Then, about to apologize, he couldn't remember who was on duty tonight. Hadn't he set up the schedule himself? Now his goddamn memory was going, too.

By the time he arrived at the newspaper building on Main Street, Henry had begun to wonder whether the time had come to pack it in. Get this case behind, then write out a letter of resignation to the Board of Selectmen—

Then what? Fish? Stare at the TV screen and lose his mind? Or, worst of all, back to the bottle? Another form of death.

If he had a choice, he'd rather die now, tonight, than sit around and wait for it to happen.

Vincent Fletcher's maroon-colored BMW sedan was not in the parking area. He hadn't really expected it to be and it was too soon to confront the man anyway. Carole probably thought all he had to do now was make an arrest. But if he did, Mark Rainer'd make sure the case never reached court.

Then what would happen to her? What would *she* do then? He should have gotten that gun away from her, somehow, even if it had meant threatening her with arrest on a concealed weapons charge.

Every muscle aching, he went inside, nodding at the girl behind the counter, and went through the double doors and into the enclosed stairwell and started up, then halted when he heard a voice from above: "Well, well, well, Sherlock Double-O Seventy himself!"

Joel White was coming down the stairs, carrying a large

cardboard carton in both arms, his gaunt, sallow face hostile and mocking, his tone derisive: "You come to arrest me, Chief? You found out where I was Saturday night?" The small young man came to a stop a few steps above him. His red hair was a curly, bushy mess; his brown eyes looked hazy and unfocused. "More questions, man?"

Henry voiced the first question that came to mind: "You said you knew someone who was so insecure that he wore both belt and suspenders—" and he let it hang there.

Joel White's face changed then. He smiled in a half-hearted way. "You heard that, then? It took till now to sink in, did it?" Now he seemed almost to be enjoying himself. "Chief, I've had a real shitty day up to now. That asshole fired me for writing the story *he* gave me, word for word. The one *you* fed him. So just tell me you're here to arrest him. Please."

"I can't arrest a man for being insecure," Henry growled. "If you suspected what you're indicating now, why didn't you say it straight out?"

Joel White cackled a mean laugh. "My boss? The man who pays for my food and rent and a jolt of coke now and then?"

"You don't work for him now."

"For that you get another little hint. Normally, he wears both braces *and* belt. Because if his pants fell down, we'd all see what he ain't got. But no belt since Saturday night. Misplaced it somewhere, I guess."

Staring up at the pale, haggard face, Henry felt a sudden stab of pity. "Now what're you going to do, kid?"

"What do you care?" His eyes were sober, still unfocused, and he was frowning. He seemed very young and vulnerable now. "I'm going to New Haven. Where I go every night after work. Where I try to cheer up the boy I love." He tilted his head sideways. And Henry caught a glint of moisture in his half-closed eyes. "He's dying. Very, very slowly, he's dying. And that's where I was Saturday night, too. But then I couldn't tell anyone that, could I? Get out of my way now, please."

Henry stepped aside. As Joel White passed him, he reached out and tapped him on his bony shoulder, unable to think of anything to say except: "Sorry, kid."

But Joel White reached the bottom, went out the stairway door, and did not look back.

Hip joint catching with each step, Henry climbed the stairs to the top, more tired now, every move an effort. Going down the corridor, he couldn't remember when he'd felt older. Or more spent and useless—

The door was open and when he went in, Miriam Bishop turned from the slanted drawing table where she'd been working, pen in hand, cigarette dangling between her lips. She pushed her horn-rimmed glasses to the top of her head and stared at him: "Hey, what's happened to you? Take the load off. Big man, you've had a busy day."

In the big, high, fluorescent-lighted room, Henry glanced around. If he could hoist himself up to one of the tall stools, he'd probably never be able to get down again, so he remained standing and said, "I've been having a chat with Joel White."

"Yeah. He dropped in here to say good-bye. Made me feel like the bitch I probably am. Honestly, Chief, I did think he might have done it. I didn't know then . . . what he just told me. How about a drink? I need one."

Henry shook his head. A drink now would probably finish him off. "You may as well tell me; he tried to."

Miriam was stooping at a supply cabinet, reaching inside. "AIDS," she said. "I feel sometimes it's closing in, like the Black Plague. His lover's dying." She produced a half-filled bottle of Haig & Haig. "And, of course, the poor kid knows he's next." Pouring the scotch, she said, "Thank whatever gods may be that I was wrong. I didn't know he'd already come out of the damned closet." She lifted the glass. "To Carole." She took a long swallow.

"You were in such a rush I couldn't ask on the phone. How is she, honestly?"

What could he say? That she'd been driven to the breaking point and that if he didn't put Vincent Fletcher behind bars, she'd probably kill him? And *then* she'd be the one he'd have to arrest. So, instead of answering the woman's question, he asked one himself: "Did you do the sketch?"

Glass in hand, cigarette still dangling, Miriam stepped to the high table. "All I know about a police composite is from watching television." She picked up a nine-by-twelve piece of heavy drawing paper. "You said it shouldn't be exact." She held up the drawing. "Does this look too much like him, or not enough?"

Henry studied the black-and-white pen sketch. It was clearly Vincent Fletcher's face, yet enough out of focus and proportion so that he had to study it carefully to recognize him. "Good God," he said. "For my purposes, it's perfect."

"Lucky for us he's at rehearsal, so there's no danger we'll hear those leather heels stomping down the hall any second. It's his theatre, you know; he built it in memory of his dear dead mother. And he's been at home sick all day. You really think he raped Carole then? I don't know why, but even I'm surprised." She lifted herself to sit on the stool. "Well, what are you going to do with my little masterpiece, Chief?"

"I'm not absolutely sure yet," he admitted. But at that moment it came to him. He remembered drinking late with a gnarled oldtimer named Pat Shea, Detective Lieutenant, NYPD—a seedy, smoke-filled bar near the docks, many years ago. *If you're at a dead end but you're absolutely positive yourself but don't have the evidence—well, kid, one way's to scare the shit out of the suspect till he confesses . . . orrrrr . . . you tighten the screws to force him to give himself away in some other way . . . orrrrr . . . he makes a break for it and you have to put a bullet in him to keep him from eluding—*

"Precisely and exactly!" Henry heard himself say out loud, imitating Vincent Fletcher, and heard Miriam laugh as he stepped to the door.

She slid down from the stool. "Chief, just so you'll be warned—Mr. Fletcher is an honored member of the National Rifle Association, wouldn't you know. He runs an editorial once a month about the constitutional right of every citizen to bear arms and have one handy when the Russkies land. He has a small arsenal in the basement of his home."

"You're saying he might be armed. So am I."

"I'm saying that Vincent Fletcher is one of the angriest men I've ever known. For all his inherited wealth and position, he thinks he's been dealt a raw deal. And for all his phony pompous charm, he's simmering with rage."

"So am I," Henry said again, realizing that it was true. "Where's the Sudbury Civic Theatre located?"

Cass is dead. You hear me? Cass killed himself.

From the house and through The Village, sitting in the back seat of the cab, Carole, numb and stunned, had heard those words roaring in her mind over and over. She still didn't quite believe them. Could Rolfe have been lying? Drunk and furious, could even he be that cruel?

If he was not lying, why hadn't Henry told her? Or Judith?

It's all your fault anyway! he had shouted.

But . . . but what had she done? Everyone was blaming her but nobody would tell her what *she* had done.

"Where to in Sudbury?" The driver's voice reached her from a distance. "We're coming into Sudbury, Mrs. Jensen."

He knew her name. How? "How do you know my name?" She heard her words in the closed car, which was warm now, the heater purring.

"Name's on the mailbox back there. And your old man

—he's so spaced out he talked all about it on the way. Said that was the reason he's been guzzling since five."

"One of the reasons," Carole said.

"Yeah. Well, like I was saying to my wife at breakfast—if it was her—I mean, if someone did that to her—I'd be on his trail some way. Something like this, honest, it makes me ashamed to be a man. I'd probably kill him."

"That's what I'm going to do."

"I know you're kidding, but I don't think anybody in his right mind'd blame you. They ought to bring back the death penalty, maybe just for his kind. Hey, you *are* kidding, aren't you?"

Then she remembered what she had to do. "Do you know where the newspaper building is? On Main Street."

"That where you want to go, Mrs. Jensen? Sure. You take it easy now, will you? Sit back and take it easy."

The man had been kind, so very kind, when she'd made the long-distance call from the booth on the highway. He'd helped her when she didn't have coins. When she couldn't remember Cass's phone number in the city, or his address, except that it was on West Sixty-third Street. When she had had to think and think, even to remember her own number, so he could charge the call to it. After he'd dialed for her, and after he was sure she had someone on the line, he'd gone back to sit in the cab and wait.

This is Tracy Farrell. Cass isn't here. Carole had heard tears in the woman's voice. *I mean—Cass is dead. Who is this?*

So it's true—

It's true all right. Who is this?

Then she must have given her name. Because there was a long silence. Cars speeding by on the highway, tires humming, the booth freezing cold—

Oh? the voice had said. *Carole. I always wanted to meet you. He adored you. And I've always hated you.*

Tracy Farrell?

You don't even know my name. It figures. We've been

living together for about two years. Except on weekends, of course. That's why I wasn't here. The voice had sounded sad and lost and incredulous then. *I loved him, too. But I always knew I was the wrong one—*

Had Carole asked when, or how, or why? She *knew* why. She remembered last night—

. . . must've been in some kind of fight. His face looked awful. He left a note. All it said was: I was cleaning my gun.

Unable to speak then, Carole had managed to whisper, *When . . . when did it happen?*

Around three this morning. He used to quote Fitzgerald, remember? "In the long dark night of the soul"—remember?

No, she had said, thinking: there was so much she hadn't known, or realized. So all that was going on and she hadn't even—

When she'd said good-bye and how sorry she was—what a puny word, sorry—and after she'd returned to the taxi, it had taken some time for the shock and grief and loss to reach her and take over. She couldn't concentrate now on what she knew she had to do, had to do because of Sandy . . . who loved Cass . . . whom Cass loved.

And he was dead.

Cass was gone.

Like all the rest of her life.

Except Sandy.

You'll nefer know when, or how. You'll nefer have a second's peace of mind for the rest of your life—

Cass . . . if nobody else, Cass would understand what she was doing, what she had to do, and why. Only Cass.

Then, realizing, she had been grateful for one thing: *she* had never, not once, *she* had never suspected Cass of raping her. He must have known that. No matter what Rolfe had accused him of, Cass must have known that she—oh God, he knew that, didn't he?

"Here we are, Mrs. Jensen," the driver said. "They work late to get out a morning paper, don't they?"

She was back in the present again. The here and now. Lights in almost every window, as the taxi stopped along the curb in front of the two-story building. "What's your name?" she heard herself ask the driver, suddenly grateful, almost overwhelmingly grateful for his kindness.

"Cliff Sackett," he said, getting out of the cab, going around its front end to open the door for her. "You want me to wait? Just in case whoever you want to see ain't here."

"Please," she said, stepping out, her knees stiff and sore, hearing the word ain't and thinking of Henry. Had he been here already? Had he already made the arrest? "And thank you again, Mr. Sackett."

She took a step, but his voice stopped her. "Mrs. Jensen, it's not my place, but . . . but listen, you don't look so good now that I can see your face. Maybe you ought to let me take you back home."

"I don't have a home," she heard herself say as she limped toward the front door of the building.

Inside, the girl behind the counter asked, "Are you okay, Carole?"

"I will be," she answered. "After I see Mr. Fletcher."

"Oh, Mr. Fletcher's not here tonight. He wouldn't miss rehearsal, though."

She thought of Miriam upstairs and realized how lonely she was. Had she ever felt so lonely, and alone? But at once her mind recoiled: Miriam would only try to stop her, too. Like Henry. Like Judith.

"Where's the theatre?" she heard herself demand, knowing he'd missed rehearsal Saturday night, knowing better than anyone. *"Where?"*

"Civic Theatre. I don't know the address. By the lake. But listen, Carole, he doesn't like to be disturbed unless it's very important."

"It's important," she said, turning from the counter toward the doors. "The sonofabitch raped me."

Then, having said it, it was as if she had crossed some

invisible line and now she was again in full control. As if that shutter in her mind had lifted and she could see everything sharp and clear and with a hurtful vividness. She went out the doors and the cold night air took her breath. Everything was now so vibrant and dazzling that, as she reached into her pocket to touch the gun, she experienced a wild sense of elation, expectation, eagerness.

Not limping now, she walked to the curb where the taxi was parked. It was like moving in another world altogether. The same world, of course, but transformed, intensified.

And in it she could do anything. Anything at all.

On the way to the Sudbury Civic Theatre at the southern end of Lake Candlewood, Henry had—finally—learned the time of death of Mr. A. L. Cassady in New York. Not yet official, the Manhattan medical examiner's office had warned: between two and five A.M. Which meant that the writer could not have seen the phony story in the local morning paper. Not that it mattered now—a moot point. But Henry felt a kind of relief regardless.

And it had been then that he knew what he could do when he spoke with Vincent Fletcher, how he could scare the shit out of him, as old Pat O'Shea had suggested all those years ago. Very simple, really: all he had to do, all he *could* do really, was to tighten the screws by making certain Vincent Fletcher learned that he—he, himself—was the suspect. Another long shot, but . . .

Now, sitting in the back row on a side aisle watching the rehearsal, which had been in progress when he arrived, Henry was hoping that, since he'd removed his cap, if and when his presence was discovered, it might not be apparent in the dimness that he was wearing a uniform. If he didn't have to stand up.

On the other hand, Vincent Fletcher would have to see him, sooner or later, but Henry was hoping he could time this so that he could observe the bastard's reaction. The first shock. How many more would it take? . . . *he also could shatter any second.* And if he did, what would follow then? *No way to predict when or how. Or what could trigger it.* Henry slumped deep in his seat and looked around.

A kid in his twenties was atop a tall folding ladder, which was straddling one row of seats, obviously repairing a light hanging on a pipe above. Except for Henry, the seats in the auditorium were empty.

The stage scenery was familiar: an apartment in an old New York brownstone. But this one had a huge slanting skylight, which appeared to be made of transparent plastic to represent glass. An attractive blond young lady, whom everyone called Corie, and a handsome young man playing her lawyer husband were acting out a scene—no sign of Vincent Fletcher yet, although Henry had seen the maroon BMW parked outside. Standing in the center aisle, a few rows back from the stage, a short slightly heavyset woman in her late forties was watching and occasionally giving directions in a deep gravel voice. The actors called her Mitzi and every once in a while she'd go up the three-step platform leading to the stage from the end of the middle aisle and change positions or discuss how one of them was speaking a line, occasionally stopping to bellow: "Quiet offstage!"

But Henry was not interested. His mind returned to his own uncertainties. What if Carole and Judith were both wrong? Carole had suspected Jerald Dixon, and David Slade, and her husband. In her hysteria, she'd even threatened to shoot Janos Petofi. And whatever information Judith had, it had to come from Mady Fletcher. Who was still a child. Who, if she was under psychiatric care and hated her father for whatever reasons, upset and bitter and maybe even vengeful, could distort reality, too. . . .

Good God, here he was, he'd come all this way and now his mind was still clouded with doubts. Where had his confidence gone? Had his age and personal involvement shot his confidence, too? But . . . what if he and Judith and Carole were all three wrong? And what if Carole did what she threatened without even the slight mitigating fact that the man was actually the one who'd attacked her?

Well, his job now was to make certain. Before he himself took action. And before Carole did.

Getting old, Henry. Showing your age more every hour.

Then he heard several tittering voices offstage and the boy on top of the ladder laughed out loud.

Vincent Fletcher had made his entrance. The blond young woman, Corie, was staring at him, beginning to smile. He was wearing a sports jacket, an ascot, and the kind of Tyrolean hat Henry hadn't seen in years.

"I begg your pardon," he said, sweeping off the hat and bowing grandly. "I hope I am nut disturping you . . . My name is Velasco . . . Victor Velasco."

More tittering from off the stage, the boy on the ladder chuckling.

Vincent Fletcher, the bastard, was actually enjoying himself. Overacting, clowning. The stage had come alive—and the bastard knew it, and loved it.

"You'll learn, as time goess by in thiss mittle-income prison camp, thatt ve haf a rat fink for a landlort."

Henry was suddenly sickened. Not shocked—sickened. With revulsion, with hate. Hate so consuming and ferocious that his right hand reached without volition to unsnap the flap on his holster and his stomach threatened to rebel. After all the bastard had put Carole through, he could still come here and play games, make people laugh. Henry's outrage streamed hotly through his blood.

"You know, uff course, that you are unbearaply pretty." Vincent Fletcher reached and placed one arm around Corie's waist. "Vhat iss your name, m'dear?"

"Hold it," the dark-haired director called. "Vincent, we reblocked that Saturday night."

Vincent Fletcher stared down on her. Eyes blinking. Still glowing. "Mitzi," he said, still using the same accent, "you vill recall that Mady and I were not here on Saturday night."

Henry's mind zeroed in. The bastard had just blown his own alibi again. And in front of witnesses. *Oh, all right, Daddy, but Miss Brewer's already mad at us because of last night.* Why the hell hadn't he picked up on that?

"I gave Mady the changed blocking on the phone this morning," Mitzi Brewer said now. "Didn't she give it to you?"

"She ditt nutt!"

More laughter.

Something in Henry shriveled. *That's where I was when the city desk here phoned to tell me what had happened to Carole.* The bastard had been giving himself an alibi yesterday afternoon when Henry had had no reason even to wonder about it. But *why* hadn't he wondered? Why, *why?*

Mady Fletcher, wearing blue jeans, not shorts, and a fuzzy pink sweater, appeared on the stage from the side. She held the same clipboard in her hand. "Daddy, how *could* I give you the changes when you weren't home all day?"

Miriam had said, *He's been at home sick all day.*

And Henry remembered Mady boasting yesterday: *Daddy has the funniest accent and he's going to steal the show.*

And Judith: *I've decided Mr. Deutsch's accent is phony.*

All doubt washed out of Henry's mind. And he felt such an invigorating charge of certainty and renewed confidence that, heart hammering, he leaned forward in his seat.

On the stage Vincent Fletcher still had his arm around Corie's waist. "I *was* here *last* night, remember?" He'd dropped the accent now. "And I did the scene precisely and exactly the way I am doing it tonight . . . and you did *not* stop me, Miss Brewer."

Mitzi shrugged and turned and came up the center aisle. "Let me see it from the back of the house. But I still think that arm bit goes too far." Then, catching sight of Henry, she stopped walking to stare over the seats at him. "Hold it, please!" she called out, and came to the last row of seats. "May I help you? Mr. Fletcher doesn't allow visitors at rehearsals."

Henry decided to stand up. He saw her eyes travel down his uniform. "Please don't stop because of me," he said in a low voice, not glancing toward the stage. "I've come to see Mr. Fletcher on newspaper business, but I'm enjoying—"

"Houselights!" Mitzi shouted. And then to Henry: "I'm ready for a break myself." Then she lifted her gravel voice again: "Vincent, you have a visitor."

Henry did look at the stage then—to see the bastard let go of the young woman and come down to the edge, placing his hand above his eyes to peer out into the dimness. At that moment lights came on all over the theater.

Vincent Fletcher's face, after one quick moment of startlement, regained its composure. "Chief Lindheim?" he said, his tone carefully cordial and guarded. "Well, you have caught me at my revels. Is it something we can discuss at my office tomorrow?"

"Nothing important at all, sir," Henry said, hating the *sir,* hating the man, and hating what he knew he had to do. And, at last, how he intended to do it. "Please don't let me interrupt. Just so we can have a few minutes before tomorrow's edition goes to press." Then he forced a cordial tone into his own voice: "I haven't seen a play in years and I've never seen a rehearsal. I insist, sir."

The bastard nodded and turned away, his back to the audience, and Mitzi bawled: "Let's finish this scene, then we'll take a ten-minute break. Places, everybody. Kill the houselights!"

Henry sank into his seat, his hip joint catching, hard. Time, he thought, was what he didn't have. What if Carole learned, or realized, where Fletcher was? But he himself needed time now. To plot his course. Now that he had some idea where he wanted that course to lead, he had to do a little rehearsing of his own.

"Take it from your entrance, Vincent," Mitzi called, just as the theater darkened, leaving only the stage lighted.

The scene began again. As before. And continued until Fletcher again placed his arm around Corie's slim waist.

"You know, uff course, that you are unbearaply pretty—" Then he stopped. Frowning. Then he looked into the wings. "Line, please!" he shouted, no accent now. "Mady, give me the line for God's sake!"

His daughter appeared on the stage again. "What's your name?" she said, in a small bewildered voice. Her face looked very pale and her eyes had that same scared look he'd seen before. "That's your line, Daddy: *What's your name?*"

"Well, *thank* you," Fletcher said, elaborately. "And if I blow a line with an audience out there—"

"If that happens," Mitzi said, "just go on, ad-lib."

"I am speaking to the assistant stage manager, Miss Brewer, not to you!" He strode to where Mady stood. "What do I have to do to get a prompt? If you can't keep your mind on the play, Mady . . ."

"Sorry, Daddy," the girl muttered, and turned to leave the stage. Henry was not close enough to see whether there were tears in her eyes.

He heard Mitzi sigh with irritation and a touch of exasperation before she shouted: "From that speech, please. Don't go back!" And then she turned her head toward Henry and whispered an angry apology: "I don't know what's the matter with him. He's had every line down pat since the third rehearsal."

From the stage he heard Corie stop in the middle of a speech and saw her step away from Fletcher, wriggling out from his grasp. "I can't cross to where I'm supposed to be if you keep holding onto me, Mr. Fletcher."

Fletcher stared after her, then growled: "If we keep

changing the blocking, we'll never get it right before opening night."

"Well," Corie said, "I think Mitzi's right—you don't have to make *love* to me just because you say I'm pretty!"

The bastard was standing stiff and straight. "I shall never touch you again, young lady." There was a distinct tremor in his voice. "You may rely on that."

Mitzi hurried down the aisle toward the stage. "Let's go back again. Try it without taking hold of her, Vincent. And look, everybody, we open in three nights. Let's hold down the tension, shall we? Now, from Victor's entrance again, and no stopping till the end of the scene, *please.*"

Henry continued to watch, without moving, letting the hatred take over, but struggling to quench the anger. While he watched, in his mind he could hear the lava simmering and bubbling deep in the crater of the volcano.

Then he began to concentrate on exactly what he could do to make sure it erupted.

The taxi came to a stop at the red brick walk leading to the front door of the theatre, which was on the outskirts of town, across a road from the southern tip of Lake Candlewood. The light inside the cab came on.

"Mrs. Jensen," Cliff Sackett was saying, "my wife's always going off without her purse. No sweat, I'll trust you for the fare. But I can't take this. It's your wedding ring."

"It's gold," she said, getting out into the cold damp air from the lake. "Please. I was going to throw it away anyway. Please take it." She was moving up the walk now, when she heard:

"You sure you don't want me to wait?"

"I won't be going home," she said, not sure he'd heard her.

The bright, light, strange stillness inside was awesome. On the way she had come to wonder why she'd never felt this way before. It was, in its way, a beautiful feeling—no doubts, no shadows, almost like drifting in a weird but pleasant dream in which everything was radiantly clear. The dark glitter of the lake across the road was lovely. And the light from over the wide entrance porch was yellowish and beautiful, too.

As she heard the taxi pulling away, she saw a sign upright and glowing on the withered lawn: PARKING. There was an arrow in luminous paint beneath the word. She stopped and turned her head. In the paved area alongside the theatre building she saw, as she'd expected, Vincent Fletcher's maroon BMW sedan. The parking lot was flooded with light from under the eaves of the theatre. She let her gaze move over the other cars, only about a dozen in all, and found it at once, again without surprise: the round light on its roof, glittering pale blue, and the spotlight on its side like an enormous burnished bullet. Henry's police car was the only one that had been backed into its slot.

If your friend . . . that police chief . . . if he comes near me, or any police—

She shoved her right hand into the pocket of the car coat. The metal of the gun felt warm.

She was distantly surprised that she felt no savage urge to rush inside, to take out the gun, to find him and empty it into him no matter where he was or who was with him. She continued on to the porch, stepped up the single step. Henry couldn't stop her now. No one could. Not even herself. She was vaguely grateful they were both here. It could mean Henry had already arrested him. Not that that mattered just so long as Vincent Fletcher was still here—

She opened one of the double doors and went inside. A lobby. Bright and warm. Empty. She stopped inside the door, hearing a voice:

"You are still unbearaply pretty. I may fall in lofe with you by seven o'clock."

It was his voice. His accent.

Yet somehow she felt no shock. Not even surprise.

Then: "I see the rat fink left the hole in the skylight."

She heard someone laugh beyond the far wall with the three entrances, one on each end and one in the middle, with brown curtains drawn together over each.

She started toward the middle entrance, hearing a young woman's voice then: ". . . he'll fix it, won't he?"

"I vould nott count on itt. My own bathtup had been running since nineteen-hundred-and-forty-nine."

More laughter. Several voices this time.

The sense of unreality carried her past the lighted box office to the curtains at center.

From behind the velvet, the same man's voice, but unaccented now, said: "Damn it to hell, Mitzi, she does that every time." Unmistakably Vincent Fletcher's real voice. "How do you expect me to play this role if she's going to keep changing her moves?"

She drew aside the heavy curtains and looked into the theater. And down the aisle. To the lighted stage.

He was standing at the edge of the stage. In the light. By himself.

Why didn't she move? Why didn't she get it over with?

Because it was not her time to move.

Yet.

He was too far away, she might miss, she had to be very close. And also, she wanted him to see the gun before she killed him. He had to know it was happening. And who held the gun—

"Okay, *okay,*" she heard a third voice, a woman's gravel voice, angry, shouting: "Take ten, everybody! I'll talk to her, Vincent, I'll talk to her. Houselights!" The woman who spoke stood up from the front row, short and heavy, as if she were very tired. "Mady, you show the officer backstage, men's dressing room. And Vincent, please—make it short, will you? It's getting late." She turned and started up the aisle toward Carole, shaking her dark head, bawling: "Houselights, I said!"

Carole felt no panic. She was here now. No hurry, no urgency. As she stood aside to let the woman pass, lights came on all over the theater and she saw Henry, in uniform, shambling down a side aisle and then across to the center in the space between the stage and the front row. She saw Mady Fletcher on the stage waiting for him.

Was he going to arrest Vincent Fletcher now?

If so, if so—

She started toward the lobby, but her way was blocked by the woman who had come up the aisle. "My name's Mitzi Brewer. I'm the director. Or at least I *think* I am. I'm sorry, Mr. Fletcher doesn't allow visitors . . ."

Carole didn't answer as she drifted into the lobby and toward the doors, hearing the gravel voice behind speaking to whoever was in the box office: "That man's driving me up the wall and now I think he's farther gone than I am tonight. That fucking accent, whatever he thinks it is, who's going to believe the character's named Velasco? It gets laughs but, oh God, why did I ever take this job?"

Carole was outside again. The air was cold but not so cold as the shimmering quiet still undisturbed inside her. Inside her whole being.

She turned and went to the corner of the building and looked down the side. A sheer brick wall. So she went to the other side, by the parking lot, and saw, at the far end, what she knew had to be there: a lighted sign protruding from the wall and reading STAGE DOOR.

They, Henry and Vincent Fletcher, would have to come out either the lobby door or the stage door.

Again she had the sensation that she was moving in a dream and was surprised at how well her mind was working.

She turned and saw a large tree, bare now, on the edge of the front lawn. She went to it, turned and leaned against it. From here she could see the lobby doors in front and, on the side of the building, the stage door, both with lights above them.

And Sandy . . . dear sveet Sandy . . . she vill be dead. Dead, dead, raped and dead—

The words seemed to reach her from a vast distance. As if they came off the lake, or from beyond the lake—

It was cold.

She should have worn a heavier coat.

Poor Henry. She wished Henry didn't have to be the one to arrest her.

Tenderness swept over her. Poor *dear* Henry, he really thought he was helping her by arresting the sonofabitch.

In a few moments she became conscious of the sound of a car's motor. Headlights flooded her as the car turned into the parking area.

She turned her head, but only for a moment.

She recognized the car. A gray Honda.

Well, let her come. Judith couldn't stop her now.

Nothing could.

Nobody.

She waited, eyes moving back and forth from door to door.

Then she turned her head and glanced. Judith had turned off the headlights and she was now coming toward her in long strides. She was wearing the gray capelike coat that Sandy had called neat.

When she was about two yards away, Judith stopped. "What are you doing out here?" she asked.

Carole's eyes were on both doors. "Go away," she said.

"I will *not* go away. I had a hard enough time figuring where you might have gone."

"It's not your business, Judith."

"Rolfe's been raving one minute and weeping the next, and drinking in between. I tried to help him but—" She sucked in a deep breath. "He's gone, Carole. He packed a few things and took the Saab."

"Good," Carole heard herself say.

She heard Judith take a step on the crisp grass. "Carole, give me the gun. Please."

"I don't have a gun," she heard herself say. "I threw it into the lake."

"Carole, you're not a very good liar." Judith stepped closer. "I must warn you," she said in a voice Carole had never heard before, "I'm not going to let you do this."

"How are you going to stop me?"

"I don't know. God help me, I don't know."

"Amateurs," Vincent Fletcher was saying, scoffing, "I wish I'd never got involved." He was pacing slowly up and down the length of the dressing room, unable to conceal his excitement, or his fear.

Henry was seated in a straight chair at the end of the long table that ran the length of the narrow room between built-in dressing shelves along the two walls. Unlighted bulbs framed the many mirrors. A tan military-type overcoat was hanging in the space for costumes at the end of the room. Henry thought of the belt at once. The time he'd wasted. Watching the man on stage, Henry had already, decided that the bastard didn't have a handgun on his person, in the pocket of either the plaid sports jacket or the tan twill trousers—but there could be one in the overcoat. "You seem right at home on the stage," Henry said. "I'll bet you once had ambitions to be a professional."

"I had to take over the paper when my mother died, didn't I?"

Henry heard the truculent, defensive note and decided on another tack. "I know just how you feel, Mr. Fletcher. This justice business can be damn frustrating, too." Henry was playing a game now, knew it, and was making up the rules as he went along—not knowing whether he'd win or lose. Or even whether he had the right to play such a game with a man's mind, no matter how much he hated him, no matter what the bastard had done—

Abruptly, Fletcher stopped pacing, sat down at the dressing shelf, looked in the mirror, not at his own image, but at Henry's, behind him. "What can I do for you, Chief? You interrupted rehearsal; we don't have all night."

"It's like this, Mr. Fletcher," Henry said, for the first

time recalling his promise. "Remember what we agreed yesterday? Quid pro quo, you said."

"I remember." Henry heard the bastard breathe a long sigh, as of relief. Just what he wanted. "I said I'd run your story and you said you'd let my paper break the news of any arrest." His eyes, glittering, were on Henry in the mirror. "Have you made an arrest?"

"What time do you put the morning edition to bed?" He saw a thin veil of perspiration on the man's high-colored cheeks.

"Midnight. On the nose. Why?"

"Because by then I'll have the name. So I thought maybe you'd like to have the rest of the story now. Then all you'll have to do is fill in the identity of the perpetrator."

The bastard was almost grinning as he turned in the chair. "By the way, Mark Rainer gave me hell for running that piece this morning." He reached for a Kleenex and dabbed at his face and forehead. "Said it accomplished absolutely nothing."

Henry realized, faintly amused, that he'd been lied to so often in the line of duty that now lying came easier to him than it had when he was younger. "There's a lot Mr. Rainer doesn't know," he said, almost tempted to wink. "For instance: the State Police now have very sophisticated laser devices— pick up threads left on the victim's clothes, human hair, not just from the head but from a rapist's hands. Pubic hairs, too. Fingerprints on human flesh. Skin under the victim's fingernails unobservable to the naked eye. Officers in the field can't keep the DA up on everything." He watched the bastard turn to the mirror again, glance at his own face, then reach up to make sure his reddish brown toupee was still in place, tapping his palm against it from above. And then, very careful to make it sound casual, Henry added: "Semen stains."

The bastard turned around to face him. The sweat had

already returned to his forehead. "Semen? I understand all that can tell you is the . . . the rapist's blood type."

Henry heard, or perhaps imagined, a slight tremor in the man's deep theatrical voice. "That's the way it *used to be,* Mr. Fletcher, you're right," he said, aware he'd only read about experiments in this area. So he lied again: "Law enforcement techniques've come a long way. Now we have what we call DNA Fingerprinting—a process in which semen, recovered as forensic evidence, is matched to its source. Today, a semen sample's a more positive ID than a fingerprint or voiceprint ever was." And then, slowly, watching it sink in: "Of course we can't do a matchup till we have the man in custody."

Vincent Fletcher stood up then. "You *have* been busy, haven't you? Well, Mark Rainer told me the footprint turned out to be a policeman's."

Henry watched the bastard almost stroll to the other end of the room. Then he said, very softly, "You've been pretty busy yourself, Mr. Fletcher."

"I take a natural interest in Carole Jensen, I told you that. And as a newspaperman—"

"We also know," Henry went on, forcing a confident laziness into his tone, "We also have determined where the belt used in the assault was purchased."

The bastard was standing, very still, at the other end of the room, his barrel-shaped back to him. "What makes me think, Chief—" he turned around, that faint grin again—"what gives me the idea you're feeding me more bullshit?"

"Why should I do that, Mr. Fletcher? Tit for tat, you said yesterday. I'm just filling you in." Henry decided to stand up then. "After the arrest, the sales records will be subpoenaed, of course."

"And you expect me to write this up and print it as fact?"

"Ego," Henry said. "Like you and this playacting. I don't mind admitting I expect to get credit in the story. Might even ask for a raise." He walked along the table to where the bastard stood. "We also have what they call a psychological profile of the perpetrator. We know he's a vain, insecure man, with a wide strain of sadism in his nature. Like all rapists. We know he was acquainted with the victim, had some kind of what the doctors call an obsession about her. That he often followed her and was following her car Saturday evening. Till he saw his chance and took it." Henry was hoping he wasn't going too far when he shrugged and added: "One of the doctors I talked to in New York said the man was probably impotent—in normal circumstances, that is."

But instead of what he'd expected, or hoped for, Vincent Fletcher's face twisted into a smile. "Listen, Chief, you took me down the garden path once. Whole town's laughing at me for printing those other lies. I allowed my mother's paper to be used, I put its credibility on the line. Witnesses, you told me, and now I know there were none. So don't ask me to do it again. There's your answer."

"I admit it, Mr. Fletcher," Henry said, hating himself for saying it. "There weren't any witnesses yesterday, but now, because of what you wrote, two have decided to come forward. So, you see, it wasn't all for nothing."

The bastard spread his legs and scowled. "You don't know who he is and you're still trying to get me to help you flush him out. That's your game, isn't it?"

"I'll have the name as soon as my beeper goes off. Then I'll know who read the story and got spooked and pushed his luck because he was scared shitless. The man gave himself away—isn't that news, Mr. Fletcher?"

"I think I should tell you, Chief—I've always hated liars."

"So have I," Henry said. "The perpetrator phoned the victim, not once but twice, and threatened to rape and murder her five-year-old daughter. I don't have to take the victim's word, either. I have an outside witness, who heard the threats because she was on an extension phone. She's positive she can identify the voice if she hears it again. Even though the subject used a phony accent."

The bastard's bulbous lips were parted. His eyes had now gone flat, blank.

There was a knock on the door. "Daddy, Miss Brewer wants us all on stage, please."

A moment passed, then Vincent Fletcher said, in a strange, strangled voice: "I'll be there, Mady." He started to move past Henry toward the door at the other end of the room, avoiding his eyes now.

"Just so you won't think I've been lying, Mr. Fletcher." Henry reached into the inside pocket of his uniform. He placed the folded sheet of drawing paper on the table and slid it down its length. "It's what we call a composite by our police artist. The face of the man our witnesses say they saw going into the woods."

The bastard's face was covered with sweat now, so much that it was dripping off his chin.

"Places," Mady Fletcher's voice called from beyond the door. "Act Two, Scene Two. Places, please!"

As he watched the bastard take the sketch from the table and leave the room, Henry experienced a quick pang of doubt—not as to who had raped Carole but as to whether, regardless, he himself had the right to do what he was doing.

But it was too late to turn back now. The dice had already been thrown.

He went to the military coat on its hanger and removed the gun that only a hunch told him would be in its pocket. A .45-caliber revolver, government issue.

Carole had not moved from her position under the tall tree on the lawn where she could keep her eyes on the lobby doors in front of the theatre and the lighted stage door on the side. A north wind, chillingly moist, had come up over the twenty-mile-long lake and was cutting through her car coat and sweater. As if trying to reach that other cold inside, that icy calm that isolated her from Judith's urgent voice and the quiet, reasonable, logical words: *You're not thinking of Sandy, you're thinking of yourself* and *Revenge is not justice, Carole,* and *Do you want to force Henry to arrest you instead of him?* And then, finally, again: *I'm not going to let you do this.*

Poor Judith—she still had the foolish idea she could reach Carole's fixed mind with words. Carole wished she could think of some way to reassure her.

How could she explain what she knew now, what she had accepted? That there was no difference between justice and revenge, that there was no meaning anywhere.

Cass. Cass had known that. And now he was dead. What had *he* done? What was *his* crime? Why had he always felt so guilty, when those who sent him halfway around the world to kill felt nothing? And still felt no regret, no remorse. Oh Cass, why didn't we talk more? I knew so little about you. And now it's too late. Why is it always too late?

The lobby door opened. Carole stiffened and her hand closed around the butt of the gun in her pocket.

Mady Fletcher appeared, called: "Anyone out here? Rehearsal's beginning."

Carole had to clear her throat to speak: "Where's Chief Lindheim?"

"He's in here. Aren't you freezing?"

"Where's your father?"

"He's backstage. We're starting Act Two."

"Let me take you home," Judith whispered.

"We're coming, Mady," Carole called and started toward the building. Why hadn't Henry arrested the sonofabitch as he'd threatened to do? Why was he waiting? Maybe she'd convinced him, after all, that putting the sonofabitch in jail would not save Sandy—

Mady was holding one of the double doors open. "I didn't know *you* were here, Dr. Judith. Hey, I gotta run!"

Once Mady had disappeared down the right side aisle,

the lobby was empty. Judith was moving toward the velvet curtains at the center aisle. She held one aside. Carole followed. As if she were still in a dream. As if everything and everyone around her were part of something weird and unreal yet sharply clear and vivid at the same time. *You frighten me,* Judith had said, at the tree. *Carole, do you realize you're almost catatonic? Oh my dear, dear child, I know where you are. I've been there. Let me in, let me help, please.*

But her words had come like the wind off the lake, and from as far away.

The theatre was lighted and Carole saw Henry at once. He was sitting a few rows from the back, on the center aisle. She saw him turn his head to look at her. His huge face looked grim and disapproving, not quite angry. She took her hand from her pocket before she sat down across the aisle from him, leaving a seat vacant for Judith. But Judith took the seat on the aisle behind her instead. Carole knew why and was distantly, vaguely saddened. Did Judith really think she, or anyone, could prevent what had to be done?

As the lights began to dim all over the almost empty theatre, she saw the tall stepladder, off to the right, straddling a row of seats. A boy was working on a spotlight overhead while a girl about his age was perched on one of the lower steps watching the stage.

Carole realized she was too far away; she should have taken a seat closer to the stage. When the time came, she would have to run down the aisle instead of standing up and taking aim. And she was much too close to Henry here: like Judith, he'd stop her if he could. In this she was alone. No one understood, yet it was so simple, really.

The stage was dimly lighted and, after Mitzi Brewer came down the steps and flopped into a seat in the front row, it was empty. "Lights, please," she called. And a faint light came up all over the apartment, with blue moonlight falling through the skylight. "Curtain!" Mitzi Brewer shouted in her gravel voice.

No curtain rose or fell, but a blond young woman rushed in from the door on Carole's left. She was wearing a man's Tyrolean hat and an overcoat, and she was breathing hard, as if she'd climbed several flights of stairs. "I beat you!" she called over her shoulder and then did a giddy half-drunken spin across the room. "I won!"

There was a silence. The blond girl stood waiting. No one appeared in the door. And Mitzi barked: "Vincent, that's your cue."

A voice offstage—*his* voice, without an accent—called: "That is *not* my cue, Miss Brewer. I take my cue from the lights and if Corie doesn't turn on the lamp, I am not going to appear on a dark stage. *Period.*" But . . . somehow his voice sounded different—shaky, loud but uncertain. "Mady! Mady, are you managing this stage or not?"

Lights came on. Then he appeared in the doorway on the left. He was wearing no hat, but a tan military-type overcoat she'd seen many times at the office.

Now. Now was her chance. She shoved her hand into her pocket.

But before she could stand, she felt a hand on her shoulder, pinning her in the seat, and heard Judith's voice in her ear: "Let Henry handle this." The hand tightened on her shoulder. "I'm beginning to get some idea of what Henry's up to. I don't like it, but give the man a chance."

It was too late then because Mady appeared on the stage from the right. "I couldn't give the light cue, Daddy, because Corie forgot to turn on the lamp."

"No excuses. Do your job or go home." He marched to the edge of the stage and peered out into the darkness. "What's going on out there?" Then he bawled: "Get that ladder out of here!" But his gaze was still searching. "I heard whispering. Who's whispering out there?"

The boy and girl scrambled down the ladder and scurried toward the side aisle, bent low, and disappeared through the door leading backstage.

"Who is it?" Vincent Fletcher growled. "Mitzi, you know I don't allow visitors! Who's out there?"

Carole heard the shakiness in his voice, saw the angry bafflement on his face—and made a decision. She took her hand from her pocket, and stood up. "It's only me, Mr. Fletcher," she said. Out of the corner of her eye she saw Henry stiffen in his seat across the aisle.

"You? Who are you?" the sonofabitch demanded. "It's dark out there. Who are you?"

"Carole," she said, her voice cool and even pleasant. "Don't you recognize my voice, Mr. Fletcher? Carole Jensen."

"Carole?" It was only a breath of sound, astonished, incredulous. Then, as if he'd been hit in the stomach and couldn't quite get his breath, he asked, "What . . . what are you doing here, Carole?"

"Just watching," she heard herself say, in the same tone of voice as before. She knew that if she returned her hand to the pocket, Judith would grab her from behind. After all, she was in no hurry now. Now, when she did it, he'd know where the bullet came from. "Do you *mind* if I watch?" And then she added, "Vincent."

His mouth opened and he looked as if he couldn't find his voice. Then he tried to smile. "You know I don't, Carole. Of *course* not, my dear. But . . . but . . . but remember, this is only a rehearsal, you know."

"All *right!*" Mitzi shouted. "Are you ready, Mady? Lights, ready? Corie, turn on the lamp *before* you take your little drunken spin. From the top of the scene, *please!*"

Seeing the sonofabitch go off on one side and Mady on the other, Carole sat down. Then, in the silence, she heard Henry's beeper. The sound went on and on, repetitious and insistent, and Henry, for reasons of his own probably, did not click it off.

Out of sight, Vincent Fletcher's voice cried out: "What's that sound? What's happening around here tonight?" And as the lights on the stage dimmed: "What's that *sound,* where's it coming from?"

The beeping stopped.

Henry hauled himself up from his seat and lifted his voice: "That's my call, Mr. Fletcher. In a few minutes I should be able to give you the name you want for the morning paper."

Henry was lumbering up the aisle toward the lobby.

Behind her, Carole heard Judith's whisper: "I *know* what he's doing, Carole. And you're helping him do it. And it's outrageous." And then, in a growl: "My job's to treat sick people, not to make them worse."

Instead of going outside to the radio in the squad car, Henry decided to use the phone in the box office—where he could hear whatever occurred in the theatre and could keep an eye on the exits from all three aisles. "Official business," he told the elderly dignified man rearranging the ticket racks.

"By all means, Officer," the old man said, and disappeared.

Henry dialed the station house in Sheffield.

"Telephone company complied, Chief. The calling number was 579-6365, Sudbury. Dialed direct to Sheffield. Phone bill in the name of Vincent R. Fletcher. Private line, unlisted number, in his vehicle. Two calls today. First at one-thirteen P.M. and another from that number to the Jensen residence at three thirty-seven P.M."

"Pendleton Day-Care?"

"Sure enough. One call, originating at same number, at one-thirty-nine this afternoon."

By now Henry was not even slightly surprised. It was what he needed, but was it enough? Even with Judith to corroborate Carole's claim that he'd threatened the child? "Anything else?"

"A number for you to call. He wouldn't leave his name but he'll be home all evening. Five-two-seven, zero-two-zero-three. He refused to talk to anyone but you, Chief."

As Henry was dialing the number, he saw the curtains of the middle aisle part and then Mady Fletcher's slight figure rushed into the lobby, panic in her childlike face. She halted, looked around, then moved, slowly now, to one of the high-backed chairs against the paneled wall. Fighting tears, she was muttering: "I could kill him, someday I *will* kill him—" Her head went down into her hands and her slim shoulders began to heave.

"Hello? This is Jeff Wilder."

"This is Chief Lindheim, Jeff." Then, with a sense of inevitability, he asked the question that he didn't need to ask: "You change your mind?"

"You better believe it, sir. No matter what Mr. Morgan does, no job's worth going to prison for, right?"

"The name, Jeff."

"Fletcher. Vincent Fletcher. He owns the newspaper."

"Any way to prove it?"

"Listen, I swear I didn't know this this morning. I have the sales slip. Mr. Fletcher bought the buckle and belt on the fifteenth of last month, but never brought the buckle back to be monogrammed."

Was it possible that, in that twisted mind, the bastard had been planning for more than a month to do what he did? Longer perhaps? Unconsciously? Subconsciously? Or with malice aforethought? Moot points now, all of them.

"Hold on to the sales slip," Henry said. "And thanks, kid."

He replaced the phone on the wall carefully so that Mady wouldn't hear, then again looked out through the grilled window. She still sat there, eyes squinched, tears rolling down her cheeks.

Henry, fighting the tenderness that was mixing with the excitement inside (he didn't have time for this now), opened the box office door and then, in the lobby, hearing voices from the theatre, he crossed to where Mady Fletcher sat.

"Mady, what are you doing out here?"

She opened her eyes. "He—my father threw me out."

"Why would he do that, Mady?"

She was staring up into his face. "Corie made the same mistake again and he blamed *me.* He . . . he called me names, the awful names he calls me at home when he's mad. Only in front of everybody." She stood up from the chair. "What'd you say to him in the dressing room? Whatever it was, he's worse than I've ever seen him. He's losing it."

"Do you want me to ask Dr. Kahn to come out here?"

"No. I'm tired of sneaking around, but if he finds out tonight that I've been seeing Dr. Judith—"

"Do you have a way to get home?" he said in a gentle whisper.

For a second Henry thought she was going to cry again. But then he saw a hard defiance enter her reddened eyes. "I'm not going home. All Mama does is defend him and tell *me* to change *my* ways. She doesn't know. Or maybe she's scared, too." She stepped around Henry and started toward the entrance to the left side aisle. Her body was very straight, rigid. "I'm not going to do what he tells me ever again. He's dirty. He's *foul!*" And she disappeared between the brown curtains.

What now? He had the evidence. Enough to go up on the stage and arrest the bastard. Which would be very satisfying; which would give him great personal pleasure. But, he reminded himself harshly, the bastard'll be on the street by morning, no surveillance, nothing to stop him then.

He's a sick and dangerous man, Judith had said. *He's capable of anything.*

And if he cracks up completely tonight? Now? Here?

Even with Judith's professional help, could Henry be absolutely sure the bastard'd be placed in a locked ward in

Fairfield Hills Hospital? No jail, no bail. No Mark Rainer making a deal with some sleazy lawyer like Jerald Dixon—how could he be sure of that?

Decision time again, Henry thought, as he went across the lobby, through the curtains and down the center aisle. He ignored whatever was happening on the stage. When he reached Carole, who was sitting in the aisle seat now, with Judith directly behind her, he reached out impulsively and tapped Carole twice on the shoulder. Then he resumed his seat across from her, still racked by indecision.

"Henry," he heard Judith whisper across the aisle. "Henry, I know what you think you're doing and I can't allow it. Have you ever dealt with anyone who's just gone off the deep end? Because I have."

From the stage he heard the bastard's voice again, almost shrill: "More whispering! Mitzi, how many people are out there? What are they *doing* here?"

Mitzi Brewer stood up in the front row and turned, without coming up the aisle. "Please, everyone. You're our guests. *Please!*" And then to the actors on the stage, only Corie and Vincent Fletcher now: "Take it from: 'How many Zuzus did I have?' And Vincent, I think you're acting a bit *too* drunk."

"I am not acting drunk at all, and as you know, I do not drink, so fuck off, Brewer. If you stop me again, you're fired. I don't take orders from *females!*"

Carole could still feel the double tap on her shoulder. Was Henry trying to say *I'm here?* Or *Please don't?* Or *Trust me?*

And she was remembering what Judith had whispered into her ear while Henry was gone, when Carole knew Judith had been tempted to follow Mady up the aisle after her father had given her a public tongue-lashing and told her to walk home. *My job's to heal people, but even I, sometimes, in spite of all my training, even I know in my bones that some people have to be punished.*

From the stage now Carole could hear his hated voice, with the accent, answering Corie's question as to how she'll feel in the morning: "Vunderful. No headache vhatsoever."

She saw Corie utter a sound of disgust, stop, and place her fists on her hips. "That's *my* line." She turned. "Mitzi, now he's reading *my* lines. He hasn't given me the right cue all evening and he keeps changing the lines, so we don't know *what* the hell he's going to say."

The sonofabitch was standing with his legs apart, glowering, trembling all over. "Listen," he snarled at Corie, "listen you stupid *cunt,* I don't give a shit whether it's your fucking line or not." Corie took several steps backward. "Ad-lib if you have to and stop acting like you're an actress when you're nothing but a two-bit whore who can be picked up on any street corner!" He strode all the way across the stage to shout through the door: *"Mady!* Mady, where are you? Isn't that my line, *'No headache'?"* He waited. There was not a sound anywhere. Then he went through the door, out of view, growling: "If I find you with some pimple-face son of a slut getting it on back here—"

There was a long silence.

From behind the wall of the set his voice rose higher, the shrill cry of some jungle bird of prey: "Evil, wicked, whores, and harlots—"

Hearing the word, Carole reached into her pocket again . . . and felt Judith's hand on her shoulder, heavy and tight.

The sonofabitch reappeared from another door. He started blindly across the room, knocking over the table with the lamp on it, and then stopped, frowning, staring around as if suddenly he didn't know where he was. Several other people—some young, some older, all curious and wide-eyed—had come onto the set from both sides. His face baffled, he looked around blindly, blinking at them.

It was then that Carole heard another voice for the first

time. It came from behind but off to one side of the dark theatre. "Daddy," it said, "you sent me home. Can't you remember?" His daughter's voice. "You told me to walk home like the streetwalker I really am—"

The sonofabitch moved, uncertainly now, down to the edge of the stage, his high-heeled, shiny shoes dragging as if he had gone suddenly weak. He stared out into the dimness. "Mady?" he asked in a slow bewildered tone. "Mady, is that you out there?"

"It's me, Daddy. And that's what I'm going to be, a hooker! I'm going to get into the first car that offers me a ride."

Another long silence. Longer this time. Carole had forgotten the gun, had forgotten why she was here.

The sonofabitch was peering in the direction of his daughter's voice, an expression of profound incredulity on his face, which had turned so white that it looked like a mime's in makeup. Then he erupted again. "Proof, proof—you're all alike!" Again he began to walk, like a blind man, in a strange, erratic pattern. "My mother—you're all like her. Sex, sex, it's all you ever think of!" His tone became a plea, almost a whine: "What have I ever done to make all of you hate me?"

Before she had time to break the impulse, or to think, Carole stood up. "You know what you did," she heard herself say, faintly surprised at her clear-cut words, her almost emotionless tone. And then, very slowly, very clearly, she said it: "You . . . raped me . . . you . . . son of a bitch."

Her hand went to her pocket, she felt Judith reaching to grab her upper arm, she heard the gasps, then the whispers, she saw Corie backing away from him on the stage, she saw Mitzi edging sideways between the stage and the front row, she felt Henry's stolid presence, and in that instant she wished the man would come down the steps toward her, so that she could kill him, or Henry could—

Instead, though, Vincent Fletcher, eyes again searching

the dark theatre, didn't move. His voice was thin and plaintive: "Carole? Carole, tell them you didn't mean that? You know I could never harm *you.* Tell them, please. I've loved you like . . . like a daughter."

Carole shrugged off Judith's grasp and took her hand out of her pocket. Without the gun. She didn't need it now.

"You not only raped me," she said, in a clear level tone, "but you threatened to rape and murder *my* daughter."

"Lies!" the sonofabitch bellowed, his voice filling the theatre. "Lies, lies, everyone's always lying about me, always, always. Envy, envy, and sloth, fornication and licentiousness, it's a wicked world, evil, evil." Then, without moving, in a demanding, desperate howl: *"Why's everyone always against me?"*

Another silence—as his voice echoed and faded.

Then a change came over him. He drew himself up again and began to move about the stage, lurching, stumbling, blind again, muttering to himself now, only a few furious, tangled words coming clear: ". . . all my life . . . my sainted bitch of a mother . . . even before I was born . . . hated me, hated me, hatc . . . oh Jesus, why do you let them? . . . If I'd had a son . . . oh God, why did you make this world . . . why is the world just *shit?"* He stopped, facing away, staring up through the skylight, his back to everyone. He put his head back, as if he might be praying. "Oh Lord, you created everything, why do you have to be so cruel?" His chin went slowly down to his chest and he made a turn so that now he was in profile. "I'm innocent," he mumbled, "you know, Lord, *you* know . . . I'm innocent."

He sank slowly down onto his knees, his legs seeming to collapse. His thick, soft body wobbled, limply, as if it might topple.

Henry, hand on the butt of his revolver, had listened and watched with mingled relief and satisfaction—and a kind of baffled awe. Judith had been right: he had never seen anyone go off the deep end. All the while, though, he had been fighting a pity that he knew he could not afford. Was it over then?

He saw the bastard's body bend forward slowly until his forehead reached the floor. The neat reddish brown toupee was at a crazy grotesque angle on his skull now.

The theatre was very quiet.

The man, bent almost double, lifted his arms high over his head, which was still down, and began, very slowly, to pound the floor with his fists. The dull thudding was the only sound anywhere. Then there came another sound: his voice again, the words spoken very softly, coming clear over the repeated thumping sounds: "I loved you, Carole . . . if only you had treated me like a man . . . a real man . . . not an *old* man, a *real* man—" His voice drifted away and he stopped pounding the floor. Still kneeling, he straightened up. His hairpiece had come off altogether now and his totally bald head looked shiny and white and naked—almost obscene. He turned his head to look out toward the seats. But his eyes had an empty, blank look. "Carole . . . Carole, I had to have you. Just once. Just once. . . ." And then his head went down again until his forehead was again resting on the floor.

"Call an ambulance," Judith whispered, and he saw her standing up to go swiftly down the aisle toward the stage.

Henry hissed her name, once, a warning, but she didn't stop. "You have your duty, Henry, and I have mine." She went up the steps and onto the stage. To kneel down alongside the madman. "My name's Kahn, Mr. Fletcher. I'm a doctor." Her tone was warm with sympathy, even kindness. "I'd like to help you if you'll let me."

Henry stood and whirled to take several steps up the aisle toward the lobby and stopped when he saw the elderly dignified man standing between the curtains—stiff with shock and bewilderment. "Dial nine-one-one," Henry snarled, under his breath. "We need an ambulance, *fast!*"

When he heard the man say, "By all means," he swiveled, took a single step—and stopped. What he saw on the stage caused him to lift the .38 from its holster, very gently, and to lower it in his hand along the side of his leg, pointed at the floor.

Judith was still kneeling but the madman had stood up and was staring down on her, speaking in a low, bewildered growl: "I know you. I know . . . who you are—"

"Mr. Fletcher, let's talk." Judith's tone was filled with understanding, yet firm. "Let's find some quiet place where we—"

But the bastard didn't move. "Turning my daughter against me—"

"Judith," Henry called—

But he saw her make a slashing, silencing gesture with one hand.

The madman seemed not to have heard. He was now searching the pockets of his overcoat with both hands, his face and actions increasingly frantic.

So Henry called out: "I have your gun, Mr. Fletcher." Slowly, cautiously, he began to go down the aisle. "It's in *my* pocket," he continued, very quietly, "not yours."

The madman stared over Judith's dark head and out into the dim theatre. He was scowling now, but wary nevertheless, eyes darting around—

"You're under arrest, Mr. Fletcher."

Then he saw Carole move. He saw her standing up without stepping into the aisle, and then he saw the gun in her two hands as they lifted.

Damn the girl, *damn* her!

Carole had decided that this was her chance. Now, before Henry could go down the aisle and up onto the stage.

The gun clutched in one hand, her other hand supporting that wrist, the gun shaking, her body quivering, she looked down the length of her arms and over the gun. She could see the sonofabitch very clearly: he was looking down on Judith, who was close, very close, too close—

But if . . . if she was very careful, if she could steady her hands and take careful aim—

"Filling that pure mind with your degenerate slime," the sonofabitch was saying. Had he even heard what Henry had said? "Filth. *Filth!* You foul-minded slut, whore, harlot!"

Hearing the hated word spoken aloud again brought it all back in a flooding rush. Carole felt a scalding, savage need tighten through her. In that blazing instant she could feel his body moving on top of hers, penis pumping, thrusting, the pain, his groans of rage and pleasure, his words, the same words—

On the stage Judith was saying, "Mr. Fletcher, we can't talk here with all these people listening, let's—"

Before Judith could stand, Carole was tempted to yell, *Judith, get down on the floor!* But she couldn't risk it. Any more than she could risk trying to put a bullet into him above Judith's head.

Did Judith know that? She'd said she'd do anything to keep Carole from doing what she knew she had to do *now*—

Suddenly then, without a sound, a word, any warning, the sonofabitch took a single long step, his arms shot out straight in front of his body and his hands closed around Judith's throat.

Her body was lifted off the floor, legs dangling, no sound, she was trying to fight, but wriggling helpless in his grip as he whirled her about, still clutching her throat, and threw her flat down on the floor without letting go.

Somewhere, someone screamed.

Carole lowered the gun, staring, and heard Henry passing in the aisle, heard his voice: "Get the hell out of here, Carole. *Please.*"

Henry did not even hear his own words, he heard another shriek somewhere, and then Mitzi Brewer's voice squawking: "Stop him, he's killing her, where are the police?"

Revolver in his grip, Henry climbed the steps and saw the bastard's back, upright, astride Judith's body on the floor, his arms stiff, her eyes bulging—

Discovering for the first time in many years that he actually wanted to kill a man, Henry stopped, facing an instantaneous decision: to pump a slug into the bastard's back, or to leap on top of him, or to bring the barrel of the gun down on his shoulder to break his grasp—

"You're under arrest," he shouted, moving, lifting the heavy weapon, his finger still hooked on the trigger, and brought the barrel down, not on the shoulder but on the bastard's bare white skull, trying to control his fury and the force of the blow at the same time.

There was a terrible cracking sound of metal and bone. He heard another shrill scream somewhere, then saw blood soaking the man's scalp, turning the white to brilliant red.

He stepped back to watch the body fall sideways to the floor, then sprawl there. He heard a groan, saw Fletcher roll onto his back.

He heard Judith coughing, gasping for breath, and saw her trying to sit up. Her eyes looked stunned and glassy and her shoulders were heaving as she scrambled, weakly, to her feet, staggering toward the door in the set. Hands reached out from the dimness—

Henry stepped to the fallen man, who was lying limply on his back, to make sure he was unconscious. Or alive. Had he killed the bastard? Did he really give a damn?

He holstered the gun, took the bracelets off his belt and, touching the bastard's body as little as possible—damned if he was going to roll him over—he handcuffed the two wrists in front of the body. The two sharp clicks of the bracelets sent a jolt of satisfaction through him.

Standing up, he called: "Judith, are you all right?"

A man's voice answered: "She'll be okay now."

So then he turned and looked into the darkness of the

auditorium, remembering Mitzi Brewer's words, shouting them: "Houselights!"

He could not see Carole. He didn't move but called her name, once, and waited.

Then he heard her voice, faint and filled with a wan defeat. "I'm here, Henry." And after a moment: "You win."

Carole was slouched low in the seat, lifeless now, shattered.

So . . . it was over. Not with a whimper but with a bang, after all—

You vill nefer know where or when. You vill nefer haf a second's peace the rest of your life—

It would never be over now.

She could see Henry standing on the stage, the sonofabitch stretched out on his back behind him, blood all over his head. But alive. Eyelids fluttering. Still alive. She should have risked the shot when she had the chance.

Slowly lights came on all over the empty theatre.

"Carole," she heard Henry saying, not moving toward the edge of the stage, "Carole. I'll have things to do now." His voice was so soft, so gentle—almost a plea for forgiveness. "Judith will drive you home."

"No," she heard herself answer, trying to stand up. "No—" for she had no home. "I'll go to Judith's."

She discovered that she was on her feet after all. The pain in both knees was worse now, in her breast unbearable.

It was then that she saw the body move. Behind Henry's back.

When she tried to cry out, her throat locked.

Vincent Fletcher had his knees drawn up to his chin, legs doubled back on his chest—

She heard herself utter a small sound then, but she still could not scream, so she stepped into the aisle, trying to run to the stage, watching in horror—

As the legs shot upward at an angle, the sharp heels plowing simultaneously into the small of Henry's back—

A look of surprise came over Henry's face, then pain, and his huge body stiffened, then arched backward for only a split second, before it shot forward, propelled toward the edge of the stage—

Carole realized then that she was screaming at last. The sound seemed to fill the universe—

Helplessly, she watched Henry's massive upright body reach the edge of the stage and fall, twisting sideways, arms groping, as it dropped into empty space. She saw, and then heard, the side of his head and face strike the wooden edge of the stage floor before his whole enormous weight disappeared onto the floor in front of the first row of seats.

She managed to move then, running and limping down the aisle, hearing a terrible thunderous thud that seemed to shake the walls of the theatre.

But even as she reached the first row, mind engulfed in nightmarish disbelief, she heard from the stage, in the eerie silence that followed, Vincent Fletcher's piteous voice: "Carole, you've got to help me."

His voice didn't stop her, nor did the wild, weird idiocy of his words.

She turned into the front row and dropped to her knees alongside Henry's body. Which lay at a grotesque unreal angle, unmoving. His eyes were closed.

Because the gun was still in her right hand, she reached with her left to touch his square chin. At her touch his head rolled to one side. The whole side of his face was turning a dark purplish black.

Then she heard Vincent Fletcher's voice again, plaintive, with amazement running thin through the words: "Carole, you've got to get me out of this."

She stood up. She looked onto the stage.

To see him standing there, only a few feet away. Her

eyes were level with his knees. She lifted her gaze up the tan coat to see—

His face was a red-streaked mask, the skull dripping blood, the eyes peering out, glazed and desperate and bewildered.

When he spoke, the mask twisted. In a dazed, hushed, hurried whisper, as he lifted his manacled hands, he said, "Listen, Carole. You and I—we can still make it."

As he took a staggering step toward her, she brought up the gun, fast, heard someone out of sight call her name—Judith's voice?—and she pulled the trigger. Once.

She heard the blast, smelled burnt powder and felt the recoil up her arms, ripping like a bullet into her left breast.

She saw his manacled hands jerk upwards and his body stiffen, and then a black splotch appeared on the tan coat just below the shoulder. Not red, black, wasn't that odd?

The impact of the single shot had spun his body sideways and now he was staggering and lurching toward the door of the set.

In panic she tired to fire again.

But before she could pull the trigger, he had disappeared.

Instantly the picture of the lighted stage door on the side of the building flashed in her mind.

So she turned and rushed up the aisle, saw Mitzi coming toward her, shouting, "Get a doctor, where's the ambulance?" and stepping aside as Carole passed her.

There were people in the lobby, also backing away, their faces a blur. Cold struck when she went out the door. It didn't stop her. Nothing could stop her. The icy calm was inside again.

A car door slammed in the parking lot. Headlights came on.

She tried to run faster in spite of the pain, along the front of the theatre, hearing an engine burst into a roar, seeing the maroon glint in the floodlight from the building, seeing the BMW back out of its slot, stop a second, then turn and charge toward the street.

She stopped where she was then, spread her legs on the gravel, bracing herself, bracing the gun in both hands again, and aimed at the rear window of the car and pulled the trigger over and over and over, hearing the explosions, then a series of *snap-click* sounds, no more blasts, no more jolts up her arms—

The red taillights of the BMW were disappearing down the street in the direction of the lake.

Suddenly she was cold, and no longer calm but quivering all over, her body beyond control, racked by violent convulsions.

And in that instant of intense silence she heard, but from far away in the distance, the sound of a siren wailing in the night.

Too late, too late . . .

Henry's mind had moved into a hazy silent world of pain. Red pain, consuming, total. But his body seemed to be drifting, no longer a part of him, detached and without weight. Somehow he knew that his eyes were shut, yet in the violent red blur he saw a face. Unclear at first, until the red faded to pink. Then the face floated close, into focus. Luisa's face. Framed in a lovely glow. The way she had looked when she was young. Had Luisa ever been that young? Then, as her face faded, another appeared. Teresa's. Young and lovely and alive. Brown eyes bright and happy and loving. When the image began to blur, something still alive in his mind reached, pleading: Don't go, Teresa, stay with me. (Maybe now he would see them both again. He'd always wished he could believe what they believed.) Teresa's face still hovered dimly, fading, but slowly, slowly, it was becoming another face, the two merging, becoming one, and then Teresa was gone and Carole was staring at him. Her face was very clear—had he opened his eyes? Carole's lips were moving. But he heard nothing. He longed to hear her voice. But there was only a vast, eerie silence. There were tears in her eyes. Don't cry, Carole. But he knew he couldn't speak. Don't cry, dear, you've had enough crying. And then he could hear—many voices, shadows moving—where had Carole gone?

A light snow had begun to fall and Dr. Judith had turned on the windshield wipers.

Over the whoosh-whoosh sound, Carole asked: "Why wouldn't they let me go with him?"

Driving fast, but not so fast as the ambulance, which had disappeared down the dark street ahead of them—the flashing red lights were no longer visible—Judith said: "If you'd told them you were a member of the family, they might have allowed you to ride in the ambulance."

"He saw me. Did you see him smile when he opened his eyes? He recognized me."

"Did you ever hear Henry laugh?"

"No. I never have—" Nor had she seen him cry. Or shared a meal with him, or a joke.

"Henry has such a wonderful laugh."

"Somehow I've always known that. Can't you drive faster?"

There was a smile in Judith's voice: "When we get there, all we can do is wait anyway, dear."

"Is he going to die? Judith, is Henry going to die?"

"We may not know that for a long while—"

"Where's Sandy? I forget, isn't that strange, where is she?"

"She's with Mr. Clive, dear. I'll phone there as soon as we get to the hospital."

A few minutes later—time passed so slowly—Carole was alone in a large, deserted, dim waiting room, while Judith was using the phone in the corridor. Huddled, her body limp and bloodless but her mind knotted, tense and taut, she was staring almost blindly out the windows at the snow, which was falling more heavily now, white and soft. Her mind was empty of images—except for Henry's huge, lopsided face, swollen and purple, his eyes opening only that one time.

"Mrs. Jensen?"

She turned and looked up. It took her a long moment to recognize Mark Rainer, who reminded her: "Mark Rainer, State's Attorney. Would you mind if I sat down? It's about Vincent Fletcher."

To her surprise, the name stirred not a recollection so much as a vague, pervasive feeling of revulsion, not even anger. But she heard herself ask, "Did they arrest him?"

Mark Rainer lowered his slim body into a chair facing her and began to speak without seeming to move his lips: "Vincent Fletcher's dead." It was all he said, his eyes on her face, fingers touching his mustache, brows lifted as if he were waiting.

Carole remembered the hate and pitiless fury she'd felt as she'd emptied the gun after the speeding maroon car, thinking then of Henry's death mask of a face on the floor of the theatre behind her. "What do you expect me to say, Mr. Rainer?" She felt no satisfaction, no relief. "I'm not sorry," she said. "I wish I were . . . but I can't honestly say I'm sorry." Nor, surprisingly, did she feel any elation, or satisfaction—only relief.

"That's what I want to talk to you about. The official report will state that he died almost instantly—of injuries suffered in what appears to have been an automobile accident. Trouble is, he was wearing handcuffs."

"What are you trying to say?" she asked, weary now, tired all through. "Are you trying to say that Henry's responsible, are you!"

"Oh, we know that Mr. Fletcher was under arrest, and with more than probable cause according to witnesses in the theatre. But according to the police preliminary report, he also had a bullet in his body—"

"Are you saying *that's* what killed him?"

Mark Rainer's smile was empty. "The bullet was lodged in the left shoulder, only a few inches above the heart. We'll just have to wait for the medical examiner's official report in the morning."

"I shot him, if that's what you're trying to say, or ask. Those same witnesses must have told you that."

"Exactly, as Vincent would say." That empty smile again. "But you misread me, Mrs. Jensen. The last thing I want—anyone wants—is to see you arrested for homicide. Even *attempted* homicide, *or* aggravated assault with a deadly weapon, which you displayed in public and had no permit to be carrying."

"I don't understand," she said, because she didn't. But she sensed the threat. "He was mad, insane, and he was trying to strangle Dr. Kahn—didn't those witnesses tell you that?"

"Let's please not complicate things. Since the man is dead, what's to be gained by prolonging the whole nasty business? According to the officer who was pursuing him, Mr. Fletcher's BMW failed to make a sharp curve and crashed head-on into one of those bluffs along Lake Road. He was cuffed and driving with a shattered shoulder, so he *seemed* to be trying to get away. On the other hand, he may have seen that bluff jutting out and he *could* have decided not to *try* to get around it."

"For God's sake, Mr. Rainer, get to the point. If you're trying to fix responsibility—"

"Responsibility? Who can say where that begins, or ends? This is much too complex for that. Let's just say, between the two of us, that Vincent Fletcher was a very confused man, sick if you will. Who can say where sickness stops and evil begins? I've known the man for years and I didn't have any idea. But no need to make all that part of the public record, is there? There'll be enough speculation —gossip—around town anyway. I'm thinking of his wife and teen-age daughter. It's over, Mrs. Jensen—for him, for you. Will anything be served by causing any more anguish and pain? You tell me."

And then when Carole didn't—couldn't—answer, he cleared his throat and lowered his voice to a half-whisper. "You were sick yourself, Mrs. Jensen, in your own hysterical way. We both know that. You even have your psychiatrist with you here tonight. But why should we have to get into any of that in a courtroom?"

Now she understood. "Justice," she breathed, hearing the subdued scorn in her tone.

"He's been punished, hasn't he? What more can happen to *him?* But there are other people who shouldn't be made to suffer any more than they have already. You comprehend, Mrs. Jensen?"

Carole took a deep, shuddering breath. "It's a deal," she said, suddenly thinking of Sandy—who would also be spared.

"Mrs. Jensen, I did not come here to make a—"

"It's a deal," she growled. "Now please leave me alone. *Please.*"

Mark Rainer stood up. "There is a weird kind of justice in it, you know." He turned and moved away. "He's not my favorite person, but I honestly hope your friend Chief Lindheim comes out all right."

She didn't thank him. She didn't speak at all, but sat back on the couch, watching him go, feeling her body relax very slightly. Justice. Death. How can death really be punishment if it comes to all of us anyway—in time?

Time. Yes, that's what death robs us of. The only thing we really have. So that, yes, death *is* the worst punishment of all.

Then why didn't she feel purged, free?

Because Henry might die, too.

What had *he* done? Except to love her—

What kind of justice was that?

"Any news?" Judith asked as she came into the room. And when Carole could only shake her head from side to side, Judith sat beside her. "Well, whether he knows it or not, Duncan Clive has adopted a five-year-old girl. Or vice versa. To get off the phone, I had to promise Sandy I'd ask you whether he can go to Maine with you."

"Is Sandy still up? What's she—it's late, Sandy should be—"

"Sleeping. She knows it and *Dunc,* as she calls him, knows it. But it's a bit much to expect in the circumstances, isn't it?"

Before Carole could answer, a tall, spare figure in a white coat came into the room. "Remember me, Mrs. Jensen? I'm Dr. Stoddard."

Carole stood up, quickly. The gray-haired elderly man placed a gentle hand on her shoulder to ease her down again, as he nodded to Judith and called her by name, before he said, "Henry Lindheim's too tough and too contrary to die." He sat down in the chair facing Carole. "He has a concussion, spinal injuries, and his face will require plastic surgery—but that can only be an improvement, after all."

Still afraid to believe it, struggling to sort out her chaotic feelings, Carole whispered, "May I see him?"

"Not now. He's sedated and sound asleep. I made sure he knew you were here. There's always tomorrow, you know."

"There's always tomorrow," Carole was saying, her mind filling with wonder now. Yes, it was true.

Driving the dark winding country road, Judith said: "Tomorrow. To make of what you will."

"I still can't believe it."

Her whole being seemed suffused with astonishment—a kind of overwhelming awe.

"Mr. Rainer was right. It is over now."

All of this that had happened had begun because she, Carole Jensen, had walked into a half-dark woods to pick sumac for her dinner table, to share her own joy with her friends, her husband.

Rolfe—if it had not been for this thing, would she have lived out her life, blind and unknowing, with a stranger who could love her and betray her at the same time, without himself even realizing the contradiction?

In her mind now she was hearing again the old Bob Seger song that she'd never really understood before: *I wish I didn't know now . . . what I didn't know then.*

No. Now that she did understand, her mind rejected the words. Because if it had not been for this dreadful, cruel thing, she might never have asked herself the questions. She might have lived all those years ahead without knowing how human beings really are . . . how the world really is . . . or the dark savagery that she, like everyone, carried inside.

Well, she could live with that. Along with a new certainty that had entered her mind somehow: the acceptance that there was no pattern overall—only chance and happenstance. Monsters lurked in the dark jungle, which was everywhere. Monsters and wild evil creatures, no matter how clean and normal and civilized and, yes, how caring and kind they appeared to be.

So . . . so that's the way it really is.

But you can't stop living, or laughing, or loving because the world's the way it is.

The snow seemed to cover everything now. The black road was white in front of the car.

And already, Carole was thinking, her life was changing. Would go on changing. Already she had begun to say good-bye. To Karen and Jerry and David and Esther and Allison, and Sudbury, and Sheffield Center, and her lovely old house that was no longer hers—

Then she saw the lights ahead. Golden lights in every window of the old barn. Beneath the slanting roof shimmering white with snow. And when the car turned in, more light flooded the wooden walkway from under the eaves and the falling snow sparkled in it.

As Judith stopped the car, Carole slid out, feeling no pain but only the stiffness in her knees, feeling the damp softness on her hair and face as she moved swiftly toward the front door.

Which burst open. And then Sandy was in her arms, her legs circling her mother's body, ankles locked behind. "Wait till you see! Just *wait!*"

But Carole did not wait—she walked awkwardly, off-keel, the quivering, excited small body fiercely glued against her, snow falling over both until she went through the open door. *"See!"* Sandy screamed into her ears, legs kicking to be released. "Did you ever see anything like it in your *life* before?"

And then, seeing Duncan Clive, big and brawny and solid and quiet, silhouetted, his legs apart, against the flare of the crackling logs, hearing Judith coming in behind her, Carole began to shake the snow from her hair, as Sandy's voice, shrill with excitement, called to her: "Look at these paintings—not pictures, *paintings!* They don't make any sense, but aren't they *beautiful?*"

It was then that Carole heard herself laughing.

She had not laughed in . . . how long? How many days now or centuries, or eons—

"Well, they're not meant to be *funny!*" Sandy scolded, fists on hips, face severe with outrage. "You want to hurt Dunc's feelings, Mommy?"

Which, somehow, because she couldn't help it, made Carole laugh more loudly, her eyes beginning to water.

As she saw Duncan Clive coming toward her, a half-filled brandy snifter in his hand, his gray eyes amused, she heard his voice—which held a solicitude that suddenly reminded her of Cass. She felt a quick piercing stab of loss. "Brandy, Carole? You need it."

Had he ever spoken her name before? "Sit yourself down now while I see what Dr. Kahn would like." He didn't reach out to touch her, as Cass had done—how long, long ago it seemed now.

She took a small sip, remembering, but without emotion, the only other time she'd been in this room. And she heard Judith reporting to Sandy and Duncan, "He's very much alive," saw Duncan's shaggy nod, heard Sandy's "I knew it, I knew it, I *knew* it!"

Then she found herself sitting in the same chair that she'd found herself sitting in then. Outside the silent snow kept coming down, but her blood was pumping warm and fast. And she saw Judith lift her glass to her in silent salute, winking over its brim. The glow of the room, and its wood scent, and the marvelous heat mounting inside her—she gave herself over to the here and now. Her senses and her mind had begun to reel slightly, but pleasantly, and she felt snug and safe and serene, as if she were floating in a strange but terribly satisfying dream.

Now Sandy was standing close alongside her chair, whispering: "Did you think about what I told Dr. Judith for you to think about on the way? About Maine? And Dunc and us."

Carole took a long, burning sip and, with the heat cascading inside, she pictured Wildwood: the log building with the huge veranda and the lake stretching away and the high dense pine forest and how the trees smelled. Was the snow falling up there, too? "I'm afraid I didn't, darling."

Then Duncan uttered a nervous, apologetic laugh from across the room, and said, "I've a daughter of my own, so I'm aware of how impulsive . . ."

Her eyes locked with Duncan's, Carole smiled, and teased: "If you didn't have a beard, I'd swear you were blushing." And then added: "Dunc."

"Does that mean yes?" Sandy screeched.

Eyes still on Duncan—the firelight burnishing the dark red of his beard, eyes amused but burning—Carole was thinking then of the vast quiet nights in Maine, and the bird sounds at first light, and the deep old-fashioned beds. And now, of all the unlikeliest of times and places, an exquisite tremor of excitement passed pleasantly through her whole body and a strange quivering, as of anticipation, began in her mind.

"We won't be going to Maine for a few days," Carole heard herself say.

"But *why?"* Sandy wailed. "Why? You *promised!"*

Carole's eyes did not leave Duncan's. She saw no change in his face, perhaps just a glint of something else besides amusement in his steady gaze. A tingling had begun deep inside her. "Sandy," she said, in her quiet reasoning mother's voice, "Sandy, when Henry wakes up in the hospital in the morning, I have to be there. You understand that, don't you?"

Sandy's stubborn crestfallen voice demanded: *"Then* we go, right? Tomorrow. Deal?"

Before Carole could answer, Duncan spoke again, but in a tone she had never heard before: very low, filled with love, but firm, with a strong, gentle urgency. "Sandy, you heard what your mother said, didn't you? In a few days."

And then Sandy moved. To cross, in a straight line, to where he stood. She turned to face the room, her body against his leg. "Yes, sir," she said, meekly, but somehow satisfied.

And then, as if something had given way inside, Carole's body relaxed and, sitting back, she thought of Dr. Stoddard. "There's always tomorrow," she said—to Sandy or to Duncan?

And Sandy said, very grave now, very sober: "Deal, Mommy. And Dunc comes, too, right?"

All of a sudden, the brandy warm and soft in her body, Carole began to laugh again.

She saw a grin begin to twist Duncan's beard, his eyes sparking, and she heard his voice: "Is there any sound in the world lovelier than a woman's laugh? If there is, I've never had the good fortune to hear it."

And then Judith also began to laugh.

Then, for no good reason that Carole could explain, Duncan was also laughing.

After a moment, looking puzzled, so was Sandy.

Laughter filled the house that had once been a barn.